THE
HUNTER
AND THE
MAGE

A Dance of Dragons

The Shadow Soul ~ The Spirit Heir ~ The Phoenix Born

Leena's Story (The Novellas)

~

Once Upon a Curse

Gathering Frost ~ Withering Rose ~ Chasing Midnight

Parting Worlds ~ Granting Wishes

~

Midnight Fire

Ignite ~ Simmer ~ Blaze ~ Scorch ~ Burn

~

Midnight Ice

Frost ~ Freeze ~ Fracture ~ Shatter

THE
HUNTER
AND THE
MAGE

2

KAITLYN DAVIS

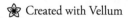

*To my family for their unconditional love,
my friends for their overwhelming support,
and my fans for their incredible enthusiasm.
Thank you from the bottom of my heart.*

THE WORLD ABOVE

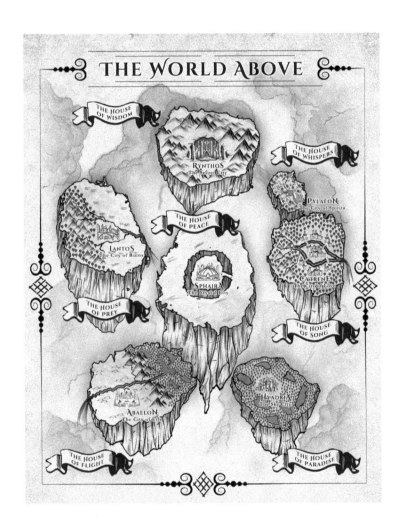

THE HOUSE OF WISDOM

THE HOUSE OF WHISPERS

RYNTHOS
The Secret City

PYLAEON
The City of Spirits

THE HOUSE OF PEACE

LANTOS
The City of Ruins

SPHAIRA
The Crystal City

CYRENE
The City of Love

THE HOUSE OF PREY

THE HOUSE OF SONG

ABAELON
The City of Mist

HYADRIA
The Sky City

THE HOUSE OF FLIGHT

THE HOUSE OF PARADISE

THE
HUNTER
AND THE
MAGE

The funeral procession passed in a blur of whispers and wails. His people mourned, their spirits clawing at him like beggars for bread, pleading for one morsel. They had no gods, no temples, no prayers to murmur to the heavens. They believed only in magic—and now, in him.

"The King Born in Fire."

"He'll save us."

"He's here."

Malek kept his head high, worried the crown would slip off his brow if he moved a single muscle. His cheeks were dry—too many tears had already been shed, and it was unbecoming of a king to weep in public. At least, that's what he'd been told.

His throat ached from holding back the sobs.

His father was dead. Not his blood father, perhaps, but the only one he'd ever known. Now he was alone with a burden too big for his young arms to carry. Already, the weight dragged at his bones like an anchor against the sand, growing heavier with each yearning soul his boat floated past. The journey through the canals was nearly complete, but the burden of his destiny had only begun to penetrate.

The boat came to a stop before the final bridge. Remembering the instructions from his councilors, Malek stood and removed the ivory rose from his jacket. For the first time that day, he lowered his gaze to the body laid to rest before his throne. It was a shell, empty of the golden spirit he knew better than his own, yet he still wished to fling his arms around his father and never let go. Instead, he swallowed his grief and stepped down to place the flower upon the late king's unmoving chest. Then he accepted the hands offered as two guards pulled his small body up over the edge of the canal and onto the wooden platform. Symbols of hope didn't have the luxury of succumbing to despair.

The air around him glittered with *agro'kine* magic. Malek didn't look as he followed his guards to the apex of the bridge—he couldn't. The insert fitting the crown to his head was precariously close to coming undone. With each step, the golden coronet wobbled. By the time the boat floated under the bridge, his father was buried beneath a woven tapestry of white flowers.

Hydro'kine magic sparked next. As the front of the boat entered the sea, an archway of flowing water emerged, sprinkling the flowers with a misty dew. Then a gust of wind barreled down the canal, laced with yellow *aero'kine* magic, whipping Malek's cloak and pushing the king away from the city. A ray of light pierced the endless fog, illuminating the boat as shadows rolled across the sea, darkening the waters—light magic and shade magic. The sixth and final ceremonial element flared across the sky, cutting through the haze to land on the boat in an eruption of flames.

A thousand eyes turned to him.

Malek knew what the crowd wanted, what they expected. They were the ones ignorant to the truth of what they were asking. The only man who might have understood now burned to ash. The only woman who one day would was no more than a few days old. He stood at the center of an entire kingdom, yet he was alone.

You must find her, Malek, whatever it takes. Those had been his father's dying words. *You must always remember who you are, who she is, and what the two of you mean. No matter how hard it is, you must find her.*

I will, he'd promised. *I will.*

He was no longer the boy prince.

No matter his age, no matter his inexperience, no matter his fears, he was now Malek, the King Born in Fire, and he had no choice but to give his people what they needed—even if it meant he would give and give and give until there was nothing left of him.

Malek opened himself up to his magic the way his father had taught him, letting the rising tide pull him under. The dull murmur of spirits turned to a roar, drowning out the world. He could feel them all—their pain and their hurt, their open wounds aching to be healed. There was a boy the same age as he whose stomach growled with hunger. An old woman whose muscles were stiff in the perpetual dampness. A man whose heart stung with loss. A woman whose body cried out beneath the strain of bringing another soul into the world. On and on it went, back and back, until his awareness stretched beyond the realm of this city, beyond all the cities, into the very core of the world where that yawning abyss waited to be sealed.

It was too much.

The hurt of the world.

The pain of its people.

The weight was too much for one boy to carry, but he had no choice. Deep in his power, Malek let go. The magic rolled off him in waves, an iridescent golden sea that flowed over the crowd, easing their pain. Yet no matter how much power he sent out into the world, it wasn't enough. For every ache he dampened, ten more rose. It was like trying to dispel a raging tempest with nothing but the air in his lungs, useless and impossible.

"My liege. My liege!"

Malek blinked rapidly, trying to return to the world, fighting to quell the power that still controlled him. The air shimmered with the fading glow of his magic. In a kingdom that had never known the warmth of the sun, he was the closest thing.

"My liege."

By the time his vision returned, he realized he was too late. The funeral pyre had long since faded into the mist. There was no last glance, no final goodbye. Malek stifled his pain—compared to the hurt of the whole world, it was nothing. He turned from the gray horizon and took the crown his advisor offered. Settling it back onto his head was like securing his own chains.

"We should make haste for the castle, my liege."

Malek nodded as his gaze dropped to the guards stationed near the foot of the bridge. They'd drawn their staffs to hold back the crowd surging forward to touch their new king, their hands outstretched as they pled with him to give them his grace.

"My child is sick," one called.

"Please, my king, my wife is ill."

"My husband can't work."

"My father won't wake."

On and on, the voices followed him as he traveled deeper into the city. No one cared that he was still a child himself. No one offered condolences for the loss of his father. No one suggested he rest his weary soul. Because no one understood, and no one would until he found her—the Queen Bred of Snow.

His partner.

His soul mate.

His savior.

1

LYANA

Lyana woke wrapped in silken sheets. For a moment, she thought the day before had been nothing but a dream. Sneaking from Rafe's room at the crack of dawn. Meeting Xander's broken gaze as he slipped his ring back over her finger. The parade through the streets of Pylaeon. The battle in the sacred nest. The man with stormy eyes and golden magic who had vowed to teach her about the new power raging beneath her skin.

But it wasn't a dream.

It was real.

She shot up, disentangling her limbs from the bed linens as she rolled from the bed to land on her feet, heart thumping in her chest. Her mating gown still clung to her skin, ebony shifting to ivory as the fabric rose up her torso, every inch decorated with precious stones. A red splotch marred the fabric by her waist—Xander's blood. He'd been stabbed and she'd saved him, then...nothing.

Where was she?

How had she gotten here?

Groaning wood broke the silence as the world around her shifted, tilting this way and that, like a leaf swaying in the breeze. She stumbled with the motion, flaring her wings for balance. The ground was...moving. She slid her gaze across the wooden walls, past the dresser in the corner, past the desk covered in papers, past the tapestry, not stopping until she found the window. The world outside was gray.

She was beneath the mist.

No—she was *in* the mist.

Lyana took off, sprinting for the door and flinging it open with a loud *bang*. She raced down a narrow hall and climbed the first staircase she could find. Two men stopped short, shock written on their faces as she ran past. Then she was outside, surrounded by gray. The air was wet as she pulled a deep breath into her lungs. She was on a ship of some kind, which meant there was an ocean—a real ocean! Not a sea of flames, but one of water. She wanted to see. She wanted to know. Someone shouted her name, but Lyana ignored it as she jumped onto the railing, pumped her wings, and—

Fell.

"Lyana!"

It was the last thing she heard before the waves pulled her under. Wings that carved so efficiently through the wind were useless in the water. She kicked with her feet and pushed with her arms, but the liquid rolled around her body, unaffected. Everything was dark and eerily quiet as the current swept her deeper. Just as her lungs began to burn, blue glitter cut through the darkness. A torrent slammed into her back and flung her from the ocean. A gust of wind laced with yellow sparks carried her toward the ship. Lyana flapped her wings, but they couldn't catch the breeze as she made a slow descent toward the man waiting on deck with a frown upon his face. He'd swapped his priestly robes for leather boots and a close-fitted jacket, but she recognized him just the same—the man from the sacred nest. When her feet touched wood, she charged.

"What did you do?"

"Morning, Princess," he drawled. "You certainly know how to make an entrance."

With her hands on her hips, Lyana narrowed her eyes and spread her wings to their full ivory glory. She was soaking wet in a bloodied ball gown in the middle of the sea, but she refused to be ignored. "What did you do?"

"Nothing permanent."

As he spoke, his focus slid to the side. She followed it and found the cause of her grounding—her primary feathers had been snipped at the ends. With a gasp, she raised her arm, prepared to slap his smug face. Golden sparks danced through the air, wrapping around her fingers and holding them still. Now growling, she pulled back her other arm. Again, magic simmered, freezing her limb.

The unnamed man stared at her with a brow raised. "Are you done throwing a fit?"

"No," she answered and kicked quickly with her foot. The folds of her gown hid the movement until the last second, and her toes connected satisfyingly with his shin.

"Ow!" He cursed and hopped on one foot.

Lyana grinned.

A stifled laugh filtered into her ear, and Lyana turned to find that a crowd had gathered around them. Men and women dotted the ship, all eyes focused on her. Some faces were amused. Others were painted with shock. A few were stoic and unmoved.

"Who are you?" she demanded, turning back to the man. "Where are we?"

"You may be a princess in the world above," he murmured as power flowed across the space between them, wrapping around her body and holding it tight, "but down here I'm king, and I don't take orders."

"Neither do I."

The words were a silent dare. She remembered the way his magic worked—the way her magic had worked. If he wanted a fight, she would gladly give it. If he wanted respect, well, that had to be earned. Lyana took a deep breath, preparing to call on the magic she still didn't understand. It was the same as her healing powers yet so much more, as though her god Aethios now lived beneath her skin. The magic was endless, unfathomable. Just thinking of it made her dizzy. Her fingertips prickled with a static charge, the barest hint of the power hiding in her soul.

"Very well," the man relented, as though sensing the surge. He swept his magic back beneath his skin, freeing her from its hold. They faced each other on even ground.

"Why did you clip my wings?"

"Because I couldn't risk you leaving."

"Why—"

"Let me ask a question this time," he interrupted. "Do you want to learn how to control your magic?"

"Yes."

"Do you want to know why you've spent your entire life certain you were meant for something more?"

Her heart swelled as her brows twitched in confusion. "Yes, but—"

"Do you want to learn about the prophecy that wrote both our fates in the stars?"

"Prophecy?" Lyana asked, stepping forward. "What do you mean?"

"Come with me, and I'll explain."

"Tell me now."

His frown deepened. "Are you always this difficult?"

"Are you always this demanding?"

He opened his mouth, then thought better of it and turned his back to walk swiftly across the ship. The fog clung to every surface, damp and cool, coating the world in a film of gray—everything except for that man and the golden aura still shimmering all around him.

"Where are you going?" she called out, unused to such blatant disregard. "We're not done here."

"I am," he shouted over his shoulder. When he reached a door, he paused and glanced behind to meet her eyes, a bit of self-satisfied mirth alight in his own. "If you'd like to talk, you know where to find me."

Then he opened the door and disappeared inside. Aghast, Lyana released a puff of air and looked around, hoping to find another person mirroring her disbelief, but they had already returned to their tasks, knotting ropes, climbing ladders, scrubbing floors. Either they were used to the whims of their king, or they were carefully masking their emotions. Regardless, Lyana was alone in the middle of the ocean, unable to fly and weighed down by questions.

Naturally, she raced after him.

When she tore open the door, he was waiting inside, leaning casually against the wall with his arms crossed and an expectant look on his face. Lyana folded her wings to fit in the tight corridor and swallowed, a little bit of her pride slipping down the back of her throat along with the gulp.

"Perhaps we got off on the wrong foot," she offered slowly.

"Perhaps." He pushed off the wall. "Now, please, if you'll follow me, I'll tell you of the prophecy, somewhere private where we won't be disturbed."

He led her deeper into the ship. With each step, she found herself bracing her palm against a wall to keep from toppling over, positive she would never get used to the constant rocking. The man, however, charged confidently forward, his steps smooth and undisturbed. He didn't stop, didn't even pause, until they reached a spot she recognized, the bed in the corner left unmade in her haste to get outside.

"My room," Lyana commented.

"Actually, it's *my* room," the man said. The ghost of a grin passed over his lips, quickly replaced with the same grim determination as before. "But I'm happy to loan it to you for as long as you're here."

"And how long will that be?"

"As long as it takes."

"As long as what takes?"

He finally turned toward her, his deep blue eyes as churning and tumultuous as the sea from which she'd just been fished. "Saving the world."

The conviction in his words made her heart skip a beat.

"But first," he continued, "a fresh change of clothes. You're dripping water all over my floor, and I can't imagine that gown is comfortable."

Now that he'd mentioned it, she was a little cold, and getting out of this corset would solve at least one of her problems. The man knelt beside a trunk on the opposite wall and retrieved a bundle of clothes.

"I had these made for you. The jacket should attach around your wings, but if not, I can have something else formed."

Touched by his thoughtfulness, Lyana took the garments. As she did, their fingers grazed, the barest brush of skin on skin. His gaze dropped to the spot. With a swallow, he stepped back and let his arms fall to his sides.

"What's your name?" she asked suddenly.

"Malek'da'Nerri."

"Malek," she repeated, testing the word on her tongue. The clouds in his eyes seemed to part at the sound. "It's nice to meet you."

"You as well, Princess."

"Lyana, please. Just Lyana."

He inclined his head. "Lyana."

Then he turned and offered his back as he strode across the room, coming to a stop before the window with his feet spread wide and his hands clasped by the base of his spine.

Lyana glanced at the clothes in her hands, at Malek, and back at the clothes. Did he mean for her to change with him there? It wasn't proper. What would—

She paused.

What would who think? Her home was thousands of miles away. It might as well have been another world, and for all she knew, they thought her dead. If this stranger had devious intentions, they would have already played out. But she'd woken alone and unharmed. Still, it wasn't every day she undressed with a man present.

The longer she waited, the more she felt a silent challenge tightening the air between them, as though he was daring her, maybe testing her limits. If he thought she'd back down, he was sorely mistaken. Lyana reached back and loosened the knot of ribbons at her back, pulling the threads free. The subtle swish of silk was loud in the silence, broken only by the creak of wood. Her skin began to heat, but she didn't stop until her dress dropped past her hips and slid to the floor. He didn't move. He just kept staring out the window, making her wonder what deep thoughts were spinning in his head.

"Can you tell me about this prophecy?" she finally asked to fill the quiet. "Where did it come from? What does it say?"

"It comes from a time before your islands were lifted into the sky, and it's survived through prayer alone, passed down from generation to generation in the hope that one day the saviors would come forward to see it through."

"And you believe *we* are these saviors?"

"I do."

"Will you tell me what it says?"

For a moment, she thought he might refuse. When he finally spoke, it was in a hushed, almost reverent voice, the words drenched in promise. "*The world will fracture, splinter in two—one made of gray, the other of blue. Beasts will emerge, filled with fury and scorn, fighting to recover what from their claws we have torn. Two saviors will arise—one above, one below—a king born in fire and a queen bred of snow. Together they will heal that which we broke, with magic and spirit, with mirrors and smoke. But only on the day when the sky does fall, will be revealed the one who will save you all.*"

"And you think I'm this queen bred of snow?"

"I know it," Malek said, spinning to face her just as she finished tying the sash around her waist. The trousers he'd provided hugged her thighs and the silken jacket cinched tightly to her hips. Lyana didn't know how he'd guessed her size so accurately, but it was just one of many mysteries to unravel.

"How do you know?"

"I know because I feel it," he said as he stepped toward her and held out his hand. Magic simmered in the air above his palm, so undeniably familiar. "The power in your skin is the same as mine. We call it *aethi'kine*, the ability to manipulate spirits, but it's so much more than that, you'll see. I'll show you."

Lyana lifted her palm, then hesitated, curling her fingers into a fist. Old fears were difficult to forget, especially ones as deep-rooted as this. In her world, magic meant death. She wasn't used to offering her secrets so freely.

Malek put his hand beneath hers. "You don't need to be afraid with me."

She swallowed and met his gaze as she brought her magic to the surface. The air around them glittered with starlight, his and hers, one and the same. The gentle trickle became a rushing river. Lyana swayed on her feet, swept up in the power, lost in it. Malek wrapped his fingers around hers, keeping her grounded.

"Quiet your mind," he whispered. "Imagine a door and push it closed."

She did as he said, listening to his gently murmured instructions. Gradually, the connection to her magic snuffed out, leaving her drained and cold, unaware of how much time might have passed. Malek steadied her as the world came back into focus.

"You should rest."

"I'm not tired."

He arched a brow as though sensing her lie. "Then you should sit here and stay out of trouble while I have food brought."

"Do people always do as you say?"

"Yes."

Well, he was in for a rude awakening. "I've never been in the mist before. I want to go on deck."

"There's a window right there." Malek inclined his head. "Though I think you'll find the view a bit monotonous compared to the world you're used to. We only have one forecast—gray."

Lyana stepped across the room to press her nose against the glass, drinking in the sight. The fog was thick, nearly opaque, and bright in the afternoon light. Beneath it, waves crashed, bubbling and wild as white spray splashed against the ship. She'd never seen so much water. How could he say this was anything except marvelous?

"I have questions," she murmured.

"Too many to answer them all today, I'm sure," he noted wryly, drawing her attention. He stood beside the door with his hand already wrapped around the knob.

A grin tugged at her lips. "Maybe."

"I'll be back in a moment, and then I'll tell you as much as you want to hear."

Lyana nodded. He was right—she was tired and hungry, the events of the last day taking their toll. How long had it been since the mating ceremony? Since she'd healed Xander? Since the fight in the sacred nest? At least a day, maybe more. Her stomach rumbled. Her body was sore. The more she thought about it, the more some food and answers sounded wonderful.

"Lyana?"

The word pulled her back to the present. Malek stood hesitantly in the doorway.

"I'm sorry I clipped your wings," he said softly, almost like a concession, the last thing she expected from this king who seemed as used to getting his way as she was. "Until I know I can trust you, I can't risk your returning to the isles above and revealing what you've learned of this world within the mist. Still, I'm sorry there was no other way to ensure you were contained."

Contained. It was, perhaps, her least favorite word, up there with *patience* and *duty* and *responsibility.* He was extending a peace offer, but now she found her guard had risen. Was she a prisoner? An honored guest? Some strange thing in between? "If you can't trust me, the girl you claim is your queen of prophecy, who can you trust, Malek?"

"No one but myself."

"That sounds like a rather sad way to live."

"Maybe it is," he said, one side of his lips curving up as a blond lock of hair fell forward, shrouding his eyes. "But that's the sacrifice we make, Lyana. The one you'll come to understand. I'm afraid the prophecy never said anything about being happy."

Without another word, he left.

Lyana hugged her arms around her midsection, fighting a sudden chill as she returned her gaze to the mist.

2

RAFE

Pain greeted him like an unwelcome morning, bright and burning as it chased away his dreams. Rafe groaned, writhing beneath the ache. What happened? Where—

It came rushing back in a flash.

Waking to find Lyana gone. The confrontation with Xander. The trip to his mother's rooms to say goodbye to his home forever. And then Cassi. His friend. Lyana's confidante. The woman who had been fooling them all.

My wings.

Taetanos help me—my wings!

Rafe shot up, vision going white as his shoulders screamed at him to lie down. But it wasn't the pain that terrified him—it was the weightlessness. His body was too light. Even through the agony, the absence was obvious. His wings were gone. She'd cut them off. She'd mutilated him. Rafe reached back, fighting against all hope as his fingers tenderly touched the wounds. His skin was scarred, and the

19

jagged edges of his bones were now smooth. He was healing —healing *over*—which meant his wings were well and truly gone.

Grief came as swiftly as a punch to the gut, stealing his breath. There was no telling how long he might have drowned in the despair if a hand hadn't swatted his fingers away, shocking him back to life.

"*Stop moving.*"

Rafe didn't recognize the voice. He blinked to clear his vision, trying to understand as a room came into focus. He was stretched out on a bed, his arms bare, his torso probably bare as well. The walls were made of wood and the air was damp. The ground swayed, bobbing with a buoyancy he didn't understand. Then he saw the blades in the corner— his twin swords, returned to their scabbards and leaning against the wall. If he could get to them, he might have a chance.

"Would you just stay still?" The voice came again as two palms pressed against his shoulders. It was a woman, he was sure, and she sounded frustrated.

Rafe acted fast. With a roll, he was off the bed, landing hard on his hands and feet. The woman behind him sighed. He ignored her and shuffled across the room to grab the hilts of his blades. Wrapping his palms around those worn leathers felt the tiniest bit like coming home. Even as his muscles screamed, he spun toward the stranger with his swords held defiantly at the ready. She was small in stature, probably around his age, with short black hair and a round face. Her skin was a pale sort of tan, as though it yearned for the sun, and her eyes were disturbingly white, her pupils a milky gray as though covered by a film. They angled up at the ends, somewhat hooded by her creaseless eyelids. What he noticed most of all, however, was her lack of wings.

"Who are you?"

She dropped her gaze to his swords, then lifted it back to him, slightly bored. "The person who is trying to prevent you from getting an infection."

"Where have you taken me?"

"Nowhere. You just sort of dropped into our laps."

He narrowed his eyes and lowered one of his swords until the point was level with her throat. "What do you want with me?"

"Nothing." She snorted and crossed her arms, seemingly unafraid of his threat. "But Captain is determined to keep you alive, which means I am too."

"Captain?"

She jutted her chin to the left. "Go ahead and see for yourself. I won't stop you."

Still facing her with his swords at the ready, Rafe stepped backward, not liking the amused grin rising to her lips as he slowly made his way across the room toward the door she'd indicated. He didn't stop until his hip hit the knob.

"Want me to open it for you?" she asked sardonically. "I wouldn't want you to drop that impressive fighting stance prematurely. Who knows what terrifying evil might await you on the other side of that door?"

With a scowl, he lifted one of his swords, then remembered the scabbards weren't attached to his back and paused. He was, in fact, naked from the waist up, but that wasn't what bothered him. The trousers around his legs were foreign, his feet were bare, and there was nowhere to secure his weapons.

"You were pretty bloodied up, so we took the liberty of changing your clothes for you." She winked. "My offer still stands, by the way. Need a hand?"

"No," he half growled before placing one hilt between his teeth and pushing the door open. The girl's laughter followed him into the dark hall, so he kicked the door shut behind him.

On high alert, Rafe crept forward, fighting to maintain his balance in this swaying world. The ground refused to stay put, and with each step the wooden planks beneath his feet groaned. A globe of soft light hung near the center of the hall, gently illuminating the space. It wasn't fire. It was unlike anything he'd ever seen—pure white and sparkling like…magic.

A door beside him swung open.

Rafe jolted and spun, keeping his blades at the ready, but his only foe proved to be loose hinges. The door swayed with the floor, slipping open then slamming shut, then slipping open, then slamming shut, blocked from fully closing by a wedge of wood. On the other side, he saw the hint of a woman beneath a bundle of blankets, her face hidden in shadow. Golden hair flashed as the door closed. When it glided open again, two black-as-night eyes watched him.

"Could you get that?" she called sleepily before rolling over.

Rafe frowned, but when the door shut again, he lifted the wooden latch and pulled until he heard it click.

"Thank you!"

He shook his head and kept walking forward. *Where in the world am I? What the gods is going on?*

A flash of natural light through an old door caught his eyes. He strode forward and kicked it open, no longer cautious but anxious to get his bearings. With a *crack* the wood splintered and the door broke off its hinges, landing on the floor with a loud *bang*. So much for subtlety. Rafe leapt through the opening, prepared for battle—and stopped cold.

The air was alive with magic.

Yellow streaks flowed with the wind. Blue sparks crackled over the wooden rails to his left and right. Flares of color danced across the sky, breaking up the endless gray. Across the way a woman stood surrounded by red glitter, her fist encased in burning flames as she stared out toward an invisible horizon. To his left, a man knelt by a box of plants with glowing emerald vines snaking up his arms. To his right, another man stood with outstretched hands. Pine-green embers burned at his fingertips and shot overhead.

"You're awake."

Rafe spun toward the voice, lifting his blades. A woman watched him from a raised deck, her hands gripping a spoked wheel. His focus went straight to the caramel-tinted wing behind her left shoulder. It identified her as a hawk, as did the sharp look in her icy blue eyes. There was something familiar about her—something he couldn't quite place.

"And you broke my door," she added.

"Who are you? Where am I?"

"Captain Rokaro, and you're on my ship, *The Wanderer*."

Ship? Rafe took in his surroundings anew—the sails overhead, the damp wooden rails, the opaque gray coating the sky. The slapping sound in his ears was the crash of water on wood, and the ground was rolling because of waves, which meant...

He was in the Sea of Mist.

Only it was an actual sea, made of water instead.

But the smoke? Where was the smoke? He'd spent his life staring down over the edge of his isle, convinced the world below was a land of never-ending flame, commanded by Vesevios, god of fire, brutal and burning. Now he was here, and it was...wet. Already a fine sheen coated his bare arms, a dampness that clung to his skin. The temperature was warm, but not overly so. Where was the churning volcanic sea? The pit of burning fire?

"Not what you expected?" Captain Rokaro asked as though reading his thoughts. "I thought much the same the first time I woke to find myself here. You'll come to learn that not everything you were taught in the world above can be trusted, especially concerning the things they fear."

"What am I doing here?" Rafe tightened his grip on the swords, not relenting at the coaxing edge in her words. "Do you know Cassi? Are you working with her? How do I get home?"

"Home." The captain sighed and turned to her side, catching the eye of the man standing a few paces to her right. He was large and burly, with olive skin, a thick black beard, and an ebony patch over his left eye. At her signal, he took the wheel. She turned back to Rafe and held his gaze as she approached. "I'm afraid you won't be going home, at least not anytime soon. As for your other questions, I know no one by the name Cassi, and I work for myself."

"I don't believe you." He forced the words through gritted teeth. She was lying—she had to be. It didn't make sense for Cassi to go through the trouble of cutting off his wings only to toss him over the edge into oblivion. What game were they playing? And what did it have to do with him?

It's not personal, Cassi had said as she'd driven the dagger into his bones and sliced them in half. *You'll survive.*

She'd wanted him alive.

She'd wanted him here.

Why?

"You don't have to believe me, but I'm telling the truth. I got an order from my king to wait in these waters for a boy to fall from the sky. I waited, you fell, and now here we are. Leech tended to your wounds, and Brighty was supposed to reapply the salves, though we both know the precaution wasn't necessary."

Rafe gripped his swords so tightly his nail beds went white. "What do you mean?"

"This world is made of magic, boy," the captain murmured as she stopped an inch from his blades, not a single drop of fear in her eyes. "You can't hide what you are here."

They knew.

Rafe could feel the eyes on him, judging, staring, sizing him up and waiting to see what he'd do next.

They knew what he was.

Captain Rokaro reached up and brushed his blades to the side as she held out her palm. Yellow sparks swirled above her fingers, coalescing into a cool breeze that stroked his cheek like a tender touch. "You don't have to be afraid of us. How do you think I lost my wing? How do you think I ended up here? I know what it is to be hunted. I know what it is to be maimed and cast aside. But I also know what it is to embrace the power that was always meant to be yours, to revel in what you were always taught to hate. If we wanted to kill you, you'd already be dead. But you're not. So put the swords away and tell us your name."

He hesitated.

The tone of her voice was earnest, but the blades were all he had. The magic in his skin had never stopped the people he loved from leaving him. His wings and the world he knew with them were gone. All he had to keep the terror mauling his spirit at bay were these sharp metal edges.

"Your name?" she asked again. "Any name will do. It doesn't have to be true. We all go by nicknames anyway. I just need something to call you other than 'boy.'"

A name. It sounded simple, but the words caught in his throat. Which one should he give? Aleksander Palleius? It was a stolen name, meant for a prince and not a bastard born in the dark. It had been his name for mere hours before Queen Mariam ordered it changed, and he'd never even known it belonged to him until years later. Alek Ravenson?

If he listened closely, he could still hear the name shouted by Xander down the stone halls of their home, trailed by boyish laughter. It made his chest contract. He'd forfeited that name a long time ago, as soon as he'd discovered the truth of what it meant. And Rafe—what of that name? It belonged to a loyal brother who would have given anything for his prince. It belonged to a man who betrayed the person he cared about most for a single night with the princess who'd stolen his heart. It belonged to a raven, something the dull ache in his back whispered he no longer was.

The boat tilted and Rafe stumbled. His muscles went slack. The swords dropped to the ground, points embedding themselves in the wood as he gripped the hilts to keep from crashing to the floor.

He'd lost his wings.

He'd lost Xander.

He'd lost Lyana.

He'd lost his very name.

The only thing he hadn't lost was his magic—a gift he'd never even wanted. The one that had kept him alive while his parents perished. The one that had labeled him as other. The one that had delivered him into the arms of a woman who could never be his. The one that had healed every wound except those that mattered most—the shattered pieces of his broken heart.

"How about Scowl, since it's all he ever seems to do?" The voice belonged to the milky-eyed girl he'd left downstairs. She stood in the doorway with her arms crossed over her chest as she leaned against the frame.

"Scowl?" the captain repeated, tossing a pointed glance at the girl.

She just shrugged.

"Rafe," he finally whispered, voice hoarse and raw. "You can call me Rafe."

"Rafe?" the girl asked. "What in magic's name is a *rafe*? At least Scowl stands for something."

"It's short for Ravenson." He swallowed, meeting the captain's eyes. Her irises darkened with understanding as she nodded. He might not have wings, but he was still a bastard born of the sky—it was the one thing about himself he could never hide, could never change, no matter how he wished it were different.

"Rafe it is," Captain Rokaro said, authority oozing from her tone. "Brighty, introduce him to the crew. I have a ship to steer."

"I still think we should call him Scowl," the girl grumbled as she stepped forward. Then she offered him her hand. "Name's Brighty, short for Bright-Eyes, which I'm sure you already noticed. My father thought I was blind when I was a kid, so he set me up to beg on the streets. When my magic came in, I started to see just fine—well enough to become the best pickpocket the king's city has ever seen, if I do say so myself. Then I got in a bit of a pickle, and that's how I ended up here, with Captain Rokaro on *The Wanderer*. Got it? Good."

Before Rafe had time to speak, or even breathe, she looped her arm through his and pointed to the auburn-haired woman across the deck, who still held a ball of flame in her hands, the stark light drawing attention to the freckles spotting her cheeks. "That's Pyro. She's a *pyro'kine*, a fire mage, and I wouldn't get on her bad side if I were you, especially since she knows you can't burn. Well, I guess technically you can, but it wouldn't be permanent. Anyway, she's a bit of a nutter, but she's our nutter, so we love her."

"I can hear you," the woman drawled, darting her seafoam eyes in their direction. She waggled her fingers at Rafe, fire flaring with the movement.

"And that's Archer," Brighty continued, spinning him toward the man with silver-streaked dark hair and evergreen magic at his fingertips. He shifted his gray-blue eyes in their direction at the sound of his name, something within them warmer than Rafe had expected. "He's our resident *ferro'kine*, or metal mage. He's a bit quiet sometimes, but if you plug him with a few shots of dragon's breath he opens right up. Just make sure there aren't any daggers close by, because funny guy thinks it's hilarious to throw them at your face when you're not looking and it'll scare the piss right out of you. And before you ask, yes, I'm speaking from experience."

Down the line she went, making Rafe dizzy with the sheer volume of words spilling from her lips. She wasn't peppy by any means, more dry-witted and energetic, with enough humor that she almost made him crack a smile.

The short, somewhat rotund man he'd seen kneeling by the plants was Leech, an earth mage who knew medicine and apparently had a nasty habit of stealing blood for experiments. Next came Spout, a water mage with reddish-brown skin and bright honey eyes who was allergic to just about everything. When she sneezed, the ocean tended to erupt and land on whoever happened to be close by. High overhead was a young boy, all scraggly limbs and shaggy blond hair, whose name was Squirrel. He had no magic—yet—just a knack for scrambling across the ropes. Then there was Jolt, who needed no introduction because as soon as Rafe turned toward her, something zapped him in the ass, making him, well, jolt. According to Brighty, she was a relentless tease, something he learned for himself as her dark-mocha gaze raked up and down his half-naked body. She sauntered when she walked, curves on full display, something charged about the deep golden hue of her skin. The bearded man he'd seen by the captain's side was Patch, the first mate and also a wind mage. Finally, hidden below deck were Cook, the cook, and Shadow, the blonde woman he'd passed in the hall. Darkness was her magic, so she usually slept during the day.

"And that's everyone," Brighty finished with a shrug. "Any questions?"

Rafe glanced quickly around the ship, his home for the time being, at least until he found land or anything aside from the thick, endless fog closing in on all sides. If he hadn't come from the world above, a land bathed in sunlight and awash in color, he might never have believed it existed. Yet he was grateful. Staring into the abyss, he could almost forget his other life—a life where his brother was now mated to the woman he quite possibly loved, a life where he wasn't needed and wasn't wanted, a life full of people who probably hadn't even noticed he was gone.

But he had to remember that life, because it held Cassi, and she held secrets—ones he was determined to uncover.

Xander and Lyana might have moved on from him, but he wouldn't let them go until he knew without a doubt they were safe. He couldn't. Somehow, he'd get his wings back. In a world made of magic, as this one seemed to be, there had to be a way. Until then, he'd do what he'd always done —he'd survive.

Putting his forearms against the rail, he turned toward Brighty, half his focus on the choppy sea visible within the mist, and half on her. "What magic do you have?"

"Stick around long enough and maybe you'll find out."

He turned back to the water. "Where are we going? To this king?"

"Eventually, maybe." Brighty shrugged and took the spot beside him, her elbow grazing his. "But we have to make a stop first."

"Where?"

"Oh, you'll see."

He snorted, uninterested in her twisted words and the wall she so clearly maintained. "Why are you helping me?"

"Because Captain asked."

His gaze slipped over Brighty's onyx tresses to the woman at the wheel, her singular brown wing outstretched to catch the wind. Beneath a wide-brimmed hat, the captain's hair was wrapped in colorful bands of fabric that covered its true color. They swirled in the breeze, almost like magic. A true hunter of the House of Prey, she kept her eyes on the distant horizon, focused on some elusive prize he couldn't begin to fathom.

"And why is the captain helping me?" he murmured, looking back at Brighty.

"Because the king asked," she answered smoothly before sliding her gaze out to sea, but not before he saw a steely glint pass over her unsettling eyes. "And because she can't help herself. Captain has an uncanny knack for collecting people the rest of the world throws away."

3

XANDER

The advisors gave Xander a day to wallow before demanding an audience. He ignored the incessant knocking on his door and paced across his room, surprised the rug beneath his feet had any threads left. Yes, he was hiding. But not because he couldn't face the truth—Lyana was gone. It was a fact. What he didn't understand was how much to reveal to everyone else. What would the people think if they knew someone with magic had snuck into their most sacred place and stolen their princess? That Lyana herself, beloved by all, possessed a power meant only for their gods? That she'd saved his life? That he'd left her?

"Lysander."

Queen Mariam's voice broke his ruminations and he spun to find her standing in his room, arms crossed with a hard look in her violet eyes. The balcony—he'd forgotten about the balcony. "Mother, I—"

"You cannot ignore this any longer."

"Ignore?" He shook his head. *Ignore?* All he'd done for a

day straight was think on this, his mind spinning into a vortex he couldn't escape. "Is that what you think I'm doing?"

"If not that, then what?"

"I—" His jaw hung open but nothing else came out. "I—"

"Princess Lyana is gone."

His heart contracted upon hearing that ugly truth on someone else's lips. "I'm aware."

"Rafe is gone."

Xander closed his eyes, remembering the horror on his brother's face before he'd turned his back and walked away. "Again, I'm aware."

"The people are talking."

"The people are *always* talking."

"They say Rafe bewitched her. They say he stole her away. They say he brought her beneath the mist, where Vesevios has claimed her."

For the first time in what felt like days, Xander stopped in the middle of his room, bent over at the waist, and laughed. Oh, if only it were so easy! Just yesterday, he'd thought the worst thing to ever happen in his life was interrupting a midnight rendezvous between his brother and his mate. Now he found he wished the rumors his mother rattled off were real. If only they'd loved him a little less, this whole disaster might have been averted. They'd be gone, yes, but only his heart would be broken and not his kingdom, which, if the truth got out, would surely fall apart.

"I fail to see the humor in the situation."

"I know," he sputtered. If he didn't laugh, he might cry
—or worse. All the rage he'd kept coiled inside for so long
had been unleashed, and now he didn't know how to bury it
away. Instead, it coursed through him, boiling his blood so
he wanted to shout and snap and do all manner of
unprincely things. But that would solve nothing. It would
only hurt his people more. So he laughed, because at least
then he could pretend the tears in his eyes were easy to wipe
away. With a cough, he cleared his throat, trying to find his
composure. "I know, Mother."

"What happened in the sacred nest?"

He shook his head, still unable to find the words.

"I need to know, Lysander. You must tell me. We need
to prepare our people for what happens next."

What would happen next? Would that man come back?
Would he bring more magic with him? And if he did, how
in Taetanos's name would they stop him? It wasn't a
problem he could tackle on his own, no matter how he
wished he could.

Xander sighed and met his mother's worried eyes.
"Bring Helen, and then we'll talk."

"I'll bring the entire council—"

"No," he cut in, using a voice he didn't often use with
his mother—one that oozed with the authority of a king.
Her brows knotted, but she didn't argue. She stared at him
as though seeing her son as a man for the first time. "No
one else. Just Helen, and together we'll figure out what
to do."

With a nod, Queen Mariam left. As she murmured
instructions to the guard stationed outside, Xander sank

onto the stool by his balcony and dropped his head into his hand. The weight of so many questions landed heavily on his shoulders. In the city spread out below, a plume of gray smoke still billowed into the sky. Scorch marks marred the streets. Stone houses lay crumbled. In some places, wood burned, a fire they hadn't yet been able to contain. And buried within the rubble, he knew, were his people—the greatest loss of all. How many had the dragon killed before it flew away? How many souls taken? How many lives cut short?

If not for Cassi, Xander would have been among them. The arrow she'd put in the dragon's eye was the only reason he was still alive. How incredibly stupid he'd been to go charging at the beast like some sort of noble hero, yet how freeing the moment had been too. He'd never felt so defiant and so strong. There'd been no fear, only foolhardy hope. Though he knew he was no mighty warrior, no dragon slayer, in that brief instant before he'd seen Cassi's arrow, he'd felt untouchable, and a part of him longed to feel that way again.

"My prince."

Helen's voice drew him back from the depths, and he lifted his head. "Let's go to the sitting room."

He was off the stool before either woman had a chance to question. They followed silently as he strode across his bedroom and through the archway. Though they sat soon after he closed the door, Xander continued to pace, his feet relentlessly marching toward some unknown destination.

"How many were killed in the dragon attack?"

"Twenty-three," Helen answered solemnly.

"How many injured?"

"Burned? Nearly three dozen. Crushed by rock? Ten, though we still have some areas left to clear. Injured while fighting? Four guards and an old man with more grit than sense."

"What of the city? How long will repairs take?"

"Months. The northern edge of the castle wall took some blows. A few houses in the noble quarters were crushed. Mostly, it's farmers who were hit—a fire still rages in their sector of the city, though my men have assured me they're close to putting it out."

"Any sight of the dragon?"

"Gone."

"And the sacred nest—is it secure?"

"We have guards stationed there now. All the priests and priestesses are alive and accounted for. Some of the ravens escaped, but most remained in the grove."

Xander sighed and ran his fingers over his chin, absorbing the updates. Then he finally stopped and met Helen's weary gaze, aware that for the first time, some of her uncertainty was turned on him. "And what do the people say?"

"Nothing good, my prince." She glanced to the queen, then back to Xander. He held her stare, a silent plea for the truth. "They saw you return from the sacred nest in bloodied clothes, alone and seemingly mad, with the princess nowhere in sight. They fought off a dragon. They spent the night frightened, abandoned by Taetanos, abandoned by you. Word spread early this morning that your brother disappeared. With everything they already whispered, it was an easy conclusion to draw. They say he ran away with the princess, that he bewitched her and turned her against the gods. And there are some who whisper that maybe he put a spell on you as well."

Xander snorted derisively, but Helen didn't crack a smile. Her expression was grim—grim and unsure, as terrible a combination as he could imagine. "Surely you don't believe that's true."

"I don't know what to believe," she answered gravely.

His mother eyed him dubiously, but he wasn't concerned about Helen. If she started lying, maybe then he would begin to question her loyalty. This brutal honesty? This was how he knew she was still on his side.

"Lyana *was* taken," he said slowly, glancing between the two of them. "But she wasn't taken by Rafe."

"Then who?" his mother asked, leaning forward in her chair.

Helen watched on, a deep groove digging into her forehead.

"When we got to the sacred nest, three people were there, two men and a woman, all dressed in priests' robes. We didn't notice anything was amiss until it was too late. They attacked as we began to say the vows, and they—they had magic."

His mother gasped.

Helen frowned.

It was enough to inform Xander that keeping Lyana's magic a secret was the right call. If she ever returned—no, *when*; when she returned—there needed to be a place for her. He was determined to save her, even if it meant he had to save her from his own people too.

"We tried to stop them, but we were no match. They knocked Lyana unconscious and held me back by force. They would've killed me, but the earthquake intensified. It looked like the sacred nest was going to cave in, so they fled, perhaps to meet with that dragon, I don't know. But they didn't have wings, so wherever they're hiding, I fear it's a place we won't be able to follow, a place only their magic can access."

"No wings?" Helen asked.

He shook his head.

"Then how did they get here?" his mother asked, voice quivering in a way he'd never heard before. "Where did they come from?"

"I don't know, but I intend to find out."

They spent the next hour going through the details and drawing up a plan. The night before, Helen had gone to the sacred nest to question the priests and priestesses. No one saw anything. No one heard anything. All they could remember was a strange force holding them against their beds so they were unable to move. Xander knew the feeling well—he, too, had been wrapped in invisible binds, forced to hold still as a stranger sauntered toward him with a knife. It was magic, it had to be, which meant it was a power he had no idea how to fight. When he found Lyana, maybe she would. Her magic had been different, a light in the dark, healing all his wounds. Even vanished, she was a beacon of hope—one he had no choice but to follow.

"So what do we tell everyone in the meantime?" Helen

asked as their meeting drew to an end. "They need an official statement from their queen."

"We tell them it was Rafe," his mother murmured, the usual malice toward his brother gone from her tone, replaced by weariness. "We tell them what they want to hear until we know more—until we know who exactly we're fighting and what exactly they want."

Both women looked to Xander for approval.

This was his brother's worst fear come to life—to have Xander confirm to the world that he was a usurper, a backstabber, a traitor. For the rest of their lives, he would never again be welcomed in the House of Whispers. His room would remain empty. No more late-night conversations. No more sarcastic retorts. No more fighting. No more fun.

But Rafe was gone anyway.

"We tell them it was Rafe." A monster gnawed at his gut as though trying to take the words back, but it was too late for that. "We tell them he took Lyana, but we're determined to bring her back. We tell them to keep quiet, to say nothing to any outsiders, so we can protect Taetanos's honor until the princess is returned. And while they curse my brother's name, we use however much time we've managed to carve out to gather as much information as possible, so that when the rest of the houses come calling, we'll have something more substantial to tell them, something that will convince them to fight with us rather than watch us fall."

It wasn't a great plan, but it was the only one they had. If they told the people the truth—that a mysterious man with mind-boggling magic came and stole Lyana away—everyone would be terrified. The city would self-destruct. Better the enemy they knew, no matter how false, than the enemy they had never even imagined, at least until he knew more.

Eventually, word would get out. Xander wasn't a fool—a secret this grand could never be kept for long. And when it was revealed, Rafe would come back. He knew his brother. When he loved, he loved with his whole heart. Self-destructive as he was, he would probably save Lyana just to leave her once more.

Was that what Xander wanted?

To be the one standing between them yet again?

He'd been an obstacle. He saw that now. Not that Rafe didn't love him—he did, probably too much. Lyana too, in her own way. But they'd met before the trials had even begun, united by a force he would never understand, drawn together by an emotion he himself had never felt. Xander wanted Lyana safe, but did he want her back, knowing for the rest of his life that he would always be her second choice?

It was another question he couldn't yet answer, but at least he knew where to start unraveling this one. Somewhere in the castle, an owl had a story to tell, and as soon as he was done with his mother and Helen, he would find her.

4

CASSI

R age was such a deliciously animalistic emotion—
so much easier than regret or sorrow or, worst of
all, love. Luckily for Cassi, she had much to be
angry about.

Malek.

She swung her sword into a bag of beans, grinning as
the force of the blow reverberated up her arms. With the
city in ruins, the practice grounds were empty of other
guards, so Cassi indulged, letting go in a way she rarely
did. Spinning around, she slammed the bag again,
allowing the fire in her blood to burn everything else
away.

Malek. And his war.

Malek. And his demands.

*Malek. And his deep blue eyes that tricked me into
thinking he saw inside my soul, saw my heart, saw all the worst
parts of me yet loved me anyway.*

Every thought was punctuated by a blow—again and

again and again—leaving her no room to think outside of her king and all the terrible things he'd said.

You're a weapon.

My weapon.

To be wielded any way I choose.

If she were a weapon, let her be the one that drove a dagger into his heart, the way he had done to her. Cassi would never forgive him for stealing her sky, for holding her down as he sailed away, for taking her best friend and all her dreams with him.

Where was Lyana now?

Did she know who Cassi was? What she'd done?

And what about Rafe?

No, don't think about him. Cassi forced the vision of his bloodied back and broken wings away, but she couldn't forget the sound—that endless scraping of metal on bones as she cut his very essence away. What was a bird without wings? To what life had she condemned him?

Cassi hit the bag so hard the practice sword flew out of her hands. Without a weapon, she kicked and punched until the skin around her knuckles began to tear.

Malek made me do it.

Had he?

It's all his fault.

Was it?

Her king hadn't been there with his magic, forcing her hands. She'd had a choice. And she'd chosen to trust his demands, to believe in him, to do everything he asked, no matter the cost of her actions.

With a cry, she collapsed against the bag, holding it to

her just to keep from falling to the ground. Breathing heavily, she forced her vision to clear, her mind to slow. This wasn't her. She was calm. She was calculating. She didn't let her emotions rule her. She was a soldier in a fight to save the world, and she had one more order to carry out.

Cassi slid her hand down her side, not stopping until her fingers traced the hilt of the dagger strapped to her waist. Was it such a leap to go from spy to assassin?

One quick blow, and she'd be done.

One strike, and she'd be on her way home.

One slice, and—

"There you are!"

Cassi snapped her hand away from the dagger and jolted upright, turning toward the voice she recognized— another voice she was trying to smother. But this one was gentle and earnest, kind and fierce, dangerous as it whispered, *It's all right. I'm here. You're safe in my home. Let it go.*

She'd been unable to get the words out of her mind all night, or the feel of his arms wrapped around her, so caring and so comforting. His touch had fooled her into believing for a moment that she mattered, that she was more than a weapon, that she was a girl who had the luxury of being vulnerable.

"Prince Xander," Cassi murmured, meeting his lavender eyes and steeling herself against the warmth radiating within them.

"Just Xander, please," he said, stepping closer. "I should've guessed you'd be in the practice yards, but I thought you'd been injured yesterday. Wasn't there blood on your jacket?"

"There was," she answered smoothly. He was too attentive for his own good. It would be so much easier if he were a fool—someone neither she nor her king needed to worry about. "From a raven I helped pull from the rubble. I was lucky to get away from the dragon unscathed."

"Lucky..." He dropped his gaze to the dagger at her waist, then the sword by her feet, then the practice bag nearly in tatters. "Some might say skilled. You saved my life."

Don't remind me.

What had she been thinking? The dragon could have ended him with one blast of flame and she'd be by Lyana's side right now. She'd be home. But something about the fearless way he'd charged the beast, no care for his own life and no sense, had made her want to save him. Maybe she'd envied his defiance. Maybe she'd wanted to act on a little defiance of her own. Cassi would be the one to decide whether he lived or died—not Malek, not a dragon, *she*.

"It was nothing," she said.

"Not to me."

"Anyone in my place would've done the same."

"But they didn't."

Did he have to be so damned nice? She flared her nostrils, but it only brought a soft smile to his lips.

"You don't need to be so tough all the time."

"And you don't need to be so noble."

"Is that what you think I am?" Xander asked, a shadow hovering in the hollows of his face. *Interesting.* Cassi stored the information away. "I'm afraid I'll have to shatter that illusion. I came here to question you for information. I'd intended to go about it with a bit more subtlety, but now I think honesty might take me farther."

He was right—the truth was a rare gift, one that so often eluded her. She had spent so much of her life surrounded by lies, she feared she might drown in them. But not today. There was still a bit of air left in her lungs and a little more deceit left on her tongue. "Information? I'm not sure what information you think I have, but I fear you'll be disappointed."

"I need to know about Lyana." He swallowed the lump in his throat. "About Lyana...and Rafe."

Lyana and Rafe—the last two people she wanted to discuss in the world. At least he was coming to her as the jilted lover and not the suspicious prince. This was a problem she knew how to handle.

With a casual shrug, Cassi murmured, "What about Lyana and Rafe?"

"I need to know how they met," Xander said, a gruff edge to his tone. "I need to know how they—how they fell in love."

"Why don't you start by telling me what you know?"

"I know the dragon attack in the House of Peace had something to do with it, and then the trials. I don't know how long they carried on here behind my back, but I need to. And I know..." He trailed off, pausing to glance from one side to the other as he leaned in close. "I *know* about Lyana."

Cassi couldn't help herself—she shifted forward,

copying his movements as she glanced side to side, mocking him. "What do you *know* about Lyana?"

"I *know*," he said again, with more emphasis.

She, of course, understood exactly what he was implying, but if she gave in too easily, it would be suspect. No matter what happened, Lyana was her best friend, and she wouldn't give up her secrets so easily, not without a little something in return. "I'm afraid I don't—"

"Look, Cassi," Xander cut in, a bit of frustration evident. She tried not to grin, though the edges of her lips twitched nonetheless. She was used to seeing him from a distance, the perfect prince, but she liked him better this way, not quite so proper. "I understand that you're in a foreign house, surrounded by people you hardly know. I understand that you spent far more time with my brother than with me. I understand we're still relative strangers. But I meant what I said—you're safe in my home. And I'd like us to be friends. You can trust me. I promise we're on the same side."

There he was again, speaking with a voice full of conviction and far too alluring. But he was also naïve, which was a weakness she could use, though she hated herself, just a little, for how quickly that thought came to mind. "What side is that?"

"The side that wants to keep Lyana safe, to bring her home."

"I'll tell you what I know, but only on one condition." Cassi paused as his brows drew together. It was a gamble, sure, but she needed to see how freely Xander would give up the information her king would kill for. And the closer she could get to him, the less he would suspect her. "You tell me what happened to Lyana first."

His lips flattened into a thin line, but he didn't look away. Neither did she. Their battle of wills lasted for a few prolonged seconds. Then he told her everything—how a mysterious man with magic infiltrated the sacred nest, how he was stabbed, how Lyana fought the strangers off to bring him back from the brink of death. That last little detail made her smile. Malek must've been furious yet at the same time fascinated to have his own magic used against him. A devious little part of Cassi wished she had been there to see him beaten at his own game. Mostly, she wished she had been there to see her best friend, her queen of prophecy, finally come into her power.

"You seem impressed," Xander murmured after he finished.

Inwardly, Cassi winced. Outwardly, she cleared her features, cursing herself for letting her mask fall for even a moment. "Lyana's strong."

"So you're not worried for her?"

"I didn't say that," she replied sharply, injecting a little fear into her tone. The sentiment was somewhat true—part of her was terrified of what would happen to Lyana the longer she stayed beneath the mist, of who Malek would turn her into without Cassi there to ground her. But what could she do now anyway? Lyana would never forgive her for the lies, for the betrayals. Their friendship was over, and sooner or later, Cassi would be forced to face that ugly truth. "I only meant she can handle herself. She'll be all right until we find her."

He nodded, a distant, hopeful expression on his face.

Cassi capitalized on the moment. "Who else have you told?"

"About Lyana?" he asked, refocusing on her. "No one. I told my mother and Helen about the man and the magic, but they're sworn to secrecy. We want to keep it as contained as possible until we know more."

Good.

She added Helen and Queen Mariam to her mental list —she'd have to watch them too, just in case. Malek had been right. Murder would be much easier, at least in theory. But she couldn't imagine Xander's warm lavender eyes as lifeless. Keeping him from learning the truth would be difficult, but not impossible. The only impossibility was the idea of snatching the dagger from her belt and plunging it into his heart right now. Everything else was within reach.

"Thank you for telling me the truth," Cassi said. "And thank you for keeping Lyana's secret. Ask what you want, and I'll tell you everything I know."

Xander sighed, a bit of relief softening his hard edges. "They met that day with the dragon? Lyana saved him. How?"

"Lyana and I were hiding in a cave beneath the sky bridge when the dragon came. We saw Rafe fight it, and we saw him get hurt. She flew out to stop it, and I chased after. I'm still not entirely sure how we managed to scare it away, but we did, and then we brought Rafe into the cave to hide him so Lyana could, well, you know."

She didn't want to mention magic, not out loud, even though they were alone. Cassi of all people understood that there was always a chance someone could be listening unseen.

Xander nodded, prodding her to continue.

"We didn't know he was a raven prince until we went back. I left the two of them alone, so I'm not sure what happened between them. Though I suspect Rafe had a secret of his own, because the next time I saw Lyana, she was claiming him as her mate. And there's only one thing I know of that could draw two strangers together so quickly."

"Your suspicion is correct."

Cassi didn't ask for more. Of course, she didn't need to. She already knew everything there was to know about Rafe's magic, but there was no reason to tell that to Xander. Let him think her uninterested. "Then, well, the trials brought them closer together, until she learned the truth of who he was, who you were, and it stopped."

"But it didn't."

"It did," she countered softly. "For a while at least. Lyana pretended to hate him. I think there was a time when she fooled herself into thinking she did. But then…"

"The earthquake," Xander said, the realization widening his eyes. They grew glassy as he sank back into his memories. "Rafe saved her during the earthquake, and she must've helped with his wings because I knew they healed too quickly, and then—" He stopped short and looked sharply at her. "The children. The victims. It wasn't Taetanos. It was never Taetanos. It was her—it was them—all along."

"Even then, they never kissed. Nothing happened, not until the night before your mating ceremony. She went with the intention of saying goodbye, and I know they made a mistake, but they did say goodbye. She came back to her room in the morning. In the end, she chose you."

"Is that how you would want to be chosen?" he asked softly, staring into a world she couldn't see. A wave of emotions passed over his face—anger, regret, and most of all, pain. What caught her attention, however, was how hard he fought them off, right arm trembling under the strain. The muscles in his jaw ticked as though biting back all the terrible thoughts his mouth ached to say.

She wanted to hear them.

Horrible person that she was, Cassi ached to know she wasn't the only one with volcanic anger spewing in her gut, threatening to consume her. She wanted to see this noble prince come undone, if only for a moment, just long enough to know she wasn't alone.

"It's all right to be angry, Xander."

He glanced at her quickly, eyes flashing at her words.

"You're allowed to be angry."

"Am I?"

"Yes." Because if this good man, this honorable man, this innocent man, was furious, then maybe she could be a little bit furious too. "Here." She knelt and grabbed her discarded practice sword before offering it to him. "It'll make you feel better."

"I'm not—"

"Just take it," she said, shoving the hilt into his hand. Xander gripped it awkwardly, holding the weapon away from him as though it might bite. She couldn't help it—she laughed.

"What?" His tone was sharp with insecurity.

"Nothing." She stepped closer, softening her voice as she fixed his grip, repositioning his fingers and nudging his feet into the right spot. "Nothing. It's just, you're holding it like you're afraid of it, but you don't have to be. I know you're not much of a fighter, but that's a shame. You have the heart of a warrior—I saw it yesterday, when you faced that dragon. I see it now. But that will get you nowhere unless you learn the first lesson of battle."

"What's that?" His breath caressed her cheek as he spoke.

She met his gaze, unsure why the air suddenly seemed thick, why her lungs felt empty. "Your weapon is your best friend. Unlike people, it will never lie to you. It will never betray you. You can fuse your secrets into every attack, and it will keep them. It will be your confidant, if you let it." She stepped back to give him space and nudged her chin toward the bag. "Go ahead."

Xander furrowed his brows. In one decisive motion he spun and thrust the edge of the sword into the bag. It was sloppy and a bit crazed, but it brought the ghost of a grin to his lips. He swung again, and again, until his perfectly coifed hair turned disheveled and a bead of sweat trickled down his throat. Cassi watched, feeling every motion as though it were her own, pulse leaping with every *whack* of wood on beans. She fingered the dagger at her hip, aware of the secrets lingering in its sharp edges, and silently whispered one more.

Not today.

5

LYANA

"I don't understand."

Lyana groaned and dropped her hands, staring at the four dishes set in a line on the table before her—one for fire, one for earth, one for air, and one for water. Colors danced across her vision, painting the world in rainbow hues she could see but not touch. The magic had seemed so easy in the sacred nest, with the power simmering at her fingertips, but now it felt like trying to capture a ray of sunlight in her palm.

Malek's gaze burned as it burrowed into her face, demanding something she didn't know how to give. They sat facing one another in her bedroom, no sound between them aside from the groaning of wood and gentle crackle of the fire burning in the first bowl. She didn't want to meet his eyes only to find disappointment swirling within them.

"You're afraid."

She flinched. "I am not."

"You are." He frowned as a sigh slipped through his lips. Why did it seem like when he looked at her, he looked *through* her, into the very depths of her soul? "You don't want to be, but you are."

Am I?

Lyana stilled her wringing hands. She had never been afraid of her magic, but the power churning beneath her skin didn't feel like hers, not anymore. Before it had been gentle and benign, a force she could smother with ease and call forth without worry. Healing was a tender sort of magic, just her and the person she was trying to fix, two souls locked together in an intimate embrace.

This new magic was something else entirely.

A few days had passed, but when she closed her eyes, those last few minutes in the sacred nest came flooding back as clear as if she were living them again. The ground shaking. The ravens screeching. The power pouring from her body, endless and immense, too much for any one person to manage. At the time, it had felt as if the world threatened to cave in around her.

But then she remembered Malek, his warm palms cupping her face as his thumbs grazed her skin in a soothing, meditative rhythm. *Listen to my voice*, he'd said. *Calm down. Someday, you'll be able to control it.*

Would she?

"You're afraid of it," Malek said, honest but not unkind. "And as long as you are, you'll never be able to control it." Leaning back into his chair, he lifted his hand and looked at his fingers. Golden sparks danced across the tips, mighty yet contained, as lethal as any blade yet as docile as a dove.

They faded just as quickly as they came. "Magic can be fickle. There's evidence it's hereditary, and yet it might show up in someone like you whose bloodline hasn't seen a mage in a thousand years, if ever. It chooses when it wants to emerge, be that the day of your birth, split across an age, or never at all. It's unpredictable, and that can make it scary, but you don't need to be afraid. I was born with my full power, so I've never known anything else. But your experience is different. You need to stop thinking of your magic for what it was and embrace what it's now become. With practice, it will be easier."

Lyana stifled a groan. These were the sorts of lessons she loathed, all mental and full of minutiae, no burning muscles or racing hearts. Just a chair, a table, and her.

If only Cassi could see me now... A grin pulled at her lip as she imagined what her best friend might say. *How horrible—you have to stay inside with a handsome king and learn how to use your immensely powerful, world-saving magic. I feel so bad.*

Pretend Cassi was right.

Whether she believed in this prophecy or not, she needed to learn how to control this magic. If she didn't, she'd never be able to go home again. Right now, that was far more of a concern than a string of pretty words. Her parents would soon start to worry. Luka, she was sure, would descend on the House of Whispers as soon as he heard she was gone. Xander was her mate, his people her people, and they were likely all reeling from her loss. And Rafe...

Her heart hurt just thinking about him.

KAITLYN DAVIS

He'd be gone by now, she was sure, their night together as burned into his memories as it was in hers. Their kisses. Their sighs. Those magical hours beneath the stars when they'd let passion consume them. Now their minds were supposed to lead them, but if he thought her hurt, he'd come back, no matter the personal cost. He would probably do something foolish and noble and brave in his quest to see her safe—the thought which terrified her the most.

Lyana dropped her gaze back to the bowls set on the table. "Please, Malek, tell me again about the magic, about what I must do."

"The world is made of elements, both tangible and not," he began, leaning forward once more. Though he'd told her all of this already, there was no tiredness to his words, just determination. He always seemed so focused. Did he ever allow himself a little time for fun? "For the purposes of our magic, the physical elements matter most—earth, air, fire, and water—because our magic is tied to the thing which connects them all. Within the molecules of water, between the burning embers, deep beneath the ground, and flowing across the sky, there is spirit—invisible to all eyes except for ours. A *hydro'kine* can manipulate the ocean waves, but you, if you want to, can manipulate the very thing that holds the ocean together." He paused as a stream of golden flecks flew from his fingers, sinking into the water and lifting a perfect sphere of liquid into the air. "A *pyro'kine* can make fire dance across the air, but you can make the spirit connecting each lick of flame soar." The water fell back into the dish, not a single drop spilling, and the aura of magic switched to the flames, urging them to go higher. "When you heal

56

people, you work directly with their spirits, which are the easiest for us to command because human souls practically cry out to be saved. But every aspect of the physical world is touched by spirit, which means every aspect of the physical world is ours to do with what we will."

Lyana shivered at his words. She wasn't sure if she wanted so much power. "And what of the intangible elements?"

"Don't concern yourself with those."

If only he knew her well enough to understand his refusal only heightened her interest. "Please. Every bit of information helps. I didn't grow up surrounded by magic like you. All of this is new to me."

He released the fire and clasped his hands on the tabletop. No sigh escaped his lips, but with her magic at the surface, Lyana thought she felt his spirit relent. "Light and dark magic are the most common, but there are others such as time and space. It's believed the woman who proclaimed the prophecy could see into the future, though I've never seen such magic myself. I met a man who could touch objects and see flashes of the past. We also know of magic that allows one to open doors to other lands. But none of that has anything to do with the spirit magic we possess."

Doors to other lands? What Lyana wouldn't give to have that magic—to get out of this room, to explore. Her attention slid to the window and the opaque gray shrouding the view. In all her years of wondering, she'd never imagined the world beneath the mist to be so dull, full of nothing but the lessons she'd spent her childhood escaping.

"Lyana." His tone was chiding.

"I'm sorry." She returned her focus to the bowls. "I'll try again."

Lyana brought her magic to the surface, letting the power swell beneath her skin. The world seemed to fade and flourish at the same time. The wood desk and walls and floor fell away, replaced by a cacophony of colors, as though a film had fallen over her eyes, giving her access to a different scene, one layered over what she knew was there. Brightest of all was Malek, a golden pulse in his chest extending out to his limbs—living, breathing spirit. His shine dulled all others, but she forced her gaze away, back to the bowls and the lesson she was utterly failing. Within the flames, red streaks flickered. Within the dirt, a deep green glittered like emeralds reflecting the sun. Within the water, swirls of blue churned. And within the empty bowl, a bit of yellow painted the air, as in the rest of the room, covering everything in a sunlight hue.

With a furrowed brow, Lyana tried to see deeper, into the spirit within, but she couldn't. All she saw was fire and water and dirt and nothing.

"Use your magic," Malek commanded.

Lyana pushed out with her power, letting the smallest streak of golden light emanate from her palm. Deep inside, the magic surged, as though aching to be used. It wanted to rush out. It wanted to consume her. With all her concentration on controlling the onslaught, she hardly paid attention to the bit of power she allowed through.

"Don't be afraid. It won't hurt you."

She wasn't worried about herself. She was worried about

everyone else—about the walls shaking, and the ground trembling, and the ravens squawking, and the sense of impending doom.

"Don't hold back. Let it go."

The simmering light of her power stretched across the table to encase the burning flames, but no matter how she tried, she couldn't hold them, couldn't move them, couldn't see any bit of her own magic within the crackling red.

"Don't think of the fire. Think of the spirit within the fire."

Her head spun. Her vision shifted, the colors growing brighter until the real world fell away. She tried to find the flames, the red, the spirit, but her power unleashed, swallowing the table in a glow as bright as the sun. The magic blinded her to everything else, so charged, so mighty, so overwhelming. More and more escaped her hold, brilliant and beautiful and beastly. There was no control. There was no thought. She was swimming in starlight, a sea of glittering gold. No up. No down. No beginning and no end. Just raw energy.

"Lyana!"

The sound of her name drew her back.

"Lyana."

His voice was forceful and demanding, yet gentle and sure.

"Listen to me. Return to me."

Warm palms cupped her cheeks. She focused on the feel of his skin on hers, on the subtle dig of his fingers in her hair and the soothing brush of his thumbs. Gradually, the world came back. She smothered the power as her vision cleared. Blue eyes stared down at her, made softer by the sunspots on his nose, still left from his days in the world above. He was kneeling over her, which meant she was on the floor.

"What happened?"

"You lost control."

She wrinkled her nose and sat up, brushing his hands from her face. "How in the world am I supposed to control *that*?"

"By listening to me."

Her nostrils flared. She was ready to wring his neck. "I *am* listening. All I've done for days is sit in this room and listen to you and stare incessantly at these bowls waiting for something to happen. I'm losing my mind!"

"You're tired."

"I'm restless!" She ignored the hand he offered and rolled to her feet. If he would stop for just a moment to really look at her, she wondered if he'd realize she was drowning in his expectations and his demands. His vision was too far into the future to see what was happening right before him. Or maybe worse still, he saw and just didn't care. "Please, is there nothing else we can do? Is there no other lesson you can teach me?"

For once, the know-it-all king didn't seem to have an answer. A groove dug into his brow as he pursed his lips, no quick retort on his tongue.

"Please," she said again.

He sighed. "Perhaps a demonstration is in order."

Her heart lifted despite her annoyance. Finally, something to see, something to do. When they reached the deck, he led her to the very front of the ship. The wind struck her cheeks and flowed through her feathers, the sensation so similar to flying it brought a smile to her lips.

"Viktor," he called. "Nyomi."

Two crew members came immediately and stopped silently by his side to await orders. Lyana recognized the man, tall and thin with somewhat scruffy chestnut hair—he was the wind mage who'd come with Malek to the world above. No recognition lit his hazel eyes, no spark of anything. The woman was unfamiliar, short and curvy, her brunette locks secured in a tight knot atop her head. The only thing the two mages had in common was their stances. Both held their hands clasped behind their backs with their feet braced, gazes sharp and lips drawn in a line. Everyone here was so disciplined. They didn't speak out of order, didn't step out of line. It made Lyana want to scream.

"Bring your magic to the surface," Malek told her as he took her fingers. "Try to see what I do with mine. Try to feel my spirit and my power as I work."

He nodded to his crew. Nyomi lifted her hands, blue sparks coming to life in an instant. Viktor turned his face to the sky, a yellow aura shimmering around his palm. The sea before her erupted. Spouts of water jetted up from the waves, droplets splashing her face as they slithered like snakes through the air. Gray vapors swished as a squall descended, wrapping her in furious winds. The sails overhead slapped with the gusts. The two mages worked together, wind tunneling into a vortex as water lifted in a cyclone, both swirling with destructive might.

All at once, the maelstrom froze.

Wind and water hung suspended in the air, broken by the spirit power surging from Malek's palm. Lyana focused her gaze, seeing with her magic, the elements falling away as saturated hues infiltrated the gray. Blue, yellow, and gold threads wove together, a chaos she didn't know how to decipher as the ship closed in on the stalled tornado. He flicked his fingers. Water and wind yawned open and the storm parted, cleaving into a tunnel. Lyana gasped as they sped through the opening, tightening her hold on Malek's hand. With the magic so close, she finally saw what he'd been trying to tell her. His power didn't touch the blue or the yellow. It carved between them and cut around them, encasing the swirling hues in unbreakable golden bonds.

"If you control the space around and between the elements," Malek murmured, no strain evident in his voice, "you control the elements themselves. The difference is small, but it's everything."

He dropped his arm. The wind and water surged, slapping the sides of the ship before Viktor and Nyomi regained control. Guided by their magic, the storm imploded, dispelling across the sea. A few seconds later, the world was calm, nothing but thick fog and waves once more.

As his crew walked away, Malek signaled for her to step forward. Lyana slid into the spot, leaning her hips against the rails and spreading her wings to catch the wind. Her view was painted in shades of gray, yet it was filled with color and possibility.

"Reach out with your magic," he whispered into her ear, breath warm against her neck as his hands came to rest on the small of her back. She hesitated and he leaned closer so his chest pressed into her wings, sturdy and sure. "Trust yourself. Let go."

She took a deep breath and gripped the rail, letting his arms hold her steady as she closed her eyes. The power was there waiting, yearning to flow free. For some reason, it made her think of Rafe. Her thoughts drifted to their stolen hours in the dark, the golden spark of her magic sinking into his skin, welcome and accepted, and the silver spark of his, new and so alluring. The magic had never terrified her when she was with him. Through his eyes, it was magnificent. Beside him, it came as naturally as breathing. Lyana imagined the hands at her waist were his, strong and defiant. She imagined the chest against her back belonged to a raven, his touch as electrifying as it was forbidden. Rafe's spirit was wild like hers, but in his arms, she'd never felt so assured, as though he were a pocket of safety within the chaos. Holding onto that feeling, Lyana let go.

The magic flowed like a swiftly moving river, surging out and showing no signs of an end. It dove beneath the sea and cut through the wind as though on wings. She felt Malek behind her, his own power calling to hers. She felt the other people on this ship like stars in the dark, their spirits bright and burning. Far away, she felt the whispers of other souls, yearning to be healed. There were no screams. Beneath her feet, the ground was still. It didn't tremble, didn't quake. All was calm, including the magic, which settled across the world like a blanket, promising safekeeping.

When she opened her eyes, the gray was coated in gold, shimmering as though the sunlight had broken through it. But it wasn't the sun—it was her. And it was glorious.

6

RAFE

As Rafe stood at the bow of the ship with the wind in his face and the breeze against his chest, for a brief moment the world gave way and a weightlessness took over—during which, for a fraction of a second, he could almost fool himself into thinking he was flying. Then wood slammed into water, jarring his knees as the floor rose to meet him, and he remembered that he was now a bird without wings, no longer a creature of the sky.

It was the only spot on this ship he felt alive.

It was also the only spot that made him want to drop over the edge, sink into the ocean, and die.

Luckily, the shifting of the ship was so frequent, neither extreme had a chance to win. Instead, he stood with his fingers on the damp rail and hovered somewhere in between, unsure if his arms were pushing him back or pulling him forward. It was a sweet sort of pain he'd grown used to, like a punishment that felt so good he kept coming back for more. It felt the same way touching Lyana had, as though it might kill him and save him at the same time.

"I see you've found my favorite spot on the ship."

Rafe tore open his eyes, finding the captain beside him. Her face was turned out to sea, angled just right to catch the wind. The colorful fabrics wrapped around her hair shifted in the breeze, and the edges of her lips crinkled with the barest hint of a smile.

"When I was younger, I used to spend all my time at the bow of the ship, not behind the wheel. And then I learned a very important lesson—living in the past will prevent you from ever seeing a brighter future."

He grunted and returned his gaze to the thick gray stretched out before him.

"It's dangerous to long for things you may never have."

A laugh escaped his lips, darker than the wings he no longer possessed. "Trust me, Captain, that's a peril I'm well acquainted with."

"And how has it treated you so far?"

Rafe frowned.

Before his parents died, he used to spend hours in his mother's room at the base of the castle imagining the royal rooms where his father lived. He wanted to see them, to sleep in a luxurious bed, to have servants bring him meals, to have free rein of the grounds the way his brother did. The wishes of a child. Then the dragon came and stole his parents, and somehow he found himself in the spot he'd always dreamed of, but in a way he'd never desired.

As a boy, learning to fight beneath scrutiny and stares, ostracized by everyone aside from the brother he held dear,

Rafe used to dream of proving his loyalty. In some visions, he'd slay the dragon. In others, he'd save Xander's life and, just like that, the ravens would forgive his sins. In a few, the most idealistic, he didn't have to do anything at all except remain steadfast by his sibling's side, and eventually his devotion won them over. Then he'd gotten his chance to prove himself, but it was by posing as Xander in the trials, a role he'd never wanted, one he'd in fact abhorred.

When he'd been saved by a mysterious dove, he'd opened a heart that had always been closed, daring to hope for a connection he'd never before thought possible. Instead, he found a mate for his brother and a recurring dream to haunt his nights—of her lips on his throat, his fingers digging into her skin, their magic sizzling between them.

Now he longed for the sky.

What twisted fate did Taetanos next have in store? It didn't matter, not really. Rafe was quite certain he had nothing left to lose.

"I was seven when my magic made itself known," the captain said, leaning her elbows on the rail beside Rafe's and staring out into the distance. "I was in the woods, training with my uncle, when I felt something stir in my chest. Before I could speak, a vicious wind tunneled down from the sky, wrapped around my limbs, and carried me away. I tried to fly out of it, but it followed me, as though it were part of me. Then I noticed the yellow sparks at my fingertips, how the storm mirrored the turmoil in my spirit, and I knew what it was—magic. When I finally managed to calm it, my uncle pulled me into his arms and let me cry against his chest. I pled with him to keep it a secret. The House of Prey is notoriously solitary. No one else was with us in the woods. We lived alone with my parents, my aunt, my brother and my cousin. I could control it, I promised. No one would ever have to know."

Despite his cool exterior, Rafe's stomach flipped. His magic had made itself known after the dragon attack, and only luck and the love of his brother had kept his fatal secret from being revealed. "How were you found out?"

"I wasn't," she said, a puff of air escaping her lips as a deep-set hurt flashed across her eyes, the sort he recognized —betrayal. "That night my uncle, my aunt, and my parents pulled me from my bed. We didn't live far from the edge and they were worried if our king found out, the entire family would be punished. It had happened before. We're a particularly brutal house. As I recall, my mother and father held me down while my uncle cut off my wing. I screamed and begged to no avail. The entire night is mostly a blur, except for the moment I glanced through my tears to hold my mother's resolute gaze. She turned her back and walked away as my uncle dug his foot into my spine. One push and I was falling."

"Your magic caught you?" he asked, turning to study her profile. The tight clench of her jaw could have crushed rocks.

"The same way it caught you." Her eyes met his, the color so blue they were nearly white, reminding him of the gleaming edge of a blade in the sun. He wasn't yet sure if the weapon was delivering a fatal blow or defiantly raised to protect his life. "I was lucky, too. There was no ship waiting in the depths to save me. If I'd landed in the sea, I'd be dead, dragged down by the one useless wing still attached to my back. But I landed at the edge of a city and despite the darkness, another *aero'kine* sensed my magic and drew me in."

"Who?"

"I believe you know him as Patch, though to me he'll always have a different name." She looked over her shoulder toward the man behind the wheel, her first mate. A warmth he hadn't seen before filled her face, not romantic but affectionate just the same.

"How did you end up here?"

She stood abruptly, the openness of her expression closing so quickly Rafe almost winced with the impact. "That's a story for another time, and maybe one day you'll earn it. My point was this. You're not the only one on this ship to have lost things. You're not the only one on this ship to want. But you are the only one wallowing in self-pity, which I'm afraid I can't allow."

"I'm not a member of your crew," he challenged, his growing sympathy gruffly quelled. "You can't order me around."

"Should I toss you out to sea then? And we'll see how well you fare?"

He didn't know her well enough to discern if it was an empty threat or a real one, but he couldn't stop himself from fighting back. "Go ahead. No fire has killed me. No sword. No dagger. No arrow. No wound. Even a building falling on my head did little to slow me down. I'm almost curious to know if drowning will finally be my magic's undoing."

The captain paused, swallowing her words, or maybe her shock at his. An empty threat then, which was good to know.

"How about a bargain?" she asked slowly, studying him. "If I remember correctly, the ravens put their faith in a trickster god. Maybe a game of chance would do you better."

"There's nothing you have that I want."

"That may be true, but I know a lot of people."

"There's nothing they have that I want."

"No?" She arched a brow. "Not even wings?"

He jerked upright. "Who? How?"

"That's for me to know," she said slyly. "I need a ship full of people pulling their own weight, and you need something to live for. Make me a deal and maybe we can both walk away from this arrangement unscathed."

"Anything," he rasped. "I'll do anything."

"Did Brighty tell you what we're doing out here in the middle of the ocean?"

"She said I'd find out eventually."

Captain Rokaro's lips quirked. "This is no trading ship. We sail for one purpose, and one alone—to hunt dragons."

"Dragons?" Rafe turned to her sharply. "You actually go out looking for them?"

"You will too. That's my end of the bargain. You see, we've been hunting a particularly nasty beast for about a month now, and until I catch it, I can't return to port. Become a member of my crew, do as you're told, and help us find it—and I mean actual help, not standing at the bow of the ship with that brooding look of yours, distracting most of my crew. In return, when we do reach port, I'll get you an audience with the king."

"Your king? He can return my wings?"

"The king has magic unlike any you've ever seen, but he can be a bastard when he wants to be, ruthless and shrewd, and convincing him to let you return to the sky will be nearly impossible. But yes. If he wants to, he can return your wings."

"Done."

Rafe extended his hand. He knew there was something she wasn't telling him, some plot unseen. It was clear this king had ordered Cassi to remove his wings, just as he'd commanded Captain Rokaro to be waiting when he fell. Why go through all the trouble to bring Rafe to the world below just to return his wings and let him go? Then again, why go through the trouble at all? The only thing that made Rafe unique was his magic, which meant it had value to this king—what sort of value he had no clue, but he intended to find out. And when he did, he'd use it to his advantage. He'd get his wings back, no matter the cost, because Xander and Lyana were counting on him.

The captain took his hand and they shook once.

"Wait." Rafe tightened his hold on her fingers. "Why haven't you asked this king to return your missing wing?"

"Who said I haven't?" She slid her hand from his and cupped it around her lips as she turned to look over her shoulder. "Brighty!"

The girl glanced over immediately, as though she'd been

waiting for the call. Watching her shimmy down the ropes and scuttle across the deck, Rafe had no trouble imagining her as the master pickpocket she'd claimed to be. Her every move was silent and assured, not a single step out of place despite the swaying waves.

"You called, Captain?" A grin played across her lips, ripe with amusement. He'd never seen her serious, never seen her without a joke upon her tongue. It made him curious as to what she was trying to hide. He, of all people, recognized a guarded heart when he saw one.

"I did. Rafe and I have come to an understanding."

"Thank magic," Brighty interjected with a roll of her milky eyes. "There was only so much moping I could take before I pushed him over myself."

Rafe frowned at her.

She winked at him.

"As I was saying," the captain gently chided, "we've come to an understanding and he'll be joining the crew for the time being. It's not easy to teach a man of the sky to be at home on the sea, but if anyone's up to the challenge, it's you. Show him the ropes. Teach him to stand on two steady feet. You know what to do."

"Aye, aye, Captain."

"Good." Captain Rokaro turned back to Rafe. "You know where I am if you need me."

She was gone with a swish of wind as the single wing she still possessed rippled the air. Before he could ruminate over the conversation, Brighty grabbed his arm and yanked surprisingly hard for a girl so petite.

"Let's go."

"Where?"

"Captain said to show you the ropes, so I'm showing you the ropes."

Rafe let her pull him along. They climbed down a set of stairs and traversed the main area of the deck, her feet steady while his stumbled.

At home on the sea. He huffed. The chances of that happening seemed even more unlikely than him ever regaining his wings. He'd never get used to this place—to the moisture always clinging to his skin, to the heaviness of the air as he breathed it in, to the constant push and pull of water. He missed the trees. He missed the sun. Most of all, he missed the sky.

"All right," Brighty said as she stopped by the main mast, grabbing a set of thickly woven ropes from where they pooled at its base. "These are the ropes."

Rafe snorted. "I don't think the captain meant to literally show me the ropes."

"Are you the teacher here? Or am I?"

She put her hand on her cocked hip. He shrugged, lacking the energy for a fight.

"Getting back to my point before you so rudely interrupted, these are the ropes." She shoved the bundle into his hands, nearly punching his gut in the process. In truth, he wasn't sure if she missed on purpose, or if a lucky undulation of the ship sent him stepping backward for balance just in time. "A sailor who can't tie a knot might as well be a stowaway, and Captain's never been fond of useless baggage, so I suggest you pay attention."

Rafe sighed. There would be plenty of time to ruminate

later. For now, it might do him some good to get his mind off things. Hours in the practice yards had always alleviated his burdens. His swords were below deck and there wasn't a target in sight, but any physical task would work.

He took the ropes. "Just tell me what to do."

7

CASSI

Sinking into her mother's dreams always felt like a falling into warm embrace. Not that Captain Rokaro was particularly affectionate, but she was familiar and trustworthy, which mattered far more to Cassi. As though she sensed her daughter's spirit, the chaos of the captain's mind slowed. It took hardly more than a thought to spin the racing colors into a scene mirroring Cassi's mood.

They stood at the highest peak of a jagged mountain range, the wind nipping their cheeks as snow battered their eyes. The sun was shrouded by gloomy clouds, and howling storms echoed from the valleys below. Toes sticking over the edge of a steep cliff, Cassi couldn't help but notice she'd forgotten to give herself wings. Or maybe that had been on purpose, her body like her mind, teetering and precarious, one wrong move from falling.

"How's Rafe?"

Her mother turned toward her, arching a brow in question. "Where have you been?"

"How's Rafe?"

"He's…" The captain paused, expression heavy as she looked back toward the blistering view. "Surviving."

"What does that mean?"

"What do you think?"

Her mother had an uncanny ability to say everything yet nothing at the same time. Cassi snarled and cast her gaze onto the rocks below. What did she think? That he was broken. That she'd destroyed him. That to be a bird without the sky was a fate almost worse than death—a fate from which the man she'd once called a friend would never recover.

What had she expected her mother to say?

He's fine? He'll be all right? He likes it better down here?

Those were just the lies she told herself to keep the guilt at bay, to prevent it from eating her alive from the inside out. Cassi was rotted to the core, and she wasn't sure how long she could keep everyone else from seeing it too.

"He had a better day today," the captain murmured softly. Sympathy churned in her frosty eyes, though Cassi was certain she didn't deserve it.

"Why?"

"I gave him something to live for, something to fight for. I think it helped."

"What?" Her brows twitched. "What did you give him?"

"Hope."

A nauseous feeling stirred in Cassi's gut, as real as if she were in her own body. The taste of bile ate at her tongue. "What kind?"

"I told him I could grant him an audience with the king."

"Mother!" The word spilled out sharp with disbelief and accusation. She knew instantly what the captain had promised. It was a cruel trick, not as brutal as the one her daughter had played, but close. "Malek will never give him back his wings."

"I don't know that."

"I do."

He would never. Not this king. Not Malek. Not the man who ordered the death of an innocent prince in the name of keeping his world a secret. Rafe had only seen a small glimpse of what the lands within the mist had to offer, but it was enough.

"Do you know what he's planning then?"

"No." An angry puff of air escaped her lips. "I wasn't privy to that information. I was just told what to do."

"Then neither of us knows what the king will or won't agree to. It's possible he just wanted to give the boy time to learn about our world and to appreciate it before recruiting him to our cause. The only way to do that with an *invinci* is to remove the wings entirely—otherwise Rafe would've already healed and flown away. I don't see much use for his magic aside from using him as a fighter, and a warrior with wings is always better than one without, especially in a war against dragons."

"It's possible," Cassi conceded. *Though I doubt it.*

Malek wasn't kindhearted. For better or worse, he was

single-mindedly focused and ruthless in his pursuit of saving the world. Oh, he had a plan for Rafe, she was certain. But it wouldn't be the pretty picture her mother painted.

"Don't lose your hope, Kasiandra." The captain brushed her caramel feathers against Cassi's arm. "Don't lose your ability to believe in people."

She looked at her hands, for a moment seeing Rafe's blood still upon them, sticky maroon spotted with ebony fuzz. One blink and the image was gone, but it was always there, lurking in the far corners of her mind. *How can I believe in people, Mother, when I don't even believe in myself?*

The captain studied her, though Cassi refused to meet her gaze. After a few moments, she finally said, "I don't usually hear you call the king by name."

Cassi folded her fingers into fists, heart racing with the memory of her king. His golden hair, streaked with highlights from the sun. The soft brown freckles scattered across his nose. His dark blue eyes, so bottomless she couldn't find a soul within them. And the grip of his magic, holding her down, stealing her sky, breaking her heart even after he'd disappeared. Seeing him in real life had made clear something her dreams had naively brushed over— Malek was not the boy she remembered. He was a man and a king, and he cared little for the Kasiandra he'd once known.

"Things change."

"Hmm." Her mother paused. The heavy silence pierced like a blade. "Is that why you haven't gone to see him?"

Cassi sucked in a breath. "How do you know that?"

"He sent another man into my dreams to ask if I'd heard from you. When I told him no, the man gave me a message from the king. He's looking for you. He wants to talk to you. And eventually he will, one way or another."

She snorted at the unveiled threat in the words. "He knows where to find me if he wants to talk, but I don't see him venturing up to my world anytime soon. So I guess he'll just have to wait."

"Kasiandra." Her mother sighed. "It's not wise to go against his wishes."

"What about my wishes?" Cassi snapped, her anger ripe and raring. Did anyone care what she thought? She didn't want to be a killer. She didn't want to be a monster. She didn't want to keep leading a double life. She wanted to go home. She wanted to be with her best friend. She wanted to be a normal girl, whatever that meant.

"Do you hold the fate of the world on your shoulders?"

She mumbled a gruff, "No."

"Then for now, I don't think your wishes matter."

Cassi opened her mouth to argue, but her mother held up a hand to stop her.

"Think of it this way, Kasiandra. What if Aethios himself came to you one day and told you a great battle was coming, and few would survive? Then he offered you a choice. If you sacrifice one man or woman now—a knife to the throat, quick and done, delivered to his feet—he would save one hundred later. Would you do it? Could you?"

"I—" She squirmed, made uncomfortable by the choice of analogy. Was Xander the sacrifice? Were innocent people the victims? Did her mother have information she didn't? "I don't know."

"The king knows, because he has to know. He makes this choice every day. Countless people need him, but there is only so much time and energy he can give. So, if sacrificing one will save a hundred, he'll do it, over and over again, to keep as many people safe as possible. You and I, Kasiandra, and others like us? We're the one. Our lives are forfeit to a greater cause. Is the sacrifice fair? No, of course not. But is it worth it? That's something you must decide on your own." She sighed, wrapping a lock of Cassi's bronze hair around her finger and tugging gently. "In the meantime, go see him. Hear what he has to say."

Cassi stared into the blizzard, watching it strengthen as her mother's hand dropped away. She didn't want to see Malek, but if she were being honest, it was about more than that.

She didn't want to see Lyana.

No, she didn't want to see Malek and Lyana, the king and queen of prophecy, united in ways Cassi could never dream to be, not even with her magic. She'd lost more than just a foolish crush. She'd lost her best friend. For, surely, Lyana would never speak to her again if she learned what Cassi had done and what she might yet do. Malek had always been able to sense her spirit outside of the dreams. Now with her new magic, Lyana might too. And the thought of facing her, of staring into her eyes and seeing hate, was too much to bear.

Had her sacrifices been worth it?

Cassi didn't have an answer to that question yet.

"Come, Kasiandra, let's not waste all our time in deep, dark thought. I do too much of that during the day as is. Do you know what scene the *dormi'kine* the king sent imagined for us?"

She turned toward her mother absently. "What?"

"My own ship! As if I don't spend enough time there already. It was all gray and cloudy. No wings. No color. No life. He was such a bore. I couldn't wait for him to leave so my own mind could twist my thoughts into something beautiful. He had none of your spirit. None of your imagination."

"Perhaps he needs to read more."

Her mother laughed, a sudden, barking thing, and then she found her daughter's eye. It wasn't their way to be overtly affectionate, yet Cassi saw the words deep in the captain's irises just the same. *I missed you.* On her lips, they came out differently, but just as warm. "Let's fly."

With a shrill shriek, the captain jumped off the cliff, letting the winds of the storm carry her, copper feathers stark against the snow. Cassi did the same, launching herself over the edge before remembering she'd forgotten to give herself wings. Instead of the wind catching her weight, she fell, plummeting head over heels as her stomach surged into her throat to block her scream. Her body had never felt so heavy. The air had never felt so foreign. It whooshed around her, empty and cold, like a lover who had turned away. The ground rose to meet her, jagged rocks like a bed of daggers, sharp and deadly.

Was this how Rafe had felt when she'd thrown him over the edge? As though his body had betrayed him? As though the one thing he'd always been able to count on was suddenly gone?

Just before impact, her spirit tore free of her mother's body and everything fell away. The mountains. The blizzard. The fall. She was back in her phantom body, surrounded by humid air and groaning wood, hovering at the edge of a four-poster bed. A soft smile played on her mother's lips while she slept, and her single wing stretched back, feathers rustling against the sheets. Somewhere deep in her subconscious, she was flying, and the last thing Cassi wanted to do was disturb her.

Instead, she drifted through the cabin door and into the dark halls she knew so well she could have lived there. The swaying did little to bother her floating spirit. Her soul bobbed with it, as though somewhere deep inside, the ocean called to her. She had, after all, been born for the sea and not the sky before fate intervened.

It only took a few minutes to find him. Cassi could go no farther than the door. She poked her spectral body through the wooden planks and froze as soon as she spotted Rafe. Tortured grooves cut into his forehead. He winced in pain, his body curled in on itself. Soaked with sweat, the sheets wrapped around his limbs like binds. This was not a man at peace. He was haunted by nightmares, and though she knew she could help—could sink into his dreams and shape them into something kind—she couldn't face him or what she'd done.

Her spirit flew back as though jerked by a string, sailing through wood and metal until she was in the mist and the ship was far away, vanishing into the gray depths. The fog was suffocating. She felt as though she couldn't breathe. Up and up and up she rose, until finally, the vapors gave way and the stars flickered to life.

Normally, entering the world above felt like waking from a dream, but not this time. Part of her was stuck in that ship, trapped in the mist. Part of her was still falling through the air, racing toward the ground. She needed a distraction. She needed a little bit of good to hold on to in a world that at the moment seemed a thousand shades of bad.

As she neared the city of Pylaeon, she found her diversion. A light in the tallest spire of the castle glowed bright against the night, large windows offering a view of the bookshelves housed within. Xander was awake. And though she knew it would only make things harder, she found she couldn't help but gravitate toward him.

8

XANDER

J ust as Xander was ready to pull yet another heavy history volume from his shelves, a little *tap, tap, tap,* sounded against his window. He spun, surprised to find Cassi hovering behind the glass. After quickly crossing the room, he twisted the latch and yanked the pane open.

"Cassi?"

"I hope you don't mind," she said and soared past him, shuffling the pages of his books as she swept into the room. It was refreshing that she didn't ask for an audience or tiptoe around him, though at the same time a little alarming that she felt free to barge into his study. He supposed he *had* opened the window for her, but still… "I couldn't sleep, and I saw your light on. What are you doing?"

"Oh, this?"

Xander turned toward his desk, thinking of the hours he'd spent roving through his library while the rest of the world was asleep, all in search of information he feared he'd never find. His books held only vague mentions of what the world looked like before the isles were lifted into the sky, the same stories he'd heard as a child—they'd been slaves to cruel masters who wielded magic like a weapon. There was no explanation of what that magic was or how to fight it, only cautionary orders to kill any who possessed it lest they anger the gods. Worse still, there were no theories as to what lands might now exist beneath the mist, and hardly any mentions of Vesevios, as though writing his name would conjure him into being.

He blinked away his frustration. "It's just research."

The owl sauntered across the room, fingering the corner of a leather-bound book. "Anything interesting?"

A dejected sigh escaped his lips. "No."

"Pity."

"What are you doing? Here, I mean?"

"I told you. I couldn't sleep." Pressing her finger to one of the maps spread across the tabletop, she traced the rough edge of his homeland, an expression he couldn't read playing across her face. Then she straightened abruptly and turned toward him. "Could I ask you a question?"

"Sure." He shrugged. "I don't see why not."

"It's hypothetical."

"That's my favorite kind."

She sighed and collapsed into one of the leather armchairs, her black-and-white speckled wings bending up and over her shoulders as she pulled her knees into her chest. It was the most childlike he'd ever seen her, except for the haunted look in her eyes, dark despite the firelight reflecting within them. He couldn't help but wonder from whom she might be hiding as he took the seat across from her.

"You're going to be king someday, right?" She finally broke the silence.

Xander couldn't stop his lips from curving. "I hope that's not your hypothetical question."

"It's not," she said. "My question is this. Imagine for a moment that sometime during your reign, Taetanos himself appears to you and offers you one of his infamous bargains. He tells you a great battle is coming, and if you sacrifice one of your people to his realm now, he will save one hundred in the future. Would you do it?"

Expelling the air from his lungs, Xander sank back into his chair. On paper, the bargain seemed easy—one in place of a hundred. But then he thought of Rafe, he thought of the people caught with magic who were brought to the executioner's block, he thought of that horrible, wet *thunk*, and the words wouldn't come. He had yet to order anyone's death—it was the one responsibility his mother had never forced upon him, perhaps fearing what the outcome might be.

He tore his gaze from where it had settled on the fireplace and flicked it to Cassi instead, arching a brow. "This is the kind of question that keeps you up at night?"

"What would you do?" she repeated, not relenting.

"Is the one person a criminal? Or completely innocent?"

"Would that matter?"

"I don't know."

"Then let's assume he or she is a little bit of both. Not a murderer, but not Aethios's chosen either. Someone who's done a few bad things, but isn't beyond redemption."

He rested his elbow on the leather and cupped his fingers around his chin, running through the possibilities. There was an answer his mother would want him to give, and then there was the truth. Alone with Cassi, no one else around to hear, he supposed it was all right to admit the latter. "No. I don't think I would."

"Why?" Her eyes widened as the word slipped out drenched in surprise, and she leaned forward, uncurling her legs to move closer. "Why not?"

"Because..." He swallowed, thinking back to that moment in the sacred nest when he'd held his forearm to that man's throat and attempted to choke the life out of him. "Under some circumstances, I can imagine myself killing a person—to protect someone I love, to protect my kingdom—an enemy, a combatant, someone trying to do me or my people harm. I know in the future I'll have to execute people to maintain our laws, though I don't relish the thought. But in the circumstance you posed—using someone as a sacrifice—no, I don't think I would. As king, I think it would send the wrong message. It would tell my people I deemed them disposable. I would rather we fight and die together, to try to save all or none, than risk a single raven ever believing I wouldn't do everything in my power to save them."

He'd said more than he'd meant to, yet somehow it seemed right. He rarely had conversations like this with Rafe—his brother lacked the patience. Lyana, too, had been more comfortable out in the world doing than inside the castle thinking. But Cassi was different. The silence didn't seem to bother her as it stretched between them. Her eyes glazed over as she got lost in her own thoughts the way he so often got lost in his.

"What would you do?" Xander finally asked.

She returned to the present at once, a smile shaping her lips, though it seemed more a mask than anything else. "Luckily, I'll never be a king, so I don't need to find out."

He laughed and shook his head. The hilt of a dagger was barely visible through her loosely bent fingers, a weapon he hadn't noticed she was carrying. "Are you telling your secrets to that instead of to me?"

Cassi stared at him blankly.

Idiot. Xander internally winced. *What a ridiculous thing to say.* "The blade, I mean, because of what you said the other day..."

"Oh." Her eyes widened and a true smile overtook her face, pinching her cheeks and softening her features. He'd thought her attractive before, but in that moment, he couldn't believe he'd ever seen her as anything but beautiful. An impish twinkle lit her moonlight eyes. "Wouldn't you like to know."

In an explosion of motion, she jumped easily to her feet and spun, her feathers nearly smacking him in the face as she left the fireplace behind her. Xander remained seated, observing her as she walked across the room. He half expected her to open the window and vanish as quickly as she'd come, her question answered, but instead, she surprised him. She paused beside one of his bookshelves and gracefully ran her index finger over the spines as she read the titles embossed on them. A slight pout rose on her lips as her hooded eyes narrowed with concentration. She seemed...interested.

"Would you like to borrow one?"

Cassi turned, surprise written across her face. "You wouldn't mind?"

"No, of course not. As you can see, I have more than enough. Too many, if some are to be believed."

"Fools," she muttered dismissively, glancing back at the shelves. "Do you have any that tell a story? I find history rather dull, and don't even get me started on trade."

Xander bit back a laugh. He was quite fond of history himself, and trade was a necessary evil to someone training to be king—though if he were honest, he quite enjoyed that too. Instead, he rolled to his feet and strode confidently to the shelves to the right of the fireplace. "This one is a love story between two warring clans in the House of Prey."

"I read that. A little mushy for my taste."

"How about this?" He pulled a larger volume off the shelf and handed it to her. "It's about a songbird who gets swept up in a storm and transported to a mystical land. Or, oh, this one is quite entertaining. It's about an owl who tries to fly all the way around the world. I also have these, all the stories of the gods before they sacrificed themselves to the god stones. If the myths are to be believed, they used to cause a lot of trouble."

Before he knew it, Xander had a stack of books balanced precariously against his hip. Cassi pulled the growing pile from his hold, seemingly unaware that her fingers brushed the rounded end of his arm, and placed the stack more sturdily on the floor.

"I can't take all these."

"Why not?"

"For starters, I might topple out of the sky the second I leave the window."

He nodded to one side with his chin. "Then use the door."

"Can I give you something in return?"

"There's nothing I need."

Cassi rolled her eyes, a playful yet frustrated move. "Why are you so honorable?"

"You say it as though it's a bad thing."

Under her breath, she half growled, "Maybe it is."

Xander pushed his brows together even as a grin tugged at his lips. She was mystifying. An expert fighter who happened to enjoy reading. An owl who'd grown up surrounded by doves. A woman who always wore a brave face, yet when he thought of her, he remembered that moment in the square, seconds after the dragon attack, when he'd held her in his arms and she'd let him.

Cassi was a puzzle—one he was determined to solve.

"Perhaps you can do one thing for me," Xander finally said, his mind still on his mating day, on the fight with that man and the battle with the dragon. In both instances, he'd been a liability, someone who was in the way while others fought to tame the beast. He didn't want to be that person anymore. He wanted to be someone who could face down a dragon with more than futile hope and an empty scream on his lips. "You could train me."

"Train you?" She frowned. "What about Helen? What about the hundreds of guards in a little place called the barracks about two hundred feet to our left?"

"I've been training with them since I was a boy, and not a single one ever thought to tell me the most important rule of battle."

"Which is?"

"That my sword could be my friend."

She snorted, though the ghost of a smile graced her lips. "I said that was the first rule of battle, not the most important."

"So, teach me the rest too."

"I don't think I'd make a very good teacher."

"That's all right." He shrugged, nothing if not persistent. A fallback of being royal—he was unused to hearing the word *no*. "I'll make up for it by being an excellent student."

"Books for lessons?"

Xander nodded.

Cassi studied him, her gaze boring into his as though searching for some reason to keep fighting. When he didn't give one, she sighed and glanced to the books by their feet. By the time she looked back at him, her mind was made. "Prince Xander, you have yourself a deal."

"Excellent."

They shook hands. It didn't go beyond his notice that she showed no hesitation in extending her left arm, not her right one, something it had taken most of his advisors some getting used to when he'd come of age. It told him she was smart, which he already knew, but also observant and quick, all traits he imagined to be perfect qualities in his new instructor. If she wanted to one day, she'd make a fine royal guard.

He was about to say so when the window shattered.

Fractured glass pelleted his side like a hundred little needles, the sound of falling shards like that of rain, truncated by the deep *thud* of something heavy landing on the rug. Xander twisted away instinctively and lifted his arms to cover his face. By the time he righted himself, Cassi was already beside the window with her dagger at the ready, her predator's eyes scanning the darkness. He rushed to her side.

"Do you see anything?"

"No."

Xander studied the shadows, but it was futile. If an owl couldn't see anything, a raven had no chance, especially at night. Instead, he left her by the window and searched for the source of the break. Hardly a second passed before he noticed a rock sitting within the pile of broken glass, a bit of black lettering only half-visible. He carefully lifted it from the floor, spinning it until he could read the message.

Kill him.

"What does it say?"

The clog in Xander's throat made it impossible to speak, jovial mood as thoroughly ruined as the window, so he simply lifted the rock overhead. Cassi snatched it from his grasp and muttered a curse. He barely heard.

Kill him.

That's what the message said, but he knew what it meant.

Kill Rafe.

His people had been angry ever since they'd made the announcement that his brother had stolen the princess. They'd taken to the streets, shouting for revenge, screaming for justice. But that wasn't enough. Now they wanted blood.

I did this.

Xander winced, closing his eyes against the truth. No matter what had happened between Rafe and him, no matter what his brother had done, Xander still loved him. Yet he'd condemned him to this. Maybe his earlier answer to Cassi's question had been false—a naïve and noble hope. He could have given his people the truth, for better or worse, so they could fight this evil together. Instead, he'd thrown his brother to the wolves.

Don't come back. Xander sent out the thought like a prayer to his god, as though Rafe might somehow hear. *Wherever you are in the world, brother, don't come back. Not yet. Not until I have a better answer to give them. Please, for your own good, stay away.*

9

RAFE

The ground had never seemed so far away. Not in the countless hours he'd spent hovering over Xander with the other guards while their prince walked the city streets. Not when he'd soared thousands of miles above the Sea of Mist. Not even when he'd fought that dragon on the sky bridge. Logically, Rafe knew it was no more than twenty feet, and that even if he fell, his magic would heal him. That did little to stop the blood from rushing to his head or his heart from leaping up his throat every time a strong breeze pushed him the slightest bit off balance.

"Come on," Brighty called from the top of the mast, having already completed the climb. "We haven't got all day."

I'm pretty sure we do, Rafe grumbled silently, latching his fists around the ropes and holding on for not-so-dear life as the ship rocked in the waves. Time seemed to be the one thing he had in abundance. Lost within the endless fog, the days passed in a blur, one just the same as the next. Life on the ship was a monotonous cycle of eating, sleeping, and learning the ropes while trying his best not to strangle Brighty with them.

"I didn't take you for someone who'd be afraid of heights."

I'm not. Or at least he hadn't used to be, but it was a new feeling entirely to know that if he fell, there would be no wings to catch him.

"If you get to the top before I count to ten, I'll answer one of your questions about the king."

At her challenge, Rafe finally looked up to where she perched in the little basket atop the main mast, a smirk on her face. He couldn't tell if she was lying, but something told him she was being honest—she just didn't expect him to make it in time.

"One."

Rafe scrambled up the net, forgetting about the ground and the fall and the wind and the waves, focusing instead on where to wrap his fingers and place his feet. The higher he climbed, the more the world swayed. The sounds of the crew fell away, replaced by whistling gusts and whipping sails. The countdown droned in his ear.

"Two. Three. Four."

He missed a step, leg falling through a hole, and panic snatched his breath. The ropes bit into his palms as he caught his weight. Gritting his teeth, Rafe righted himself.

"Five. Six. Seven."

The net grew narrower as he neared the highest point. It wobbled unsteadily beneath him, making his biceps and thighs burn in the best way. His abdomen fired up as he fought to keep his balance, his body blazing with life.

"Eight. Nine."

Then he was there, pressing his fingers against the small wooden deck and pulling himself over the edge.

"Ten."

"I made it."

"Did you, though? I mean, as I was saying *ten* your feet were technically still on the net, so I'm not entirely sure that counts."

"I made it," he growled and collapsed against the mast, letting his feet dangle over the edge. He closed his eyes and breathed, calming himself now that there was some sort of floor beneath him.

"Fine, you made it." For a moment, he thought she might leave it at that—no jab or jibe for the first time ever. Then, under her breath, Brighty added, "It's not like you'll ask a very good question anyway."

He opened his eyes to glare at her as his head dropped to the side. Then he asked the first question that came to mind, unable to stop himself from jumping in without giving his brain time to think. "What kind of magic does the king have?"

Brighty snorted, the sound dripping with superiority. "*Aethi'kine.*"

"What's that?"

"I don't think my deal included a second question."

"Come on. I don't know what any of this means, and you know it."

"I do, and your ignorance is adorable."

Rafe clenched his teeth to keep from barking back, remembering one of Xander's former lessons about catching flies with honey or some such nonsense.

"Your anger is adorable too."

"Brighty!"

"I may look like an honest member of a dragon-hunting crew, but once a thief, always a thief, Rafe. No one steals from me, not even something as simple as an extra answer, and I don't give anything away for free. You want more? You'll have to earn it."

"How?"

"I'm glad you asked." She grinned, pulled a rope from behind her back, and tossed it into his lap. "For every knot you tie correctly, I'll answer another one of your questions, with one caveat."

He fingered the rope. "What's that?"

"No questions about me."

It was Rafe's turn to snort. "No problem."

Her gaze bored into his side, but Rafe kept his attention on the fog as the ship rolled back and forth, the movements more pronounced from this height. It would take most of his energy not to be sick, especially as his focus dropped to the wooden deck far, far below, making him dizzy.

"We'll start easy. Show me a square knot."

Rafe tightened his grip on the rope, trying to remember the endless stream of information Brighty had been doling out ever since his conversation with the captain. He switched his hold, grabbing the two ends in his fingers before twisting them around each other twice.

"Good. Ask away."

"What's an *aethi'kine*?"

"You're so obvious."

"Just answer."

"A spirit mage."

He waited, giving her the chance to say more.

She didn't.

"Brighty, if all I'm going to get are one- and two-word answers, I'm not playing your ridiculous game. Go find another person to annoy. Oh, wait—you can't. You're just as stuck with me as I am with you."

"There's one difference," she commented, voice so smooth it immediately raised his hackles. "I'm not the one in need of answers."

His hands balled into fists, accidently tightening the knot. How in the world had he tumbled out of the sky just to find someone more frustratingly stubborn than his brother? Even Taetanos didn't have a sense of humor this cruel.

"Sailor's knot."

With a sigh, he untied the first knot, then looped and twisted the rope around into the new one before holding it up for inspection. Brighty nodded.

"What's a spirit mage?"

"Before you learn that, you need to understand what spirit even is," she said, dropping her head back against the mast but keeping her attention on the sky. Rafe expected her to stop, but instead of tossing out the name of another knot, she kept going. "When you look at this view, you see fog and water and wood. But if an *aethi'kine* looked at this view, they would see beyond all of that, into the very essence of what the fog and water and wood are, into the unseen force holding them all together. Did you ever wonder why no one else could see your magic in the world above?"

Rafe nodded, though in truth one person had seen his magic—the same person who had let him see hers, a moment so special to the two of them yet so benign to someone of this world, where magic freely lit the air. Brighty would never understand.

"It's because people without magic can't see it. They're not attuned to it. It's a form of energy invisible to their eyes. There's a similar divide between those with and those without *aethi'kine* power. We don't sense spirit, so we can't see it, but they do. And spirit is in everything. The air we breathe. The food we eat. The water we drink. Nothing in the physical world exists without a little bit of spirit holding it together. And *that* is what a spirit mage sees, what they touch with their magic. There's no limit to what they can do, including giving a raven back his wings."

Rafe snapped his face to the side. "What makes you say that?"

"You're an easy mark, Rafe," she said, meeting his eyes, her own expression inscrutable. "You wear your every emotion like a new bauble on display. Now, show me a dragon's nostril."

He didn't bother to press her, but instead focused on the rope, tying it into a new shape. As soon as Brighty nodded, another question rose to his lips. "What's my magic called?"

"*Invinci*," she said without hesitation. "We think it's a form of spirit magic, but no one knows for sure. I've never met anyone else who has it, but don't let that go to your head."

Invinci, Rafe thought, mulling over the word. It was strange to finally have a name for the magic he'd spent his entire life hiding, to bring something so secret into the light —strange, but not, he was surprised to find, unwelcome.

"Show me a serpent's noose."

Rafe tied it, earning another nod. "What do you think the king wants with my magic?"

"Ooh, finally an interesting question," she murmured, grinning as she studied him. Rafe tried to smooth his features, but it was no use. She could read him as easily as Xander did his many books. "Unfortunately, it's also a question I can't answer. I don't know what the king wants, though I agree, it must have something to do with your magic."

"We had a deal. Make a guess."

She pursed her lips as though considering, then relented. "If I had to guess, I'd say he wants the same thing he wants from everyone with magic—another soldier in his army."

"Captain!" A shout cut through the silence following her words, rising up and over the whipping sails as though carried by the wind. Pyro stood at the front of the ship with both hands extended, her fingertips sizzling with flames. Rafe couldn't see her face, just her auburn hair swirling in the breeze. "I feel something!"

Brighty was on her feet in an instant.

"Wait!" He grabbed her hand. "What army? Who is he fighting?"

"Dragons, Rafe." An almost sorry expression crossed her face before she twisted free of his hold. "In the end, it always comes back to dragons."

Then she was gone. Brighty grabbed one of the ropes attached to the mast and launched herself off the platform, looping her foot in such a way as to slow her fall so she landed easily on the deck. Rafe scrambled down the net to follow.

"Where?" Captain Rokaro shouted.

"Port side," Pyro answered.

The ship heaved, and Rafe flew backward as the mast tilted with the sharp turn, leaving nothing below him but the choppy sea. One of his feet lost its grip. He snaked his elbows through the net and hugged it to his chest as he dangled, afraid he might lose his breakfast. The wind changed direction, air flecked with yellow sparks of magic, and the ship righted itself. Rafe held tightly to the ropes, not yet willing to move as they raced forward. On deck, Brighty was already by Pyro's side with her fingers raised.

A white light shot through the fog, so brilliant it made his own vision spot. Brighty stood at its center, a black figure silhouetted by the glow. Pyro had turned away, holding her forearm to cover her face. Rafe wanted to watch, but he couldn't stand the burn. Instead, he found the captain, staring ahead with a wild look in her eyes. She kept her focus on Brighty—the only one on the ship who seemed to do so. He waited until the white gleam in her pupils faded before spinning back around.

The mist was gone.

Not all of it, of course, but it looked as though a tunnel

had been carved through the gray, revealing an endless stretch of choppy ocean waves, the blue of the sea almost as vivid as the sky with the ivory glow of Brighty's magic still clinging to the air.

She had burned the fog away.

"Do you see anything?" Captain shouted.

"No!" Brighty called back.

"Do it again!"

This time, Rafe turned before she fired her magic, noticing how the sails caught her light first, then the mast, then the nets and the ropes and the rails. Where before there had been a dull sort of shine from the shrouded sky, leaving everything muddled, now the deck was marked by shadows, dark lines cutting across the wood and drawing patterns. The grains were a rich cedar, more vibrant than he'd ever seen them. And the captain's single wing, arched back like a falcon's on the hunt, shone caramel in the glow.

As quickly as it came, it faded.

Rafe flipped his head around to find another tunnel carved through the mist, the first one nearly gone by its side as the fog rolled back in. But unlike the last time, at the very end he caught sight of something black and sharp, gliding through the fog and emitting a subtle orange hue. It took another second before he realized what it was—the tip of a wing.

"Dragon!" Captain Rokaro shouted as a blistering gust rolled over the ship, snapping the sails so tight he feared they might tear. "All right, you lazy sluggards, let's move!"

LYANA

A knock sounded at the door and Lyana turned from the window, swallowing a groan. Using her sweetest voice, she chimed, "Come in."

Malek strode inside, amusement twisting his normally stern features. "You sound cheerful."

"Do I?"

"Excited for our lessons?"

Lyana dropped her gaze to the bowls resting on the table, unmoved from the day before, and the day before that, and the day before that, on and on for she didn't know how long. She'd lost count. Her mouth curled before she could stop it, and something sounding strangely like a laugh escaped Malek's lips.

"You look at them as though they might bite."

"I almost wish they would," she mused, unsure how to read his expression. "At least then something interesting would happen."

"Are you bored?"

"Aren't you?"

He sighed, the small hint of humor leaving his face. "These lessons might be tedious, but until you can master your magic, we've no hope of seeing the prophecy through. And the first lesson you must learn is control."

"I know, Malek," she cut in, uninterested in another lecture. He so loved doling them out. She needed to practice her magic. She needed to control her magic. According to him, she needed to do so many things, but leaving this room to enjoy the fresh air wasn't one of them. "I know."

He frowned but let it go. "As it happens, you're in luck."

"What do you mean?"

"I didn't come here for a lesson. I came to tell you we're arriving at my home."

A thrill raced through her. "Your home?"

"Meet me on deck as soon as you're dressed."

"What is it? Where are we? What's it called?"

He shut the door in her face, effectively ending her stream of questions, but Lyana was too excited to care. Finally, she was going to see more of this world than the endless curtain of gray always stretched across her window. What would it be like? Would there be people? Would they have magic?

With haste, she dug through the trunk of clothes Malek had left her, searching for something to wear. Back home, she would have been draped in jewels, her dress so complicated it required the help of servants to secure, her hair so intricately designed she would need Cassi's assistance to later undo it. Visits to foreign palaces were no small thing. But here, she would have to make do with clean leather trousers and slightly worn boots. The jacket she finally pulled from the bottom of the trunk was a rich jade to match her eyes, embroidered with golden threads reminiscent of her magic. Lyana secured the buttons, admiring how the silk cinched her waist only to flare around her hips like a skirt. On her way out the door, she grabbed a few of the pearl-studded pins left over from her mating day and threaded them through her hair.

Malek was waiting for her at the bow of the ship, his gaze on the mist. As she took the spot by his side, he spared a glance her way. For better or worse, he didn't comment on her appearance, a fact which didn't surprise her. He rarely said anything without a purpose behind the words, and a statement as frivolous as *you look beautiful* would sound almost silly spilling from his lips. After a few moments, he pointed into the gray.

"There. Do you see it?"

Lyana squinted and leaned over the rail, as though the few inches might make all the difference. She saw nothing.

"That bit of shadow," Malek murmured, his eyes now expectantly on her. He always looked at her like that, as though wanting more. She worried he would forever be kept waiting, needing something she didn't know how to give.

The thought fled when an outline of dark gray emerged from the haze, expansive and wide, far larger than a castle. "It's a city!"

His lips twitched with a grin. "It's Da'Kin."

"Da'Kin," she repeated, playing with the word as the view sharpened, ship masts and wooden spires becoming more visible through the fog, dreary yet dazzling to her eyes. Something new. Something unlike anything else she'd ever seen. A city that floated on water instead of on air. "What does it mean?"

"Most people call it the King's City, though that's not quite the translation from the old tongue. *Kin* has multiple meanings. Some believe it was a precursor to the word *king*. Others think it means *family*. More believe it used to be *kine* or *mage*. Da'Kin—the city of the king, the city of the people, the city of magic. All three apply here."

The city emerged from the mist as though from a dream, gray giving way to wooden buildings, carved bridges, gliding boats, and most of all, people. Hundreds stood in wait, their eyes on the ship sailing toward them. Some stood on decks, many on floating walkways, others poking their heads through the windows of their homes. Nerves swarmed in Lyana's stomach like a flock unleashed. Were they all there waiting for her?

"Time to make our arrival," he said with a sigh that sounded weary in a way she didn't quite understand. "Please, Lyana, don't use your magic. Your control has improved, but the open ocean is much different from the concentrated quarters of the city. Look with your spirit eyes if you'd like, but don't touch the power, not until I tell you. You'll understand soon, I promise."

He offered his hand, waiting.

She took it with a nod.

Raising their joined palms overhead, Malek released a

wave of spirit magic. The golden power arched across the sea to settle over the crowd at the nearest edge of the docks. A cheer emerged, cries and screams mixing as the masses turned into his power, soaking it in like the rays of the sun, their cheeks upturned to bask in the might of their king. Lyana watched through her spirit eyes, the world a swirling rainbow of light and magic. He was healing them, she realized quickly, the prickle of power so familiar yet so foreign. Restorative waves of magic sank into their bodies, not as concentrated as the magic she'd once poured into Rafe's wings and Xander's chest, but a more diluted form that gave off the sense of vitality without its force.

"Can they all see it?" she asked, so used to magic being her dirty secret.

"Most can't," he said, still letting his power flood across the water and crash over his people. "But even those without magic themselves can feel my touch, and that's why they cheer. For the promise of our power, for the hope it brings."

As they neared, more magic lit the skies, so dazzling her only wish was for Rafe to be there and see it. Nearly all the sailors on the surrounding ships sent shimmering swirls into the air—blues and greens and yellows and reds exploding in celebration. Among the crowd, there were far fewer displays of power, but the occasional spark of color flared. Even the swathes of people without magic looked on with awe. Their faces held no fear, only joy. No hesitation, only pride. Glistening cheeks caught the light. Tears of happiness. Sobs of relief. Every eye seemed turned on her with that same expression Malek always held—as though waiting for more.

They wanted their Queen Bred of Snow. They wanted someone she wasn't sure she knew how to be, but beneath the weight of their stares, she needed to do something. Guided by instinct, Lyana flared her wings as wide as they could go, her white feathers bright against the dreary gray.

The crowd roared.

Malek squeezed her fingers in silent approval, a gleam in his eyes unlike any she'd seen before. Despite the strain of his magic, he was content. For the first time since she'd met him, there was a hint of satisfaction woven through his spirit, a sense of peace.

The ship came to a halt by the mouth of a canal. A richly painted boat bobbed in the middle of the water with two gilded thrones resting at its center. Lyana couldn't for the life of her see a pathway through the crowd, a means of getting to the spot. But Malek seemed unbothered. He cleared his throat as the din quieted. Shouts gave way to soft weeping, which gave way to nothing but the gentle slap of waves, the creak of wood, and the subtle howl of wind.

"People of Da'Kin," he said, no strain in his voice. Magic followed his words, carrying the sound on the wind so all those gathered could hear. "I, King Malek'da'Nerri, the King Born in Fire, present to you Queen Lyana Aethionus, our long-awaited Queen Bred of Snow. For generations, we have suffered, but the time of the prophecy is finally upon us. Together, we will see the dragons defeated and our people liberated. Together, we will see the world healed."

A flurry stirred in her chest, making her dizzy.

She wasn't ready for this—ready for the hope in their

eyes shining brighter than Malek's magic, the collective held breath of so many people waiting for her to speak, hanging on her every word, the weight of all their dreams settling like a plug in her throat. Malek had been right. The open ocean was different from the city. Out there, the prophecy seemed little more than words and myth, prattle she could ignore while she focused on learning to use her new power. Here, it seemed as real as her gods, as powerful as Aethios, as terrifying as Vesevios, as double-sided as Taetanos. Here, there was no escaping this destiny she wasn't ready to accept.

Lyana opened her lips, but no sound came. She inhaled sharply, throat dry, chest burning, eyes wide. A shout saved her.

"To the queen!"

"To the king!"

"To the prophecy!"

The words crashed over the crowd like a tidal wave, drowning out the stillness and leaving chaos in their wake. Malek leaned close, his nose brushing her cheek as his breath warmed her skin.

"Hold on."

Deep green magic peppered the air. She recognized it as *ferro'kine* power just as the metal disk they were standing on lifted free of the deck. Malek placed his arm around her waist and held her tightly to his chest, still pushing his healing force out into the crowd. Lyana wrapped her arms around him, not afraid per se, but aware of her clipped feathers and the very real possibility of falling. Out of habit, her wings adjusted to the slight undulations as they rose over the edge of the ship and above the crowd. Their destination was clearly the smaller boat bobbing in the canal, and as they neared, a circular cutout by the base of the thrones became clear. Malek waited until the metal disk sank fully into the spot before taking his seat. With a gulp, Lyana sat beside him, feeling more of a farce than ever as he rejoined their hands, continuing the illusion of their shared power.

The water in the canal moved with a current made of magic, pushing them deeper into the city. Not once did the crowd thin. The platforms to either side teemed with people. Every bridge they floated past groaned with the weight of moving bodies. At first, Lyana marveled at the architecture—the wooden docks, the elegantly carved rails, the endless canals, the boats of various shapes and sizes, also filled with people. Glowing orbs penetrated the haze, the same light magic she'd seen on the ship. As they drifted deeper into the city, spots of color emerged—islands filled with flowering trees, painted signs above shop doors, intricate designs along peaked rooflines, and windows made of saturated glass. The skies were gray, the hues drab, the air so wet every surface held a sheen, and yet, against all odds, Da'Kin oozed with life.

But as Lyana turned her attention to its citizens, she realized that wasn't quite true. Most of the children they passed were rail thin, their clothes hanging off their feeble forms. Most of the adults had shadows under their eyes, expressions drawn despite their joyous smiles. She'd grown up in a frozen tundra barren of life, the land too harsh for plants or animals, yet her people had never starved. They'd

THE HUNTER AND THE MAGE

known hardship, but not like this. With its golden sunshine and diverse isles, the world above had been bountiful. Within the comfort of shared peace, all the houses had prospered. The world below was made of little more than ocean and mist.

Questions came unbidden as she forced a smile to her lips, looking everywhere yet nowhere, unable to meet the eyes surrounding her on all sides. What did they eat besides fish? How did they grow crops without sun? How did they find so much wood with no trees? How did they drink when their only water came from the sea? There were so many things she'd taken for granted growing up in her crystal palace—food appearing every night, endless water for baths, all the weapons she could want, all the dresses, all the jewels. Knowing now what hid within the fog, she almost felt greedy, a new sort of shame burning in her chest. All her life she'd yearned for nothing more than adventure —the childish dream of a princess unaware of her own privilege, which she'd given up the moment she and Xander had walked into the sacred nest to make their vows. She'd been prepared to be his queen, with all the responsibility it entailed.

Glancing askance at Malek and the shimmering aura dancing along his skin, Lyana wondered if it would be so different to accept the role of his queen instead. These people needed her, just as the ravens had, and they not only accepted her magic but praised it. Was swapping one cage for another so difficult? Like any bird, she longed for open skies. Like any royal, she knew the dream to be unattainable. Down here at least, she would be free to use her magic, no longer forced to hide the very essence of her soul.

Lyana didn't know what she wanted, but for the first time since her arrival in the world below, she was open to new possibilities. She tightened her hold on Malek's hand. With his magic still freely flowing, she wondered if he felt the change in her spirit as a smile widened his lips. He turned toward her, studying the planes of her face, a slight furrow to his brow.

"I'm ready," she whispered for his ears alone, bringing her power to the surface. The magic sizzled beneath her palm, aching to be used.

"We're nearly there."

He jutted his chin to the side where a towering castle sat heavy in the fog, the gray stones nearly invisible in the misty folds. An imposing wall hid most of the base from view, but behind it, Lyana saw mossy cliffs and roughly hewn towers, as though an island of rock had been carved into a fortress. The canal spilled into a dark tunnel blocked by an iron gate, through which still waters and a small dock were barely visible.

As they neared the entrance, *ferro'kine* magic guided the bars to open and the boat spun toward the crowd yearning for one final glimpse of their king and queen. Malek nodded subtly, a flicker of uncertainty in his eyes. As soon as Lyana opened herself up to her magic, she understood why.

A gasp escaped her lips.

Malek tightened his hold on her fingers.

The world dissolved into golden spirits, no bodies, no

buildings, no boulders—only magic and the many souls yearning for her touch. She felt them all as though she held each one in her arms, their pain screaming out to be healed. A thousand aching stomachs. A thousand gaping wounds. A thousand pining hearts. Lyana released her power, drowning in the need, unable to focus her magic or her mind. No matter how much she pushed, they kept pulling like a yawning abyss impossible to fill. Time ceased. Awareness ceased. Unable to ride the wave, Lyana succumbed to the torrent, getting swallowed by it instead.

11

RAFE

Catching sight of the dragon had transformed the ship. Instead of idle time and banter, solitary workings and bored pranks, there was order. Every sailor had a role. Every magic had a purpose. Even Shadow had risen from her afternoon slumber to take her spot by the rail, darkness curling around her fingers like gossamer snakes prepared to strike.

Rafe was the only one who seemed out of place as he dangled on the net, unsure if his presence on deck would be a hindrance or a service. Even with the twin swords attached to his back, what could he do against a dragon? Unlike the gusting winds striking the sails and the tunnels of pure light carving away at the mist, his magic was useless to all except himself. In the end, he decided the best thing he could do was stay out of their way.

Climbing back up the net to the perch at the top of the mast felt like running from a battle, the coward's way out, but he didn't know what else to do. Was he still a warrior without his wings? Or had Cassi taken that too?

"We need to catch its interest," Captain Rokaro shouted, drawing Rafe's attention away from his own dark thoughts. "We'll lose it in a chase."

Catch its interest?

Rafe turned back to the bow, spotting a flash of tail through the mist. Spout's water magic dusted the sea with sapphire glitter, churning the current in their favor, but even with Captain's and Patch's forceful gales, they were no closer to the beast. The rest of the crew acted almost immediately. Pyro sent waves of flame to either side of the ship, so warm Rafe's cheeks burned and the air felt nearly dry. Darkness rolled over the ocean, a blanket of thick ebony that swallowed the fog. Lightning crackled, making the water splash where it struck, not far from where Jolt stood on deck. Everyone with magic sent it soaring aimlessly into the sky. There seemed to be no purpose behind the display, just raw might, as though baiting the beast to come closer. Brighty shot another beam of energy into the mist, revealing the curved edge of the dragon's backside as it continued to soar away.

Catch its interest? Rafe thought again with a frown, eying the power surging all around him, potent enough to sting as he sucked in a sharp breath. *Magic—magic must be what the dragons want, what draws them in, what calls them.*

His mind spun with the realization.

Suddenly Rafe was a boy again, back in his mother's rooms at the base of the castle, shivering before the fire as chills racked his small frame. He'd been ill all day. It was the last time he could remember ever feeling sick, yet he still remembered how odd the sensation had been. Not like the coughs that sometimes came with the winter chill. Not like the fevers that sometimes spread in the warm summer months. This had been a burning in his chest, a tingling of his limbs, as though every nerve in his body were being formed anew.

Maybe they had been.

Before the dragon, he'd been a normal boy. After, not a single day had passed without the magic stirring beneath his skin. At the time, he'd been lost in grief and afraid for his life. With Xander's help, he'd buried the magic and all that had come with it. He'd cursed the power for keeping him alive—he'd never thought to blame it for killing his parents, too.

Was he why the dragon had come that day?

Was his magic to blame?

Had he called it?

Rafe gripped the rail to keep from slipping off the platform as the boat swayed, as he swayed, his muscles going slack. He thought of that day on the sky bridge and the beast that seemingly manifested out of nowhere. Had he been using his magic? Sometimes he did it subconsciously, if his body was tired, if aches needed to be healed. Was he to blame for that fateful morning, too?

He had to know.

He was desperate for an answer.

Brighty sent another beam of light into the mist, burning it away to reveal the shadow of a dragon moving just out of reach. Before Rafe knew what he was doing, he was on his feet with his sword in his hands, the point aimed at his gut. With one swift jerk, the metal carved into his skin, sinking deep enough to slash vital organs. His magic stirred immediately, power flooding to the spot and working swiftly to heal the wound. Not a sound escaped his lips as he pulled the blade free and slumped against the mast, his body going weak. No one seemed to notice. No one seemed to care. They were too focused on the beast to see the man bleeding out high atop the ship.

But something noticed.

Something cared.

Not a minute later he heard the roar, and for the first time in his life that nightmarish sound was accompanied by a smile. Dark laughter spilled through his lips as he held his palm against his stomach, blood pouring over his fingers.

It worked.

The idea broke him and remade him at the same time. Both an agony and an ecstasy came with knowing all the hardships of his life had happened for a reason—all the losses, all the pain, all the heartache. He was responsible. Not Taetanos. Not Vesevios. Not an invisible dark cloud hanging over his head, determined to smother the light. Just him, and his godforsaken magic.

Another roar shattered the sky.

"Where is it?" Captain Rokaro shouted. "Where—"

A bubbling cloud of fire emerged from the mist, cutting her off as the heat blazed like a furnace, ready to burn them alive. Pyro acted swiftly, red sparks infiltrating the churning orange as she used her magic to keep the flames at bay. The beast carved through the inferno, unbothered by the heat, and turned its red eyes on Rafe. Those massive jaws opened to reveal a throat bright with volcanic fury.

Just as another blast of fire was released, a geyser laced with magic exploded from the ocean surface to smack the beast in the face, sending the blaze harmlessly into the sky. Steam sizzled from the dragon's skin, its scales wet yet burning. Chains rattled. At first, Rafe thought Captain had loosed the anchor, but then a man-sized arrow pierced one leathery wing. The beast wailed. Just as Brighty had said, Archer never missed his mark. But it wasn't enough. The dragon clamped its jaws around the stem and yanked the weapon free. A few pumps of its wings, and the beast disappeared into the fog.

"Find it. Now!"

Brighty acted before Captain even finished speaking, sending a blast of light into the sky. Nothing. Again, and nothing. A prickle in the air raised the hairs at the back of his neck. The dragon wasn't gone—it was hiding. And it watched them through the mist.

Rafe pulled his hand from his stomach, shirt sticking to his skin from the blood, and staggered to his feet, keeping one arm around the mast for balance while the other gripped his blade. The sword was as useless as his magic, but he felt better with that worn leather hilt between his fingers. The wound no longer bled, but it still hurt. Beneath his skin, his magic worked to fix the damage.

"There!" Pyro called, sensing the fire before it struck and once more using her magic to halt the blaze.

Jolt raised her fist into the sky as purple sparks danced

around her fingers. Bolts of lightning cut through the fog and fractured out into a web. Invisible to his eyes, the dragon shrieked. Another blast of flames lit the endless gray, only to be held back by Pyro again. Brighty shot concentrated beams of light into the mist, searching for ebony scales, but the beast retreated again. Compared to the agility of wings, the ship was cumbersome, leaving its crew exposed as the dragon circled unseen.

I should have let it go, Rafe thought, watching all this from above, apart from the scene despite having created it. *I should have let it fly away.*

Even as he thought it, the beast came roaring back, diving from above. Archer released another arrow, and it struck true. Before the dragon could pull it free, he wrapped the loose chain around its stomach, trying to tie down its wings. Shadow released her saturated darkness, wrapping the ebony folds around the beast's head, shrouding its eyes as Archer worked a new set of chains, this time tightening the metal bands around its neck to cut off air.

Rafe, a creature of the sky, recognized the subtle shift in the dragon's wings before anyone else. "No!"

Captain, seeing what he saw, shot a gust of wind across the sea, but it was too late. The dragon closed its wings tightly to its body and dropped out of the sky, slamming into the ship with the weight of a falling star. Wood crunched. Sails caught fire. Someone screamed, though in the chaos there was no way to know who. Rafe hugged the mast to keep from falling as the floor jerked. Gray skies quickly turned charcoal with smoke, and the acrid smell of char burned his nose. He'd never thought he'd long for the sight of uninterrupted fog, but in that moment, he did.

The dragon's tail whipped to the side, slamming into Archer and sending him overboard. The chains fell to the deck with a heavy *thud*. Red sparks glittered as Pyro worked to control the flames burning across the ship, but so distracted, she didn't notice the beast was freed. Spout was too busy searching for Archer in the water. Brighty sent a beam of pure energy into the dragon's hide. The beast spun on her, rearing back its head. Her eyes lifted and those strange milky irises found Rafe's across the distance, filled with a pleading he'd never seen from her before. In that moment, he remembered he had more than just his healing magic.

Even without wings, he was still a raven.

He was still a fighter.

Rafe released his godly cry.

Within the crackling flames and crashing waves, everything stopped. The dragon paused. The crew stood still. His shriek filled their ears and mulled their brains, and no one moved except Rafe. He watched the attack as though in a dream, as though his spirit were floating above the fray, and it wasn't his legs that pushed off the edge of the platform or his body that arched across the air or his feet that landed on the dragon's skull, boots melting on impact. Distantly, he knew his toes were burning, but all he could focus on was the blade in his hands. Twice he'd faced a dragon, and twice he'd lost. But this time was different. There was no whisper of Vesevios in the back of his mind. The dragon hadn't been sent by a vengeful god, controlled by a force greater than any mortal could ever understand. Rafe had summoned it. And there was a comfort in knowing the creature beneath him was just an animal led by pure instinct, not a mythical beast after all.

Rafe used all his strength to slam the sword into the dragon's skull. The blade cut through scales, sinking all the way to the hilt—once, twice, three times. He twisted it for good measure. For the first time in his life, luck was on his side. The beast went slack beneath him. They fell together, the dragon landing with a lifeless *thud* as it tossed Rafe across the deck.

Just like that, the calm evaporated.

Agony struck like a dagger and he clenched his teeth to hold back his scream, the scalding of his feet too much to bear as his vision flashed white. Time raced forward. Boots pounded, growing louder, and Brighty dropped to her knees by his side.

"Rafe."

There was something unnerving about the breathy quality to her voice, the way her gaze flicked to his legs before swiftly returning to his face, the utter lack of sarcasm in her tone.

"You can thank me for saving your life later," he muttered through the pain. "Right now, I need you to cut off my boots so I can heal properly."

Her lips drew into a thin line, but she nodded and pulled a dagger from her waistband.

"Wait," Captain said from somewhere over his shoulder. "Leech!"

The man was already scurrying across the deck, his arms

full of bandages and glass jars. A grim expression clouded his features as he took the spot opposite Brighty and scanned the wounds. He glanced at Rafe. "This is going to hurt, but there's no way around it. I can give you a little something to dull your senses before we get started."

Rafe nodded.

Leech opened a few jars before grinding leaves and flowers, mixing them with a clear liquid that Rafe hoped was water. "Here."

"What in magic's name was that?" another voice sputtered as Rafe downed the potion. "It whispered of darkness."

Shadow stared at him, her inky eyes wide and her blonde hair swirling in the breeze. He had a feeling she wasn't talking about the bitter taste currently singeing his tongue.

"It was raven magic," Captain Rokaro muttered, an exasperation to her voice he didn't quite understand. "Power I wasn't aware you possessed."

"Raven magic?" Shadow asked.

"Animal magic, from the bird his soul was bonded with. Humans aren't the only living things with a tie to the elements." She cut her gaze toward the dragon. "Is it dead?"

"Dead," her first mate answered.

Captain Rokaro cursed.

Rafe's senses were not dulled enough to prevent the shock from coursing through his system. "You wanted it alive?"

She ignored him. "How much damage?"

"I'm holding off water from both sides of the hull,"

Spout answered, then sneezed. A splash lapped over the side of the railing. "Bloody dragons."

"She's allergic," Brighty whispered. "To everything."

"I'm not—" Spout broke off to suck in a wobbling breath, fighting off another bout as the blue surrounding her fingertips sparked. "It's something about the scales. I can't be around snakes either."

"Or cats," Brighty muttered, making Rafe's mouth twitch with amusement. His body grew more relaxed as the drugs sank into his system. "Or dust. Or flowers in the spring."

"Enough," Captain barked, shutting them both up. "Spout, downstairs now and keep the water from leaking into the ship as best as possible until Leech can repair it. Archer, go with her and use some metal sheets to temporarily seal the holes. Pyro, put out the fires. Jolt, take Squirrel with you, and go find the backup sails—"

"We burned those two months ago," Patch interjected.

"What about the backup, backup sails?"

"Last year."

Captain wrinkled her nose. "The sheets then! I don't give a damn what it is as long as the wind will catch it. What's the nearest city?"

"Da'Kin," the first mate replied, finding Captain's eyes. Something passed between them, something Rafe didn't quite understand, but the world was becoming fuzzy around the edges, colors turning brighter and sounds growing duller. "We need supplies."

"I'll speak to the king."

"The king?" Rafe said. Or tried to say. His tongue felt

fat and his eyes heavy. They began to slip closed, the world falling away, blissfully taking his pain with it. He rushed to finish, aware the words came out as nothing more than a garbled slur. "I want to speak with the king. You promised after the dragon you'd take me to the king."

"If you can walk by then, I will."

12

LYANA

Lyana stood on the balcony, staring out over the sleeping city. She'd awoken a few hours ago and had done little else but walk across her richly adorned room to stand in the damp air and think. Afternoon gave way to evening, the fog shifting from a downy gray like that of her brother's wings to the deep black of night. White lights bobbed, undulating with the tides, casting an almost eerie glow through the mist. Nothing was still in this world except the castle beneath her feet, sitting heavy on the rocks, an anchor keeping an entire populace from drifting out to sea.

"You missed dinner."

She didn't turn to greet Malek. "I'm not hungry."

"I brought food anyway," he said, the gentle *clink* of a tray being set down on wood following his words. Soft footsteps sounded, subtle on the rug and shifting to a scuff as his boots brushed against stone. He came to a stop beside her, placing his hands on the rail, close enough for her to feel the heat of his skin but not so close that they touched. "You should eat something, to preserve your strength."

She didn't say anything, instead keeping her focus on Da'Kin. He scanned her face, his gaze as tangible as any touch while the silence stretched between them.

"Lyana—"

"Is it always like that?"

Malek sighed, a heavy sound with more weight than air had any right to hold. He leaned forward to rest his elbows on the rail, his body collapsing beneath the invisible burden. A lock of blond hair fell over his brow as he turned toward the city.

"Yes," he said, his voice edging on hollow, surprisingly vulnerable. "Yes, it's always like that."

"So much suffering, so much pain."

"There's joy too, but it's harder to feel. We're healers. The hurt calls to us—the bruised, the broken, yearning to be saved. With time, it will become easier to manage. I can teach you how to guard yourself against it, to put a wall between your magic and your heart, so the wave won't pull you under as it did today."

"I want to help them," she whispered, throat clogged with the memory of their pain. "I want to heal them."

"You will—"

"No," she interrupted, blinking so that her spirit vision took over. The shades of black-and-white, of night and fog and rolling light, gave way to brilliant color, every element coming alive in her eyes, the yellows of the wind, the greens of the wood, the soft blues of mist and sea. But what shone brightest of all were all the souls spread like a carpet of golden starbursts, visible in her mind's eye even if they were hidden behind walls and rocks and shadow. But her magic stayed beneath her skin as it tickled the underside of her palm, longing to be used. "I want to do something now. First, you kept me stuck on that ship. Now, you keep me locked in this castle. I want to go out into the city. I want to—"

"You can't."

She blinked her magic eyes away and turned to him. "Malek—"

"Listen to me," he said, taking her hand in his, willing her to hear him. "I know how you feel. Trust me, I understand. And there was a time when I thought if I just used my magic swiftly enough, I could heal them all. But you can't, Lyana. And you never will. Even if you knock on every door in this city and cure every wound, come morning, there will be more. Humans are fragile creatures. We fracture easily, and there are some pains even magic can't heal. Broken hearts. Empty bellies. Lost dreams. The only way to help them is to spend your time learning to control your magic, so one day soon we can stop the source of their suffering together."

"And what's that?"

"The mist. The dragons. Our divided worlds."

"The prophecy."

He nodded.

"I've been thinking on that, too."

She hadn't asked him much about the poem that claimed to seal their fates. Perhaps it seemed blasphemous to believe human words could carry the weight of divine proclamations, an affront to her gods. Instead, her time on the ship had been spent preoccupied with magic—what had seemed a more immediate concern, and one she was sure Aethios approved. He had gifted her this power, after all. Now her curiosity beckoned.

Beasts will emerge, filled with fury and scorn, she thought, replaying the line from the prophecy. *Fighting to recover what from their claws we have torn.*

"What did we take from them?" she asked on instinct. "The dragons, I mean. And how do they plan to get it back?"

He let go of her fingers. "I don't know."

"You must have suspicions."

"I'm not sure if you're ready to hear them."

His lips thinned and a distant look gathered in his eyes as he stared into the dark. The stern expression he usually wore had returned, as hard as the stone wall surrounding his castle, as impenetrable too. Luckily, getting past people's defenses was one of her specialties.

"That's a shame," Lyana commented softly. "Because my feathers will grow back eventually, Malek. And if we can't learn to trust each other, if you can't learn to trust me, then I don't see any reason to stick around once they do."

His eyes cut sharply to her. "You can't leave."

"Why?" She snorted. "Because you say?"

"No. Because the world needs you."

"Without honesty, I won't stay."

"What about all the people you just said you want to save?"

"How can I save them if I don't know what I'm fighting?"

"By doing what I tell you."

Lyana laughed, the barking sound escaping her lips before she could stop it. He flinched as though struck. *Good.* "You don't want a queen, Malek. You want another soldier in your army, someone who will listen to everything you say and blindly take orders, but if you knew me at all, you would know I'm not that person and I never will be. So you can either treat me as your equal, as the queen you say I am, or you might as well send me home now."

"Lyana—"

"Make a choice." She shrugged, her tone far lighter than her words. "According to you, the fate of the world depends on it."

He ground his teeth, the muscles in his jaw flexing, until finally he relented. "You want the truth?"

Lyana nodded.

"I think they want your god stones."

She gasped. "Why?"

"Because they're not what you think they are." He paused, gaze drifting to the sky before returning to her, the tiniest bit softer than before. "I know what the avians of your world believe, that godly hands lifted your isles into the sky, but it's not true. The stones you all pray to hold nothing more than pure, concentrated magic. Seven stones for the seven most prominent elements—earth, air, fire, water, light, dark, and spirit—all bound together in a spell the likes of which this world has never otherwise seen, magic even I don't understand. I believe the power in that spell is what we took from the dragons, a power they would do anything to retrieve."

"But…" Lyana's gaze darted back and forth, fixed on no point as her mind spun. She'd been in the sacred nest—she'd felt the power of Aethios, raw and potent, absolutely real. She'd seen babies venture into those holy grounds and return with wings, a gift from their gods. How could magic do that, without at least a divine hand to guide it?

"Have you ever wondered why your island sits so much higher than the rest?"

She snapped back to the present. "It wasn't my place to question Aethios's will."

"Of course not." He laughed softly, an empty puff of air, then lifted his hand, his palm facing up. "Six of the isles all hang on the same plane." He indicated his fingers, and then lifted his other hand above them, as though holding a bit of string. "Your isle, the House of Peace, creates an apex point high above the rest. But there's an eighth point you don't know about that resides at the perfect opposite of your homeland, the lowest cornerstone of the spell, buried deep beneath the sea." He arced his hand in a perfect circle, until what was above shifted below. "And in place of a god stone, there is a door. The spell holds it closed—or at least, it once did. But with every passing year, the magic weakens, and more dragons break through." He dropped his hands to examine her. "Do you remember the earthquake you experienced in the House of Whispers and how it worsened with each new wave of magic you unleashed?"

She could only nod.

"The spell exists in a careful equilibrium, and large

bouts of power close to the stones disturb the balance, which in turn leaves the isles less stable. When dragons come to our world, they come in search of one thing—magic. The power calls to them, and they chase it. We're not entirely sure why, but I think it has something to do with their desire to weaken the spell until it breaks, so the door will open, giving them the opportunity to flood our world in search of what was lost."

Her mind came to a halt, focused on a single word. "Breaks?"

"*And only on the day when the sky does fall—*"

"*Will be revealed the one who will save you all,*" Lyana finished softly, her heart lurching painfully in her chest. "You think the isles will fall?"

"I know they will. It's only a matter of when and how."

She swayed on her feet and gripped the bannister to keep upright, dizzy as she thought of all those people in her world above, living in ignorant bliss, unaware of how close to disaster they teetered. Could what he was saying be true? Could it possibly be real? And if it was, what did that mean for the home of endless skies and wings and freedom she held so dear?

"Why should I believe you?"

"If you want proof, I can give it to you. Take my hand."

She did, no argument left in her body.

"Open yourself up to your magic, and let me guide you."

They brought their power to the surface at the same time, a golden aura surrounding their joined hands, so beautiful, so divine she had to believe it came from her gods. Malek pushed with his magic, and she followed, extending her awareness and reaching toward the city before them. The onslaught of burdened souls hit immediately, so forceful she staggered back, nearly falling if he hadn't been there to steady her.

"Harden your heart and think beyond them," Malek instructed.

Lyana tried not to care, not to crumble, but she was buried in the avalanche of so many aching human souls. Her vision grew spotted, the scene shifting in and out of focus, gold then black then gold, her power too slippery to control.

"Lyana!" He dug his nails into her palm, the bite bringing her back. "Push your mind past the city, into the ocean and the sky, into the fibers of the world. And you'll feel it."

"Feel what?"

"The door."

She tried, digging deeper into her strength, forcing her magic to listen and move beyond the bounds of the city, to ignore the cries and search the mist for wounds instead. But it was impossible to focus her mind and drown out the noise.

"Let me lead you," Malek urged. "Stop fighting me."

"I'm not."

"You *are*. You always are."

Maybe her soul was too used to rebellion, to independence. She liked to lead, not to follow, but this was uncharted territory. His power pressed into her skin, tugging on her spirit, willing her to relent. Though it went against her every instinct, she finally gave in.

Instantly, Malek wrapped his power around hers, fusing their two magics together so their spirits shot across the night, racing farther than her eyes could even see. She had no control, no will. He commanded it all. They were within the mist, within the ocean, carving between sea and sky, then deeper still, into the water and into the air, into that invisible substance binding all the elements together, the beating heart of the earth. And there, surrounded by spirit, she felt it—the gaping absence, the void, a dark stain on an otherwise glittering world, not a shadow but something empty, completely vacant of all life.

He released the magic and they snapped back to the present.

"What was that?"

"The door," he said darkly. "It's a rift between worlds, a fissure we need to seal before it swallows us whole."

"How?"

"The same way we might heal any other wound—with patience, and control, and precision."

Lyana frowned, aware of the chiding undertone to his words. "The three things I lack?"

"The three things you'll learn," he said gently, the hint of a smile on his lips. "If you stop fighting and let me teach you."

"I don't want to be cooped up in a room all day long, staring at bowls, willing something to happen." He opened his mouth to retort, but she lifted a hand to stop him.

"Please, Malek, it drives me mad. Take me out into the city. Introduce me to your people. Show me their magic. Open my eyes so I can see, like you did tonight. Some lessons, yes, and I will do my best to pay attention. But I'm not like you. I can't be focused all the time. I need some space to breathe."

"A compromise?"

"If that's what you want to call it."

He took a deep breath, studying her until a bright spark lit his stormy eyes, like a break in the clouds. "We have a deal."

13

MALEK

She was more infuriating than he'd ever imagined, yet so much more exciting too. It had been a long time since anyone dared question him, a long time since he'd allowed it. Part of him wished she would just be quiet and do as he said—the world perhaps would be better for it. Yet another part of him, a dying ember her presence had breathed back to life, was glad of her insolence. He did want a queen. He did want an equal. He did, after so many lonely years, want someone by his side who understood the burden and could carry it with him. Maybe that was why this newfound protectiveness surprised him most of all.

"Good night, Malek," Lyana whispered, her body mostly concealed behind her door. Those emerald eyes had regained their spark, a fact for which he was wondrously grateful, even if it might cause a headache come morning. Earlier that afternoon when she'd first opened herself to her magic and felt the onslaught of humanity, all the light had fled her gaze. It'd been the first time in his life when he'd regretted being a king in need of a queen, the first time his thoughts hadn't been on saving the world, but instead on saving her from it.

Maybe that was why he'd finally given her the truth.

To remind them both of the battle ahead.

"Good night."

He waited until she closed the door to turn his back, drinking in these last few moments of the buoyancy her presence brought. She looked at him as though he had all the answers, a peaceful thought until he was alone again and reminded himself that no matter the authority he'd learned to ooze, he was just as uncertain as the rest of them.

No one bothered him as he traversed the dank castle halls, footsteps loud in the silence. He missed his ship, the constant groan of wood, the steady drum of waves, the serenity that came with isolation. Here, in the heart of his city, even without using his magic, he felt it—the steady pull of his people, their yearning like a hum in the back of his thoughts, only heightened by the quiet. But he needed the people to see her, to believe in her. For once, he wanted their hope to drown out their pain.

"My liege."

Malek returned from his wandering thoughts in an instant. Lord Ferris, a member of his high council and the overseer of Da'Kin, stood by his door. He'd forgotten their meeting entirely, but monarchs never apologized. That was another lesson his father had taught him.

"Come in," he ordered as he strode inside his antechamber and made his way to the heavy wooden desk in its center. Only after taking his seat did he incline his head, indicating the other man should as well. "What news?"

"My liege," Lord Ferris began.

Despite his weary bones, tired from the long day and the use of so much magic, Malek sat forward in his chair, listening intently to the report on the welfare of the city. Overpopulation was a problem, as always. With the constant threat of dragons, there was safety in numbers. Each city in his kingdom was fortified by weapons and mages to keep the beasts mostly at bay. Those living on isolated islands or in the open sea were most vulnerable to attack. But with the crowds came other problems. More homes were needed, more supplies, more food. Disease spread quickly, violence too. Keeping his people safe was a constant game of push and pull, magic the only thing that kept them going. Earth mages were put to work in the floating farms, tirelessly cultivating crops the sun failed to reach. Water mages pulled the saturation from the air, drawing it into freshwater cisterns that flooded through a complicated network of fountains and pipes managed by a team of metal mages. Fire mages were on standby in case of dragon attacks, but also in case of wild blazes that might raze a city made of wood. Some mages worked to keep the seas surrounding the cities calm, others to fix the rot eating the buildings away, more to create medicines and weapons and technologies vital to life within the mist. Without magic, they'd be lost. Even with it, his people struggled, the number of mages dwarfed by the number of humans with no magic in constant need of aid. There was only so much one person could do, even if that person was the most powerful man in the world.

By the time Lord Ferris left, Malek was utterly exhausted.

Unfortunately, his dreams rarely provided solace.

The work required of a king, at least in a world such as this, was never-ending. Even in sleep, he labored, no time to rest his mind. Maybe one day he would trust Lyana enough to share all these burdens. Maybe one day she would understand the true cost of being queen. Maybe one day they would together make the difficult decisions that came with saving the world.

Today was not that day.

The dream wrapped around him quickly, shoving aside whatever peace his sleep had brought. By the time he opened his eyes, the antechamber had formed anew around him—the heavy desk, the thick rug, the stone walls, and the chandelier powered by mage light. Malek allowed himself a brief moment of disappointment before turning to face his spy. Kasiandra always wove the most vivid scenes, smells and tastes and sights so real they reminded him of warmer days made of laughter and imagination and fun. But Kasiandra wasn't here.

"Gaspar," he said with a commanding voice. Like his other spies hidden in the world above, the man chose to appear before his king without wings. "What happened?"

"I just met with Captain Rokaro." The spy glanced to the floor, hesitating in a way that promised bad news.

Malek stifled a sigh. It would only make him appear weak. "And?"

"They found the dragon, but it died in the attack."

"It died..." He arched a brow. "Or they killed it?"

"There was an unforeseen complication. Captain Rokaro failed to inform the raven of the true purpose of the hunt. She didn't deem it necessary, given the nature of his magic. But the dragon got onto the ship, and he used a raven cry to distract it, then put a sword through its skull."

Malek bit back a curse. The raven was becoming a thorn in his side. Despite the worth of his magic, he seemed nothing more than a nuisance—winning Lyana's affection, turning Kasiandra from her mission, even getting through Captain Rokaro's otherwise stalwart defenses. Malek had learned of the promise she'd made the raven of a meeting with the king, an offer that wasn't her right to give, but he found he didn't entirely mind. A curiosity he couldn't deny made him want to face the man. Maybe it would finally make him understand why Kasiandra now betrayed him with her insolence, why ever so often there was a distant look in Lyana's eyes, one filled with a warmth and longing she hadn't yet turned on him.

"They need to stop for repairs to the ship and supplies for the crew," Gaspar continued. "And the nearest city is Da'Kin."

Now that *was* interesting.

Malek cupped his hands behind his back, walking out from behind his desk to take a moment and consider the options. He hadn't intended on meeting the raven so soon, but perhaps he could use the opportunity to his advantage.

"Tell Captain Rokaro I'll allow it," he said slowly, still mulling over this new plan. "But I want eyes on the raven for as long as he's in this city. I want to know everywhere he goes. No surprises. And tell her I'll agree to a meeting. She'll get the details next time we speak."

"Yes, my liege."

He forced the formulations to stop spinning—there'd be time for that come morning. Right now, he had other matters to attend. "And what of our little rebel in the world above? Did Kasiandra get the message you sent?"

"She did. But I'm not sure it had any effect."

"Hmm." Malek pursed his lips, thinking of the playful girl he'd grown up with, whose dreams of candied stars and rainbow skies once made the night his refuge, and the strong woman she'd become. Part of him was a little proud, he'd admit, but it was a part he had no choice but to silence. He could live with her hate if he had to. He couldn't live with the cost of her failure. "Perhaps it's time to send her another message, one heavy-handed enough to incite action."

Unlike Kasiandra, Gaspar didn't ask questions. He simply nodded and said the three words Malek so longed to hear. "Yes, my liege."

14

XANDER

The halls were silent as Xander exited the dining room and made for the practice yards, no sound but the steady echo of his boots. Many of the guards were still busy repairing the city and their stations had been left unmanned, a fact for which he was grateful. Right now, he didn't want their stares—the questions in their eyes, the suspicions, the fears. Breakfast with his mother had been bad enough. People were still rioting in the streets of Pylaeon, their grief and anger now a weapon turned on him, which was exactly why he had to get out there. The note thrown into his library had been a threat, but instead of instilling terror, it had given Xander newfound purpose. Before he could focus all his energy on the mysterious man with magic, he needed to show his face outside these stone walls and prove to his people that he was still the prince they knew. No matter what had happened on his mating day, he would never abandon them. He just needed to round up an escort first—hence his focused march toward the barracks.

Perhaps if he'd been paying more attention, he would have noticed the movement in the shadows and the subtle shifting of feathers before an attack.

Alas, he was caught completely unawares.

Fingers grabbed his good hand, twisted his arm behind his back, and pressed him forward so he stumbled chest first into the nearest wall. A blade dug into his throat, the metal cool against his skin. The motions were rough, but the touch was soft and feminine.

Xander sighed. "Cassi, is this really necessary?"

She said nothing. The point of her dagger angled a little deeper as she breathed easily behind him, the warmth of her body sinking into his back—not entirely unwelcome despite the circumstances.

"Cassi, I don't have time for this right now."

"Do you think that would stay an assassin's hand?"

"Then it's a good thing no one is trying to kill me."

"Yet."

Xander snorted and tried to wrestle his arm free. It was no use. "Cassi. This isn't exactly what I had in mind when I asked for lessons."

He could feel her shrug against his wings. "I warned you I'm not the most conventional teacher, but I'm effective."

"And what exactly am I supposed to be learning?"

"You tell me."

Xander turned his head to the side, his cheekbone digging somewhat painfully into the stones as Cassi relentlessly pushed into his back. A grin widened her lips. "You're enjoying this."

"It's not every day I hold a prince entirely at my mercy." She leaned over a little, finding his eyes, a wicked gleam lighting hers. "Now, tell me how you'd escape."

"If I knew that, I would've done so already."

"Don't think of it as swordplay. Think of it like a riddle. You're good at solving those."

Xander frowned but tried to reason through it, testing different muscles. Distantly, he knew this was the most undignified position in which he'd ever found himself. To his surprise, he didn't care. Sometimes it was nice to feel a little less like a royal and a little more like a regular man—a lesson Cassi seemed all too pleased to impart. While he went through the options, he held her gaze, trying to distract her. "So, do you like the book?"

"Hmph." She rolled her eyes. "Tassos is a fool. He made it halfway around the world, beyond the Sea of Mist, over the mountains, to a great ocean, and then couldn't wait for the storm to pass before launching over its waters? He deserved to drown. And don't even get me started on Nyara, betraying the secrets of her people to pull him from the waves to save his life. As soon as he wakes up, he's going to deceive her. I know it."

"You're enjoying it then?"

She muttered a begrudging, "Maybe."

"Come on," Xander implored, unable to stifle his grin. "You don't think it's at all poetic for a man of the sky to fall for a woman of the sea?"

"She has a tail." Cassi wrinkled her nose. "Where would they live? It's impractical."

"That's why it's romantic. They love each other despite the obstacles stacked against them. They love each other even as it ruins them."

"Why must love destroy you to be real?" She frowned, a dark shadow passing over her luminous eyes. "Why can't it save you instead?"

He didn't have an answer to her question. The pieces of his heart were still shattered and rattling in the hollow cage of his ribs. Love should be easy—as simple as breathing, as steadfast as his pulse, as lovely as slipping into a beautiful dream. Too often it wasn't, as his own sorry life had proved.

In the silence, her breath brushed his cheek, the warmth making his skin tingle. His throat was tight when he finally managed to give a response, one meant to lighten the mood. "Because that would make for a rather boring read."

Cassi returned from her thoughts to focus sharply on him. "Stop trying to distract me, and tell me how you'll escape my hold."

"If you were an attacker, which you aren't, and I had no qualms about hurting you, which I do, I suppose I'd start by throwing my head back in an attempt to break your nose. Then I'd flare my wings to try to loosen your hold and use my right arm, which you left unrestricted, to elbow you in the gut."

"Close, but no."

"I really do have some place I need to be."

"First," she said, tone a bit haughty as befitted someone holding him against a wall, "you call for help. Because you're a prince, and guards around nearly every corner of the castle swore an oath to protect you. There's no shame in knowing when you're beat. It takes a shrewd mind to admit defeat—only an idiot fights a losing battle when they have a winning hand yet to play. Then, while the guards are on their way, you use one or both of your legs to push off the wall, since you have a height and weight advantage on me. If you're lucky, I'll fall and you can roll free. If you're not, keep pushing back until my wings slam into the opposite wall, and the pain will likely force me to let you go. The elbow idea was good too. That might work, especially since most attackers would underestimate your right side as your weak side. I wonder if we could fashion some sort of metal plate to be sewn into your clothes."

"I don't think that will be necessary."

"The people are rioting for Rafe's head right now. Need I remind you that you look just like him?"

Xander scowled. "No."

At his tone, Cassi finally loosened her hold, pulling the knife from his throat and unraveling their limbs. Without her so close, the air felt cool and a shiver raced down his spine as he turned to face her head-on. She was shorter, though not by much, and he might've been heavier only because of his bones, whereas he had the sense that the body hiding beneath her clothes was made of muscle— supple and smooth.

Don't think about that, he chided, heat gathering at his collar.

"I didn't mean to offend." She mistook his response for annoyance and glanced down to play with the dagger in her hand. "The people want blood, and they might be fine replacing one brother for another if the true target of their frustration can't be found."

"I know." He put his fingers gently against hers and she froze, staring at their hands. He hastily dropped his away. "That's why I'm going out into the city right now, to show my face and ease their fears, to prove I'm still the prince they know. You can come if you'd like, to watch my back. Though I'm afraid another lesson will have to wait. I doubt the people would approve of you tossing me up against the castle walls. At least, I hope they wouldn't."

A smile passed over her lips, there and gone. She flipped the dagger in her hands so that she held the blade and offered it to him. He couldn't help but feel there was a veil over her eyes, guarding the truth. "Take this. You should always have a weapon on you, just in case. To hold your secrets, if nothing else."

Their fingers grazed as he took the blade. It felt cumbersome in his hand, as though it might do more harm than good. Xander gave it back. "I'll get one from Helen. I don't want to leave you defenseless."

Cassi arched her brow dubiously.

"I will," he insisted.

With a shrug, she slipped the dagger smoothly back into her belt. "At least keep more aware of your surroundings, especially out there." She jerked her chin toward the window. "In the meantime, I'll see if Nyara surprises me and kills Tassos in his sleep, the way I'm sort of hoping she will."

He laughed and shook his head. "You're terrible."

"You have no idea."

With that, she left. Xander watched until she turned a corner, black-and-white speckled wings disappearing around a bend. Even then, it took a moment for him to move, still considering the hollow tone of her voice. He'd only been joking, but Cassi's response was all too real. Another piece to the puzzle of her, one he wouldn't solve today.

Xander turned in the opposite direction to make for the practice grounds, his original destination before he'd been sidetracked. Helen was already there waiting with an escort when he arrived, his message from breakfast having reached the spot before he did.

"We start with the wounded," Xander ordered, then took to the sky.

His guards flanked him on both sides as he soared over the castle walls and into the city beyond. A group still gathered near the main gate, tossing rotten fruit at the wall and cursing Rafe's name. But if they meant real harm, they would have used their wings to storm the castle itself. This was more frustration than fury, which meant he still had time to remedy the situation.

They traveled to the homes of the wounded first, those burned by dragon fire or crushed by falling stone. He said prayers to Taetanos with the families, offering what little comfort he could, as well as food and money to ease their burdens. The healers followed soon after, sent from the palace itself, with salves from the House of Paradise to help with the pain. Xander had already met with the relatives of the few who'd passed, but he stopped by their homes again to leave flowers by their doors, not interrupting their grieving, but not ignoring it either. The bouquets were made of fragrant lilies, the same he put under the spirit gates, using the scent to guide lost souls to the river, where the entrance to his god's realm was waiting. His final stop was to the rubble, buildings crushed by dragon claws and burned by dragon flame. He did what he could, struggling to help clear debris. Soot stained his clothes and skin, mixing with his sweat. There were no speeches that could cure their pains, so he didn't give any, choosing to work beside them instead. It meant so much more than empty words. He could see it in their eyes—the burgeoning respect, rebuilt much like the houses around him by placing one stone at a time.

People whispered, of course.

Fire cursed.

Where's the bastard?

What'd he do with the princess?

The gods are angry.

Taetanos help us.

Xander listened without comment. He couldn't defend Rafe—it would only bring more questions. Yet he found he couldn't damn him either. Oh, he was still furious. His invisible fist trembled by his side, his anger so much harder to tame now that it had tasted freedom. Perhaps it was unfair, but there was a part deep down in him that reveled just a little in hearing people curse Rafe's name, that was still livid with his brother, not only for stealing his mate, but for leaving him alone to pick up the pieces. Sometimes at night he found himself going to his brother's rooms, forgetting for a moment that he wasn't there, an old habit that wouldn't die. He didn't know who he was without Rafe there to act as a foil. It was so much easier to be carefree with Rafe by his side to carry his troubles, so much easier to be happy in the face of Rafe's perpetual grouchiness, so much easier to focus on his studies with Rafe there to guard his back. They were two sides of the same coin—as much as he loathed Rafe, he loved him, and maybe that hurt most of all. Missing Rafe felt like missing a piece of himself, one he'd never get back, and Xander had no one to blame but himself.

Weary and ravenous, Xander returned to the castle in a solemn mood, needing peace and quiet and a chance to rest his mind. He skipped dinner with his advisors and ordered it brought to his study instead. He wanted to lose himself in his books, in other worlds and other lives far different from his own.

When he stepped through the door, wind ruffled his feathers. With a curse, Xander ran across the room to grip the sheet that had torn loose from the broken window, sending a draft throughout the space. Moisture already wrinkled the pages of his books, nothing a fire wouldn't cure but still an annoyance he didn't need. The shifting pages only made his hackles rise.

They better not be damaged, he thought as he dropped to the ground to see what had ripped the curtain loose from its nails. *I ordered the window sealed.*

Xander frowned.

The nails hadn't ripped loose. They still bit into the curtain, securing it to the floor and the walls. He ran his hand up the fabric, searching for the source of the tear. That was when he found the perfectly straight line cut through the center as though with a knife.

An arm came around his throat.

"Cassi—"

The grip tightened, cutting off air as something sharp bit into his side. Pain flared, followed by a warmth spreading across his jacket. Blood. His blood. Xander jerked in surprise, disbelief outweighing the ache as a heavy body wrestled him to the floor, crushing him against the rug. Instinct took over—instincts he wasn't aware he possessed —and Xander threw his right elbow into the assailant, remembering Cassi's advice. The man groaned but didn't let go. Still, his grip loosened just enough for a scream to break through.

"Help!" he cried. "He—"

"Be still," a deep voice growled as the arm clamped tighter.

Think, he thought. *Think. My mind is my greatest weapon. What can I do?*

He needed time. He needed an opening, a distraction. With a burst of inspiration, Xander kicked his desk as hard as he could. The books stacked near its edge toppled over to land heavily on both him and the stranger, and the arm around his neck slackened. Xander slipped his hand beneath the man's elbow, freeing the pressure on his vocal cords. Just as he opened his mouth to scream, his attacker howled and let go.

Xander scrambled forward, glancing back to find the hilt of a blade protruding from the man's thigh—a hilt he recognized, one he'd held only just this morning. Whipping toward the door, he found Cassi at the frame, lethal and poised to strike.

The stranger stumbled through the torn curtain, falling out the window and into the night. Without a moment's hesitation, Cassi vaulted over Xander and dove after him.

15

CASSI

It was Malek. Not physically, she knew, but the attack had her king's name written all over it, a message drawn in blood. Xander would be fine. If the man had wanted the prince dead, he would be. No—this was something else. Not an assassination attempt, but a reminder of her king's power, the very same power she was now even more determined to defy.

The attacker's ebony wings blended into the night. Though he was little more than a shadow on the move, Cassi's sharp owl eyes tracked him through the darkness. He dove as soon as he reached the edge of the castle, plummeting toward the Sea of Mist. Cassi followed, her predatory wings far faster than his in a free fall. The jagged cliffs of the isle passed in a blur. Just as she was about to catch up, the man cut to the side, swooping under an outcropping of stone. Cassi copied the maneuver, but her wings weren't quite as agile. By the time she reached the spot, he was gone.

What?

A hand wrapped around her ankle. Cassi kicked wildly and flapped her wings. The fingers clamped down harder.

"Stop fighting, I want to talk," the man ordered.

"Then why'd you run away?"

"To make sure we weren't followed."

As if to prove his point, he let go. Cassi whirled around, surprised to find the entrance to a shallow cave. The stranger stood inside, looking not at her but at her dagger, which was still lodged in his thigh. With a gasp, he pulled it out, then wrapped a length of torn fabric around the wound to slow the bleeding.

She didn't apologize. Instead, she landed beside him on the ledge and crossed her arms. "Who are you?"

"That's not important."

"It's important to me."

The whites of his eyes caught the moonlight as he looked up. "I'm you, Kasiandra, as you're meant to be."

She'd known, of course, that he had to be another of Malek's spies, a dreamwalker caught between two worlds, not quite of either. Still, her lips parted in surprise. All her life, she'd felt alone with her secrets, yet here was a man who carried the same burdens, and he'd been so close. A raven. Living in the House of Whispers this entire time. And never once had her king mentioned his name. Never once had he given her the chance to talk to this man who might have understood her.

Now, they stood on opposing sides.

"Why did Malek send you?"

"The king wishes to speak to you. He says he's waited long enough, and his patience is wearing thin."

That's not my problem. Cassi clenched her jaw, taking in the sapphire glow of the mist and the endless stretch of stars across the sky. A whole world rested at her fingertips. Why then did she feel so ensnared?

"You could have killed Xander tonight." She returned her attention to the man silently watching her, his expression a lesson in control.

"Those weren't my orders."

"Why? What game is he playing? What does he want from me?"

"Obedience."

Cassi snorted, though the lump in her throat betrayed the true weight of the word. She'd spent her entire life doing everything Malek said. Now, just this once, she wanted to live for herself. Why was that so difficult for him to understand?

"And if I won't do as he commands? What then?"

"That's not in my power to say."

She snarled, disgusted by the man before her. Was this what she had been like before? *Yes, my liege. No, my liege. Whatever you say, my liege.* He was empty. No emotion. No personality. No thoughts aside from the ones Malek had put there.

Cassi refused to be that way again.

"The king demands you visit his dreams tonight. If you want to beg for the raven prince's life, it's your last chance to do so, or his next orders may not be so friendly. He also told me to remind you what exactly it is we're all fighting for."

"And what's that?"

"The world."

Her hands were a silvery tan in this light, yet all she saw were the bloodstains on her fingers, a vision no bath could wipe clean. The mark was internal, a wound carved into her spirit, something not even Malek's magic could heal.

"What's so great about this world?" she asked as she folded her fingers into fists. The unnamed man stared back at her like a mirror, reflecting all her awful deeds. "If we're willing to kill honest men, good men, then we're no better than the dragons. Why are we worth saving?"

"That's not up to me to decide."

"If the knife is in your hand, it should be."

A flicker passed over his eyes, there and gone before she could see exactly what it was. Maybe they weren't so different after all. "Speak with the king tonight. Your answers lie in him. When you return to the castle, say I got away and all you saw were my raven wings. My family lives in a village far away from Pylaeon, where they won't think to look. In the meantime, the royal family will believe one of their own has turned against them, a rebel after the crown. They won't suspect it was an assassin sent by our king."

Cassi nodded.

No matter Malek's beliefs, she was still loyal to the prophecy and to Lyana, if nothing else. The avians wouldn't learn the secrets of the lands beneath the mist from her. She did want to save the world—she just didn't want to lose herself in the process.

The man left. Cassi waited for his outline to disappear into the night, then followed suit, making her way back to the castle and its tallest spire, still lit by a soft orange glow. The wrong end of a sword was the first thing to greet her upon her return. She frowned at the blade and landed inside the broken window, arching her brow at the guard with unmasked disdain.

"Put the weapon away, Dimos," Xander drawled.

He sat shirtless by the fire, a healer kneeling by his side while the queen watched with a furrowed brow. He was thin, as expected, but not in an unpleasant way. The ridges of his abdomen caught the golden glow of the flames, muscles lean and defined, forming two distinct lines that disappeared into his waistband. Shadow and light danced across his skin. It took more effort than Cassi cared to admit to shift her attention to his wound, which was already cleaned and nearly bandaged. Not quite able to hide his grimace, he rested his head in his palm, his onyx hair in disarray as it spilled over his forehead.

"How do we know she can be trusted?" Queen Mariam asked her son, a sharp look in her violet eyes as they cut toward Cassi. "All we know about her is that she came with the princess. A bird without a flock can be a dangerous thing."

"Mother." Xander sighed with a heaviness Cassi felt to her bones. "If she wanted to kill me, she's had ample opportunity. She's given us no reason not to trust her."

I'd be a terrible spy if I had, she thought, stifling her

frown. His was the worst sort of reasoning, foolish and naïve, and if they were alone, she would have throttled him. Yet part of her envied his infallible ability to see the good even in a viper about to strike. *I'll have to add this to the long list of things to teach him.*

"Put it away, Dimos," Xander ordered again, a bit more forcefully this time. The guard glanced between his prince and his queen, then slowly sheathed his weapon. Xander shifted his attention to Cassi. "Did you catch him?"

She licked her lips and swallowed.

If she were a good person, like Xander, maybe she'd offer him the truth—explain the prophecy, the war, and the civilization surviving beneath the mist. He would understand, she was sure. He would do the right thing. He'd try to help her, and Malek and Lyana and everyone fighting to see the dragons undone.

But she wasn't a good person.

She was a liar.

It was the only thing she knew how to do.

"No." The word came out as more breath than voice. "No, I didn't catch him."

Xander's disappointment was swift, his shoulders falling, his expression too. There wasn't an ounce of doubt anywhere on his face. He believed her. He trusted her. Just as Rafe had. Just as Lyana did. Deceit came more naturally to her than breathing. Malek would have called it a skill, but to Cassi it was a curse, something she couldn't stop, didn't know how to end, almost hoped would be caught.

"Did you see him? Was he a raven? What did he look like?"

"I never saw his face, but yes, he was a raven, wings as black as the night. That's how he got away. He flew over the edge, and I lost him in the shadows of the cliffs. I don't know where he went after that."

Xander nodded, taking her at her word.

She wished he wouldn't.

"Very well." He shared a look with his mother laced with unspoken meaning, then turned to the guard. "Dimos, get Helen and tell her to come here immediately. She can send a team to search the cliffs without her. Understood?"

"Yes, my prince."

"Good. Go. Cassi—"

"I'll just get out of your way."

"You're not—"

"It's all right, Xander. The game of politics isn't for me, and there's a bath somewhere in this castle with my name on it. Whatever you and your advisors decide, and whatever it means for me, will be fine."

"If that's what you'd like."

She turned toward the door, spotting the book she'd dropped near the entrance still open on the floor. Taking a moment to retrieve it, she carefully smoothed out the pages and folded it closed before handing it back to Xander. "I was just coming earlier to return this to you."

"Did you finish it?" He took the book from her hands, swallowing as their fingers touched. Queen Mariam quietly studied his reaction while Cassi nodded. "And? What did you think about the ending?"

"She gave up everything to be with him. Her tail. Her home. Her people. The very essence of herself."

"She gave it all in the name of love."

"And what did he give up?"

Xander tilted his head to the side, brows pinching together.

"He still had his wings, his sky, his home," Cassi continued. "Why did Nyara have to surrender everything and Tassos nothing? Why must women always be the ones to sacrifice for men? What's romantic about that?"

"I—" He paused. "I never thought about it like that."

Cassi laughed softly, unable to stop herself, though her anger was with a very different man somewhere far beneath the mist, who still had his magic and his kingdom and his queen, while she was lost in the aftermath. "Why would you?"

The queen caught her eyes as she turned away, a curious spark igniting, but Cassi ignored it and kept walking. The last thing she needed was that spiteful raven as a kindred spirit—two women torn apart by love. No, her story wasn't over yet, and she was determined to write a different ending from the one her king had planned.

Tragedy just doesn't suit me.

Her lips curled into a grin as she made for her room, longing to lose herself in a tub of steaming water. She hadn't been lying about the bath. Her muscles ached and she needed time to think before she released the magic gathering beneath her skin. Malek would get his visit. There was no doubt about that. But first, she needed a plan—some way to convince her king that a decent, kind-hearted man like Xander was anything except a liability.

16

XANDER

Her words lingered long after she left, while the healer finished dressing his wounds and his mother looked on with concern. The fire crackled, breaking up the silence.

Who had she loved?

What had she sacrificed?

Xander didn't doubt the venom in her voice had come from experience, but what? And when? And perhaps more importantly, why did it matter? A dangerous emotion crept its way up his right arm, like a spider crawling out of hiding, breaking free of the tight hold he kept on all those unpleasant feelings he didn't want to face. Anger on her behalf. Anger at himself. Logically, he knew she couldn't possibly have been talking about him, and yet, he couldn't help but wonder. Lyana had been prepared to give up everything for him and for his people—her freedom, her dreams, her heart. In return, Xander would have gotten everything he'd ever wanted. A worthy queen. A loyal mate. A hopeful future. All the while, Cassi had lurked in the periphery, watching the scene unfold.

Was that what she thought of him?

Worse still, was she right?

"I'm not sure I approve of how much time you're spending with that owl," his mother murmured as soon as the healer left.

He eased his shirt back over his shoulders and around his wings, wincing at the dull ache in his side. "I'm not sure I care."

"Lysander."

"Mother."

"What is she still doing in our home?"

"She's helping me find Lyana."

"How?"

"She's— She's—" In truth, aside from tossing him up against walls and stopping by to steal books from his library, Cassi wasn't offering much assistance. But then again, what else could she do? He didn't even know where to begin the search, so how could she? "She just is. And besides, we couldn't very well let her leave. The doves would know something was amiss the second she stepped foot on their isle, and the whole ruse would be undone."

The queen tsked.

Xander was saved by the sound of the door opening behind him. Helen strode into the room, a grim look on her face. "My prince."

"We need to discuss our next course of action."

"I agree."

"Cassi lost track of the assailant, but she says he was a raven. She's sure."

"And you believe her?"

"I do. I saw the man for a brief moment, and I thought his wings were black. Her words just confirmed it." He frowned, wiping his palm over his face and into his hair, the heavy weight of that truth starting to sink in. "Did you— did you see this coming?" he asked, allowing all the shock and doubt and hurt he'd been hiding to leak into his tone now that the three of them were alone. "Today, while I was in the city, I swore I felt a change in the air, a shift. I thought they were starting to trust me again, to believe in me, but now… I don't know."

"I did *not* see this coming," Helen said as she leaned her hip against his desk and crossed her arms. "And that's what worries me more."

"Do you think he was working alone?" Xander asked.

"I don't know."

"Do you think he'll attack again?"

"I don't know."

"We need to call the guards back to the castle immediately," his mother cut in, voice flustered with fear for her son—a feeling he appreciated, but also couldn't accept. "We need to double their shifts. We need people shielding Lysander day and night. I don't want a single window unwatched."

"We can't do that, Mother."

"Last time I checked, I was still the Queen of the House of Whispers, and I say we can."

He and Helen shared a look.

"We can't pull the guards from the city," he tried to reason. "There's still too much work to be done, with the wounded, with the destruction. The people need help."

"You're their prince, and someone is trying to kill you. I'm sure the people will understand."

"And what will they say?" he asked, remembering her warning. *Frightened gossip has the power to bring a kingdom to its knees.* The statement had never been truer. "That we're more concerned for ourselves than for them? That we're greedy? That we don't care? Our reign is fragile enough as is with everything that's happened. Until we have Lyana back, we can't risk bringing more contempt upon us."

"What would you have me do? Dangle my only son— my heir—as bait?"

"Of course not, I just..." He sighed. "There's got to be another answer."

"I might have an idea." Helen's tone was soft, but the statement rang loud against the silence. An ominous pulse slipped down his spine.

"What?"

"You're not going to like it."

"When has that ever stopped you before?"

Helen pursed her lips while his mother frowned. She'd never appreciated their relaxed relationship, but the last thing he needed in an advisor was another person tripping over to please him.

"Fine." His captain of the guard stood, unfolding her arms as she met his gaze unflinchingly. "You could leave."

Xander recoiled. "Leave?"

"It would solve both our problems. The guards would

be free to continue rebuilding the city, and you would be safely away where no disgruntled ravens could harm you. It's not so strange for a newly mated royal to explore the other isles. Now that the trials and the mating ceremony are over, at least according to all the other houses, you're finally allowed to travel freely between the kingdoms."

"And what message would that send?" his mother drawled, clearly unconvinced. "That we're ready to abandon the people further?"

"I don't think so." Helen shrugged. "No one needs to know what happened here today, no one except for the guards. We can say he's working on a trade agreement, that he's presenting offerings to the other gods in our favor, that he's looking for our lost princess. Whatever we believe will work best. If the people are clothed and fed, they'll be happy. And in the meantime, our prince will be safe."

The scrolls sprawled across his desk sent him back to another time not so long ago when he'd stood in this very room with Lyana, saying much the same thing—that he longed to see the famous libraries in the House of Wisdom, to study their maps and ancient texts. At the time, he'd promised to take her with him, the mere idea bringing a dazzling spark to her eyes, so infectious, so spirited, so...

A dull ache pinched his chest and he pushed the memory aside with a quick shake of his head. His problems were much bigger now than a few mismarked charts, but maybe the solution wasn't so different.

"I could go to the House of Wisdom," Xander murmured.

"Lysander, you aren't seriously considering this—"

"Why not, Mother? Helen's right. It's the perfect solution. And besides..." The shelves surrounding him on all sides showed him leather spines as familiar as the lines etched into his palm, not a single cover unopened, nor a single word unread. "There's nothing here that will help us. The owls have ancient tomes, some from a time before the isles were lifted into the sky. There might be information we can use to get Lyana back." He lowered his voice. "Information on how to fight magic."

She sank back in her chair, a frown on her lips, but he recognized the calculating gleam in her eyes—it was the same one he sometimes caught in his own reflection, violet streaks of awareness coming together to form a plan.

"What would we tell the advisors? The nobles? The city?"

He clicked his tongue against the roof of his mouth until inspiration struck. "Tell the advisors and the nobles I go for diplomatic reasons, to make amends with the House of Wisdom now that my mating ceremony is complete. When Lyana chose me, the owls were snubbed, so you thought it prudent I visit the royal family to smooth things over and ensure none of our relations have been affected. And tell the people I— Tell them—"

"The truth?" Helen offered.

"Yes." Xander snapped his gaze to hers, feeling invigorated by this new plan, by the sense of purpose he'd been lacking these past few days. "At least, a version of it. Tell them I go in search of a means to bring our princess back. Give them a reason to celebrate my departure rather than denounce it."

Give them the same feeling surging through me now, he thought, a foreign sense of optimism bubbling in his chest. *Hope.*

They spent the rest of the night hammering out the details before parting ways with an agreement to meet with the rest of the advisors in the morning. He considered sneaking off to Cassi's room to inform her of the plan, but with Helen ushering him back to his room, he thought better of it. She scanned the halls until they reached his door, then went in first to scout for intruders.

"I'm stationing someone on the balcony overnight."

He sighed internally but nodded.

"And by your door."

Again, he understood.

"Xander." The informal use of his name surprised him. Insecurity hovered in the shadows of her brown eyes. "I hope you don't think— I hope you—" She broke off and swallowed, then straightened her shoulders, the captain he recognized. "My oath is still as strong as the day I took it. I'm your sword and shield. I always will be."

"I know, Helen." He reached out and placed his palm on her shoulder to squeeze it softly, confident in her loyalty. She nodded, clearly out of her element. He decided to take it easy on her rather than tease her for the unusual display of affection and offered a warm, "Good night."

With a slight quirk to his lips that he couldn't entirely stifle, Xander entered his room, leaving her to her duties, and made for the trunk by the foot of his bed. Cassi had said he should always have a weapon on him, and the truth was he did have a dagger, one gifted to him a long time ago.

He hadn't looked at it in ages, hadn't even thought about it since the moment he tucked it into his old fighting leathers and stored both away. But maybe it was finally time to face the past and all the memories he'd buried.

Xander removed the books and the blankets, searching for the bundle hidden at the bottom. As his fingers brushed smooth hide secured by a belt, relief coursed through him and he quickly unraveled the fighting gear now too small for his grown-up body. The hilt of the dagger had been carved to resemble a raven in flight, and at its base gleamed an obsidian stone, as opaque and inscrutable as his god. The weapon was a gift from his father.

Rafe had one just like it.

They'd been in the practice yards, one of the few places in the castle where his mother had allowed Rafe to visit him, perhaps because it was one of the few places where she never ventured. His father was there too often, and she loathed the sight of him. At that point in his life, however, just a boy with no awareness of grown-up things, Xander had been in awe of the man—his prowess, his power, his stature. When he looked back, it was hard to believe there'd been a time in his life when he'd wanted to be just like his father, but he had. That was before he'd discovered the wonders of reading, before he'd realized he would never possess the sort of strength his father valued, before he'd stopped trying to be someone he wasn't and learned to accept the person he was.

"Enough," the king had said, interrupting the fight that had broken out between Rafe and him, the two of them rolling around on the grass as boys did. If memory served, his brother had had him in a frustratingly efficient headlock. "I have a gift for you boys."

They stopped in an instant, turning to him eagerly.

"What, Father?" Xander asked while Rafe remained silent, happy to let his brother speak for him.

"The same thing my father once gave to me," he said, pulling the twin daggers from behind his back. "I'll show you how to wield them, but you must promise me something."

"What?" they said in unison that time.

"No more fighting." Rafe frowned at Xander, who elbowed him. "You're brothers. You're blood. There's no one you can trust more in the world than each other, no one you can rely on, no one you can depend on, not even me. And I want you to remember that."

"We will," they chorused, already grabbing for the blades. The response had been more to appease him than anything else, and they'd spent the rest of the day in the practice yards ignoring the advice and competing for his attention. But in the years that followed, after he was gone and nothing remained to fight over, the heart of his statement had sunk in.

Xander eyed the dagger.

It had been too big for him then, but it fit his hand now. And he imagined that if he walked to Rafe's room, he'd find its twin hidden at the base of a similar trunk, abandoned but not forgotten. He knew his brother. Even though it might be the only gift their father had ever given Rafe, he wouldn't have taken it with him when he left. He wouldn't have wanted the reminder that he had been the son their father favored, or the son to first break their promise to remain true to one another.

But had he been first?

Cassi's words came back to haunt him, words about sacrifice and love, and one person always giving while the other did nothing but receive. She'd been speaking of a different sort of love, but it wasn't that different, not really. And in this matter between brothers, Xander knew which role he'd played. Rafe had given up all memories of their father, though most of his had been good. He'd given up his life, pledging it to his prince instead. In the end, he'd given up his love, his home, his very place in the world.

Now Xander would give up something—his pride.

The plan with the House of Wisdom wasn't just about finding Lyana, he wanted his brother back as well. Rafe could never return to the House of Whispers, not with what the people now believed, but a part of Xander hoped his brother would learn he had traveled to the home of the owls and would come running. They had much to talk about before all could be forgiven, but he wanted to have that conversation. He owed it to Rafe, to himself, and to the long, complicated history between them. If his brother didn't come, then somehow, someway, he would find him. That was a promise.

Xander stood and tucked the dagger into his belt. Tomorrow, Cassi could show him how to use it. Until then, he would confess his secrets to the blade, the way he would have confessed them to Rafe had his brother still be there to listen.

17

CASSI

Stepping into Malek's dream was like stepping into the past. His spirit wrapped around her, so strong and familiar, a warm embrace, until she remembered the hard look in his eyes as his magic held her down and the orders on his lips, until she remembered that his affection had been as false as the world she now crafted around them.

Cassi stopped spinning the tendrils of his mind into his preferred meeting spot, a castle room with stone walls and a heavy iron chandelier, dreary and drab and dire. Instead, she imagined blue skies and a lush grassy plain that extended as far as the eye could see. Wildflowers, as sweet as they were beautiful, covered every inch of the ground. In the distance, lavender hues hinted at far-off mountains topped by cones of white. They stood on the roof of a stone keep, heavy and impenetrable, the winds whipping around her legs. Crumbled buildings littered the grounds below, remnants from a time long ago, once homes and shops and an imposing city wall, now nothing more than moss-covered rocks and ruins.

"This is new," Malek murmured by her side, his feet braced against the breeze and his hands clasped behind his back. In the dream, she imagined him the way she'd last seen him in the House of Whispers, with a sun-kissed glow to his skin and golden highlights in his hair, those eyes as inscrutable as a stormy sea.

"I thought it was time for a change."

His brows lifted inquisitively. "Are you trying to send me a message, Kasiandra?"

"No message."

"Then what is this place?"

"It's Lantos," she said, stepping forward so her toes extended out over the edge of the building. Her wings shifted, feathers ruffling in the breeze. There was no more reason to hide them from him. He'd seen the real her while she pleaded for his mercy, desperate and broken, still covered in Rafe's blood. And she'd seen the real him. "It's the capital of the House of Prey, commonly referred to as the City of Ruins. I've been told it was once a vibrant city that fell to waste when the isles were lifted into the sky. The kings and queens of these lands have always been solitary creatures. They never trusted their subjects. In turn, their people never trusted them. They keep to their fortress, and their people keep to their homes in the open plains. Without citizens, the city crumbled."

"Ah." He stepped beside her, not afraid of the height. Perhaps he mistakenly thought she'd catch him if he fell.

"So it *is* a message then. You think I'm too wary. I've been told as much before."

"I never said it was the right or wrong way to be. I just answered your question. Interesting, though, that you drew that conclusion."

"Why else are we here?"

"Because it's the first place I thought of, and while you might be in control of every aspect of our waking lives, dreams—even your dreams—are mine to command."

Malek laughed softly, the edges of his lips pulling up. "I missed you, Kasiandra."

His voice brought a shiver to her skin.

Cassi clenched her teeth and stared hard at the horizon as thunder rumbled overhead. She had been sending a message in coming here, but it hadn't been a message meant for him.

Led by childish notions of family, she'd flown her spirit to the House of Prey innumerable times as a girl to study the eagles circling the skies and to search for falcons in the mountains, wondering which might be her grandmother or her uncle. She knew every inch of this isle, maybe better than all the others except the House of Peace. Her spirit had haunted the halls of the fortress, had lain with the ruins, had flown alongside the hunters, and had even run with the buffalo while they scattered for safe haven. Then, one day, her mother told her the truth of her past. No accident had sent her over the edge and into the mist. Her own family had severed her wing and tossed her out. Cassi had never come here again, not even in her dreams...until today.

These vast skies and open plains were a reminder—love

was a gift wasted on the unworthy. It was foolish to yearn for someone who would never want her in return.

"I'm not going to kill him," she whispered.

"That remains to be seen."

"I refuse."

He sighed, as though bored. "What is it about him that has you so enamored?"

"It's not about him, Malek. Can't you see?" She caught his eyes, hating the pleading sound of her voice. Why couldn't she be strong around him the way she was with everyone else? What was it about him that always made her feel so weak? "It's about me. I don't want to be a killer, a murderer. I've never drawn a line with you before, but now I am. And I won't cross it."

He took a moment to study her face, something almost sorry in his expression. With a blink, it disappeared. "Tell me, if someone were coming at you with a knife, would you just stand there and let them strike? Or would you fight to defend yourself? Would you kill someone if it was the only way to save yourself?"

"That's different."

"Why?"

"Because Xander's not a threat." A laugh escaped her lips at the absurdity. "He couldn't even stab me if he tried. And he never would."

"He's a threat, and the fact that you can't see that has me more concerned than anything else you've said today, Kasiandra. What do you think he would do if he learned the truth about us, about our world, built on the very power they fear? If he knew there was a prophecy that foretold the falling of the skies, the destruction of his homeland, of his people? You think he would just stand there and watch it happen? Or do you think he might tell more of the avians, might rally them to his cause? And what would happen if he did? We're barely surviving as it is. Our people starve. They ache. Every ounce of magic in our world goes to providing them food, to building them shelter, to keeping them safe. We're already fighting a war on two fronts, our mages stretched thin. We can't afford a third. If the avians came, what do you think would happen? They're stronger than us, better fed, better educated, trained to be fighters from birth. If we brought our hunters back to fight them, the dragons would ravage our cities, called by the magic we must use. If we turned the magic we need to survive against them, our people would die of hunger, of illness, of drought. There's no greater threat we face than the world above discovering the secrets of the world beneath the mist."

He was right, of course. She'd heard it all before. And yet, Xander had known the truth about Rafe and loved him still. He'd learned about Lyana's magic and now fought to retrieve her. He didn't have the same prejudices as the rest of the avians.

But he might.

If it weren't his brother or his mate, if it were people he'd never met, with a power he thought an affront to his gods, who claimed the end of his world was near, he might find cause to destroy them. Even if he didn't, he might tell someone else who did.

Cassi squeezed her eyes closed, shutting out Malek and

the words he wielded like knives cutting straight into her soul.

"He's a good person," she murmured weakly. "He's honest and kind. He's just... He's good, Malek. I don't want him to die."

"The only people who have the luxury of being so-called *good* in this world, Kasiandra, are the ones who aren't important. Power comes with responsibility. Do you really think I want to kill him? That I wouldn't pick another option if I had the choice? I don't want him to die. I *need* him to die. There's a difference, one I thought you understood."

She did.

And she didn't.

Malek had her confused. His presence, his steady gaze, his uncompromising words, they compelled her, the same way they always did, as though his magic were there, digging into her skin, drawing her closer. It was why she hadn't wanted to see him. She was worried he'd pull her back into his web, just like he was doing.

Cassi searched her thoughts for the plan she'd come up with, all the arguments she'd been ready to make, all the reasons she'd so carefully outlined in preparation for this very conversation. All of them were gone, cowering in the shadows beneath her king's glorious might.

"What if—" She swallowed and blinked, trying to focus on the skies and the grasses and the stones, on anything except Malek and the power he still held over her—the power of being the only person alive, except for maybe her mother, who truly knew her.

You are a weapon. My weapon. To be wielded any way I choose.

That was what he thought of her.

That was all she was.

What if she made him think that was all Xander was as well? What if she put his life in terms her king might understand?

"What if we can use him?" she finally said.

Malek pressed his lips into a thin line, but said nothing.

"Before I came to visit your dreams, I overheard a meeting between Xander, his mother, and his captain of the guards. They fear for his safety, and they've devised a plan for his protection. They're sending him to the House of Wisdom."

Lightning flashed across Malek's stormy eyes. He was undeniably intrigued.

"I'm certain I can convince him to take me along," Cassi continued, words spilling out as a new plan came together. "I've been there in spirit, but never in body. There are rooms there with texts older than the isles themselves, from the time of the prophecy. I know. I've seen them. I've lurked over the shoulders of scholars as they've tried to decipher the old language. If I came as the guest of a prince, no one would suspect me. I could sneak in. I could copy the scrolls. I could maybe even bring you one. There might be information we could use against the dragons—knowledge we've lost to time, knowledge that the owls don't even realize they've preserved, knowledge only magic can access."

"What makes you think I don't have a spy in the House of Wisdom already?"

"Do you?" she asked, fully aware of the answer. "There's a reason I was given owl wings before I was deposited in the world above. I couldn't be a dove, because I needed to stand out enough for Lyana to take notice. But why an owl? Because I needed to be an orphan with nowhere else to go. If I'd been any other bird, my house would've taken me back. The owls are the archivists, patrons of Meteria, the god of intellect. Every child born in their house is recorded. The life of every citizen is carefully logged. No one steps into or out of their underground metropolis without their rulers knowing. So a strange owl girl showing up in the House of Peace was cause for alarm, not pity. They knew, they've always known, there's something not quite right about me, which is why they let the doves keep me, and why you've never been able to sneak any other child into their house."

Malek stared at the clear sky, at the sun shining overhead, at the floral tapestry splayed out before him, vivid colors the likes of which his waking eyes had never seen. He stared and stared and stared, studying every detail, until Cassi thought she might go mad. Then she remembered that she had control here.

With a single thought, the plains disappeared, replaced by stone walls without windows or doors, everything gray except for the single flame burning overhead to light the room. Her king stood opposite her, staring into her eyes as shadows danced along his cheeks.

"I can use him, Malek."

"And when you're done?"

Cassi didn't have an answer. Malek stared as she

dropped her eyes. In the silence of the prison she'd spun, he circled her, steps echoing against the stone. It took all her focus not to let the forests of the House of Whispers rise around them, to keep the blood from staining her clothes, from coating her hands, to keep the memory of that fateful day at bay.

When he came to a stop before her, he slipped his index finger under her chin, forcing her face up. There was a time not so long ago when she'd longed to feel his hands upon her. Now the touch just made her ill.

"I'll let you play your game, Kasiandra," he said in the voice of her king, the voice of her friend, the voice of a man she wasn't sure she would ever understand. "But the raven will only be able to hide among the owls for so long. Soon, the rest of the houses will learn of Lyana's disappearance. Soon, they'll come calling. Soon, the people of the world above will demand answers—ones we both know he can't be allowed to give. And when that happens, I trust you'll make the right choice. If you don't, I'm afraid I'll be forced to make it for you."

Time.

She'd bought time.

For now, that was enough.

When Cassi slipped out of her king's dream, she didn't linger. She didn't wait for him to glance her way, didn't wait to hear his real voice or her name upon his lips.

She fled.

Racing through the mist and across the sky, she returned to her body and woke with a start, her heart thumping. It was the middle of the night, but sleep never came. She lay on her back with her wings spilled over the sides of her bed and her skin covered in goose bumps, shivering from a chill no blanket could warm. Indigo shadows stretched across the ceiling, turning gray, then pink, then yellow faster than she could even believe. When the knock came, she rolled to her feet to answer the door, already aware of who it would be.

"Cassi—" Xander paused as soon as he saw her face, a frown curving his lips. "Are you all right?"

"I'm fine."

"Are you—"

"I'm fine," she repeated, more adamant this time.

Concern flashed across his irises, the light of a shooting star passing over a field of lilacs, there then gone. Unlike Malek, he wouldn't press. He would let her have her secrets, her space. He wouldn't ask for things she didn't want to give. "I can come back."

"No." She shook her head. Xander, of all people, had done nothing to earn her ire. "I'm sorry. I just had a rough night."

"Do you miss Lyana?"

She closed her eyes to keep him from seeing the truth within them and bit back a dark laugh, covering it up as a sigh instead. "I do. I really, really do."

Not a lie. Not quite the truth. Her specialty.

"Cheer up, then. I have a new plan to get her back."

Cassi met his eager gaze, trying to muster up the intrigue he desired.

"Imagine my library, only bigger, underground and endless, full of more books than you could ever hope to read, enough stories to last a lifetime, and you'll have the idea."

"The House of Wisdom?" she asked, infusing shock into the words.

His grin was as pure as his heart. "Exactly."

18

RAFE

"Captain told us not to leave the ship," Rafe griped, digging in his heels. Brighty tugged on his hand, trying to pull him from the room that had become his refuge. He'd had four blissful days without her incessant pestering. It was almost a shame it hadn't taken him longer to heal.

"Since when do you care about doing what the captain told us?"

"Since she's the one who agreed to take me to your king."

Brighty rolled her eyes. "Anyone can take you to the king. His castle is on a towering isle in the middle of the city. It's sort of hard to miss. Besides, don't you want to stretch your legs? You've been on bed rest for ages."

"Four days." He grinned. "Four glorious days without you."

She snorted. "Please. You've been bored out of your

mind. Shadow told me she caught you doing exercises in the storage room downstairs."

"I was looking for a snack."

"Fine. Then maybe I *will* tell Jolt you've been dying for some company. I hear she's been trying to sneak into your room at night, hoping to cure your aching heart with her aching—"

"Brighty!" he snapped, fighting the flush rising to his face.

"Oh, Rafe." She stopped yanking on him and turned around to pat his cheek. "It's only fun because it embarrasses you."

"Fine," he muttered gruffly. "Let's go."

"Excellent," she chirped, linking their elbows as she led him into the hall. When they reached the steps, she leaned in conspiringly. "By the way, you might want to consider Jolt's offer. You're wound so tight. It wouldn't be the worst thing in the world to let someone loosen you up a little. And you could do far worse than Jolt, trust me."

"How do you know?"

"The ocean can be a lonely place." She winked. "And the woman does have electric hands."

Rafe stumbled on the steps, nearly falling over as the image of the two of them entwined in bed smothered the rest of his thoughts. Brighty's laughter followed him up the stairs as he fought to recover his footing.

She was impossible.

Still, when he reached the main deck, he raced after her fleeting form as it disappeared down the gangplank. In Captain Rokaro's absence, Patch had been given control of the ship. Rafe waited for him to call them back, but no such order came.

"Why are you in such a hurry to leave, anyway?" he asked as soon as he reached her.

They stepped onto the floating wooden docks and into the strange city. The fog created a dismal atmosphere, leaving everything wet and dreary. With each step, the ground rose and fell in gentle swells, so it still felt as though he were on a ship. Men and women pushed carts along the planks, the creaking only adding to the eerie air. Their cheeks were hollow, their eyes focused and hard. The only vibrant parts of the city were the grandiose ships sitting along its edge, magic painting the skies above them. Some of them were hunting ships, like *The Wanderer*, but he'd been told even the trading ships were manned by mages. No one ventured into these misty, dragon-infested seas without magic.

"I want to see her," Brighty said, slipping around a bend and weaving her way through the crowds.

"Who?"

"The queen of prophecy. She's here."

"Who?"

Brighty stopped so short he nearly barreled into her.

"The queen of prophecy?" She studied his face for a reaction. "The Queen Bred of Snow?" He remained blank. "The person we've been waiting hundreds of years for?"

Rafe shrugged. "Never heard of her."

"What did they teach you up there? Aside from how to brood?" She scowled. "Magic alive, you're like a newborn babe. You know nothing."

"What's so great about her?"

"She and the king are going to save the world."

"I didn't realize it was in peril."

She made a disgusted sound and snatched his hand. "Just come with me."

Rafe let her pull him along, his attention wandering to his surroundings. The city was divided into various floating segments, with streets and homes and shops, all connected by an elaborate system of canals and bridges. Small boats floated along the waterways, transporting people and goods. Every so often, magic flashed in his peripheral vision—a man kneeling by a bed of plants, a woman ushering the waters of a fountain, a man casting toward a glowing lantern, a woman bending metal to patch a hole in a building. The children they passed were thin, but happy the way children were, playing with small wooden toys or chasing each other down the streets. The adults seemed... tense, weary even. Though he supposed that wasn't so unusual. Still, it irked him, like an itch at the back of his neck prompted by something he couldn't quite place.

"Do you even know where we're going?" he asked after a while, trying to ignore the unsettling feeling. "I want to be back before the captain, just in case she calls on me."

"I know these streets like the back of my hand," Brighty scoffed. "We're almost there."

"Where? How do you know where to go? How do you know this queen is even here? We've only been docked for a few hours, and you never even left the ship."

"A thief always has her ways." She yanked on his arm so that he stumbled through the narrow opening at the end of the alley and onto a new street. With a smug look on her face, she said, "We're here."

Rafe spun to find a courtyard filled to the brim with people, voices a hushed whisper, all their faces turned in the same direction.

"Let's find a good spot."

Brighty swerved through the throng as seamlessly as a bird through the open sky. Rafe followed boorishly after, his larger size forcing him to elbow people out of the way to keep up, leaving grumbles and hastily whispered apologies in his wake. Buildings surrounded the open space on three sides, but the fourth was edged by a wall made of stone, behind which the spires of a castle peeked through the mist. Built straight into the cliffs, the castle was imposing and imperial. A massive wooden door closed off the entrance to the public. Men and women stood along the wall, not in any uniform he could see, but the sparks at their fingertips labeled them mages, and the squared placement of their shoulders hinted at soldiers. An arch of deep green *ferro'kine* power sailed overhead, landing somewhere behind the wall in a spot he couldn't see.

"We made it just in time."

"In time for wh…"

The words died on his lips as a wave of gold exploded across the sky, spilling over the edge of the wall and washing over the crowd, brighter even than the sun. All at once, an excited clamor filled the air. Rafe swayed on his feet as the magic sank into his skin, so familiar, too familiar, subtly healing the aches in his bones. He'd felt this power before, the memory of it burned into his soul like a brand.

It can't be—

It can't—

The rest of the world faded away as she emerged from the mist, just as stunning as the first time he'd seen her, the sight stealing his thoughts, his words, the very breath from his chest. Her ivory wings peeked out from behind her shoulders, tucked close to her back, but there was no mistaking them—no mistaking her. Loose braids framed her face, enhancing her high cheekbones and plush lips. Those emerald eyes shone through her magic, filled with purpose, with pride, though in his memories they were filled with passion instead.

Ana.

"What? Who's Ana?" Brighty muttered, staring curiously at his gobsmacked expression. Rafe hadn't even realized he'd spoken out loud.

"Lyana," he corrected, out of habit. Lyana—not Ana. Even in this world, she was his brother's mate, so close yet so far away.

"How do you know her name? I only just learned it this morning. Lyana Aethionus—the Queen Bred of Snow."

He wanted to laugh. He wanted to cry.

What was she doing here?

What was she doing with him?

The man by her side must have been the king he'd heard so much about. The captain had called him ruthless and shrewd, and he seemed it, staring down his nose at the crowd without a smile on his lips. He gripped Lyana's hip, and she clutched his waist. Rafe forced a tight swallow down his throat when he noticed their joined hands bursting with magic, a power the two of them clearly shared, a power he would never understand.

Pain seared his chest, and he closed his eyes against the ache. In the darkness, he saw her, with moonlight dancing on her cheeks and starlight in her eyes as they held their palms together and studied each other through the gentle glimmer of their magic. It had been deeper than a physical touch, as though their souls had kissed, and then their lips, a night he would never forget, never trade, not even for Xander. The only night of his adult life when he'd felt for a moment as though he belonged.

And now she was here—sharing her magic with someone else.

"Rafe." Brighty tugged on his arm. "Are you all right? You look ill."

"I'm—" He shook his head and stared at Lyana, at the king, at the two of them floating majestically through the fog. They came to a stop atop the wall to address the waiting crowd. "What is she doing here?"

"Do you—do you know her?"

Do I know her?

He knew the taste of her, sweet and intoxicating, like bubbling hummingbird nectar laced with the sharp pang of citrus. He knew the feel of her, smooth skin and supple muscles, thighs strong as they wrapped around his waist, her hair tickling his cheeks. He knew the sound of her, sighs like the sweetest music, his name on her lips the most wondrous song.

But did he know her?

Ten minutes ago, he would have said yes.

Now, he wasn't so sure.

Lyana was Cassi's best friend. Cassi, who cornered him in the base of the castle. Cassi, who cut off his wings. Cassi, who threw him over the edge and into the world below. Cassi, who'd been working for the king now standing with Lyana, their fingers laced together and their magic flowing, the two of them joined for the whole world to see.

Had they been working together? All three of them?

Had she only been pretending the whole time?

Blood pounded in his ears, drowning out the crowd, the magic, the city, until there was nothing but the rapid thumping of his heart. The king was giving some sort of a speech, but Rafe couldn't hear it. The man hoisted his and Lyana's joined hands over his head. The crowd around them cheered, nothing but a distant roar to Rafe's ears, as though he were sinking below the ocean and they were on land. More *ferro'kine* magic flared, and then they were in the air again, standing on some sort of metal disc that hovered over the crowd. Lyana spread her wings to keep her balance, and that's when he saw it.

They'd been clipped.

The pearlescent plumes at the far ends of her wings, her gorgeous primary feathers, were gone. The people surrounding him probably didn't even notice—hers might have been the only wings they'd ever seen—but Rafe did. He recognized the abnormality in an instant. Just as quickly, the confusion and despair flooding his veins ignited, turning to fury instead. The king had done this to her. Rafe knew it. With Cassi's help, he'd grounded her. She was as much a prisoner of this world as Rafe was, and he was just as determined to set her free.

"Lyana!"

His shout was lost to the din of the crowd as the disk carrying them touched down in the center of the courtyard. The golden flecks in the air brightened, magic stretching and strengthening with their nearness.

"Lyana!"

Rafe shoved people aside, uncaring, all his focus on the tips of her ivory wings, which were still visible above the masses. She and the king were moving. The crowd seemed to part before them and meld behind them, as though a bubble encircled them, allowing people to get close but not too close, a strange sort of magic.

"Lyana! Lyana!"

He was only a few bodies away now. Through a break, her face flashed, something in her expression so drained it made him wish he could bear the silent burden for her. Digging his shoulder into another man, Rafe pushed past. Two or three more people and he'd be there, beside her. He was close, so close, so—

Rafe froze.

Invisible binds fastened around him, as though a hundred hands held every inch of his body, keeping him still. No one else moved. The magic in the air sharpened, wrapping around the crowd like gilded chains. He tried to shout, but no sound passed through his lips. His jaw didn't even open. No matter how hard he fought to take a step, to reach out, he was trapped where he stood. Lyana came closer, and closer, only a few feet away.

See me, he silently willed, pushing the thought out like a prayer. *Please, Ana. Hear me. See me. If you ever loved me, please don't walk away.*

Her feathers bristled.

Her movement slowed.

She paused, and the whole world seemed to pause with her.

LYANA

The back of her neck tingled. Lyana stopped, turning to the crowd as the sensation slipped down the length of her spine, making her stand tall. There was something undeniably familiar about one of the spirits grasping for her magic, something recognizable about the deep-rooted pain aching to be healed, its touch and taste and feel like a phantom haunting her thoughts.

Rafe?

She narrowed her eyes, scanning the faces all around her.

Rafe?

It felt so much like him, that gently throbbing ache her magic had never been able to heal, not in the cave as she'd fixed the burns covering his body, not in his room when she'd repaired the broken bones of his wings, not even later, when she'd tried using her lips instead. There had been a moment as they'd lain entangled in each other's arms, his wings a warm blanket, her breath against his chest, their hearts beating as one, when she thought maybe his pain had gone. A peace had settled over him, over them both—a serenity the rising dawn had shattered.

Where had he gone after she'd left his room?

Was it possible he'd come here?

Her heart convulsed. Lyana scanned the fog for the telltale flash of onyx wings, hope a painful beast inside her chest. There was nothing, just thick gray mixed with the glimmer of magic, most of it Malek's. Every spot of ebony along the rooftops made her nerves flutter, but no raven lurked in the shadows. If anyone in the surrounding crowd had wings, she would have seen them from atop the wall. Still, it felt so much like him.

Rafe?

The thought had a little less conviction this time, a little less certainty. Maybe her mind was playing tricks on her. In his presence, she'd always felt as though she could do anything. He'd always made her feel strong. With the weight of so many pleading souls pressing in on her, it was only natural she wished he were there.

But he wasn't.

In the lands above, she was Xander's mate. Down here, she was Malek's queen. There was no place in the world where she and Rafe would ever be anything more than a memory, and she had to remember that.

"We should go," Malek murmured into her ear, his lips so close she felt his breath on her neck as he squeezed her fingers. "We shouldn't linger."

When she turned to face him, a flash of black hair caught her eye, the short strands ruffling in the breeze.

Lyana froze, willing the crowd to part. If she could just get one look, one glance, one—

"Lyana." At the commanding tone, she flinched. "If you want to visit the infirmary, we need to keep moving before you burn out."

He was right. Already, the small bit of power she was using threatened to overwhelm, her control a precarious thing. Thoughts of Rafe had opened her heart, and she had to fight to shut down her emotions, to keep them contained, lest her magic overpower her again. Surrounded by so many people, she couldn't afford to let their aching souls inside. The maelstrom would consume her, and she was eager to get to the infirmary. As part of their newfound compromise, Malek had promised to let her practice her healing magic on his people, a way to endear her to them, but also to boost her confidence by using a power she already knew how to wield. This entire outing was a favor to her, and the least she could do was respect this one request.

"Of course."

He put his hand to the small of her back, easing her forward. Lyana searched one last time for the wisp of onyx, but whatever she thought she'd seen was gone.

Forcing her face and her thoughts ahead, she followed Malek's lead, fortifying her walls and separating her magic from her heart the way he'd taught her. As they made their way down crowded city streets, she couldn't help but marvel at his control, his precision, his apparent effortlessness. He moved the crowd around them, wrapping the people in his golden magic and forcing them aside, so no one got close enough to touch her or blocked their path.

Yet no one shouted. No one complained. The only looks she saw were of devotion, as though his magic, even when used to restrain them, were a precious gift.

Part of her was envious—of his expertise, of their love for him, of the idea that if she'd been born to this world, maybe her magic would flow just as easily, just as freely, since she never would have had to hide.

Another part of her was wary—reverence such as this should be aimed only at the gods. Normally, she basked in attention, but this made her skin crawl. She was just a woman. Malek was just a man. What if they weren't the king and queen these people hoped for? What if, in the end, they couldn't give the people what they needed?

Nausea coiled like a snake in her gut.

It took a moment for Lyana to realize it wasn't her own. The air was sick, and as they turned a corner she knew why.

The infirmary loomed before her. Even though she'd never set eyes on the building, there was no mistaking it. Unlike every island sector they'd crossed before, this one had no paths, no walkways, no open bridges waiting for pedestrians to cross. The building was a fortress, its wooden walls slick and lacking handholds, and the windows mere slits with iron bars across them. There were no balconies and no doors. The sides sank straight into the canal, and the only way over the water surrounding it was the drawbridge being lowered in anticipation of their arrival. The people of the city kept their distance, the crowd around them thinning as the foot of the bridge drew near.

"We have to keep the sick contained," Malek whispered,

as though sensing her sudden trepidation. "But inside it's not as bad as it looks. Trust me."

She did.

Or at least, she was starting to.

When they were halfway across the canal, the door to the infirmary eased open, and a man in a billowing evergreen cloak stepped outside to welcome them.

"Your Majesties." He bowed his head. "You honor us with your presence."

"Lord Daegal, the honor is ours."

He led them through the entrance and into a dark tunnel made of solid stone, the way illuminated only by globes of magic light. Their boots clicked in the silence, each step echoing around the chamber, softened only by the dampness hanging in the air. An ominous feeling crept up Lyana's spine, worsening as they crossed the suffocating space, until finally the door at the other end swung open.

She gasped.

It was...beautiful. The darkness gave way to an explosion of color—swatches of ivy, blooming flowers, vibrant leaves, towering trees, as though the jungle had fallen out of the sky and landed in this sorry space, carrying life with it. There wasn't a single stone in sight. The walls were living gardens, cultivated by the men and women standing within them, green sparks flaring at their fingertips. Lyana's wings opened on instinct, the urge to explore too difficult to contain, until she remembered that because of Malek she couldn't.

She snapped her wings closed.

"Unexpected, isn't it?" Malek murmured.

Lyana swallowed the emotion clogging her throat. "It looks exactly how I always imagined the House of Flight might look. Abaelon, the City of Life, sits in the middle of a vast desert, but the walls themselves are said to breathe, every inch of the oasis covered in foliage."

"It's funny you say that, because I've been told all the seeds for these plants were stolen from the hummingbirds hundreds of years ago, after the isles first rose into the sky."

"Really?" A note of wonder rang in her tone as her mind filled with clandestine expeditions. "How?"

"Much the same way I visited the isles to find you," Malek said. It was interesting, she couldn't help but note, how he reframed their first meeting as though he'd happened upon her rather than stolen her from her home. "The ocean offered little by way of food, even less by way of medicinal herbs, so our people had to steal them. Using powerful wind magic combined with metal magic, they lifted four vessels into the sky—two to the House of Flight and two to the House of Paradise. In the dead of night, they stole as many plants as they could, digging them out from the roots or plucking off seeds. Then they returned to Da'Kin where our earth mages turned a handful of scattered scraps into this. Though I assume it took more than one trip and likely multiple lifetimes for us to establish the floating fields and fruitful gardens we now maintain across the sea. Every city in my kingdom has an infirmary, and within every infirmary hides an oasis of plants chosen specifically for their medicinal uses."

"And where are the people?" Lyana asked, fascinated.

"Inside the walls, though each room has a view into the

courtyard. I've been told there are some who injure themselves just to be able to peek at the splendor hidden within."

"Right you are, my liege," Lord Daegal said as he continued leading them down a winding path. "And when they do, I give them a smack on the head and a kick out the door. A healer's time is never to be wasted, as I'm sure you both well know. Shall we start with the children?"

"Let's."

He ushered them through an open door and inside the building to where a group of men and women were waiting. The air was warm and dry, the work, she suspected, of a *hydro'kine* or perhaps a *pyro'kine*. But it was also stuffy compared to the fresh air of the gardens, and almost immediately, the pain and suffering of the desperate souls she'd felt before clawed at her again. Lyana nearly collapsed as they led her into the first room. A young girl rested there, buried in blankets, her skin flushed with fever and her pupils so dilated only a thin sliver of amber hinted that she had any irises at all. Before Malek could even speak, Lyana took the girl's hand and unleashed her power. The world fell away as she pushed her magic into the child's skin. All she saw was spirit.

This wasn't a lesson spent playing with bowls. This wasn't a display before the masses, meant to sway hearts or gain loyalty. This wasn't magic for magic's sake. This was power with a purpose, and it filled her with a sense of determination all her days in the mist had thus far lacked. With her focus on this single task, the ache of the other spirits slipped away, no longer a burden too heavy to carry, but an afterthought.

The healing came more quickly than it ever had. Her magic ruthlessly ate away at the dark stains littering the girl's soul, the foreign bodies that never should have been there. Before she knew it, she was done, skin still buzzing, her power charged and aching to be used. So they went to another room, and another, and another, until Lyana lost count of the innocent souls she looked upon, the bodies she healed, the lives she saved. The sky darkened and her energy waned, but she didn't want to stop when she had so much to give and they were in so much need. How could she claim to be tired when they were dying around her? How could she rest her mind and close her eyes when theirs might never reopen?

Finally, Malek grabbed her by the elbow. "Lyana, it's time to stop."

"I'm fine."

"Lyana."

The command in his tone pulled her back to the world. She cleared the magic from her vision, turning to face him and nearly falling over as her knees gave out. Malek caught her in his arms. The child she'd just healed was asleep in his bed. The mages waited on the other side of the door. They were, for the moment, alone. Maybe that was why she let him keep his arms around her as he peered down at her, so much sorrow and understanding in his eyes.

"You can't save them all."

"I can try."

"And what would it accomplish?" He brushed a

wayward braid from her eyes, tucking it behind her ear. "The infirmary will be full again in a month's time. You can exhaust yourself here, working tirelessly night and day to save a handful of these people. Or you can save more, maybe not from every illness or injury, but from the plague that matters most. You did as much as you could today. You must save some of yourself for tomorrow."

"Will we be coming back here?"

"Eventually."

She straightened and pushed away from him. "I want to come back tomorrow."

"No." The word came too quickly to his lips. "There are more important things to do, more things I need to teach you."

"What? Bowls and invisible doors and legends? These people are dying now. And I can save them. What is more important than that, Malek? Tell me."

"What if you did?" he countered, just as used to getting his way as she was. "What if you came back every day, exhausting yourself and learning nothing of the true extent of your power? What would happen when the spell holding the gateway shut finally unravels? I'm not powerful enough to close it on my own. I've tried. If you don't know how to use your magic by then, the isles will fall, the door will open, and there will be nothing to stop the dragons from invading our world, from taking it over. How many would die then? How many of these people you spent your days healing would survive? How many, Lyana?" He echoed her words, her tone, the final two landing like punches to the gut. "Tell me."

She didn't have an answer.

She didn't know.

All she knew was a small child in the next room felt a pain so violent it cut into her like a knife, and she wanted to heal him. In this moment, nothing else mattered. Not a prophecy. Not a gate. Not philosophical questions that might never matter.

"Our magic is a curse as much as a gift," Malek said, stepping closer and taking her hand, drawing her back to the room and his words. "It's no easy thing to hold a life in your hands, let alone thousands. In matters such as this, who are we to say who lives and who dies? Sometimes it's better to let nature decide."

He rubbed his thumb over her knuckle, a brief flash of magic simmering at the spot before disappearing into her skin, soothing her aches. She'd never felt the warm trickle of healing magic before, like honey in her veins, delivering sweet relief.

"My father told me a story once," he continued, voice softer than she'd ever imagined it could be, no unspoken orders or rough edges. "Of a king who'd been overthrown. The rulers of this world are always selected by magic, the crown given to any living *aethi'kine*, and if none exist, then to the strongest mage by way of competition. But powerful doesn't mean invincible, and even magic such as ours doesn't guarantee safety. Some have been replaced throughout our history, bested by other mages or betrayed by their heirs, but only one was taken down by revolt. By all accounts, he was a kind soul. He spent his days much the way you'd like to, healing whom he could, leaving little time for everything else. Da'Kin flourished, its people happy and healthy and in debt to their savior king. But in his neglect for his other responsibilities, the other cities, especially those farthest away, deteriorated. People grew resentful of his seeming favoritism, grew jealous of this thriving city, grew bitter at their own misfortune, until finally, they led an attack and overthrew him. After that, very few kings spent their days in the infirmaries. It was better to use their healing magic as a blessing on rare occasions, making it a wondrous gift instead of a dangerous expectation. We cannot save them all, as my father used to tell me, so sometimes it is better to save none."

"But—" Lyana shook her head. *That can't possibly be right. I don't believe it. I won't.* "Even if we can't save them all, we should do what we can. Surely one is better than none."

"To that one, maybe." He dropped his gaze to the boy asleep on the bed, then shifted it to the wall separating them from all the other desperate souls housed within this place. "But if you're not that one, if your child or your sibling or your friend is not that one..." He shrugged, meeting her eyes, the rough look of choppy seas back in his. "Then I'm not so sure."

As he led her to the courtyard and through the tunnel, across the drawbridge and to the inconspicuous boat waiting to return them to the castle, his words followed her. She wasn't sure if she believed them, but she was consumed by them—so consumed she didn't notice the tingle at the back of her neck urging her to turn around, whispering that something else chased her through the night.

20

BRIGHTY

"Rafe, this is madness."

"You're the one who said, and I quote, 'Anyone can take you to the king. His castle is on a towering isle in the middle of the city. It's sort of hard to miss.'"

"One, I do *not* sound like that," she said, digging in her heels, or at least attempting to, but the man had about a foot on her and magic knew how many pounds, so the effect was completely lost as he continued to pull her along. "Two, I was being facetious."

Rafe snorted.

"You can't sneak up on the king. Did you feel his magic?"

"I have no intention of sneaking up on him," Rafe growled, a venom in his voice that made her wince. His hands curled into fists. "What I'd like to do to him requires that we meet face to face."

Brighty rolled her eyes. Why were men so quick to

jump to violence? Especially when confronted with impossible odds? If he showed even a bit of sense, she might have been willing to tell him he was going the wrong way, and had been for quite some time, but not when he was in a mood like this. "Rafe—"

"Gods alive!" he snapped as they reached a street that opened into the canal, no bridge, just water, and no royal boat in sight. "Where did they go?"

While he scowled, she sighed, wishing, and not for the first time that day, to get back to the ship. Da'Kin was her city, but it was also her past, littered with memories she'd rather not face and people she'd rather not find.

This is what I get for breaking Captain's orders.

Her intentions had been to see the queen, wander through the market, and perhaps make a quick stop at the gambling hall, then return to the ship. Instead, Rafe had chased the king and queen across the city, and she had chased him. They'd spent hours standing outside the infirmary—well, Rafe had been standing, his arms crossed while he stared daggers at the raised drawbridge. Brighty had scaled a building to take a leisurely nap on the roof. Still, not her ideal afternoon. When the king and queen had finally emerged, she'd watched from above as Rafe sprinted down the street like a lovesick fool, only to freeze in his tracks as a golden power wrapped around his limbs. It would have been comical if it weren't so sad.

Like she'd said, it was impossible to sneak up on the king.

Cursing the dead end, Rafe picked a direction, seemingly at random, and started running. Brighty followed. She almost wished she could say jealousy led her to chase after, as it was a much easier emotion than the one stirring in her chest, but he was decidedly not her type. Too handsome. Too tall. Too male. No, this was something far, far worse, something she'd thought she'd cured herself of—compassion. He was, perhaps, the least charming man she'd ever met—always grumpy, always moping, always talking back. But there was something about him that almost pleaded with her to take pity on his soul.

For magic's sake. She shook her head, as though trying to dispel the wayward feelings creeping up her spine and infiltrating her common sense. *What is happening to me?*

It was his damned eyes—those deep, tortured eyes. He reminded her of someone she used to know. Before the day that had changed everything, before she'd been delivered to the king with that wretched stain on her soul, before he'd cleaned his hands of her, these streets had been her home. There had been a boy who used to beg beside her when she was just a girl, back when her eyes hadn't fully worked. He'd been whip sharp and sneaky as hell. After her magic came in, gifting her a new kind of sight, she'd spent months quietly studying his sleight of hand, trying to copy his tricks. Clearly, that shrewd bastard wasn't anything like Rafe. But his constant companion had been a loyal hound, floppy ears and droopy eyes, the perfect ruse to lure people in. *That* was who Rafe resembled. He was just like that dog, loyal and steadfast, honest and somehow pure, so undeniably sad with those big brown eyes that were impossible to pass by and ignore. Rafe's eyes were blue, but it was the same thing. They were so broken, so fractured, that for some inexplicable reason she wanted to protect him.

Brighty sighed and shook her head, still racing after Rafe, his pounding boot steps probably waking the entire neighborhood. Even if they weren't, the occasional frantic shout of *Lyana* would do the trick. Apparently, she needed to teach him how to live on land as well as on the sea. Were they all like this in the world above? So rash and loud? Had the thin air messed with their minds?

You should go right, she thought as they reached the next fork in the street.

Rafe went left.

The bridge is two blocks in the opposite direction.

He kept going.

The rooftops are so much easier to navigate.

He remained firmly on the ground.

Aren't you a bird? Shouldn't you inherently know how to move north?

He went south, toward the docks, decidedly away from the castle, and ran into another dead end. A thin line of chain was all that kept him from toppling over the edge and into the canal.

"Rafe," she finally said, taking pity on him.

He spun, eyes blazing. "Brighty, how the gods do I find this bloody castle?"

A delighted gasp escaped her lips as she put her hand to her chest. "Rafe, you're talking like a sailor."

"Please." With a hasty step forward, he grabbed her hands. "Please, no more jokes. No more watching me run aimlessly through the streets with a smirk on your lips. No more games. You know where to go. Please, help me." He stared at her, the imploring expression nailing her to the spot and weighing her down with its familiarity. "Please, Brighty. I have to see her."

Just like that, she knew who he truly reminded her of— not the dog, but someone else, someone far more important. The memories of her were buried so deep it had taken Brighty a moment to realize it. Back in the square, when he'd first seen the queen, an emotion had filled his eyes, warm and burning, brighter than the light magic in her veins, more powerful too and edged with yearning. She'd seen that look before. It was the reason she'd decided to guard her heart, to stop caring about other people, to stop giving them the chance to hurt her.

That look had once destroyed her.

She didn't want it to destroy him too.

"Rafe," she said softly. Hope pooled in his gaze, the sort of light she didn't need her magic to see, yet it touched her just the same. Brighty mentally scolded herself. *It's his heart he's playing with. His life. What's it to you?* The answer should have been *nothing*, but it wasn't, and she didn't care to linger on why. Instead, she stifled every instinct screaming at her to return to the ship and said the very thing he wanted to hear. "Follow me, and I'll take you to the king."

This was his mistake to make.

Maybe the best thing she could do was to let him.

21

RAFE

With Brighty's help, he made it to the castle wall without mishap. She really did move like a spirit, shifting through the shadows as fluidly as a phantom, quick and lithe, so silent he almost wondered if there were magic involved. But there wasn't—he would have seen it. In fact, he might have even complimented her, if she weren't so frustrating. It was a shame, really, that her attitude surpassed even her skill.

"You're such an oaf," she muttered as they crossed the last set of rooftops, not a single of her steps out of place, while he clambered after, accidently kicking a shingle loose. They both winced when it crashed against the courtyard below. "Watch where you're going."

"I am," he grumbled. It was just, he was used to the sky, to the stealth of wings, the ease of them. He'd never had to climb anything in his life, not really.

"Watch harder."

Gritting his teeth against a reply, Rafe followed her to

207

the edge of the roofline, nothing but open air between them and the looming wall, which stretched just high enough to block his view of the other side. The gods, what he would give for his wings. It would be so easy. A few quick pumps and he'd be over the edge, on the other side, and on his way to Lyana, to the king. The mere thought of the man made his blood boil.

"How do we get over it?"

"I said I'd get you to the castle." She shrugged. "I never said I could get you inside."

"Brighty!"

She remained unperturbed. Rafe rubbed his hand over his face and into his hair, grabbing the strands as though to yank them from his head. His instincts screamed at him to take action, to make a running leap and hope for the best. If he fell, well, he might break his legs, but they'd heal. If he made it…

Rafe shook his head.

That's a horrible plan. He frowned. *I am an oaf.*

What would Xander do? He'd come up with something. He'd reason it out. He'd use the knowledge from his books and his endless theories to put some semblance of a plan together. Of course, Rafe had little awareness of those books or theories. Still, he had his fight and his strength, and he'd spent enough time with his brother. Surely something must have rubbed off.

Think. Think.

"You look like you need to take a shit."

He glared at her. "You're not helping."

"Why would I, when this is so entertaining?"

Rafe ignored her, mumbling, "I guess I could—no. But maybe—no. What if—"

"Don't hurt yourself."

"Could you just, for once, not talk unless you have something useful to say?"

"Something like this?" Her tone was too cheerful by half. Rafe snapped his face to the side, surprised to find her standing there with a rope he'd never even noticed her holding. "It's not my first break-in. I grabbed this as soon as I saw it, about three islands back. Just stay here and I'll toss it to you."

"But how are you going to get to the top?"

She scoffed in response and disappeared over the edge of the roof. Rafe could do nothing but watch as she landed in the courtyard below and glided silently to the wall, the creak and groan of the city more than enough cover. Then she simply...climbed. His eyes nearly bugged out of his head as she scaled the wall, hands gripping invisible holds, feet somehow finding perches, moving as easily as a spider up its web. Before long, she vanished over the top, reappearing a moment later to toss him the rope.

Rafe caught it easily and jerked it once to test the weight. It wasn't long enough to reach the ground beneath them, so instead he jumped. Gripping the rope between his hands, Rafe careened toward the wall. Never since his first flight had he felt so precarious in the air, dangling like a fish on a hook as the rocks raced closer. At the last second, he lifted his feet, landing with an *oof* against the stone. As he climbed, he searched for the grooves Brighty had used, but for the life of him, he couldn't find a single one.

"Took you long enough," she muttered as he pulled himself over the top.

His heart sank when he saw what waited on the other side—water. The castle was built into jagged cliffs, surrounded on all sides by a calm pool. In the darkness, there was no way to tell how deep it sank, no doubt too deep for a bird who'd never learned to swim. Across the way, a boat was anchored to a small wooden dock. A staircase had been carved into the rock, leading all the way up to what must be a door. If he could just reach it…

All he needed to do was keep his head above the surface. Swimming couldn't be that hard.

Brighty read his mind. "Before you take a diving leap off the wall, can you please ask yourself one question—why has no one tried to stop us?"

"I don't care."

"Why not?"

"I just—" He squeezed his eyes shut, Lyana's face rising through the darkness. No one had ever looked at him the way she'd looked at him. No one had ever treated him the way she'd treated him. As an equal. As worthy. As someone to love. If she was hurt, if she was imprisoned, he had to help her, consequences be damned. She would do the same for him. He knew it in his bones. "I know it might be a trap," he finally said, his voice gritty. "I know this is probably idiotic. And I know there's a good chance it won't work. But I have to try. I have to. So, are you going to help me or not?"

"Well, I've come this far." She sighed and nodded toward the water. "You first."

Rafe jumped.

The water devoured him on impact. In the darkness, he couldn't see which way was up and which was down. He kicked and flailed his arms, struggling to find the surface as his chest burned. The ebony folds smothered him, impossible to fight.

A beam of light cut through the shadows.

Hands grabbed his arm.

Rafe kicked his feet, following where Brighty led, until finally they broke the surface together and inhaled deeply. With his head above water, swimming came more easily. His movements were still rushed and jerky, probably the strokes of a child, but they did the trick. Brighty slowed her pace to stick with him, keeping a hand on his shoulder as she went, just as nimble in the water as she was on land.

When they reached the dock, Rafe pulled himself up first, then lifted her beside him. Not waiting, he raced up the stairs, taking them two at a time and grabbing the metal rail when he slipped on the moist stones, not letting it slow him. Brighty was right behind him, he was sure, but as he got to the top, he didn't stop to check. The door was a few feet away. He sprinted for it, reaching for the knob, so close, so close—

The entrance yawned open.

Rafe barreled inside, unable to stop himself as he skidded over smooth tiles and fell to his knees, off balance in this new body with no wings to catch him. Brighty put a hand on his shoulder to steady him, then froze as a voice echoed across the darkness.

"I admit, I didn't think it would take you quite so long to get here. If you would, please, Thalyia."

He felt more than saw her flinch.

Thalyia? Rafe thought. *Is that her real name? Does the king know her?*

Light pooled around Brighty's hand, illuminating the hall and chasing the shadows away. With a flick of her fingers, ivory sparks sailed across the room to land in glass encasements. The space almost reminded him of home— thick stone walls, heavy woven tapestries, a grand staircase leading deeper into the castle. Rafe's attention went straight to the man standing before him with his hands joined behind his back. They were the same height, yet somehow the king managed to peer down at him, reeking of arrogance. Rafe longed for nothing more than to wipe his smug expression from his face.

Still on his hands and knees, he pushed off the ground and launched himself at the king. Golden sparks blazed at the man's fingertips and shot across the divide to wrap around Rafe's limbs. He froze in place with his hands outstretched for the king's throat. Using every ounce of muscle he possessed, Rafe fought against the binds, until his heaving breaths echoed across the hall. No matter what he tried, it was useless.

"Where's Lyana?" he asked, still fighting, not giving up. "Is she safe? I demand to see her. Take me to her."

The king arched a brow. "I really don't believe you're in any position to be making demands."

"Where is she?" He strained until he thought the veins in his neck might burst. "Tell me."

"Is he always like this?" The king turned to Brighty.

She swallowed and nodded. "Yes, my liege."

Rafe's eyes about fell out of his head when she dipped her chin to stare at the floor. Who was this girl by his side? Meek and subservient? What the gods had this king done to her?

"Fascinating," the man murmured, his gaze on Rafe once more. "Predictable, yet fascinating."

"Stop talking about me as though I'm not standing right here," Rafe spat, not backing down. "What have you done with Lyana? I saw her wings. I know you—"

Invisible fingers pinched his throat, cutting off the words. Rafe hoped his glare said everything his voice no longer could. *I know you clipped them, you vile cad.*

Maybe the sea was rubbing off on him.

At the moment, he couldn't say he minded.

"The queen is perfectly safe, I assure you," the king said, unperturbed. "She's asleep in her room, recovering from a long afternoon of healing her people. I won't have her rest interrupted. I will, however, make you an alternate offer, as a sign of good faith. If you agree to leave her in peace for the evening, you may follow me to my study and we can have the meeting I hear you so desperately long for. If, however, you refuse to be silent and insist on shouting her name down the halls, I'll be forced to remove you at once. The choice is yours, though I'd take a moment to think before you answer. This opportunity won't come again."

The vice around Rafe's throat unclenched.

He caught the refusal before it slipped out—but just barely. It wasn't in his nature to back down, but for once he had to be smart, to think first and act second. This king thought Lyana was the queen from some prophecy. Even if she was down here against her will, he wasn't planning to harm her. At least, not yet. And difficult as it was to accept, Rafe had no way to get past this man tonight.

But with his wings, maybe they'd be on a more even playing field.

"I—" He paused, fighting the overwhelming feeling that this was wrong—so, so wrong. But what other choice did he have? This wasn't about winning one battle. It was about winning the war. "I accept."

"Good." The binds around Rafe fell away as the king's magic winked out of sight. "Thalyia, I trust you can find your own way out."

Brighty spared a quick glance at Rafe. "Yes, my liege."

They left her by the entrance and walked deeper into the halls, which were somehow warm and dry despite the dankness outside. Rafe followed the king up stair after stair. Built into the rock, the castle was towering and narrow compared to the sprawling palaces he was used to in the world above. He didn't know where to begin searching for Lyana. There were so many levels, so many doors, so many twists and turns. He wasn't even sure he could find his way out without assistance. When the king finally opened a door, he was just relieved to stop moving.

The relief faded the moment he saw what waited inside.

"My wings!"

Rafe raced across the room and stopped dead. His hands trembled as he reached for the bundle of onyx feathers on the table. They were wrapped in cords and coated in a thick layer of blood, now dried and glimmering in the firelight, but there was no mistaking them.

My wings.

He nearly spilled his lunch on the floor. The room spun, the air growing too light. He swayed on his feet, overcome by the brutal reality before him. His hands dropped to his sides. He didn't want to touch them, didn't want to feel his own feathers but not *feel* them, to know they were truly gone.

My wings.

Spine bending forward, Rafe wilted, all his fight seeping out of him as efficiently as if the king had swiped a blade along his stomach, sending his entrails to the floor. He was empty, gutted, nothing but a shell of the raven he'd once been.

"I hear you'd like them back."

With a snarl, Rafe turned, the fire in his heart furiously erupting. A loathing unlike any he'd felt before burrowed into his soul, like a brand, like a promise. He didn't know when, but somehow, someway, he would destroy this man.

"Sit, please."

Magic pressed into Rafe's chest, forcing him to sit. While Rafe seethed like a rabid animal ready to break free of its cage, the king took the spot opposite him, the picture of ease with his hands folded in his lap and his foot casually balanced on his knee.

"You might not believe me, but I don't take pleasure in your pain, Aleksander. Everything I do is for the good of the world. It's inevitable that there should be some hurt feelings along the way."

Rafe flinched, understanding how Brighty felt at the sound of her real name—as though an arrow had slipped through a small break in his defenses to pierce his heart. He wasn't that person anymore. Neither was she. Of course, that was the entire point. It allowed the king to give the first strike.

He didn't ask how the man knew. Maybe Cassi had learned it. Maybe he had other spies in the House of Whispers. It mattered little.

"I'm at a disadvantage," Rafe said instead, thrilled at the hint of surprise written on the man's face. "You know my name, but I've yet to learn yours."

"King Malek'da'Nerri, though you may call me *my liege*."

"You're not my king."

"Until you have the means to return to your world above the mist, I'm afraid I am, which brings us to the point of this little gathering. You want your wings back. I have the magic to return them to you. But I won't, unless you do something for me in return."

"What?" What could he possibly do that this man couldn't do already?

"I've tasked Captain Rokaro with catching a dragon alive and bringing it to me so that my mages and I might study it. We'd like to learn how they communicate with each other, how their magic and their fire work. I want you to help her, to learn about her crew and about this world, to listen to her instructions and do as she says. And when you come back to Da'Kin with a dragon in tow, we can see about your wings."

"That's it?"

The king shrugged. "What can I say? I'm a simple man."

Rafe snorted. He'd spent his life praying to the god of chance—he knew a trick when he saw one. There was no way the king had gone to so much trouble bringing him down to this world just for help catching a dragon. The gods, he was more a hindrance on the ship than a help. They might have caught the last one if he hadn't leapt into action, or they might have all been killed, but still. What could he do that a whole crew of magical sailors couldn't?

Nothing.

"Give me a dragon," the king murmured, dangling the words like bait. "And I'll give you back the sky."

"What's the catch?"

"No catch. My promise is true."

My ass it is, Rafe silently cursed.

The king leaned closer, sensing his wavering mind. "A man is only as good as his word."

"I know a lot of men who think otherwise."

"Not this man." He straightened, gaze boring into Rafe as though he could see into his soul, into all the dark thoughts and insecurities he'd spent his life trying to hide. "I grow tired of this debate. Give me an answer, now. Do you agree or not?"

No.

No.

No.

No.

"Yes." The black wings resting on the table were ripe for

the taking, too good to pass up. The king was toying with him, Rafe was certain, but he would deal with the consequences when they came. If it meant getting his wings back, the price hardly mattered. "I agree."

"Good. Jacinta!" The door opened and a woman walked in, her long black hair as straight as a sword's edge, the bangs across her forehead severe against her pale skin. "Please, escort our guest back to his ship. We're done here."

The binds clasped around him again, this time yanking him to a standing position.

"Wait!" Rafe fought against the magic, even as his feet took step after step against his will. "I have questions."

"And I'm sure someone else will answer them for you. I lack both the time and the desire to do so."

"What are you doing with Lyana?" Rafe said anyway, expecting to be cut off at any moment. "Please, I need to see her. I need to speak with her."

"Don't worry, Aleksander," the king said, voice just as steady as ever, though a light pierced his dark eyes, giving them a wicked gleam. "One day soon, you will."

"Wh—"

He didn't have a chance to finish. A band of metal wrapped around his lips, sealing off the sound, as four more came around his ankles and wrists. Green sparks filled the air and the woman pulled on the cuffs. The last thing Rafe saw was the slight curl to the king's mouth as he was dragged forcefully from the room.

LYANA

His chest rose and fell beneath her palm, up and down, up and down, in a mesmerizing rhythm. Nestled against his side with her cheek pressed to his skin, Lyana listened to the steady beat of Rafe's heart. He was deep in slumber while she lay wide awake. Her mind buzzed too wildly for rest, and she slipped her gaze down the length of his bare chest, over the defined ridges of his abdomen, down, down, down to the very tips of his toes, and back up.

How could he sleep at a time like this?

Lyana trailed her fingers over his skin, amazed at the feel of him, hard and smooth. His muscles flexed at her touch, as though stirred to life, and a light trail of goose bumps followed her movement. In the deep grooves of his abdomen, light and dark battled, gaining and losing ground with each breath. She traced the shadows, wanting to linger in the night, in this moment. Every inch of his body was like untouched terrain, a new world just waiting to be explored. All her life spent searching for adventure, and here in his arms, for the first time *she wondered if maybe it wasn't a place she should have been yearning for but a person instead, a man with enough mystery and wonder to fill the rest of her days.*

She knew the moment he woke up.

His entire body tensed and his heart thundered. Lyana took her time swirling her rogue hand up his abdomen and his chest, until her fingers found the soft tendrils of his hair and she looked into his face. Two eyes watched her, as blue as the clearest sky, as warm as the sun, more tempting than any distant horizon.

"Ana?" His voice brought a shiver to her skin.

"Rafe."

She moved against him, inching closer, until their noses nearly touched. His gaze was steady and waiting, almost unsure, and she realized he didn't know what was coming next. There was a hint of fear, as though he worried she was about to say goodbye. But the moon still hung low in the sky, dawn a faraway thing, and she preferred to keep it that way.

"I think..." Those three sacred words hovered at the edge of her tongue, fighting to be said, just as they danced across his eyes, bright and burning. Had they gone mad? Was that what this was? They'd only known each other for a few short weeks, mostly in stolen moments and secret meetings, yet here they were, free-falling into unknown territory together. Maybe it was love. Maybe it was something else. They'd never know for sure, their time like a dream cut short, like a blossom clipped before it could bloom, the smallest hint of something that could've one day been so much more. Saying those words would only make things harder, so she covered her sorrow with a grin.

"You're snoring."

Disappointment flashed across his face, quickly replaced by relief. He, too, wanted to pretend their hearts weren't on the cusp of breaking. "I am not."

"You are. It's horrible, like a monster clawing at my ears. I can't sleep."

"Poor princess."

"There's only one solution."

"What's that?"

Lyana shifted her face to the side, lips grazing his cheek, the softest caress, before she whispered, "You must stay up all night with me."

He inhaled sharply. She pulled back in time to see a slow smile spread across his lips, his eyes growing full and heavy with desire. Before she could move, his arm came around her waist and he rolled, pinning her beneath him. His wings fanned out above them, two black curtains shielding them from the coming sun.

"Is that so?" he asked softly, more playful than she'd ever heard him. The very sound brought a wicked grin to her lips. She scratched a nail down his chest, just to see the silver glimmer of his magic upon his skin.

"I dare you."

He kissed her, long and deep, as though they had nothing but time, his hands moving over her curves as if she too were a wonderland he ached to explore...

Lyana woke with a start, her breath coming fast, the memory hovering at the edge of awareness, so real and so vivid even as it slipped away. Sweat dampened her skin. A fever burned within her, but it wasn't the sort of illness she knew how to heal.

Rafe.

She pressed the heels of her palms to her eyes, not sure if she wanted to return to the dream or push it away. She was supposed to forget him. When she'd left him that morning, she'd promised herself she would. For Xander. For the ravens. For her own good. But how could she, when her heart, her soul, and her mind all rebelled against her?

Air, she thought. *I need air.*

Pushing off the blankets, Lyana stood, then strode across the room to the balcony. It was small, with hardly enough room to stand. If she opened her wings here, they'd be cramped against the walls of the castle, without enough space to beat. Like so many aspects of this world beneath the mist, the balcony gave the impression of freedom without the weight of it.

Across the slumbering city, lights bobbed in the water. The never-ending fog swallowed the brilliant globes, leaving most of the buildings in darkness. Gentle strains of music caught her ear, though she couldn't tell from whence they came, each note overwhelmed by the eerie groans of straining wood. It was funny to think how afraid everyone in her world was of what waited beneath the mist— Vesevios, dragons, an ocean of molten fire. Now she knew the truth. It was a world full of people struggling to survive. Somehow, to Lyana, that seemed scarier than the nightmare.

A golden sheen settled upon her palms as she brought her magic to the surface, practicing the way Malek had shown her, building a wall to separate herself from the onslaught of pain careening toward her. Cutting them out seemed counterintuitive, though, especially in light of her afternoon at the infirmary. Helping those people had left her feeling better than she had in days, and all she wanted to do now was jump from this balcony, soar over the castle wall, and dive into the pain reaching toward her.

Even without her wings, she supposed she could try to sneak outside, steal a boat, and somehow break through the gates separating her from the city. It wouldn't be easy, but that had never stopped her before. If Rafe were here, no doubt he would have been by her side as he had been those nights in Pylaeon, to protect her if nothing else. It would be dangerous and adventurous and reckless—all the things toward which she usually gravitated.

Yet it was Malek's voice in the back of her head that stopped her.

You can't save them all.

She wanted to—oh, how she wanted to—but in a strange, soul-crushing, horrible way, he'd been right. Logic had always been her greatest enemy, it seemed, and his was sound. In the world above, the risk she'd carried when using her magic had been entirely her own. If she died, people would mourn, at least she hoped they would, but life would go on. Down here, so many futures, so many dreams, so many innocent souls all depended on her. What if she did sneak out but got hurt or injured or worse? Was Malek right? Would the isles fall without her? Would this gateway open? Would the world as she knew it be over? Was one night, one risky, selfish night, worth all that?

"Are you leaving?" a voice asked, shocking Lyana from her thoughts. She spun to find a girl standing in the room behind her, short and petite, with straight black hair and eyes the milky white of an opal. "I only ask because I've seen a lot of things in my life, but I've never seen a person fly, and magic alive, I want to."

"What? No, I—" Lyana broke off with a shake of her head. "Who are you?"

The girl ignored her and stepped closer. "If you're not flying, what are you doing?"

"Thinking," Lyana answered, turning back to the view. "What are you doing? Here in my room, I mean? Are you a servant?"

"Sure. Why not?" The girl shrugged and leaned her shoulder casually against the bedroom wall, stopping just inside the entrance to the balcony. Her face was half-shielded by the curtains. "Can I get you anything?"

"No."

"Good, because I doubt I'd be much good at serving."

"Why are you here then?"

"I wanted a closer look at our queen."

"Oh." Lyana's heart sank with the words. That was all she was to these people—a queen of prophecy, a figure of legend. They didn't see the woman underneath the title. It seemed like ages since she'd spoken to anyone who saw the real her—not what she could be, but who she was. "And?" she asked, putting on a brave face. "What do you think? Do I live up to your expectations?"

"You're skimpier than I thought you'd be."

Lyana frowned. She knew she wasn't the tallest person, or the most overtly muscular, but the girl before her didn't exactly have a leg to stand on. "You're one to talk."

"I'm not a queen of prophecy. Can I?" The girl's hand darted out, brushing over her wing and tugging sharply on one of her feathers.

"Ow! Those are attached to me, you know."

"Now I do." She shrugged. "You want to know what I really thought when I first walked into this room?"

Lyana crossed her arms, tone biting. "What?"

"I thought you seemed lonely," the girl said, eyes gaining a probing sheen as they studied her expression. Lyana swallowed—that wasn't what she thought she'd say. "Is there someone you were looking for up there in the sky?"

"I…"

"Someone you miss?"

Rafe's face filled her thoughts—the sharp edge of his jaw, the slight wave to his onyx hair, the intensity of his gaze. His lips had been pursed with frustration more often than not, but in her imagination he smiled, full of all the happiness his real life had failed to provide, all the joy she wished she could have given him.

"Someone you maybe loved?"

The image shattered. "No."

"No?"

Lyana spun to escape the girl's scrutiny, turning her attention back to the city, though all she saw was Xander's face the morning of their mating ceremony, the hard look in his eyes, a reflection of her own betrayal. "Please leave."

"I didn't mean to upset you. I won't tell the king, if that's what you're worried about. We're all allowed our secrets. You just seemed like you could use a friend."

Was that what she was missing?

A friend?

Between Malek, Xander, and Rafe, she clearly had more men in her life than she would ever need. But what about a friend? Maybe that was why she felt so lost in the clouds. Cassi wasn't there to ground her.

"Tell me his name," the girl said, almost cajoling.

Lyana opened her mouth. *Rafe.* But she couldn't say it. The word clogged in her throat—too painful to voice, as though if she spoke it, all the yearning she was trying to erase would be real. Instead, she took the coward's way out, or maybe just the loyal one. "I had a mate in the world above. His name was Xander."

"Xander?"

"Lysander Taetanus, the Crown Prince of the House of Whispers."

"Hmm," the girl muttered. "A prince?"

"Yes," Lyana whispered, voice failing her. "I miss him very much."

And she did. She really did. She missed Xander's kindness and the warm smiles he offered so freely. She missed his hope and the way he always seemed to believe everything would work out in the end. Mostly, she missed his acceptance. There had been an honesty between them, an understanding. Maybe he hadn't known about her magic until the very end, but even before that, he'd known her—all the ways they fit together, and the many ways they didn't. Despite it all, he'd been ready to accept her as his queen.

Yet, she missed Rafe more.

Therein lay the problem.

"I—"

Lyana broke off as she turned to find nothing but an empty room behind her. The girl was gone, just as mysteriously as she'd come. It hurt more than she thought it would to have this brief moment of friendship stripped away, a reminder of how much she craved it.

Cassi, she thought, staring back out at the thick fog as she wiped her tears away. *Where are you? Why haven't you come? Why haven't you found me?*

That was the truth of it, at last.

She didn't just feel alone—she felt abandoned.

Lyana had spent her life preparing to leave her home in the House of Peace, to say farewell to her brother, to walk away from her family. She'd spent weeks trying to say goodbye to Rafe, and then finally one morning she'd done just that. She'd even shared a parting moment with Xander in the sacred nest as her magic swirled around them, a mutual understanding.

But leaving Cassi had been sudden.

One moment she had been in the House of Whispers, and the next alone in the middle of the sea, surrounded by strangers. There had been no time to prepare for life without her best friend, no time to fortify herself for the absence. If she were being honest, a small part of her didn't think she'd have to. If the roles had been reversed, nothing would have kept Lyana from ripping apart the skies in search of her friend.

What was Cassi doing in the world above?

Where, in Aethios's name, was she?

Lyana studied the sky one more time, waiting for something, anything, to break up the impenetrable darkness.

Nothing came.

After a while, she retreated into her room, a hollow void in her heart. It had been naïve, maybe, but in all her hours dreaming of adventure, she had never once imagined that when she finally found one, it would leave her feeling so alone.

23

XANDER

When Xander walked into his study, he was surprised to find Cassi there waiting, the whites of her wings painted pink by the dying light of the sun. She looked a million miles away, staring out the window with her soft lips slightly pursed and a wrinkle in her brow. Whatever thought had been in his mind fled at the sight, replaced by the sudden urge to make her smile.

"If you meant to catch me by surprise, you succeeded," he murmured into the silence. Cassi started and turned toward him. "Though I admit, I enjoy this sort of surprise far more than your usual sort. No daggers. No chokeholds. Some might say you're losing your touch."

"I thought your dignity could use a break to recover," she drawled, then quickly eyed the door behind his back. A wicked gleam flashed across her irises. "But if you want me to toss you up against another wall..."

He fought a rising flush as the image filled his vision—Cassi up against him, her hands on his chest, their bodies pressed tight, their breath mingling as the fire crackled across the silence.

"No. No, I don't think that's necessary," he stammered, stifling the thought and focusing on safer ground. *What the gods was that?* "Are you here for a book?"

"Actually, no."

"No?"

"I have something for you."

Eyebrows raised, he found himself unable to keep his gaze from straying to her face. She was grinning now, the sight drawing him in like a flower stretching to the sun, something innate, almost physical in the pull. "What?"

"A present," she replied coyly.

His lips curved into a smile. "You bought me a present?"

"Well, no. Not quite. I asked Helen to have something made, which she did, using the crown's resources. So, really, you bought yourself a present."

"A technicality."

"Precisely."

He waited for her to give him a box or move to the side or do anything really, but she didn't. She stood there and stared, an unfamiliar sensation in the air. If he didn't know her better, he'd say she was nervous. But Cassi never got nervous. Did she? The very idea made him want to laugh. "And am I allowed to see this mysterious item I bought myself?"

"Oh, right."

She bent to retrieve a box from the floor and handed it to him. He recognized the insignia immediately. Metal ore and precious stones were his house's largest exports, the blacksmith's guild its richest, and he'd seen this emblem many times before, just not burned into gifts meant for him. It belonged to the wealthiest shop in the city, and for Helen to have spent that much royal coin, Cassi's design had clearly been deemed more than worthy.

Xander opened the lid, heart thumping with an eagerness he couldn't quite explain. The last few weapons he'd been presented left him feeling nothing but dread, yet this was different. For whatever reason, his fingers trembled ever so slightly as he removed the bundle from the box and unwound the cloth, a giddy excitement fluttering beneath his skin.

"After I agreed to teach you, I asked Helen to take me to the storerooms to see what sorts of weapons you'd previously been trained with," Cassi explained as he undid the wrappings. "Broadswords. Bows. Clubs. Staffs. There was a whole array of special devices for your hand, all manner of strange contraptions, and none of it seemed to suit you. So I thought I would have something made instead."

Xander finally removed the last bit of cloth, revealing a matching set of steel cylinders with leather straps. "They're...arm guards?"

"Of a sort." She stepped forward. "If I may?"

Xander nodded and held out his arms as she removed the guards from his hold. It was only when she started attaching them to his forearms that he noticed how easily the gesture had come. He tried to hide his disability from most people—keeping his right arm by his side, holding it behind his back, shrouding it from view. With Cassi, he didn't seem to mind putting it on display. He was comfortable, he was shocked to realize, as she leaned over the rounded end of his arm and touched him, a focused look in her eyes and not a single ounce of hesitation.

"When I saw all the weapons your mother had made, it became obvious to me that she was trying to pretend you were no different from everyone else. She was trying to make you fit the weapons," Cassi continued softly, a distracted sort of quality to her voice while she concentrated on securing the guards. She normally seemed so careful about everything she said, each word precisely chosen to maintain the walls around her heart. Right now, she seemed open and honest, perhaps just as strangely comfortable as he. "When, really, the weapons should have been made to fit you. You'll never be an expert swordsman or an archer, and it's not because of your hand. It's because you lack the drive to become one. You don't want to learn how to attack people, how to cut them or maim them or deliver a killing blow. You're not a soldier or a guard or a fighter—"

"I think I was enjoying this more before you started talking."

Cassi rolled her eyes. "Let me finish."

"By all means, continue describing my shortcomings in excruciating detail. There's nothing I find more enjoyable than listening to you list all the qualities I lack."

"I never said they were shortcomings." She tightened the final strap and looked across the narrow space between them. "You're kind, Xander. You have a tender heart, a noble one. I bet the first thing you thought after that raven attacked you was, *What did I do to deserve this?* when most people in your position would've cursed his name and demanded his head. I meant it as a compliment when I said you'd never be a fighter. The world would be a far better place if there were more people like you in it, and less people like me. But there aren't. So the best thing I can teach you is how to protect yourself, and the best thing I can do is give you weapons that increase the possibility of your survival, ones designed not to attack, but to defend."

They stared at each other for a moment, breath mingling in the silence, until a single word escaped his lips. "Oh."

"Yes, oh." She huffed and stepped back, giving them much-needed air. Why was she so annoyed? Why wasn't he? Before he had time to understand, she sighed, releasing whatever emotion stirred within her. "I wasn't— I mean, I didn't—" She turned toward the window, as though worried he might see something in her eyes she didn't want to reveal. "We all have differences we need to learn to work with. Why do you think I picked archery? My sight is best at far distances, and I can see well in the dark when others can't. Both advantages, yes. But I'm also a woman, which means it's in my best interest to pick a weapon that provides a safe distance because half of my foes are probably stronger or bigger than me. And my wings are cumbersome in a close fight, not made for agility but for soaring. Most of all, arrows match my personality, sneaking in unseen rather than facing things head-on—just like Lyana's daggers match hers, flitting and flighty, full of too many options and too much excitement, the outlet she needs. And Rafe was drawn to his swords for the same reason. They provide a steadiness he lacks, and the exercises focus his mind, giving his isolation a purpose. We each have weapons that are best suited to us, and all I meant to say was I think these will be best suited to you. They're sturdy and dependable and easy to underestimate, which in turn makes them more powerful than anyone would ever expect." Cassi swallowed, silvery eyes inscrutable before she blinked the headiness away. "Anyway, how do they feel?"

He wasn't sure what to make of her words or the sentiment thickening the air between them. Instead of trying, he bent his elbows and rolled his arms, testing the guards. The metal molded perfectly around his forearms and biceps, like a second skin, while the looser sections at his elbows allowed for movement. They were heavy, but not overly so, an extra weight he could easily get used to. "Good."

"I told Helen to have the blacksmith incorporate some filigree into the design, so they appear ceremonial from the outside, something you could wear to any formal occasion without people thinking twice. But they're crafted from the strongest steel, able to withstand any sword, and most importantly, they hide a secret."

"A secret?"

"I thought a lot about what you said that day in the hall, about how I'd left your right side unguarded when I jumped you, and how you'd elbow me in the ribs to break loose. The truth is, I didn't leave you that opening on purpose. It was a mistake, one you were smart enough to notice. And it got me thinking that it's the sort of mistake a lot of people might make, the sort of mistake you could take advantage of."

Xander narrowed his eyes. "How so?"

"Bend your elbow like this," she said, lifting her forearm so it pressed against her biceps. "Not too close to your face, make sure there's empty space above the guard. Good. Now, turn your fist so it faces out like this."

He rotated his forearm and *click*. Xander flinched as a blade sprang free, slicing into the empty space above his shoulder. He returned his focus to Cassi, finding a wide grin across her lips.

"Neat trick, right?"

A puff of air escaped his lips, something between a laugh and a relieved sigh. Thank the gods she'd told him to move his arm. Two inches to the left and he might be missing an ear.

"If someone is holding you from behind, you could stab them before they ever saw it coming. And there's another blade at your elbow, in case you missed it, so you could also catch an assailant on their side. It's on a spring, so all you have to do is push the blades back inside the guards and they'll be hidden again. We thought about a button release, but that might be too cumbersome in a real fight, so we came up with this instead. It'll only release with your arm fully bent, because the first latch is in the nook of your elbow, and the second latch is unhooked by the turn of your wrist. It's unnatural enough I didn't think the motion would ever happen by chance, but I could change it if you think something else would work better."

He twisted his arm to see the sharp point protruding from his elbow, then used the metal guard on his other arm to press the blades back in. They were on the same gear, it seemed, because pushing one in also moved the other back into place. When they were re-secured, he bent and flailed his arm, trying to unleash them, but the design was flawless. After lifting his forearm, he twisted his wrist and *click*—the blades sprang free. That subtle ring of metal made him feel powerful. Perhaps not like a warrior who could chase down a dragon, but in his own way, that of a prince who was stronger than the world might have him believe.

Xander met Cassi's eyes over the sharp point of the blade, acutely aware of how much careful thought had gone into this gift, the hours of planning, the sheer consideration. "They're perfect."

The rosy hue flooding her cheeks might have seemed a trick of the light if she hadn't glanced away to hide it. "Shall we run through some defensive exercises? Just in case any more ravens decide to come smashing through the windows?"

"That shouldn't be a problem."

"Oh?" She turned back to him. "Why?"

"The owls replied to our request. I was going to come find you. We leave for the House of Wisdom in the morning, so the rest of the evening should probably be spent preparing for our departure." Was there a little disappointment on her face? Did he want there to be? "Though I suppose one quick lesson couldn't hurt."

"I can be quick."

"Then—"

He broke off as the ground beneath them trembled. With a pump of his wings, he was in the air. So was Cassi. They hovered by the window as the castle shook. Books toppled from the shelves, landing with heavy *thuds* against the floor. Dust collected in the sky above the city, the debris from the attack and the soot from the fires stirred by the vibrations. Just as he was about to fling open the latch and race outside, it was over.

"An earthquake?" Cassi asked, voice thick with disbelief.

"Same as the last." His tone was grim.

"The last? What do you mean?"

"Didn't you feel it? Two weeks ago? It woke me in the night. I thought it was just a lingering effect from everything that had happened in the sacred nest, but now..." Out the window he spotted the river running through Pylaeon, following it back and back, across the valley cast in gold by the setting sun, all the way to the brilliant white spot at the far end, Taetanos's Gate and the god stone hiding within. *Now I'm not so sure*, he finished silently. To Cassi he said, "I should go."

"Of course."

"I need to discuss this with my mother."

"Of course."

He willed his feet to move, but they adhered to the stone. "I—"

"Xander?"

Her hesitant question was the very excuse he'd been

looking for, a reason to stay beside her for one moment longer. "Yes?"

"Before you go, I just want to make one thing clear. The gift, the lessons, the training—I'm doing it because you asked. I'm not doing it because there's something in you I find lacking. I'm not doing it because there's anything about you that needs to change. I'm not doing it to fix you or shape you or mold you. I'm just—I'm doing it because you asked."

He studied her as she studied him, the sincerity in her eyes, the slight clench of her jaw, the tense curve of her brow. A lock of hair slipped across her face, shining bronze in the sunlight, and he fought the urge to brush it back behind her ear. She was Lyana's best friend. Lyana was his mate. The lines were drawn, and he knew better than to cross them.

Instead, he allowed the edge of his lip to lift in an uneven grin. "And here I thought you were doing it for the books."

"Right." A bit of relief played in Cassi's smile. "Those too."

"Good night." He stepped back, forcing his feet toward the door and the responsibilities waiting on the other side of the threshold. "I'll see you in the morning."

After turning his back, he strode across the room and into the hall. His mother would want to see him. Helen and the advisors, too. This newest tremble of the isle made his departure all the more complicated. There was so much to do, and so little time. Plans whirled—orders and calculations and every kind of scenario. So distracted, he barely heard the words that chased after him. It was only later, as he lay down in bed, that they registered, and even then, he was sure he'd heard them wrong. Still, it sounded almost as though she'd whispered, "I'll see you in your dreams."

24

CASSI

Cassi was a coward.

As she let sleep take her, the magic stirring beneath her skin as her spirit slipped free of her body, the truth had never been clearer.

She was a coward.

An outside observer might not see it. They might be fooled by the suppleness of her muscles, the predatory grace of her wings, the bow leaning against her nightstand or the daggers resting on its surface, their metal polished and gleaming in the moonlight. But she saw the girl asleep before her differently. The bow was a shield, the daggers a pretense, and the toned body a carefully crafted disguise, all designed to hide the ugly truth—she was broken, and rotting, and above all, afraid.

If she were the strong woman she purported to be, she would dive into the Sea of Mist right now and spit at Malek's feet. She would refuse to go along with any more of his schemes. She would refuse to kill Xander. She would slip into Lyana's dreams and reveal her king's vile orders. She would expose him, and herself in the process. She would give her friend the honesty she deserved. After all that, she would go to Rafe and apologize for her horrible act, knowing all the while it would never be forgiven.

But she couldn't.

Invisible and free, not confined by walls or by the elements or by the gods, Cassi still felt stuck. Her fears were a cage she couldn't escape, and there was only one person she wanted to visit tonight, one person whose very presence made her feel brave and defiant and seen. Those sentiments were, of course, a lie as well. But they were ones she told herself, which made them a different thing entirely.

With the stars and the moon as her confidants, and the crisp air as her guide, she drifted outside and let a breeze carry her aloft. When Cassi slipped into his room, Xander was asleep with his left arm flung over his head and his right arm across his stomach, the rounded end tucked beneath the blankets. His onyx wings fell over either side of his bed and his lips were slightly parted, his expression serene beneath the dark hair spilling over his forehead.

In her many years of watching people at their most vulnerable, she'd learned that the way a person slept said a lot about the way a person lived. Malek always kept his legs straight and his arms rigid by his sides, his body controlled and composed, as though even in sleep he couldn't afford to be vulnerable. In the few times she'd visited Rafe, he'd been on his side with the sheets wrapped around his legs and his face hidden beneath his wings, his body as trapped and tortured as his heart. Lyana, on the other hand, usually curled on her side with her wings arched as though in flight and her arms outstretched, always reaching for something more. Even if she'd never met Xander, watching him now she'd know everything there was to know about this prince. He was laid bare, honest and inviting, at peace in the way only decent people could be, hiding the only part of himself that left him unsure. Sometimes, she wondered what her sleeping position said about her, but the revelation was just another thing she was too afraid to face.

Cassi drifted closer to the bed.

Distantly, she knew she should probably be using this time to study the god stone, to see if there were any noticeable changes, any cause for the earthquake that had shaken the isle earlier that day. These were just the sorts of things Malek would want to know, the sorts of things he would want her to track. Maybe that was the very reason she didn't. Besides, he had a raven spy who could do it for him.

No, tonight she had other plans.

Tomorrow, she'd be in the House of Wisdom and all her time would be dedicated to studying the secret libraries of the owls. Those nights would belong to Malek and his war, to his orders and his needs, to the world and the lives he so longed to save.

Tonight was for her.

Wrapped in the safety of her magic, she felt like doing something she never did, something her dual life never allowed, something reckless and wild.

For once, she felt like letting go.

Cassi pressed a phantom palm to Xander's forehead and slipped inside his dreams. Like the mind of anyone without magic, his was easy to guide. Still, she took her time wrestling his thoughts into submission and painting a picture of her own making, letting his spirit surround her, letting his sheer goodness push all the doubts and fears away. She'd been inside his mind once before, on the eve of his mating ceremony, when she'd come to whisper dark thoughts into his dreams, turning them to nightmares. He'd woken with a gasp and rushed to Rafe's room, only to discover the tricks his mind had played weren't tricks at all. Well, at least not tricks of his own making. This time, though, she wanted to bring joy instead of dread.

When the dream solidified, Cassi opened her eyes to find they were sitting side by side on a sandy shore with the surf tickling their toes and the sun shining overhead. Waves crashed. Birds cawed. The place was unlike any she'd ever visited, pulled straight from her books and her imagination, the perfect spot in which to pretend.

"Where are we?" Xander asked, his mind trying to come up with some story to justify her sudden entrance into his dreams, to explain it away. Their clothes were wet, their wings too. A rush of water flooded the ground beneath them, surging over their ankles, warm and not unpleasant. He dug his fingers into the sand, lifted his arm, and watched the wet particles drip slowly back into the sea.

She met his eyes above his wrist. "Where do you want us to be?"

"It looks like the island where Tassos washed up after

Nyara saved his life. At least, this is what I always imagined it to be."

"Well, this is your mind."

"True." He grinned, and that was all it took for her to convince him this was nothing but a dream. "I wonder why I brought us here."

He didn't. Neither had she, really. The story of Tassos and Nyara was the furthest thing from her thoughts. She'd just wanted to be somewhere that wasn't the avian realm or the foggy seas beneath the mist, somewhere neutral. Still, the mind had a funny way of spotting symbols in the dark. "Why do you think?"

Xander frowned.

Cassi eyed him curiously. "What?"

"Nothing."

"You can tell me."

He shook his head.

"If you tell me one of your secrets, I'll tell you one of mine."

Facing the horizon, he absently drew a circle in the sand, over and over, until finally, with a sigh, he folded his arms across his bended knees. A rolling wave washed the shape away. "I don't want to be like Tassos. I don't want a love born from sacrifice. I want to be able to give as much as I receive."

"This is about Lyana?"

"No, it's about me."

She put a hand on his arm. "I wasn't talking about you when I said those things."

"If not me, then who?"

This wasn't the conversation she wanted to have. Cassi turned back to the sea and studied the reflections glittering across the surface of the water. "Let's just say you're not the first man to step into one of my dreams."

"I thought this was my dream."

The ghost of a smile passed over her lips as she collapsed against the shore, letting the water soak her hair and her back, enjoying the scratch of sand in her feathers. Xander fell beside her.

"You owe me a secret," he said.

She dropped her head to the side. "Ask me a question and I'll give you an answer."

"Promise?"

"I do."

He studied her face as though it were a map with no labels, searching each groove, each curve, for a path to the hidden treasure. "What are you so afraid of?"

Cassi flinched.

Before she could look away, he took her hand. "There. I see you doing it again, putting a guard up, raising your walls, as though afraid I might see. But what? What are you so worried I'll see?"

She held his gaze unflinchingly. "Me."

I'm afraid you'll see the real me.

A wave rolled over their legs and up their chests, then splashed against their faces, washing the conversation away. Cassi jumped to her feet and pulled him up, a laugh on her lips as she kicked at the water. This was a dream. Xander didn't have magic. He wouldn't remember this night, not the way she would. And she'd been right before. He made her feel brave—brave enough to let him see a part of her only one other person ever had. She had, after all, promised him a secret. It wasn't her fault he'd forget it as soon as he opened his eyes.

"Imagine something, Xander. Dream of something wonderful, and whatever you dream will come to be."

"What do you mean?"

"Don't you remember being a child, when every shadow held a secret and every sound a story? When your blanket was a fortress, and the candle by your bed a fire-breathing dragon, and your pillow a shield while you slashed at the air with a sword no one else could see? Pretend with me. Play with me. Please, Xander. I want to forget the world for a little while. It's been so long since I've had fun, I'm not sure I remember how."

"I'm not sure I ever did."

"Not even in the pages of your books?"

A secret smile played across his lips.

Cassi squeezed his fingers, enlivened by the spark burning behind his lavender eyes. "Show me."

He glanced to the sea, lips pursed and determined, his thoughts poking at her hold on his dream. She relented, giving him the option to take over. As a girl, her favorite game had been to see what dreams another mind might weave. With Malek, it had been almost a relief to give him the reins, to not have to fight for dominance every second she lived inside his head. But Xander was more hesitant, as though asking permission, his thoughts gentle and probing. She cajoled him closer, inviting him in.

The first shift was small, little more than a test. A warm breeze blew in from the east, wrapping around their torsos and making their feathers flutter. Out of the corner of her eye, she saw his mouth gape open in wonder. Then the sea before them transformed, no longer a deep blue, but a golden citrine. Xander bent down and dipped his palm in the liquid before raising it to his lips. Hummingbird nectar, she realized as it fizzed above his fingers. Cassi laughed and dropped to her knees beside him to take a long drink. He put his hand on her shoulder, and a ripple pulsed across the air. He didn't need to touch her for the magic to work, but she didn't correct him. She just lifted her face to the sky as raindrops kissed her cheeks, tasting of sugar and honey.

"We can go anywhere?" he asked.

"Anywhere."

"We can do anything?"

"Anything."

Water clung to his lashes and dripped down his face as he turned to meet her eyes, something wild simmering in his. He pulled his bottom lip between his teeth, tasting the rain as he grinned.

The ground gave out beneath them.

Cassi clutched his fingers as they fell, tumbling through the shadows until a new world materialized in bright color. They were perched on a branch in the middle of a great forest, the leaves twice their size and the bark as blue as a jay's wings. Xander dove, plummeting through the foliage, and she followed. As they sank, the world twisted, until down was up and up was down, so when they fell into the underbrush, they sank through it as well, dispelling leaves and emerging on a freezing mountain peak, the skies above them green and the ground an ivory blanket of snow. In unison they raced across the land, ice changing to sand and cliffs to rolling hills. A sapphire strand hovered on the horizon, and when they reached it, they dove through, splashing beneath the waters as their wings vanished and their legs turned to tails. They swam through the sea like birds through the sky, his imagination leading the way—and what a wonderful imagination it was. Readers always made the best dreamers. At least Cassi liked to think so. After all, reading was simply dreaming with open eyes.

His mind was so beautiful she didn't want to leave.

Yet there was no magic so strong it could stop the sun.

Through the little strand of spirit still tied to her body, Cassi distantly felt the warmth on her skin, whispering of morning. Though she knew it was time to release him, she held on tighter, clinging to his thoughts even as his body fought her magic. Only when the dream began to fall apart around them did she finally, reluctantly, let go.

Xander opened his eyes immediately, a gasp on his lips. He clutched his chest as though reaching for his heart. Taking a few moments to fully wake, he blinked and scanned his room, perhaps searching for her. But she was nothing more than a silvery gleam on the wind, a wisp of spirit his eyes would never see. He rubbed his palm over his face, wiping the dream away as he slowly rose to a seated position and dropped his legs over the side of his bed. With a single shake of his head, he stood, no longer an eager soul in a boundless world, but a prince with duties to attend. Cassi slipped through the balcony and let him.

She'd had her one night of freedom.

Now it was over.

And as far as Xander was concerned, it had been nothing more than a dream.

25

XANDER

She wouldn't look at him. Xander had spent most of the flight to the House of Wisdom peeking over his shoulder toward the owl at the back of the flock, yet throughout the entire journey, she'd only twice met his gaze. The first time with a curious smile on her lips, eyes empty and unknowing. The second time, though, he swore he saw a brief glimmer of awareness before she turned her head away. But what could she know? What exactly was he searching for in her expression? Was he seeing things that weren't there?

As they landed in the frigid tundra of the owl kingdom, Xander suddenly realized there was a distinct possibility that she was acting normal while he'd completely lost his mind. It was just...the dream had felt *so* real.

Real and invigorating.

Like his first breath of fresh air since exiting the sacred nest.

Like coming back to life.

A cough pulled him from his thoughts. Two owls walked toward them, two sets of speckled copper wings visible behind their backs. Though it was late in the evening, this far north the sun never truly set in the summer, leaving more than enough light even for a raven. They stopped a few feet away and bowed.

It took Xander a moment to realize it was his turn to speak. Normally, he had his mother or Helen by his side. But the queen was needed back home, along with the captain of the guards. He'd traveled with a merchant flock bearing gifts from the crown. For the first time in his life, he had to rely on himself.

"I am Lysander Taetanus, Crown Prince of the House of Whispers," he stated, not entirely sure what he was doing. The only time he'd ever traveled to another house had been for the courtship trials, and he'd been so concerned with hiding his face, he'd let his mother do the speaking. "And I come with the blessing of your king and queen."

At his words, the two owls stood and turned, signaling to a spot behind them. "Welcome to the House of Wisdom, Prince Lysander. We've been expecting you and your guests. Please, follow us, and we'll show you to your rooms. The king extends an invitation to dinner if you're not too tired from your travels."

"Please tell the king I accept, and I'd like to bring a guest, if I may." He felt Cassi's eyes on him then. This time, it was Xander who refused to glance her way.

"Of course. Now, if you will..."

They spread their wings, kicking up snow and dirt as they rose into the sky. Xander and his flock followed. With the ground a patchwork of ice and rock, he didn't see the opening until they were almost flying through it, a simple hole carved into the side of a cliff, dark in the shadows stretching across the land. The inside was lit by lanterns, the golden glow guiding them farther underground. As they sank deeper and deeper, the air turned moist and warm, leaving the wintery world above nothing but a memory. When the tunnel opened into a wide cavern, Xander gasped.

A city twice the size of Pylaeon nestled in the center of the vast hollow, glowing amber in the darkness. Along the ground, buildings wound like rivers through the stones. In the center sat a castle, its walls smooth and polished, with no decoration aside from the subtle layers of sediment, markings drawn by time. What caught his eye the most, though, were the broad columns stretching back and back and back, like godly arms holding the ceiling aloft. Staircases coiled around the outsides, carved into the stone. At various levels, they flattened to platforms containing doors. The library, he realized, catching the quick flash of book spines. The longer he stared, the more hidden alcoves he spotted, a network of rooms and halls only one born to this place would ever understand. Clearly, they did. Owls flew in every direction, paying their visitors no mind, simply going about their business. The constant flutter of wings echoed off the walls, a comforting hum that surrounded him like a warm embrace, the scent in his nose one of crinkled pages and undiscovered stories.

This was Rynthos, the Secret City, in all its glory, and the sight left Xander speechless.

In all my dreams, I never could have imagined this.

Cassi smiled suddenly, as though hearing his thought. A silent understanding passed between them, like a shared memory, drawing up images of blue trees and green skies and castles in the deepest corners of the sea.

Xander shook his head.

Stop being a fool.

It had been a dream—a figment of his imagination. They couldn't reminisce about an experience they'd never had, an experience that existed solely inside his mind, no matter how real or vivid it might have felt.

He hastened to follow as their guides continued deeper into the city, his wonderment providing an easy distraction. The guest accommodations were housed inside the castle, a place of twisting halls and dancing shadows, of stillness and seams. Owls were nocturnal creatures who thrived in dark corners and quiet. It took all Xander had not to trip over his feet as they traversed the barely lit building. His footsteps were loud in the underground calm, with no winds or rustling leaves or rushing water to cover the noise, just the steady hum of wings trickling in through the occasional window.

The first thing he did when he reached his room was ignite every wick he could find. He wanted to collapse onto the bed. He wanted to stand at the window and stare unabashedly at the mysterious city resting outside. He wanted to jump through the opening, soar through the first open door he could find, and spend the rest of the night lost within the pages of a book.

He did none of those things.

Instead, he washed his face in the basin provided, changed out of his traveling clothes, and switched into a velvet jacket, leather trousers, and polished boots. Every inch of his body was as black as his wings, except for his uncovered face and the silvery guards molded to his arms. The chance for danger was low, but he found he just wanted to wear them. A knock sounded far too soon. With a sigh, Xander opened the door and—stopped still.

"Are you ready?" Cassi asked, tawny skin a rich golden in the soft candlelight of the underground castle.

He'd been expecting an owl, but not this owl. Had he ever seen her in a dress before? Surely he must have. She'd come to dinners with Lyana and had attended the princess's birthday celebration, yet he couldn't remember a single time. He must have been blind not to notice her, since now he couldn't look away. The gown was a deep burgundy, hugging the narrowness of her waist, ending just below her collarbones, with diaphanous sleeves floating around her arms. Her wavy hair was twisted into a bun atop her head, leaving the graceful curve of her neck exposed. A silver chain hung low around her hip, holding a sheathed dagger, the sight of which made him smile. Cassi stared at him with a somewhat bored expression across her face.

"Xander, are you ready?"

"What? Yes, of course."

She raised her brows mockingly, as though stifling a laugh. "I told our welcoming committee that I'd retrieve you. I thought you might want a break from all the preening—I know Lyana would have. Anyway, they're waiting down the hall to escort us to dinner."

"Excellent," he said, the word coming out a little louder than he'd intended. With a gulp and a slight frown, he offered her his arm—friendly, casually, as any prince would do. The way his heart leapt inside his chest when she took it was anything but. He coughed. "I, um, like your dress."

"Oh, this?" She clutched the skirt with a little sashay. "Being best friends with a princess had its advantages, I suppose, a nice wardrobe being one of them."

"You hate it, don't you?"

"I'm already looking forward to returning to my rooms to change."

"Well, you look beautiful, regardless."

He hadn't meant to say it—the sentence just slipped out. Cassi tripped over her feet, as though it had been a slick of oil and not words that had spilled from his lips. Before she had a chance to respond, they reached their escort. A silence descended as they made their way to the dining room, broken as soon as they stepped through the door.

"Lysander Taetanus, Crown Prince of the House of Whispers," their guide announced. The heads at the table turned. Xander recognized a few of them from his time in the House of Peace. King Sylas wore a rich ivory overcoat, his dappled wings peeking out from behind his shoulders, eyes the reddish brown of a rusted blade. Queen Areah sat beside him in amber silks, the two colors of their house, though her wings were the warm honey of a female from the House of Paradise. Across from them was Prince Nico, his gaze hesitant and unsure but kind. By his side sat an unknown owl in a rich gown with a delicate tiara nestled on her brow. "And his guest, Miss Cassi Sky."

The king wrinkled his nose at the sound of Cassi's name —or surname, really. *Sky* was the name given to orphans in the House of Peace, the surname of a dove, as clear a reminder as any that though she looked like an owl, she wasn't one of them, even if through no fault of her own. The urge to squeeze her fingers in comfort was overwhelming, but Xander stifled it. Right now he was a prince, and to the rest of the world, he had a mate waiting for him back at home.

When they reached their seats, Xander dropped her arm and slid into the empty chair closer to the royal family, the position of honor. The king watched his every move, eyes sharp and cunning, like a hunter following its mark. Suddenly, Xander was acutely aware of what had happened at the courtship trials—events that seemed a lifetime ago to him, though in truth only weeks had passed. This man's daughter had been his chosen mate until Lyana intervened, her actions a slap in their house's face. In the end, shocking them all, his son had been the one left unmatched, a dishonor Xander was sure they had all believed would fall on him. Though as he watched Prince Nico meet his mate's warm expression with one of his own, Xander couldn't help but wonder who'd gotten the better end of the deal. His match had been doomed from the start.

"Welcome to our kingdom, Prince Lysander," the king said, his tone anything but inviting. Xander had the distinct sense he was being welcomed to this isle like a lamb to slaughter. This visit would be a test of his diplomatic skill.

"And to you, Cassi Sky, though I suppose in your case, we should be saying welcome home."

"We thank you for your generous hospitality," Xander cut in before Cassi could speak, seeing the muscles in her jaw clench. "I've spent much of my life dreaming of the libraries in your glorious city, and I find I'm quite overwhelmed now that I'm finally here. As thanks from our house to yours, and in honor of your god, Meteria, guardian of history and purveyor of intellect, we come bearing gifts, which my merchants are now delivering to your storerooms. Metal ores and precious gems, blessed by Taetanos, to be used as you see fit."

"And what of the new Crown Princess of the House of Whispers? I was surprised to find that she declined our invitation."

"Unfortunately, the princess is indisposed."

"So quickly?"

Those two words were ripe with hidden meaning—that Lyana was pregnant, that it couldn't possibly be Xander's, that his daughter wasn't the only victim to Lyana's free spirit. The truth, of course, hit a little close to home. Managing to keep a pleasant smile on his lips almost amounted to a heroic deed. "A dragon attacked our homeland not too long ago, as I'm sure the rest of the houses have learned. The princess is still recovering from the trauma."

"I've heard you had some recovering to do as well."

The king glanced to where Xander's right arm sat perched on the table, his missing hand visible for all to see. He and his mother had agreed to let that information slip, using a bad situation to their advantage. It was the perfect way to explain why Prince Lysander was no longer quite the gallant warrior they remembered from the trials—well, the warrior they remembered, in any case. Rafe had never been gallant a day in his life. Grouchy and gruff, maybe, but not gallant.

The thought made it easier for Xander to smile as he slid his wrists beneath the table and answered the king's unspoken question. "These are trying times for my house, indeed."

"Such a shame, after your decisive victory at the House of Peace. *The warrior prince from the House of Whispers.* You were all anyone wanted to talk about for those few short days."

"Yes, well…"

"The heart makes a warrior, don't you think?" Cassi cut in, her voice far too sweet. Xander's hackles immediately rose, even as a warmth spread across his chest at the sound. "Bodies age and wither, as I'm sure you know. But a good heart, a noble heart, never weakens—a lesson even an owl raised by doves somehow learned."

Xander stifled a groan. She'd managed to call the king old and feckless in the same sharply crafted sentence. He could practically see the fury simmering in the man's eyes.

Well, this is off to a fabulous start.

I'll be lucky if I get out of here without starting a war.

"Too true," Xander said before Cassi could continue. Dragon fire might be beyond his capabilities, but these sorts of blazes were ones he luckily knew how to quench, assuming the woman by his side could remain quiet long enough to stop igniting them. "And with Meteria their patron, every owl in the House of Wisdom knows this lesson as well, I'm sure, their king and queen most of all. I look forward to seeing what other lessons this noble house might teach us. After our long journey, however, I confess I'm most curious to learn more about your fabled cuisine. I must admit, I'm starving."

Cassi's glare could have bored through his cheek. Prince Nico, though, threw him the grateful look of a son tired of his overbearing parent, a feeling Xander knew well. A moment of kinship passed between them, there and gone. But it was something, a bead of hope to build upon, which was exactly what Xander intended to do as the first course made its way into the room.

26

CASSI

The gods, she didn't know how Xander could stand it. All these pretty words hiding ugly jibes, all this smiling and forced laughter, not to mention the food. Cassi was an owl, but growing up in the House of Peace meant growing used to a dove's diet—fruits and nuts and berries and breads. The meat roiled in her stomach, heavy and nauseating. As dinner came to an end, she couldn't get out of that room fast enough.

"That guy was a jerk," she snarled as they stepped into the hall, well aware they were in a foreign house where their every move would be watched, and not caring. King Sylas had spent most of the night mentally dissecting her, making Cassi feel every inch the strange owl girl raised by doves as he searched for her secrets. It was best to pretend she had nothing to hide.

"What did you expect?" Xander laughed softly, subtly shaking his head. "Lyana dishonored his daughter by picking me at the trials and breaking our match. His son was made a fool by coming home without a mate. We're lucky he agreed to let us into his city, let alone invited us to dinner. The least I can do is bear the brunt of his frustration. It's the first step to smoothing things over."

"Can you please, just this once, not see the good in everyone?"

He cast a sidelong glance in her direction. "Would it make you feel better if I called him an arrogant ass?"

"Yes. It would."

"Very well. He's an arrogant ass."

As she opened her mouth to applaud him, Xander continued.

"But he's also a king, which means he's an arrogant ass whose wrath I have no choice but to suffer. It's one of the pitfalls of diplomacy—you don't always get to choose whose feathers you need to preen."

"Then thank the gods I'm not royal."

"I shudder to think what would happen to the kingdom if you were."

Cassi rolled her eyes and elbowed him gently in the ribs. "Lyana would've thought the same as me had she been here, and she would've said as much."

"I know." A frown passed briefly over his lips before the edges twisted up. "But Lyana would've done so in such a charming manner the king would've walked away not knowing if he'd been deeply insulted or heartily praised."

"Are you saying I lack charm?" Humor colored her words.

Xander stopped walking and turned toward her. "I'm saying you're honest, and I mean that as a compliment."

If you only knew.

It took every ounce of strength she possessed to hide how his words struck like a well-placed dagger, cutting straight to the core. Before her façade cracked, she turned to the side and stared out the window at the city of Rynthos. It was so much more vibrant than she recalled, her spirit body not quite able to experience the richness of the world the way her true body could. Amber light flickered over the stone formations, stalactites and stalagmites created from water long since dried by the isles rising into the sky. The flutter of wings sent a warm vibration through the air, the sensation wrapping around her like an embrace. No matter if she'd grown up in another house, no matter if she'd never before stepped foot in this underground world—something about this place whispered to her soul. For the first time in her life, she was an owl among owls. She belonged. Perhaps most importantly, the musty smell of books called out to her, murmuring of stolen lives and borrowed adventures, a scent that almost felt like home.

An idea sparked as she stared at the winding staircases of this hidden library, almost as though Lyana were standing right next to her, poking her in the ribs.

She turned to Xander. "Come with me."

"Where are we going?"

"You'll see."

With two steps and a leap, Cassi soared out the window. Her wings caught her, and she glided over rooftops, making for the column nearest to the castle. She landed easily on the steps carved into the stone, smiling when she heard the scuffle of feet on the stair behind her. She hadn't been sure he'd follow.

"Cassi," Xander hissed, voice alarmed.

Oh, Xander, you sweet, rule-abiding prince, welcome to my world.

"Cassi, what are you doing?"

Instead of answering, she raced up the steps to the first platform she came upon and tested the door. The knob didn't budge.

Damn.

Cassi bit her lip, darting her gaze left then right. No one from the castle had come running after them, though they'd undoubtedly been seen leaving. It was as much permission as she required. Cassi slipped her hand into one of the pockets hidden along the seam of her gown, pulled out a thin needle, and stuck it inside the lock.

"Cassi!"

"What?" She wriggled the pick. "Don't you want to see what's inside?"

"Yes, but..." A battle took place within his eyes, the good boy versus the eager scholar, two warring sides of equal strength, though a little push from her might tip the scales.

"Haven't you ever done anything you're not supposed to?" Most of her life had been defined by her doing things she wasn't supposed to, usually with Lyana by her side.

"I— I'm not—" His brow furrowed into a deep groove.

"Come on, a little rule-breaking can be fun."

"Fun?" He curled his lip as though a foul odor laced the air. "Fun? The last time I broke a rule it was to let my brother pretend to be me during our most sacred ritual, and we both know how well that turned out."

"I said a *little* rule-breaking," Cassi scoffed. "Not challenging the gods."

Xander sighed heavily. "I'm already in thin air with the owls."

"Well, I'm an owl, and you're not in thin air with me."

He opened his mouth to respond, but a gentle *click* sounded, stealing his words. The uncertainty on his face turned to excitement, and she grinned. With a little push, she eased the door open and slipped inside. Xander paused at the threshold, but with the light seeping in through the gap, illuminating a wall of leather-bound spines, it was only a matter of time before he relented.

One second passed.

Then two. Then three—

Xander gulped audibly and entered. Cassi closed the door behind him, shrouding them in darkness. It took a moment for her eyes to adjust, but when they did, she stepped easily across the room toward the sheen of glass in the corner. Her spying had taught her how to light the special lanterns used in the library. Instead of requiring a candle or torch to ignite the wick, the metal tops used miniature flints, which contained the fire inside the lantern and kept the collection protected.

A *bang* drew her attention, followed by a hastily whispered, "Ow!"

Cassi glanced over her shoulder to find Xander hopping on one foot, his wings flapping to keep him upright as he clutched his toe. The air circulated, rustling pages and tossing up dust. She laughed softly and spun the dial to light the lantern. Within seconds, a warm glow revealed curved walls lined with books. Three worktables sat in the middle of the space, one of their legs having been his invisible attacker.

Xander froze.

With as much dignity as he could muster, he slowly dropped his foot back to the floor and folded his wings against his back. "How much of that did you see?"

"I have perfect night vision."

"Right."

"Your toe all right?"

"Never better." He pursed his lips and sucked in a breath, then slowly expelled it. "Anyway...how'd you know how to use the lantern?"

"Woman's intuition."

He stared at her, unconvinced.

Damn you and your frustratingly attentive mind.

"There was one in my room." Cassi shrugged and turned to the shelves, hoping that was explanation enough. "I'll take this side and you take the other. First one to find something interesting wins. Deal?"

"You're on."

As she ran her fingers over the spines, Cassi scanned the titles—trade logs, supply records, interhouse agreements, and various merchant contracts. She had, it seemed, stepped into what was quite possibly the most boring room in the entire library. Still, even the most boring room was still a room. The smooth brush of leather against her fingertips calmed her heart. The slightly musty, almost sweet smell of old pages cleared her mind. Back in the House of Peace, Cassi had spent hours in the royal library, a dismally small room compared to the one she was in now, but it had meant so much. It had been her shelter from the lies, from the double life, the only place where she could be herself—or escape herself, as the case so often was. Books had always been her haven, and even surrounded by tomes filled with nothing but numbers and lists and useless data, she found peace.

"I think I got something."

"Really?" Cassi spun, unable to hide the shock in her tone. "Let me see."

Xander held out the book and Cassi snatched it from his hold. *Punishments and Executions in the First Age. Volume 1.* After reading it three times in disbelief, she looked up to find complete sincerity etched on his face.

"I thought I said *interesting*."

"This *is* interesting."

"Clearly, you're much darker than I ever gave you credit for."

He rolled his eyes, snatched the book back, and took a seat at the table closest to the lantern before staring at her imploringly. "Well?"

"Fine. Enlighten me."

With a sigh, she collapsed into the chair by his side. Xander eased the cover open and flipped quickly through the first few pages before landing on something he liked. "See? Read this here."

Cassi followed the line of his finger, but the words were too small, nothing but blurred shadows of black across a sandy page. In all their time spent together in his library, she'd never actually sat down to read in front of him. Book spines, yes, and maps with large type, but not the meat of the story. Maybe she hadn't wanted to appear weak. Maybe she was self-conscious. She wasn't sure what it was exactly, but her fingers trembled ever so slightly as they dipped into the folds of her skirt and retrieved another item she'd hidden inside. As soon as the glasses slid up her nose, the words became clear.

"*Colston Anastos. Aged nine. House of Flight. Witnesses claimed to have seen water floating about him in a blasphemous manner. Suspicions later confirmed in the form of a flood when confronted with the accusations. Beheaded for his crimes.*"

A plummeting sensation turned her stomach. "Magic?"

"It must've been."

"That's not new, though." She swallowed, carefully measuring her words. "We've always known it exists. You and I more than most."

"True, but I want to know about more than just its existence, and this is a good place to start. Every day my thoughts turn to what happened in the sacred nest, replaying what I saw, trying to understand it, to approach it like a scholar. One man had power unlike anything I could imagine, but the other two were more obvious to compartmentalize—

one seemed to manipulate the wind and the other metal. It got me thinking about what kinds of magic there might be, and a book like this might tell us everything we need to know. It might not tell us how to fight magic, but it will tell us what magic is, and that could be half the battle."

"That's..." Her voice failed her, trailing into silence. The words across the page swam despite the clarity her lenses provided. *That's genius. That's dangerous. That's too close to a line I'm not sure I should let you cross.* In truth, she'd thought Xander's quest for information was foolish from the beginning, believing the only books that might have had value were locked deep underground in vaults only owls could access.

Now she wasn't so sure.

"Smart, right?"

She coughed to clear her throat. "Yes."

"By the way," he murmured cheerfully. "I like your glasses."

"Oh." She shook her head, pressing her fingers to the frame, the nervousness from before nothing but a trite memory. "Really? Lyana always teased me mercilessly."

"No, they—" He paused, studying her face as the edges of his lips quirked. "They suit you."

Despite the dread curling her insides, her heart made the slightest leap at the words, reminding her of the other dangerous game she was playing with this prince—matters of the heart she had no right indulging.

Cassi shut down the feeling, whatever it was, as she read the name again—*Colston Anastos.* He'd been a *hydro'kine*, she was sure, but what else? Who had he been, the person and not the mage? What might he have become if he'd been born to the sea instead of the sky? They were questions without answers, but right now, she knew one thing. He was a reminder not only of the world beneath the mist, but of the other souls hidden here in the clouds who needed her help.

There were fewer mages born to the world above, magic tending to flow in bloodlines, but there were still some. What was it Xander had said to her those few weeks ago, when she'd asked him about sacrifices and deals with the gods, about what choices he would and wouldn't make, which lives he would save? *I know in the future I'll have to execute people to maintain our laws, though I don't relish the thought.*

Cassi's heart sank.

Malek had been right.

Xander's brother had magic. His mate had magic. But he loved them despite their power. To him, magic was and always would be the enemy. Whether he knew it or not, whether she wanted to face it or not, that made her his enemy too.

"Do you think they have parchment and a quill anywhere?" Xander asked, oblivious to the revelations wrapping around her like binds. "I would love to keep some notes. I wasn't prepared to start researching tonight, but I suppose there's no harm..."

As he stood from the table to search, Cassi read the name one more time, committing it to memory—*Colston Anastos*. He had no face and no family. He was just a name. Yet he stayed with her long after she and Xander returned to the castle, long after they bid each other good night, long after she slipped into her dreams. He was there beside her as her spirit explored the underground workings of the library, searching for a way into the rooms that held the information her king might need. He was there, guiding her down a path she wasn't sure she was brave enough to follow on her own.

27

LYANA

"Where are we?" Lyana asked as she emerged from the interior cabin, surprised to find nothing but open waters and endless fog before her.

When Malek had come to retrieve her, she'd been so relieved to see him without those blasted elemental bowls, she hadn't even cared where they were going. As he'd led her into the depths of an unadorned boat, shielding them from the crowds she was starting to grow used to, she'd been admittedly curious. Now, standing at the edge of the city, its sounds dulled by the fog, with the ocean to her left and a plain wooden structure to her right, she was downright intrigued.

"I have it on good authority that one of your favorite things to do before coming to this world was train."

"Whose authority?"

"So." Malek ignored her. "I thought we might try something new."

"New?"

He stepped onto the dock without looking back. Lyana jumped over the side of the boat and landed easily on the damp wooden planks, then followed him toward the nondescript building. The front door was ajar and the white glow of mage light seeped through the opening, giving no hint as to what waited inside.

"While you're making progress with the bowls, it's not happening fast enough."

A snort slipped out before she could stop it. *You think I don't know?*

Every lesson was like torture. Those four bowls mocked her as they sat unmoving on the table. Malek's eyes judged her, his every disappointment written across his face. The sight of ripples passing over still water was the greatest thrill she'd had in days. It was hardly the stuff of legend, not nearly enough to heal the world.

Lyana tried to think back to that day in the sacred nest, with the power swirling all around her, a manifestation of Aethios's might, his hands guiding her as she pushed Malek away and fought him to save Xander's life. She'd been powerful then. Strong. Unstoppable. Wild, even. Recently, the only thing she felt was tamed.

"I know you're an impulsive person," Malek continued, either unaware or unmoved by her silent insolence, his voice as focused as ever. "You like to do. You like to act. I think maybe you need real stakes to awaken your magic, not always, but now, while you don't yet know how to bend it to your will. I probably should've brought you here sooner, but I wanted to try the other way first. It's more, well, more humane, I guess you'd say. But we don't have that luxury any longer."

With a slight push, the door swung all the way open and Lyana followed him into the brightly lit corridor. As they stepped through the archway at the far end, for the first time in what felt like days a true smile fluttered over her lips. It was a training arena. What she'd thought was a building was truly a wall, surrounding a flat field of packed sand with the open skies above. Her muscles flared with the sweetest heat. She'd been stuck in the castle for days, and it would be such a relief to finally move.

"When new mages come into their power, we bring them here to train," explained as they approached the small group of men and women waiting in the center of the arena. Lyana recognized them from her days on the king's ship—Viktor, the wind mage, Nyomi, the water mage, Jacinta, the metal mage, and Isaak, the fire mage. "Teaching control isn't always the safest thing, so we like to do it away from the city centers, in a somewhat isolated location. You don't need to hold back here. In fact, I pray that you won't, because none of my mages will hold back with you." Malek flicked his gaze to the side. "Viktor, why don't you go first."

"Yes, my liege," the lanky man answered with a nod, stepping away from the group and unclasping the hands behind his back. Yellow sparked menacingly at his fingertips, but that wasn't what caught her attention. It was the look in his hazel eyes, laced with lightning despite his rigid stance. He was controlled but not broken, composed but not contained. He was exactly what she yearned to be.

They lined up to fight, and she turned toward Malek. "I have no weapon."

"You *are* the weapon, Lyana." His smile was as charged as the air after a storm, electric enough to make her feathers prickle. "Your magic is the only weapon you'll ever need."

With a gulp, she brought her spirit eyes to the surface, letting the world dissolve into a rainbow, as though a fine layer of colorful dust were sprinkled across every surface. Thrumming between the elements and alive in each human heart was the same golden spark now glittering along her fingertips. Still, without her daggers she felt naked. Distantly, she knew the metal was more a liability than a defense. Jacinta could easily send them shooting for her heart. But they were a comfort, a shield. They made her feel unstoppable, and even if the sensation were false, it was something her magic had yet to achieve.

"But with a sword—"

"No."

"A dagger—"

"No."

"A—"

"Viktor."

A gust of wind barreled across the field and slammed into her chest. She was on her back before she knew what happened, rolling across the sand. Digging her fingers into the ground, she searched for a handhold, some way to fight. The claw marks mocked her as the wind dragged her back. She pumped her wings, but the air slid through her feathers, the clipped ends making them useless. She couldn't fly. She couldn't stand. She could barely hang on. How in the world was she supposed to fight?

"Your magic, Lyana!"

Healing was the only magic she knew, the only magic she trusted. The wind pressed against her and swirled around her, glittering with yellow *aero'kine* magic and something else, buttery swirls marking the elements themselves, a color only her eyes could see. Lyana tried to see deeper, into the spirit connecting the elements together. She tried to hold it, to stop it, to turn it, but the sky had a spirit like hers, wild and free, not meant to be controlled.

Her feet hit the wooden boards at the end of the arena. The gusts didn't stop. They pushed against her chest, pounding her again and again, until her body rose and her wings spread and she was pressed flush to the wall like a painting made of flesh.

Lyana waited for Malek to stop it.

As the wind crushed her, she waited for his voice, for his command.

It never came.

Tears leaked from her eyes. They burned. Her exposed skin stung as pellets of sand caught in the maelstrom struck her like a million tiny knives. She fought to lift even a single finger, her arms shaking from the exertion. A scream tore through her lips instead. It was useless. She couldn't focus her magic, and any minute Malek would realize it too. All she had to do was wait, was endure. All she—

Lyana paused.

Somewhere in the pain and the panic, a force unfurled like a new flower in spring, not made of magic but of thought, carrying warmth and awareness down her veins, to the very tips of her toes, so every nerve tingled with its might.

When have I ever waited for a man to rescue me?

What happened to the bold girl who'd saved Rafe from a dragon? To the daring dove who'd chosen a raven as her mate? To the confident woman who'd agreed to be taken into the mist? She'd gotten herself into every one of those messes, and she'd gotten herself out of them too. The weight of this world beneath the mist, with its people and its prophecies, had buried her spirit. It was time for Lyana to set herself free.

Stop.

Lyana released her magic, sending the word out like a command.

Stop.

Through the watery film covering her eyes, through the whipping gales and the swirling sands, she saw Viktor freeze.

Stop!

She pushed the thought across the arena like her own raging tempest, letting it slam into his chest in an explosion of golden magic. He stumbled back and back and back, until he too stood flat against the wall, wincing despite the steely focus in his gaze. Still, his magic came.

"You must stop more than his body, Lyana. You must stop his power."

Easy for you to say, she snapped, letting the feistiness wrap around her like a shield. Deep in her magic as she was, the thought spiraled out, as physical as an arrow, striking

Malek in the chest. He flinched, but it was excitement, not anger, that lit his eyes.

"Spirits are simple to control," he said, the slightest challenge in his voice. "It's the elements that are the hardest to contain."

The elements. The elements.

Lyana stared at the wind pummeling her body and sank deeper into her power, trying to see beyond the magic, beyond the invisible tendrils of air, into the very essence of what held it all together, the matter that connected the world, united it, the very same thing which flooded her veins—spirit.

Viktor's spirit was easy to see, like a golden star planted beneath his skin, oozing vitality and life. She could sense his pains and his desires, the loneliness creeping across his limbs, the deep void at the center of his soul, filled with nothing but ebony loss. Malek was right. Human hearts were easy to understand, and she recognized every bit of agony and ecstasy painting his essence. But what did the air want? What did the sky yearn for? What desperate hopes were carried in a breeze?

The elements lived differently, but maybe they weren't so hard to understand. The air was wild, always blowing, always gusting, always searching for new lands. Sometimes it wanted to rage in a tempest that made the earth tremble. Sometimes it was tender, the softest breeze against a cheek like the touch of a long-lost friend. Right now, the wind barreled into her like a prisoner pounding at the walls, forced and coerced by human hands, but wanting nothing more than to be free.

A golden sheen flashed across the air, like a jewel catching the sun. Lyana gripped the spirit with her power.

Go, she commanded. *Fly.*

For a moment, nothing happened. The world was still, including the wind, which had paused, trapped between two warring forces of magic.

All at once, it exploded.

Wind lashed across the practice grounds, tossing Malek and his mages onto their backs, slamming into Viktor's chest, and whirling up into the sky. Lyana crumpled, landing on her hands and knees in the sand as the air released her. Her lungs burned and she panted, but she didn't feel tired—not exactly. Exhilaration struck like a dagger on flint, igniting something within her. She found Malek's eyes across the field.

Had Cassi been there, she would have been waiting with a wisecrack on her lips. If it were Xander, there would have been cheerful praise. Rafe would have been beside her on the wall, panting next to her on the ground, stuck in a mess she'd dragged them both into. But Malek was different, and she wasn't at all surprised to see him simply stand, wipe the sand from his trousers, and cross his arms, a delighted glimmer in his stormy eyes.

"It's a start," he said, breaking the silence. "Nyomi, you're next."

With a grunt, Lyana stood and crossed the field for a face-off against the water mage. Her body ached, but what did that matter? When the time to save the world came, she hardly imagined the dragons would wait for a day when she was well-rested and at peak strength. Fighting through exhaustion was just part of the job.

The woman across from her was a few inches shorter than Lyana, though that meant nothing. Malek surrounded himself with the best, which Nyomi undoubtedly was. Her dark brown hair was knotted atop her head like armor, and there was something steely in her golden eyes. Sapphire glitter danced at her fingertips. Just like that, the match was on.

A tunnel of seawater rose over the edge of the wall and splashed down, a liquid snake slithering closer, ready to swallow Lyana whole. She sprinted out of the way, then dove behind Malek and the three mages watching beside him.

Stop.

The command shot across the field to wrap around Nyomi like a vice. But it was just her body that froze, not her mind and not her magic. Another jet of water shot over the walls, smacking into Lyana's face and knocking her over. Whatever hold she had on Nyomi's spirit vanished in an instant. By the time she got to her feet, another liquid serpent charged. Lyana dove, using Malek as a shield again. Instead of touching him, the water parted around him, then rejoined. The last thing Lyana saw was his cocked brow before the stream slammed into her chest, barreling her over.

Stop.

Nyomi froze.

Turn around, now, Lyana commanded, gripping the woman's spirit, ignoring how wrong it felt to bend someone to her will. This was what Malek wanted, what he commanded. This was what her magic was for. *Walk to the wall and put your face to the stone, keeping your hands behind your back. Close your eyes.*

The swirls of water didn't stop, but they became chaotic and confused. Without her sight, Nyomi didn't know where to aim the magic. Lyana danced easily between the circulating currents, grinning at her own genius.

The smile vanished a moment later as the entire ocean seemed to swell above the walls, spilling into the arena as though it were a ship swallowed by the sea. Lyana flapped her wings, but the sky refused her. Water clawed at her ankles, then her calves, rising over her knees. An invisible shield protected Malek and the others from the spray, leaving them perfectly dry. The water was up to her hips, now her waist. Nyomi remained against the wall where Lyana had put her, her aura calm and unafraid of the flood. Lyana stared into the water, trying to see between the liquid molecules, within them, searching for the golden hint of spirit her magic could latch onto.

Nothing.

It was at her shoulders now, her neck, kissing her jawline, brushing her lips. Arching her head back, Lyana sucked in one more panicked gulp of air and the ocean swallowed her. The rush of water filled her ears, then the thunder of the waves splashing into the arena. With a kick, she pushed off the ground and dragged her arms through the water, trying to swim, but her bones were too light and her feathers too heavy. She wasn't strong enough to haul her wings behind her. A ringing started in her ears. Black spots dotted her vision. The warm glow of her magic lit the sea, but she didn't know what to do or how to hold it. Pressure pushed in at all sides. In desperation, her lungs screaming at her for air, she opened her mouth, hoping somehow to find a pocket of something she could swallow. Liquid swirled down her throat instead. She was getting cold, so cold, so—

A tunnel of air cut through the water, and Lyana dropped like a rock to the sand. On her hands and knees she coughed, vomit spewing through her lips as her stomach emptied itself. Malek emerged from the liquid wall, perfectly dry compared to her drenched limbs, and knelt beside her.

"You got overconfident."

She didn't know why she had even for a moment expected concern. All he cared about were results. "Only for a second."

"You let your fear overwhelm you. You forgot about your magic."

"Did you miss the part where I was drowning?"

Malek simply shrugged, his pristine golden hair mocking her as it fluffed dryly in the breeze. "I told you, this method isn't easy."

"I think you called it inhumane."

"Yes, well…" He trailed off, watching the water descend as Nyomi ordered it back over the wall and into the sea. The whole arena was nearly dry now. He stood, his shoulders hunched in dejection. "Perhaps we should call it a day."

"No." The word popped out of Lyana with such vehemence it surprised her.

She swallowed and met his curious gaze head-on. She

didn't want to go back to the castle, back to her rooms, back to her lonely isolation. She was a fighter. She wasn't used to backing down. And no matter how dangerous the place, she hadn't felt better in days.

On the other side of these walls, her problems seemed insurmountable, so immense she didn't know how to face them, where to even begin an attack. Staring at those bowls, she'd only been able to think about the weight of the world on her shoulders—so many lives, so many souls, so much hurt and pain and loneliness had overwhelmed her defenses.

Here, it was different.

Here, two people were in a duel—just one foe to think about, one soul to overcome. This wasn't her learning how to save the world. This was her learning how to save herself, and somehow that made all the difference.

"Again," she growled as she climbed to her feet. "I want to go again."

RAFE

"I have to admit," Rafe said as he dropped his head back against the main mast and let his feet dangle over the edge of the platform, no longer afraid of the height but rather enjoying the feel of so much wind and sky all around him. "Hunting dragons is far more frustrating than I ever thought it would be."

"That's the problem with dragons." Brighty sighed, her shoulder brushing against his as they sat side by side, looking at the mist. "They can fly away."

It was a problem he'd never before considered, having once been able to chase after them. Now that his feet were planted firmly on the ground, he found it was true—for the time being, at least. Dragons could fly away, and fly away they did. Since leaving Da'Kin, the crew had come upon three different beasts, or perhaps the same beast three different times. Either way, they'd been unable to catch one. Injure or hurt, yes, but as soon as the tides changed in their favor, the dragons simply retreated into the fog, disappearing without a backward glance. It was maddening.

"How do you usually catch them?"

"We usually don't."

"Have you ever caught one?"

"Me? Once. The captain, I think, has caught a few. The king likes to study them. He wants to understand how their magic works and why they're so damn attracted to ours. I'm told the previous king was the same way. But as far as I'm concerned, the only good dragon is a dead one."

"Humph." Rafe crossed his arms, scanning the endless gray. All he needed was one dragon and he'd have his wings. One measly dragon. The damn things had been haunting him his entire life, and now, when they would finally be of use, they had vanished. "What magic *do* they have? Other than the obvious, of course."

"Just let me go check my notes."

He turned toward her then. "Really?"

"No, not really." She scowled. "As if the king would talk about that sort of thing with me. Honestly, Rafe—"

He cut her off before she could launch into a tirade. "You must've heard rumors."

"Sure, everyone's heard rumors. That the dragons eat the magic. That they absorb it. That they're hoarding it somewhere, waiting to launch their final attack. But it's all ridiculous. Based on fear, not facts. When you're out here fighting them, you see the truth. Our magic hurts them, the same as it would any human. They're made of flesh and blood, just like us."

He stared into the fog as though it held the answers. It

didn't, of course, but against that opaque backdrop, memories of the fights played through his mind. Brighty was right. When she blasted them with concentrated light, they burned. When Archer pierced them with metal arrows, they bled. The waters Spout splashed against them sizzled on impact. The darkness Shadow wrapped around their eyes made them blind. Pyro was the only one whose magic didn't seem to have any effect, yet it was no surprise that fire couldn't hurt a dragon.

There had to be something to it.

Why else did they chase magic? Why else were they drawn to it? Why else did they stick around these stormy seas when they could soar to any other place in the world and be free?

Rafe sighed. He wasn't a scholar, and he'd find no answers today.

"All right, tell me this then," he finally said. "How the gods do we keep finding them? The seas are vast, the skies more so, and yet somehow they keep falling into our laps."

She snorted. "That's easy. Dragons like magic, right? Our cities are teeming with it. They attack the cities. Our mages shoo them away. Word travels to the king. He tells it to us. And, simple as that, we know where to look. Then we use a little magic and, usually, they come to us."

"Yeah, I know all that. But how does the king tell us? That's what I don't get. We go to bed clueless and by the next morning Captain is on the hunt again."

"Oh, it's the *dormi'kines*."

"The whats?"

He could practically feel her eye-roll.

"The dreamwalkers. They can separate their spirits from their bodies and dive into people's dreams. A little creepy, if you ask me, but the king values their power because they're his little messengers."

"Messengers?"

"Or spies."

"Spies?"

"Are you a parrot or something? Stop it."

If his mind weren't so busy spinning, he would have glared at her. Instead, his mouth gaped open in a manner that would certainly earn some teasing from her later, but he didn't care. Dreamwalkers. Messengers. Spies.

Cassi.

Fury ran white-hot through his blood, bringing a sneer to his lips at her very name. That was how she'd done it—she'd been spying on them with magic. That was how she'd known he would run. That was how she'd known he would go to his mother's rooms. That was how she'd known about his magic. What else had she learned? Whose secrets had she stolen, apart from his? And where was she now?

That last question stopped him short. Rafe thought back to the day he'd seen Lyana in the city crowd. Cassi hadn't been there. It hadn't struck him as odd until right now, but the two of them were inseparable. Why would the owl have sent the princess down here alone? Why hadn't she followed? Why stay in the world above?

Xander.

The fear was unfounded, he knew. What could the king possibly want with his brother? Xander had no magic. No power that might threaten. No desire to attack anyone. Still, it was as though someone had grabbed hold of Rafe's insides and twisted them in a fiendish grip, refusing to let go. *If Cassi wants Xander— If she's trying to hurt him— If she—*

"Oh no," Brighty interrupted. "You've got that look. I hate that look."

"What look?" He cut his eyes to her, still fuming.

"*That* look. That self-righteous, idiotic, sacrifice-it-all-in-the-name-of-love look. The only thing that look ever brings is trouble."

Rafe started, surprised to find his fists clenched against his thighs. Reality came crashing down, leaving him deflated, like a sail without winds, until his arms hung limply by his sides. *There's nothing I can do. If Cassi is after Xander, if she does try to hurt him, there's* nothing *I can do.*

The realization left him empty.

All his life, he'd sacrificed himself for his brother, protecting him from foes both real and imagined. And one lapse—one night of passion, no matter how worthwhile—might have undone it all. What if Xander was vulnerable? What if Rafe was gone when his brother needed him most? What if something happened because he wasn't there?

"Magic alive, Rafe, that look is even worse. It's like I just told you your puppy died. If I'd known dreamwalking was going to send you over the edge, I never would've mentioned anything."

"No, it's just—it reminded me of home, of the people I left behind, people who might need me, who might get hurt without me."

She scoffed.

"What?" he snapped, unable to take any more of her attitude when it seemed as if everything he held dear might be caving in around him. If Xander got hurt, he'd never forgive himself. Never.

"Nothing." The word came out far too lightly.

He glowered. "What?"

"Nothing, it's just—you seem to be worrying an awful lot about people who probably aren't worrying all that much about you." She said it nonchalantly, as though unaware it would cut him like a knife.

His denial frantically fought to keep the wound from bleeding. "You don't know them."

"I don't need to. I know you. I see you day after day, your head in the clouds, worried about all the people you left behind. Well, I have one question for you. If they're so worried about you too, where are they? Last I checked, we haven't seen any ravens in the skies, scouring the seas for their lost brother."

"They don't—" He broke off, hating the way her words needled past his defenses, landing with a sting. "It's not that simple."

"Why not?"

"Because it's just not."

"Great argument. You convinced me."

"Brighty!"

"What?"

He glared at her again, unsure how to even begin to explain. It wasn't simple—not by a long shot. Xander was a prince. He couldn't just leave his people to go searching the skies for his bastard brother. Sure, he could have sent a search team, but the ravens wouldn't dare sink beneath the Sea of Mist in an effort to find Rafe. They'd call him dead and be done with it. Not to mention that they'd parted ways in the wake of Rafe's betrayal. Xander thought he'd left of his own accord. His brother probably had no idea he'd been injured.

The situation *was* complicated.

Yet as he continued to stare into Brighty's opal eyes, a trick of the mind turned them lavender, and suddenly it was his brother sitting before him. All the anger he'd been ignoring came brimming to the surface. Justifiably or not, he was mad at Xander, and he'd been hurt by him. Before the fight with Cassi, back in that royal room that had never felt quite his, Rafe *had* left—but Xander had let him. And had the roles been reversed, Rafe liked to think he wouldn't have let his brother go so easily. He would have at least demanded answers. He would have tried to find some speck of forgiveness to hold onto. He wouldn't have silently let Xander walk away.

"It's not cowardice to put yourself first, Rafe. You have to know your own worth, and if other people don't see it, then screw them."

Maybe that was the problem.

Xander hadn't fought, but neither had he. Rafe was the one who offered to go, who left without saying a word. He could have stayed. He could have tried to explain himself, to explain how he and Lyana had met before the trials even began, how their magic had united them, how they'd been drawn together as though by the gods' own hands. But he'd spent his whole life believing himself to be worthless, and in truth, he never thought his leaving would matter. Fighting for Xander had always been easy. Fighting for himself was another thing entirely.

"You have more to offer the world than being someone else's punching bag," Brighty continued softly. "Sometimes, you need to live for you."

He would never abandon Xander, or Lyana for that matter. It simply wasn't in his nature. But maybe he could do things differently—maybe while he fought to save their lives, he could learn how to fight for his own too.

Rafe blinked away the heaviness in his heart, retreating from his thoughts to find Brighty watching solemnly. The urge to take her hand surged through him, to simply hold it for comfort against whatever plagued her mind. But that wasn't what they did. They took jabs at each other in an effort to wrangle out the truth. "If you're so good at putting yourself first, how'd you end up on a dragon-hunting ship, risking your life for a cruel king and trying to erase your own name?"

He expected her to roll her eyes and scoff. Instead, she turned toward the sea, a sadness he didn't understand playing over her features. "We're not talking about me."

"Maybe we should be."

"There are worse places to be than this ship."

"Like where? Tell me. Maybe I can help."

"I don't want help, Rafe. I don't need it. I found my escape, and all I'm saying is, maybe you can too. You have options. Despite your best efforts, the people on this ship actually like you. And I know that all you're thinking about is getting your wings back and storming the castle to save your lost princess, but you should take a moment to ask yourself if that's really what you want. I saw her in the square. She didn't seem trapped to me. She seemed like a queen standing next to her king, and you don't have to live stuck in their shadow. There's a room below deck with your name on it, and Captain can always use another man, especially one with wings. If the people from your past don't want to fight for you, we'd be happy to take you instead."

"Careful, Brighty," he murmured, unable to stop the smile spreading his lips. "You almost sound like you care."

"Don't get used to it."

With that, she gripped one of the loose ropes, leapt off the platform, and glided easily to the deck, ending the conversation with admirable efficiency. But if Rafe's downfall was that he cared too much, so be it. One way or another, he'd uncover her story. He'd help her whether she wanted it or not—that was, after all, the same *offer* she'd given him. A fact for which he was grateful. Rafe didn't know what he would have done in this world without her.

"Who wants to test their luck in a game of dice?" she called to the rest of the crew. "Winner gets the pride of not losing, and Rafe will do their laundry for a week."

"What?" he shouted, still on the mast. No one heard him. Or if they did, they ignored him. *Jerks.* Despite his hurrying down the net, the game was underway by the time he stepped foot on the deck.

Brighty elbowed him in the side when he tried to plead his case. "If you're so beat up about it, get in the game. If you win, I'll do your laundry. How about that?"

"I'm in."

Rafe took his spot in the circle, sizing up the rest of the crew. He'd watched them play a few times but hadn't yet joined them. Dice was one thing, but magic dice was a different game entirely. Two players rolled and the higher number won. In the case of a tie, it turned to a duel—first to retrieve the dice won, the loser was out—and those were a sight to behold.

The first few rolls were uneventful. Coins were exchanged, some murmurs and jibes, but nothing more until Pyro and Spout each hit a four. They grinned at each other, then chaos ensued. Spout pulled water from the sea. Pyro latched onto fire from the lantern she kept hanging near the door. The two forces slammed together, erupting in a blast of steam. The particles must have tickled Spout's nose, because she sneezed, and just like that it was done. Pyro rolled underneath the water, grabbed the dice, and won.

"No one say a word." Spout glowered, staring particularly hard at Brighty, whose cheeks puffed with barely contained laughter. "I'm allergic—"

"We know!" they all said in unison, breaking out in guffaws.

She stomped off and the game circled on. Rafe lost his first toss and won his second. Jolt and Archer dueled. He wrapped a chain around her ankles and yanked them out from underneath her. Before he reached the dice, she sent a bolt of lightning toward his chest. He dove to save his life, and she snatched them for the win. Fairness wasn't exactly a huge part of the game. Brighty and Leech had the next match up. Palm high, she blinded him with her light. Well, blinded them all. Rafe thought it would be an easy victory, but by the time the spots in his vision cleared, Leech held the dice and she was nowhere in sight.

"What..." He trailed off when he noticed the gaping hole in the deck, an opening that quickly sealed with a flick of Leech's wrist, his earth magic stretching the wood back together.

The door behind them slammed open and Leech caught Rafe's eye with a wink.

"Every time," Brighty spat from somewhere behind him. "You get me every damned time."

"You always jump in too quickly."

"Clearly, I don't jump quick enough."

She hunched against the rail with her arms folded to watch the rest of the game, out of spite if nothing else. Rafe managed to squeak by a few more rounds, losing some coins and gaining some coins. Jolt took out Leech. Pyro took out Jolt. Then there were only two—him and Pyro. They rolled back and forth for a little while, passing coins between them, until finally they each rolled a two.

Pyro smirked, lifting her hand to catch the flame shooting toward her from the lantern. Everyone seemed to hold a breath. No one had expected him to get this far. No one had even expected him to play.

"No shame in backing down," Pyro murmured, eyes flashing with wild delight. "I wouldn't want you to get burned."

"It wouldn't be the first time."

Rafe dove for the dice. A wave of flames descended on

the spot, encasing them in an angry glow, and he snatched back his hand. Pyro sauntered closer, as though without a care in the world, only missing a whistle on her lips. He knew it was stupid, and he knew it would hurt, but in the back of his mind he imagined Brighty's face while she washed his dirty underwear, and that was all the motivation he needed. Rafe stuck his hand in the fire, ignoring the pain, and grabbed the dice.

"You can't be serious!" Brighty erupted.

"For magic's sake, Rafe!" Pyro quickly snuffed out the flames, the crazed look in her eyes instantly replaced by fear. "I didn't think in a million years you'd actually— I mean, it's just a game. Did I hurt you?"

"I don't hurt so easily." He shrugged and held up his hand. Silver magic glimmered beneath his skin, already healing the subtle burns along his fingers. They all watched him, not with fear or loathing, but with respect. It was the first time he thought maybe Brighty was right—maybe life on this ship wouldn't be half-bad. He tossed the dice to Brighty, and she caught them with a scowl. "My laundry bin is downstairs, and it's full."

Her lip curled and she growled.

"All right, men," Patch cut in, and they all jumped. Where had he even come from? Last they'd seen, he had been at the wheel, taking lead while the captain napped.

"And women," Jolt said quickly.

He rolled his eyes. Well, eye. Come to think of it, Rafe had never seen what was underneath his patch—an empty socket, maybe a scar. He wasn't in a hurry to find out.

"I meant 'men' in the generic sense."

She shrugged. "I'm just saying."

"All right, men, *and women*, Captain just got a direct order from the king. We're switching tactics. Catching a dragon out in the open doesn't seem to be working, so we're going to the rift. Playtime is over. Understood? Leech, fix the scorch marks on the deck, and the rest of you, get back to work."

They scrambled.

Well, everyone except Rafe and Brighty.

"The rift?" he asked.

Eyes twinkling triumphantly at something new to hold over him, she murmured, "You'll see."

29

LYANA

With his arm around her waist, Malek helped Lyana back into the interior of the boat, carefully minding her twisted ankle and the burns bubbling over her exposed skin. Using him as an anchor, she limped down the steps and into the privacy of the closed room where no one in the city would see them as they floated back to the castle. It had become something of a ritual. They didn't need words as he quietly closed the door behind them and she stripped off her jacket. By the time she was seated, golden magic already shone between his fingers.

Malek eased her leg onto his lap and used a dagger to cut away the trousers Isaak's fire magic had burned, revealing her scarred flesh. She sighed as his magic sank into the wounds, delivering a coolness to quell the flames, relief so sweet her eyes fluttered shut as she sank back against the pillows. In her former life, she might have been scandalized at finding herself half-naked and alone with a man, or rebelliously pleased. Now she was too tired for either. Her soul was already laid bare by his magic. Did it truly matter if her body was too?

"You did well today."

"Was that a compliment?" She opened her eyes just wide enough to see his lips twist in a smile and felt her own do the same. "I don't believe my ears."

"I've been known to deliver a few."

"And now a joke?"

He shook his head softly, which only made her grin widen.

"Did you expect me to simply say thank you?"

"No, never. That would be as shocking as my praise."

"True."

"I push you because the world demands it."

"I know, Malek. I was only—"

"And I hold back my approval until you've earned it, so then you know it's true." His fingers tingled with power as they drifted over her ankle, the magic reflecting in his midnight eyes. Though his mouth still held the slightest curve, his jaw was clenched in concentration. A groove marred his brow, slightly hidden by a wave of his golden hair. "I find little use for pretty words that mean nothing. I'd like you to know that when I tell you something, I mean it. And today I do. You did well."

"But not great," she added, unable to stop herself. With her power near the surface, she felt his spirit brighten.

"Not yet."

"Thank you."

He darted his guarded eyes toward her. "For what?"

"For the truth."

In a way, he reminded her of Cassi. While her teachers had always boosted her ego, giving praise where it wasn't necessarily due, her friend had been there with a sharp word to bring her right down to size. Not in a bad way, but in a way that made her yearn to improve. It was the same with Malek. She was getting better. Today she'd fought Isaak and Viktor together—stopping the wind, holding back fire, doing things that had seemed impossible only a few weeks before. Her defensive magic was improving, but she still lacked the control for a strong attack, which was how they'd beaten her down in the end. Today she *had* been good, but she wanted to be great. She needed to be great, for the world, if not for herself.

"There's something I want to try tomorrow," Malek said, drawing her back. "I think you're ready."

"What?"

"I want you to touch the rift."

"Really?" She jerked up in surprise, hissing as the burns on her thigh flared with heat. Malek's hand was there in an instant, the cool tingle of his magic dousing the fire.

"Yes. You're not ready to attempt to seal it. Not even close. You've started to learn how to tame the elements, how to command them, but I want to see how in tune you are with the spirit of the earth. Not just the elements themselves, but with the essence binding them together. I want to see if you're strong enough to sense the rift on your own."

"But the—the bowls." The word slid through her lips slick with disdain.

A bit of air escaped his lips, sounding suspiciously like a laugh. "Yes, the bowls. Your greatest enemy."

He wasn't wrong. Inside the arena, her magic was starting to become second nature—with her adrenaline pumping, with her heart in her throat, with her instincts leading the way and her mind finally silenced. But in the quiet hours of the night, as she stared at those bowls beneath Malek's probing gaze, her thoughts raged like a mighty storm, sweeping her magic into pure chaos.

"The lesson of the bowls is tame compared to some of the feats I've seen you manage these past few days. It's your mind that betrays you, not your magic. You need to learn how to focus without death staring you in the face."

"I know."

"You need to separate your spirit from your heart, to build a wall between your emotions and your magic so they won't consume you."

"I know."

"Lyana," he murmured, somehow the chiding tutor and the understanding confidant all at once. The shuffle of fabric was the only sound in the room as he brushed the backs of his fingers along her cheek, leaving a tingling trail in their wake. "I, of all people, know the burdens you carry, and I don't want them to bury you. You might not think it, but I've been overwhelmed by our destiny too. There are choices we must make that no one else will ever understand, and they can undo you if you let them. So don't. Control your heart. Don't let it control you. Discipline is the only way to keep the world from crushing you."

For just a moment, she leaned into his touch.

Then she turned away, staring at the wall but seeing something more.

The truth was she couldn't compartmentalize her actions —she couldn't simply remove her emotions from the equation, and she didn't understand how he could. She couldn't feel the pain of his people without also yearning to heal them, and she couldn't concentrate on sealing a rift, on saving the world, without also feeling guilty for all the destruction that so-called rescue would bring. Most of her life had been spent testing limits, not caring about consequences, but lately the repercussions were all she could think about.

"What do you think will happen?" she asked softly. "Once it's closed. The rift, I mean. When we've won, what do you think will happen?"

The question had been on her mind more and more. The longer she was away from home, it seemed, the more she ached to protect it—the isles, the houses, their way of living. She'd spent so much of her life desperate to get away, to explore. She hadn't appreciated the beauty of her own world until now, knowing that any day it could be gone.

"The dragons will be trapped in their own world, and we'll be free of them."

"I'm not talking about the dragons, Malek. I'm talking about the people. What will happen to them? Your people have never known the sky. Mine have never known the sea. Yours depend on magic to survive. Mine curse the very thought. And what of the god stones? When the rift is sealed and the spell is broken, what will happen to their magic? Without Aethios, without the stones, who will give wings to the next generation?"

"You."

Her eyes snapped back to his. "What?"

"You, Lyana. You'll give the next generation wings."

"I don't—"

"What did I tell you before? The stones are made of magic. Your god Aethios, he's nothing but concentrated spirit magic. Everything he provides through the priests and priestesses, through whatever mechanism the spell designed, you can deliver tenfold. Spirit joining is similar to healing magic, but instead of restoring a single soul, you're weaving two souls into one. *Aethi'kine* power gave your people wings long before the isles were lifted into the sky, and you can keep your kind alive long after they're returned to sea."

Lyana stared at her hands as though seeing them anew, the golden aura shimmering like a halo of sun in a dark sky. Malek might not believe in her gods, but she did. If this was Aethios's power, then he'd chosen her. He'd seen something in her the moment she was born—something great, something worthy. Maybe if he were there with her, she'd see it too. As it was...

She dropped her palms back onto her lap.

"Is that what's been holding you back?" Malek asked, dipping his chin until he caught her gaze and not letting go. As always, he looked not into her eyes, but through them, to all the secrets she was trying to hide. "Fear of what will be? You can't think like that. There is no use worrying about the future until we know for certain there will even be one. First we must seal the rift. Everything else will be dealt with as it comes."

"I can't shut it off, Malek."

"You can. Bury it away. Lock it behind a door. Toss it over a wall. Do whatever you have to do, but living in hypotheticals solves nothing."

"That's easy for you to say."

"Why?"

"Because—" Lyana broke off, taking a deep breath. This wasn't how she'd wanted to have a conversation she'd been thinking about during all the hours alone in her room staring at the fathomless mist. Malek was stubborn, perhaps even more stubborn than her. If she didn't say it right, he'd just shut her down. But she was tired of biting her tongue. "Because your people have nothing to lose."

He froze with his fingers on her thigh. The magic still sinking into her skin was the only part of him that moved. His throat bobbed as he slowly swallowed. "They're your people too."

"I know." She covered his hand with hers, willing him to look at her. He wouldn't. "And I want to end their suffering, but I can't abandon my home. When the rift closes, your people will get the sun and the sky. The mist will clear and with their magic, the possibilities will be endless. But my people? They'll lose everything. Their gods. Their homes. They'll find themselves in a world full of magic, a world they don't understand, a world they've spent their entire lives dreading. Unless they have some warning, some way to prepare, there'll be war, and—"

"No."

"Please, just—"

He dropped her hand and stood. "I know what you're asking, and the answer is no."

"Malek—"

"If there is war, so be it." The coldness in the words hit her like a winter storm, stealing the breath from her lungs, leaving a burning ache behind. "The rift is all that matters."

Not to me.

She could already see it—*ferro'kine* magic slashing swords at their throats and *pyro'kine* fire burning their wings. The people of her world were afraid of magic, and after living in the mist, she realized they had a right to be. If it came to war, they'd lose. But Malek's people didn't want more suffering. They wanted salvation. If she could keep her people from attacking first, if they had some warning, if she could show them there was nothing to fear, maybe the worst could be prevented. To Lyana, it was worth trying, at the very least.

But Malek would crush those arguments in his clenched fist until they came out as nothing more than dust to be discarded on the wind.

Instead, she said, "I thought you wanted a queen."

"I do." His brows squeezed together as he took a breath. She could almost see his wall lower then go back up, blocking the light from his eyes. "In all decisions except for this."

"That's not how it works," she said, tired of only being heard when it was convenient for him. "The day we met, you said you trusted only yourself. Maybe that's the problem. Even if I master my magic, we'll never save the world, Malek. Not like this. If you can't learn to trust me, then all of this is moot. I'm not the only one who has some learning to do. You need to listen to me. You might not always agree, but you need to let me have a voice. Part of being a king or a queen is being a leader, and if we can't come together, then our people never will. I don't want to save one world only to destroy another."

"Lyana—"

"I don't want an answer now," she said, finally the one to cut their argument short. The sound of shuffling feet and clanking metal announced their arrival at the castle. At any moment the boat would come to a stop. "I wouldn't believe it. Like you said, pretty words are useless. Practice trusting me like I practice my magic. Let it build bit by bit over time. Come to my room tomorrow. Let's see if I can touch the rift. And we'll take the rest from there."

They stared at each other across what seemed an impassable divide.

With a sigh, he turned and left. The door closed behind him, and she listened to the pounding of his boots as he strode across the deck and disembarked. Only when it was quiet did Lyana finally stand and lift her arms over her head, stretching both her body and her wings, easing the last of the aches away. Her ivory feathers were the tiniest bit longer than earlier that day, a side effect of sitting so long in Malek's magic.

Rebellion drifted across her thoughts like a long-lost friend. After a quick glance at the door, she gave in to that purring call and flapped her wings. A wind swirled, rustling her feathers as they caught the air. Her body rose, one slow inch at a time, until only her toes grazed the floor, then higher still, so that for a brief glorious moment she was flying.

It ended far too soon.

Her wings gave out and she dropped back to the ground. But as she slid her jacket around her shoulders and smoothed the fabric with her palms, a grin widened her lips, one no amount of control could stifle. When Malek had brought her to his world, he'd clipped more than just her wings—he'd clipped her spirit. And with each passing day, she was relieved to find they were both coming back.

There was still so much to learn about her magic that she didn't want to go, but she would if she had to. She refused to be controlled. She refused to be silenced. Maybe she was being emotional, but so was he. His way wasn't the only way, and she wouldn't let the fate of the world be determined by his pride. If leaving was the only way to make him understand, to make him see her as his equal, as his partner, well then, to steal his words, *so be it.*

30

RAFE

A s dawn stirred, Rafe woke expecting more of the same. They'd been at the rift for days, and so far it seemed a lot like the middle of nowhere. There was no difference between this and any other unnamed spot in the foggy sea aside from the subtle current of magic in the air like a constant prickling against the skin.

This morning, however, was different.

He woke to a warmth against his cheeks as light penetrated the darkness behind his closed eyes. A familiar scent filled the air, one that haunted him. For a moment he thought it was the sun, and he was in the sky, and she was there—that maybe these past few weeks had been nothing but a hideous dream. Heart thumping, he tore his eyes open and rolled over, further knotting the sheets around his legs, but Lyana wasn't there. The spot beside him was empty. The walls around him were not made of stone but of wood, and the air was heavy and damp, not light and inviting. Most of all, there was no ebony wing he could fold over his shoulder to cocoon under in an attempt to block out the day.

The day?

Eyes narrowing, he paused. A subtle golden sheen lit the air, warm and radiant, but it couldn't be the sun, not here within the mist. He spun again and kicked the sheets away, disentangling himself from the bed as he lurched to his feet.

Ana.

It was crazy. It was impossible. They were in the middle of the ocean, nowhere close to land, but somehow she was there. He could feel her in the air as surely as if she were standing beside him, her magic like a piece of her soul whispering in his ear, *I'm here. I haven't forgotten about you.*

He wanted to shake the words from his head but he couldn't. They'd spent more time apart than together. Weeks upon weeks had passed since their brief hours in the dark, weeks she'd spent with another man in a new life, weeks he'd spent trying to piece together the shambles of his. They were two different people by now, he was sure. Still, the subtlest hint of her presence sent him reeling back to those nights in Pylaeon when they'd walked the city streets under the stars, and she'd taught him a lesson no one else possibly could—that magic was a beautiful blessing, not a curse. It had been the first time in his life when he'd thought maybe, just maybe, the gods had chosen him for something more. Then Cassi had carved the thought from his mind just as thoroughly as she'd removed his wings. Lately, though, he was slowly gaining it back.

A pounding at the door startled him from his thoughts. "Rafe, come on or you'll miss all the fun."

"Fun?" he asked as he yanked open the door.

Brighty immediately grabbed him by the arm and started tugging him toward the staircase. She was small, but surprisingly strong when she wanted to be. "Don't you feel it?"

"The only thing I feel is your nails digging into my arm."

"Oh, I'm sorry." She wrenched them in deeper. "Am I hurting you?"

He peeled her fingers away. "I'm not even dressed."

Brighty refocused her eyes, as though noticing his bare chest for the first time, then shrugged. "Clothes won't stop a dragon anyway."

"A dragon?"

"Magic alive, Rafe, haven't you been paying attention? The king is calling one out for us. Don't you feel his magic?"

"His…" He shook his head. "What?"

"Can't you feel the *aethi'kine* power in the air? It's the king—it has to be. He's poking the rift and hoping the dragons will poke back."

"You still haven't deigned to tell me what this blasted rift even is."

She stared at him with a frown across her round face and shook her head. "Just throw on a shirt and meet me on deck. Captain's waiting."

Not glancing back, Brighty scurried up the steps and rushed out the door.

As he watched her go, he couldn't help but note she was wrong—it wasn't the king's magic. It was Lyana's. Rafe would have bet his life on it. For some reason, that difference gave him an impossible hope. Maybe somehow she'd learned of his deal with the king. Maybe she knew he was out here waiting. Maybe she was trying to help him get back his wings.

The chance was small, but the fact that it was even there was all the motivation he needed. Rafe ran back to his room and yanked a shirt over his head, not bothering to tuck it in before he jammed his feet into boots and tossed his scabbards over his shoulders. Still securing the buckles, he stumbled out into the hall and hustled up the stairs.

By the time he spilled onto the deck, the crew was in full swing. Pyro stood at the bow, a flame burning above her fingers as she studied the misty air. Brighty stood by her side, her palms glowing so ivory that a mere peek her way left spots in his vision. The wind was eerily still, as though waiting for some invisible current to stir it back to life. Squirrel sat in the crow's nest, gaze sharper than his young age should allow. Archer, Jolt, Spout, Leech, and Shadow all stood by the rails, power simmering at the ready. Cook was the only one below deck, though Rafe hardly saw the man outside of the kitchen or the storerooms. And he knew Captain was at the wheel with Patch by her side even before her voice carried to his ear.

"Brighty, I want you to light this whole ocean up. Not an ounce of fog in the air until we spot the dragon. We don't want to miss it. Pyro, as soon as you sense something, alert the crew. Patch, you're on the sails while I'm on the wheel. Oh, Rafe, so nice of you to finally join us."

He spun at the sound of his name. Captain's icy eyes

held that wild spark of oncoming battle, though he couldn't for the life of him see the dragon they all assumed they were fighting. She gripped the wheel in both hands, magic glimmering at her fingertips and leaking into the air. It was only then he noticed how unnaturally silent the world was. No groans of wood. No snaps of canvas. No splashes of water. The boat beneath him hardly moved. The sea was flat. The sails were raised, yet drooped against the mast like old, saggy skin. The stillness was eerie.

"You so much as reach for those swords, Rafe, and I'll have Archer chain you to the mast. Understood? All I want you to do is stand there and look pretty."

Rafe sighed. So much for his earlier sense of purpose and conviction. His magic was as useless as ever. "Yes, Captain."

A few more commands were doled out, but he stopped listening and instead eyed the men and women parked by the ship rails. Whom would he have the best chance pressing for information? Shadow slept most of the day, so he knew her the least, but she always seemed kind when they interacted. Leech, he was sure, would tell him what he wanted, plus far more that he didn't. When it came to science or learning of any kind, the man was insatiable. Rafe would get answers, but probably not until the battle was already long over. Archer had just been given an order to lock him up for insolence, and Spout would probably just sneeze on him before she could speak. In the end, he sidled up to Jolt.

"Can I ask you a question?"

A smile twisted her lips as she turned toward him with

brown eyes so dark they were nearly black. The shimmer of spirit magic in the air highlighted the golden tone of her skin, though it was the amethyst magic sparking at her fingertips that most caught his attention.

"Let me guess," she said. "Brighty wouldn't tell you what the rift is."

"No," he growled.

"Oh, Rafe." Jolt pressed her finger to his throat and drew a lazy trail down his chest, delivering a static charge against his skin that made his hairs stand on end. When she reached the ties on his shirt, she pulled back with a sigh. "We could've had a lot of fun, you and I, but you chose Brighty as your mentor, and the last place I want to be is stuck in the middle. That's only fun in a few very select circumstances. But I will tell you this. The answer is right there in that handsome head of yours, if you'd only just open your eyes and see it."

With a scowl, he dropped his forearms to the railing and stared out to sea, watching the flecks of spirit glitter through the fog. Xander was the brains and he was the brawn. All his life, his brother had done the thinking for him, and truth be told, it was exhausting trying to solve so many puzzles on his own.

"Lips that perfect weren't made for so much frowning." She nudged him with her hip, though he couldn't be certain it was on purpose since she was always swinging them about. The woman had more curves than a winding mountain stream, and she knew it. "Cheer up."

"Why?"

"You're about to get your answer."

"Captain!" Pyro shouted at almost the same moment, the fire around her fingers blazing brighter as she pointed east. "There! I feel one coming."

"Brighty!"

"On it."

They all turned away as her *photo'kine* magic blazed through the mist, burning it away and clearing the sea. Gales swept across the deck, whipping their clothes and snapping the sails. The ship surged forward, Spout working the current as Patch controlled the wind. Captain stretched her wing back, the muscles in her bare arms straining as she held the wheel on target, following Pyro's direction. A leather vest cinched around her waist, dyed as red as blood, and he wondered if it was a promise or an omen.

"It's close!" Pyro shouted.

Captain fixed her steely eyes on the sea. "Where?"

"I don't—"

"There!" Brighty interrupted, sending a new wave of light across the ocean.

As soon as the brightness cleared, Rafe gripped the rail with both hands and leaned forward, straining to see what they all saw. The air was clear. There was no dragon, no hint of a leather wing, not even the barest ember in the sky.

"Archer," Captain called. "As soon as it emerges, attack. That's our best chance of catching it unaware."

The *ferro'kine* nodded, all focus and concentration, his magic ready to strike. A man-sized arrow hovered beside him as he ran for the back of the ship, gathering the chain on the way. Leech had spent the better part of a week growing enough wood to piece together the makeshift raft they'd attached to the aft deck so they could haul the dragon back to Da'Kin. It had been covered in a protective layer of metal that wouldn't burn, but doing so had used most of the ores on the ship, and unfortunately for them metal wasn't like wood—when it ran out, Archer couldn't simply grow more. The mage would have one arrow and one chance to catch his prey. If he missed, this dragon would do what all the others did at the first sight of danger and fly away.

"I have an idea," Rafe shouted.

The captain sighed loudly enough for the whole ship to hear. Beside him, Jolt winked encouragingly. Maybe he wasn't a scholar like his brother, but every so often, genius struck. Before he could tell them that genius idea, however, Pyro intervened.

"It's almost here!"

Rafe continued searching the curling tendrils of fog for the flash of wings. If not for Jolt leaning over and whispering a little direction in his ear, he might have missed it.

"Stop looking up," she murmured. "Not every marvelous thing drops out of the sky, you know. The sea has its wonders too."

He gasped. Where moments ago the ocean had been a deep midnight blue, still and clear beneath the force of Spout's magic, it now boiled. Bright aqua bubbles popped along the surface, large and slow at first, then faster and faster. A flash of orange burned within the shallows and then, before his eyes, flame and teeth and scales burst forth, emerging with a screech so piercing he stepped back as though struck. Leathery wings pumped, dispelling burning flecks of water that evaporated as soon as they hit the air. Billows of white heat spilled across the ship, burning them and blinding them as the dragon swept into the sky, nothing more than flashes of fire and darkness within the steam. Metal clinked as the arrow was released, but there was no responding cry. Archer had missed.

They'd lost. Unless…

"Everyone cover your ears," Rafe shouted above the chaos. "Now!"

Giving no more warning, he sucked in a breath and screamed. His raven cry echoed across the water, but unlike last time, the magic saturating the air around him didn't pause, only the dragon, which slowly became clearer and clearer as the winds blew the steam away. Seizing the moment, Archer turned the arrow around and shot it through the beast's wing. A grotesque crunch broke the silence. Rafe winced, recognizing the sound. The arrow had struck bone. Unlike the others, this dragon wouldn't get away, though he doubted it would quietly succumb either.

Time zipped forward as his cry dissipated and the dragon lurched back into motion, no longer held by the thrall. A blast of flame hurtled toward them, only to be swept away by Pyro's magic. Despite what must have been agonizing pain, the beast thrashed its wings, pulling against the chain latching it to the back of the boat. The telltale *crack* of splintering wood cut through the madness. Leech was there immediately, pressing his hands against the deck and fortifying the ship. Archer hurled more chains at the beast, which whipped them away with its tail. Brighty sent a blast of penetrating light into its stomach, earning a keening cry, as Shadow wrapped her darkness around its eyes.

For a moment, Rafe almost felt sorry for the dragon as Jolt rained lightning down from the sky, stunning the beast so it dropped onto the waiting raft. Dragons had killed his parents, and nearly him. Dragons had delivered him to Lyana's waiting arms. Dragons had ruined his life. And yet, for an instant, all he saw was another living thing wrapped in chains—its snout muzzled shut, its body tied down, its wings bent and broken. All he saw was another creature of the sky being forced into submission upon the sea.

The moment passed.

Spout crashed a wave upon its back, dousing the flames seeping through its scales. The best slumped against the raft, alive but unconscious, and Rafe remembered all the lives it would have claimed had it escaped. Dragons were the enemy, and this was war. There was no in-between.

Next stop, Da'Kin. A sudden sense of triumph flooded his chest. He could already feel the wind in his feathers and the welcome sting of crisp air against his cheeks. *Next stop, my wings.*

XANDER

I f the past few weeks had taught Xander anything, it was that he and Cassi made a good team. While she scanned the shelves, he studied the pages. As she read aloud, he took notes. When she started a sentence, he had a habit of finishing it. They were so thorough, in fact, that he felt as though he'd learned nothing aside from their own efficiency. For every argument he made, she had a perfect retort. In every theory he voiced, she found the crushing weakness. Round and round they went, in endless circles that left them nowhere. Though he had a mountain of notes about the magic and the isles and the mist, Xander felt no closer to rescuing Lyana than he had the day they'd stepped foot in Rynthos. The frustration was beginning to show.

"Cassi, you can't honestly believe this means nothing," he said, staring at her over the mound of unrolled scrolls sitting between them on the table and feeling slightly crazed. It took everything for him not to yank his hairs out as he smoothed his palm over the top of his head, pushing a stray lock back into place. "Every isle aside from the House of Peace has been shrinking, so slowly no one is noticing, but quickly enough that each map holds changes. It can't mean nothing."

"If it means something, then why is the House of Peace unaffected? Why would one isle remain the same while all the others changed?" She shrugged, crossing her arms and leaning back in her chair.

"Maybe it's Aethios," Xander suggested, leaning over the maps as he ran his finger around the outline of the inner isle of the dove kingdom, then brought it to a stop above the city of Sphaira. "His god stone is the most powerful and it protects their home, but the rest of us receive a diluted share." He tapped the parchment as the possibilities spun. "Maybe... Maybe he's losing strength, and our isles are bearing the brunt of the loss."

"For argument's sake, let's say you're right. Why does it matter?"

"Why..." He trailed off into silence as his eyes just about jumped out of his head. "Why does it matter? Our homes are dropping bit by bit into the Sea of Mist. I should think that's cause for some alarm."

"Why?" She shrugged, unimpressed. "If it's happening so slowly no one else can even tell, what's the big deal? We've been up here hundreds of years, and if the isles keep shrinking at this rate, we still have hundreds more to go before there's a problem."

"But...but..."

Xander released a frustrated breath and dropped into his seat. Letting his chin fall into his palm, he stared at the maps. Was she right? Was he looking for problems where there were none?

No. A nagging feeling poked at his thoughts, whispering something was there, something he was still missing. *It can't be nothing. It can't be.*

His thoughts drifted back to that day in the sacred nest, magic swirling invisibly through the grove, a current he'd been unable to see but had undoubtedly felt. The man, his two minions, and Lyana locked in a battle around him and not with him. Then the ground shaking, the ravens screeching, the cave cracking and snapping.

It wasn't a coincidence.

On instinct, he reached for his notes, scanned the list of executions, and cross-matched them against some of the larger earthquakes the owls had kept on record, then aligned those with the changes to the maps. Some dates overlapped, but they were associated with all different magics—some he and Cassi had been able to tie to the elements and some from sources still unknown. There was no clear pattern. Xander flicked his gaze to the maps, then back to the notes, then the maps, then the notes, over and over until the two began to blend. What if he'd been looking at this all wrong? What if it wasn't the type of magic that mattered, but the location?

He jumped to his feet.

"What?" Cassi tilted her head to the side, studying him.

Xander was too deep into his breakthrough to answer her. "This girl here, there was an earthquake in the House of Song around the same time her magic was made known. Where was she? Where did she live?"

"I don't..." Cassi swallowed, her brows knotting into a frown.

He grabbed a volume from across the table and flipped it to the page on her execution, then read aloud. "*First discovered in the city of Cytrene on the tenth day*—Cassi, do you see what this means?"

"No."

Was her voice strained? Xander paused for a moment, noticing her face had gone slightly pale. Fear, maybe? But fear of what? With a shake, he returned to his notes. There would be time for that later.

"What about this earthquake in the House of Flight? It says here, the man was first seen using magic in the heart of Abaelon. And here, this woman, in the House of Prey. It was the first earthquake recorded on their isle in nearly two hundred years. The second-born princess was found in possession of magic, which meant she lived with the royal family in Lantos. Has there ever been an earthquake in the House of Peace? Yes, one. It happened—" As his finger came to a stop beside the date, he found Cassi's eyes. Their color reminded him of molten metal churning in the kiln while the smithy stood watch, still deciding whether to form a dagger or a shield. For some reason, his voice dropped to a whisper. "It happened eighteen years ago, I'm guessing on the day Lyana was born."

"I heard talk of it as a girl," she said in a grave tone. "The people claimed it was Aethios showing his approval with a reminder of his might."

"Whenever people came into their magic close to the god stones, there were earthquakes," he said slowly, the discovery forming as he spoke. "We grew up learning to fear magic because it had once been used to enslave us, but what if there's more? What if magic challenges the very strength of the gods? What if that's why we've been taught to hate it and to fear it, to cast it out as soon as it's found? Because its presence weakens the very foundations of our world. We loathe Vesevios, but he's still a god. He must know this. And that must be why he sends people with magic to our world, why they took Lyana as soon as her full power came to fruition. The answer is so simple I don't know how it took me so long to see. That man didn't just want Lyana. He wanted to see our world come crashing down, and he was going to use his magic to do it."

"Then why—" The words came out jagged and torn. Cassi coughed, finding her voice. "Then why did he leave? If magic could so easily disrupt the might of the gods, why not stay in the sacred nest until Taetanos was defeated?"

"Because..." Xander's brows knotted as he stared at the maps again, information flowing even faster into his head than the waters to Taetanos's Gate. Was she right? Was he reading too far into things? Was this like all the other theories he'd spun, undone by a few of her carefully chosen words? "There were three people there, four if you count Lyana, all with magic. There are seven god stones. Maybe he needs three more people, one for each stone. Maybe they need to bring them all down at once. Maybe it wasn't the right time. Maybe...I don't know. Maybe..."

Cassi leaned forward, her forearms flattening the ridges of the scrolls as she stretched across the table, holding his gaze with unwavering ferocity. "Do you really think seven people could take down the gods? Even with magic? And do you really think Lyana would ever submit to their cause?"

She was right, of course. Lyana would never betray them like that. Xander knew her heart. Though she yearned for adventure, in the end she'd chosen duty. She'd placed his people and his kingdom above her love, above her desires, above her dreams. The fire god would never beat Aethios in the war for her affections. Her heart was too noble, too strong, and too stubborn to allow it.

Xander slumped back against his seat. He'd been so positive he was finally onto something, so sure he was on the right track, but did a few correlating dates actually lead to his conclusions? If he removed his heart and his yearning for answers from the equation, what did he have, really? Nothing, except a gut instinct and the awareness that his intuition had been wrong only a few times in his life.

"It's a good idea, Xander, really," Cassi continued, a bit of levity back in her tone, though it sounded forced to his ear. "We should look into it more. But we shouldn't get ahead of ourselves either. We need to base our arguments on facts, and we don't have enough of those to draw any sort of conclusion."

"I know," he murmured, still staring at the maps.

In his mind, the parchment had turned to a white blanket of fog stretching as far as the eye could see. There was a whole world beneath the mist, a world his people knew nothing about. Before that day in the sacred nest, he would have said it was nothing but barren rock and fire, perhaps an ocean of flames, inhospitable to life. Now, he wasn't so sure. If that man lived in the Sea of Mist, and the two other mages with him, there could be more. What if the silvery carpet weren't hiding an angry god, like they all believed—what if it were hiding that god's vengeful army instead?

"One option we haven't yet considered..." Xander said slowly. Cassi licked her lips and swallowed, giving him her full attention. "...is that the answers we seek aren't in these pages or our endless debates. They're waiting beneath the mist, and we have wings, don't we? Maybe we simply need to do some infiltrating of our own."

"Who would go? You? The crown prince with the weight of an entire kingdom on his shoulders?"

"No, of course not." Xander frowned. "I would send someone, a team—"

"No raven will risk Vesevios's wrath, especially not now, when they doubt you, your family, and your very reign."

"One raven would."

The words hung between them as though suspended in the air, thickening it until it became difficult to breathe.

"Rafe," Cassi finally whispered.

Xander nodded.

"But he's gone."

And where had he gone? That was another question that plagued Xander. His arrival in the House of Wisdom with Cassi instead of Lyana was something of a scandal, one he was sure the owl king had wasted no time in spreading to the rest of the isles in a fruitless effort to regain some of his lost respect. The rumors must have gotten out by now, yet Xander had been here for weeks, and there was still no word from his brother. If Rafe truly loved Lyana, he would know that nothing would have kept her from going on this journey with him, from exploring someplace new. He would know something was wrong. So…where was he?

Unanswerable questions were usually Xander's favorite kind, but this one hung in the back of his mind like an executioner's blade poised to strike. His head was on the chopping block, his thoughts the ones threaded with futile denial.

"There *is* one other option," Cassi spoke into the silence. "Me."

A sharp pang of fear suddenly shot through his chest. "You?"

"Yes, me," she said with a bit of self-righteous indignation. "You don't think I'm strong enough? You don't think I'm smart enough? You don't think I have more drive than anyone to find out what happened to my best friend?"

"Of course I do. It's just—just—"

I don't want you to go.

The thought came swift and sudden, like a palm slapping his cheek, leaving him reeling. He'd grown used to her presence by his side, the warm rumble of her voice, the subtle way she clicked her tongue when she scanned the shelves for a new book, the graceful movement of her fingers as they gently flipped the pages, the slight purse to her lips when she was lost within the words. He'd spent his entire life aware of the peace to be found in a library, yet here in Rynthos he'd discovered an even better sort of silence, the kind that existed between two souls perfectly in tune with one another, a rare sort of comfort that didn't need words.

"Just what?" Cassi pressed.

Xander opened his mouth to speak, but he didn't know what to say. They were friends—just friends. That was all they could ever be.

The words upon the maps and scrolls scattered across the table swam. He tried desperately to force the unfamiliar feeling down his right arm the way he'd done with so many other uncomfortable thoughts. But this time it wasn't anger or frustration or hate he was trying to ferret away. It was something bigger, the sort of force that could move mountains, an emotion even his invisible fist was unable to contain.

If Cassi saw his arm trembling, she didn't say. "Let me do this, Xander. I'm the perfect person. I have no house, no family, no place. No one will miss me while I'm gone. No one will even notice my absence."

"I might."

She sucked in a breath, the force of her eyes like a torch pressed against his cheek, burning with a fire he was too afraid to face. "Xan—"

The door behind them burst open, sending a piercing light into the darkness of the lantern-lit room. They both flinched and turned toward the intruder, an owl with the same black-and-white speckled wings as Cassi.

"Prince Lysander," the man announced, "a messenger has arrived from the House of Whispers with an urgent matter to discuss. I was told to fetch you immediately."

"Yes, of course." Xander stood, his heart still in his

throat despite the rush of relief washing over him. He'd take any emergency if it meant getting out of this room and away from those knowing silver eyes he still couldn't meet. "Excuse me, Cassi."

Without another word, he followed the man from the room and into the glowing amber dome of Rynthos, a city ablaze with activity. Tracking the hours underground was nearly impossible, though Xander assumed it was dinnertime based on the stirrings of so many wings in flight and the rumbling of his own stomach. They flew straight for the castle, not bothering to go through the front entrance, but instead soaring through the window to his guest quarters. The man departed with a quick bow, leaving Xander alone before his door.

For a moment, he wondered if maybe it was finally Rafe coming to call. The speed and haste would be so like his brother. The messenger, however, was not. Rafe would have ripped the library apart before allowing someone else to come fetch him.

With a sigh, Xander pushed the door open and stopped short. "Helen?"

She turned at the sound of her name, offering him a look as sharp as the daggers she so deftly wielded. "Can we speak freely here?"

"Yes." He shut the door and swiftly crossed the room, the tone of her voice making his features twist in concern. "I've discovered no spy holes or secret doorways. As far as I know, the room is sound."

"Good, because a lot has happened in your absence, my

prince. We have much to discuss before the night is done, and much to do before morning comes."

"What?" His heart thumped in his chest. "Helen, what?"

"Luka Aethionus brought an army to our doorstep. He arrived in Pylaeon this morning with a hundred armored doves to demand an audience with his sister. If we can't produce her, safe and unharmed, he promises the wrath of Aethios will descend upon us. Whatever time we thought we had is gone. You need to come home, now, before all is lost."

32

CASSI

uka. Luka. Luka. Cassi sighed. Well, as much as a spirit could sigh. It was more of a subtle wilting, the tendrils of her phantom body drooping lower and lower. As soon as Xander left, she'd slipped into her magic and followed him, just as surprised as he to find Helen waiting in his rooms with the last news she wanted to hear. *Valiant, brave, protective Luka. I should've known you'd ruin everything.*

She'd expected Lyana's family to be concerned as soon as they learned of her absence in the House of Wisdom. She thought they'd send a letter inquiring about her health, or perhaps a messenger, positive there would be some diplomatic back-and-forth before it got to this point. Never once had she expected Luka to arrive unannounced with an army at his heels, though she supposed that was one way to keep the peace.

Of course, Malek would want to hear of this immediately, but Cassi was in no rush to see him. She already knew exactly what he'd say. *This has gone on long enough. The doves can't learn of our plans. Kill the prince and come home. I'm tired of this game. Blah. Blah. Blah.*

He wasn't wrong, just predictable, and she still had one more move left to make. If they were leaving for the House of Whispers in the morning, then her time was well and truly up. Tonight was her last opportunity to sneak into the vaults.

Cassi snapped back into her body, returning to the dimly lit library room where a mess of scrolls, loose parchment, and bound volumes was piled high across the table. When she lifted her head from where it had been resting, a page stuck to her cheek. Peeling it away derisively, she glanced about the room. She couldn't leave it like this. The Cassi who was an orphan owl and loyal best friend to a missing princess would never abandon the curated notes upon which said best friend's life depended. The Cassi who was a spy with some thieving to do wanted to punch the first Cassi in the face. With a groan, she stood and started organizing. Books returned to shelves and scrolls to cabinets. The scattered parchments were bundled and neatly tied. There was no telling how long the process took, but when she finally doused the lantern fire and emerged from the room, the city of Rynthos was far quieter than before, which actually suited her needs just fine.

Using speed to her advantage, Cassi leapt from the platform and flew across the sleeping city, making straight for her rooms in the castle. After the notes had been carefully deposited beside her bed, she dug through her trunk for the item she'd hidden at the bottom—an archivist's robe. They were the senior guardians of the library, and the only ones allowed in the rooms she intended to visit. If she were confronted, of course, they'd know she was lying immediately. But she hoped that from a distance in those darkened halls, wearing the robe would deter notice. The members of the royal family were archivists by default, and she'd taken this from the prince's room the week before while everyone else was at dinner.

Cassi strapped two daggers to her hips, another to her right thigh and one to her left arm, then stuffed the flowing amber silks into a bag, which she slung over her shoulder. Her bow, unfortunately, would draw too much notice, and it stayed behind. There was no way to get out of the castle unseen, so she took the path of least resistance and jumped off the balcony, hoping any onlookers would assume she was doing the same thing she and Xander had done every other day they'd been there—venturing out for research.

She swooped across the city, gliding over rooftops and rock formations, watching lantern light flicker over stone. Only when she reached the farthest column from the castle at the far edge of the city did she stop, coming to a smooth landing on the steps carved into its side. Circling until the castle was out of view, she counted to fifty, but no one came. If a guard had been watching, they'd assume she found a door and stepped through. Instead, she put her hands to the rail and gracefully vaulted over it, arching her wings high in a death dive. Air sifted soundlessly through her feathers as she plummeted. The ground came up swiftly. With one strong pump, her body slowed and her feet dropped quietly to the stone. She remained crouched on the ground for a few moments, listening for voices or soft steps or the subtle whistle of wings in flight, but she heard nothing. Quickly she donned the robe and stood, pulling the hood low over her head as she made for the entrance to the tunnels a few yards away.

Mere steps into the labyrinth, she was swallowed by darkness. The archivists carried lanterns when they traversed these halls, following coded signs through the maze, but the risk of being seen was too great. Cassi would have to rely on memory alone. Every night in her dreams she'd studied the path. At the first fork, stay left. At the second, go right. At the next, stay straight. On and on, like a phantom in the shadows, only this body was real and the stakes were too.

At the first hint of a voice, she froze. With her owl eyes, it was easy to spot the dullest halo of lantern light coming closer. Pressing against the wall, she watched immobile as an archivist approached from the other end of the hall, nothing but one fork and one choice between them. Her fingers found a dagger, just in case. She held her breath as the woman paused and held the light to the sign, reading which way to go. The leather hilt grew warm against her palm.

Come on. Come on.

The archivist went left.

Cassi released her breath and remained still until the glow of the woman's lantern disappeared. After that, she moved quickly, her soft-soled shoes brushing against the stone, the swishing like the beat of flying wings. She ran into three more people after that, getting lucky the first two times with conveniently placed breaks in the tunnels. The third time, however, a man approached from behind, leaving her no other choice but to race ahead and pray he was too buried in his thoughts to notice the subtle changes left in her wake—the specks of dust stirred by her wings, the shift in the air, the scent of sweat, all drowned out, she hoped, by the loud clanging of his keys and the rustling of his robes. At the next fork, she hid in the shadows, waiting to see which way he would go. Leaving a body would only incur questions, something she hoped to avoid. When he went right, she continued down her path, until finally, it ended at a door.

Now for the fun part.

The doors this deep into the archivists' realm had not one but two locks, which needed to be opened at the same time with two different sets of keys. Perhaps unsurprisingly, incorporeal items were much easier to steal than the more banal kind. In the night, she stole secrets aplenty, but in her body, just taking the robe now draped over her shoulders had proved difficult. Securing one archivist's key, let alone two, would have been impossible. Instead, she crouched down and pulled two picks from her pocket. One in each hand, she jiggled, jabbed, and twisted, then jiggled some more, until—*click!*

Cassi eased the door opened and slipped inside. In total darkness such as this, even owls were blind. She didn't need a lot of light to see, but she did need some. It took a few moments of fumbling around with her palms pressed to the wall, but eventually, she found the lantern. Wasting no time, she rushed to the shelves in the corner, searching for the small, unobtrusive book she'd spotted a few nights before—a diary. Written in a language she couldn't understand, by a person she'd been unable to identify, in a time she'd been unable to ascertain, it could've seemed like an odd choice. But to Cassi, it was perfect.

Malek had other spies trained in the ancient languages their people had either lost to time or simply abandoned in order to keep consistent with the world above the mist. She had no doubt *dormi'kines* far more learned than she had spent hours in these rooms, floating over the shoulders of archivists, freely reading the secrets the owls worked so hard to protect. There was little written in these rooms her king didn't already know, but a diary contained all manner of unwritten things.

She'd been eight the first time she observed the *skryr* at work. He had been an old man even then, and the only of his kind still living. Malek had mentioned the mage in passing one dream, wondering, as any orphan would, if maybe he should make a visit to his shop near the outskirts of Da'Kin. The former king had left a multitude of items behind—swords and clothes and jewels. He'd believed there might be memories lingering in the worn threads, the scuffed boots, the polished gems, the sorts of messages only a *skryr* could read.

Cassi had wanted to ask if he had anything of his mother's, something that had maybe survived the fire, but she kept her mouth shut. It was easier, she thought, for Malek to simply erase the woman who'd birthed him beneath a barrage of dragon flames, into a life of prophecy her son had never wanted. Easier, at least, than forever asking questions that had no answers, which was, of course, what Cassi did. Who was her father? Where was he? Why had he gone? Did he know she existed? She'd tried once to ask her mother—but only once, those icy eyes enough to wipe her questions clean. Captain Rokaro was a strong woman, a proud woman, but the mention of that man had left her as defenseless as a child. Her walls had crumbled, leaving her bare and broken and bleeding. A moment later, they'd fortified, but that single vulnerable second had provided one kind of answer—whoever he was, he wasn't the sort of man Cassi should ever want to know. Still, curiosity was the enemy of logic, and she'd wondered if maybe there was a memory buried within her mother's things with all the answers she'd need.

Periodically, she'd visit the *skryr*'s shop, watching people as they came and went. They'd present their trinkets, and he'd take them in both hands. Sometimes, he managed to close his eyes. Other times, the visions came so swiftly, he sat there as his pupils darted back and forth, his white hair like a cloud stuck to his head, voluminous and slightly wild. It always seemed the closer to a person's soul the object was, the more deeply the man could see. A jacket that was just a jacket held little. A jacket that had been hand sewn by the wearer and embroidered with a special decoration or even a message held a whole world inside. The magic was sort of like Rafe's in a way—too rare to be fully understood. Malek was convinced it was a form of *chrono'kine* magic, or time warping, but Cassi thought maybe there was some spirit at play too. She of all people knew souls could exist outside of bodies—who was she to say a piece of a person couldn't linger behind in objects too?

At least, that was what she was hoping with this diary.

Hundreds of years had passed since the creator had perished, but what object held more of a person's soul than the one into which they'd poured their innermost hopes and dreams? None that Cassi could imagine. And if there was even a chance the *skryr* could see something that might help them defeat the dragons, she had to take it.

Cassi slipped the small book from the shelves and pressed her nose to the pages. To the simple mind, maybe dust was the only particle lingering in old parchment, dust and worn ink. But to the creative mind that dust held secrets, and as Cassi breathed it in, images flashed across her thoughts, of dragons and danger and dazzling magic, of prophecies and fallen worlds, of women with wings and men with power and the invisible strings stretched between them in a tangled mess called fate.

This diary had an important story to tell.

The only question left was which one.

With a sigh, Cassi closed the book and retied the worn leather binding, then slipped it inside her pack. The answers were waiting in Da'Kin, but first she had to make it out of Rynthos. Though she could have spent hours scouring the volumes lining the shelves, Cassi turned off the lantern and slipped from the room. When it came to thieving, the quicker the better. She wouldn't feel safe until she was back in her room with the diary tucked deep at the base of her trunk, ready to be smuggled from the city.

Her trip back through the labyrinth passed quickly. A few archivists crossed her path, but she snuck by unseen. It wasn't until she was almost at the end of the tunnels that a sight shocked her so thoroughly she stopped dead in her tracks. Her stomach leapt into her throat as her heart hammered. A hunched figure sat blocking her path. He hung his head between his bent knees, his crossed forearms providing a sort of pillow while his wings drooped along the floor. Even without seeing his face, she recognized him immediately. There was only one type of feather so black she could hardly make it out in the dark, and that feather belonged to a raven.

"Xander?" she hissed. "What are you doing here?"

His head snapped up immediately, but his gaze slid past her. Though he heard her, he couldn't quite find her in the shadows. "What am I doing here? What are *you* doing here?"

"Shh," she chastised as she yanked the stolen robe over her head and hastily stuffed it into her bag. When he started to stand, she crossed the distance between them and lowered her voice. "Someone might hear you. How'd you— I mean, why— I mean…Xander!"

"I was on my way to your room when I saw you soaring across the city, so I followed you. How was I supposed to know you'd go sneaking into the archivist's vault—which is, I might add, the only place in this city we've been expressly forbidden to enter. I tried to catch up to you, but I couldn't see a thing. I figured I'd sit and wait and hope I found you before you did something incredibly stupid. So, did I?"

"Did you what?"

"Find you before you did something incredibly stupid?"

"That depends on your definition of stupid."

"I'm not interested in a debate."

"Since when?"

"I already have one war banging on my door. I don't need one with the owls too. What were you looking for? Did you touch anything? Did you"—he gasped, as though the very thought were a scandal in itself—"did you *steal* something?"

"Of course not." Thank the gods lies came so easily to her lips. "And what are you talking about? A war?"

"That's why I was going to your room. The dove prince, he—"

Cassi clamped a hand over his mouth, silencing him as the jingle of keys made its way to her ear. "Someone's coming."

The echoes stemmed from a spot around the bend, the soft light of which had allowed her to spot Xander. They weren't far from the entrance of the tunnels, but if an archivist had just stepped inside, they had no chance to get out unseen.

To their right, only darkness waited. It wasn't far to the first fork in the hall, but could the two of them be quiet enough to hide? And if they were caught, what then? It was one thing to have an owl snooping around the vaults, even one as unwelcome as her, but it was another thing entirely to have the prince of a foreign realm sneaking around their most sacred corridors.

What to do? What to do?

Think, Cassi. Think.

Beneath her palm, Xander moved his lips as though to speak. She clasped his cheeks harder, trying to ignore the subtle brush of their skin, the way it almost felt like a kiss.

A kiss?

A kiss!

Cassi stumbled forward into Xander's chest and pushed him until his back hit the wall. With her hand still covering his mouth, she leaned close to his ear. "Don't say a word. Tuck your wings as close to your back as you can and hide your face against my neck. Please, trust me. Just go with it."

33

XANDER

At first, he had no idea what she was doing. Xander froze as her palm slid from his lips to his cheek, then up into his hair, gripping the back of his head. Her other hand clutched his chest, pulling him closer even as she pressed him against the wall. The uneven stones pushed uncomfortably into his feathers, but he jammed his wings as tightly together as he could, following her lead.

"Ca—"

"Shh," she whispered, her breath brushing over his open mouth, leaving him warm and tingling.

In the darkness, he couldn't see her face, but knowing she was right there did something to his blood he couldn't quite explain. Her nose grazed his, the brief contact making his heart lurch. The subtle shuffle of feathers was the only clue he had that she was lifting her wings, stretching them high and wide, like a curtain to shield his body. Then he understood.

She's protecting me.

"Put your left arm around my waist, and hide your right one between us."

He listened, sliding his hand across her slender back and trying to ignore how natural the gesture felt as he held her close. Despite the clothes between them, his body warmed with a heat he tried desperately to suppress, a feat that proved impossible as she gently arched his head so his face nuzzled her neck. He folded his lips into his mouth to keep from kissing her skin, swallowing a gulp as she positioned herself in the same manner, not taking the same precaution. Her breath washed over him like an undulating tide, stirring memories of the vivid dream he'd been unable to shake, of the two of them sitting side by side on a sandy shore.

Velvet-soft lips brushed against him while she spoke. "When I give you the signal, run."

Then she sighed. He was so close he felt the subtle vibrations work their way up her throat, a tingle slipping down his spine in response. The light in the corridor brightened enough for him to discern the golden glow playing softly against her skin, the loose hairs in her braid flashing bronze. She sighed again, wriggling gently against him. He bit his lips to stifle a very real groan.

Pull yourself together.

She's only acting.

This is pretend.

Then why did it feel so real? Why could he feel her pulse racing beneath his nose, the *drum, drum, drum* moving faster with each passing second? Was he only imagining that the hand she still held against the base of his neck was growing warmer?

Cassi sighed again.

Just as he was about to lose himself in the lie, a giggle spilled from her lips, so high-pitched and girlish he barely contained the laugh surging up his throat. She pinched the back of his neck in response, which only made his body shake more. She giggled again, but this time her body trembled with true mirth, the sound a deep rumble in her throat.

What in Taetanos's name was happening?

This was ridiculous. This was absurd. This was perhaps the most fun he'd ever had while breaking the rules.

A stern cough interrupted their rendezvous, and they froze. Again, Xander wasn't sure what was real and what was fake, but he was suddenly reminded that he was a prince trespassing on foreign grounds. His heart thundered, no longer with passion or pleasure, but fear. The doves were already furious with him and his kingdom. The ravens couldn't afford to earn the owls' ire too.

Gods alive, what was I thinking following her in here? I should've waited in her rooms. I should've stayed outside. When did I lose my sense? What if this man recognizes me?

What would Lyana think?

That last rambling thought took him by surprise. What *would* Lyana think? Did she have a right to think anything when he'd caught her with his brother the night before their mating ceremony? That had been real. This was just pretend. Wasn't it? Or was it? Did that even matter? Lyana had been kidnapped. She was trapped in some foreign world with an evil man. And he was here, pressed up against her best friend, feeling things no mated man should feel with another woman. What was he doing? What—

Cassi touched her lips to his neck, a kiss so soft he might have imagined it if the shape of her mouth hadn't lingered on his skin, the spot burning as though hot iron had pressed against him. Before he could do anything, she shoved him to the side as she spun around, twisting her wings so they crashed into the archivist and sent his lantern skidding across the stones.

Xander ran.

Muffled voices followed him, one angry and one frightened, a sure sign Cassi was playing her part well. When he burst through the exit, he stayed low, sprinting for the nearest column. Luckily, the city was still in that quiet part of night. The streets close by were empty, but taking to the air would be too noticeable. Having always lived as one raven among many, he found it strange to be in a place where his wings were so conspicuous. Funnily enough, Cassi must have had the same feeling now too, except for the first time in her life she blended in.

Rather than stand out in the open, he hid inside a library room, leaving the door slightly ajar while he waited for her to reappear. Before long, she emerged from the tunnel, her black-and-white speckled wings stark against the russet backdrop.

"Psst," he whispered as she neared. "Psst."

She found him immediately, needing no more prompting than the briefest whisper, reminding Xander once again of her lethal grace. Though she stepped easily, a slight sway to her hips, those eyes couldn't hide their cunning. Cassi was sharp, and he'd do well to remember that, especially with the doves knocking on his door, people to whom she owed far more loyalty than to him.

As she approached, he slinked back into the shadows of the room, remaining out of sight while she slipped inside. Despite the hint of light seeping in beneath the door, he couldn't see anything until she flicked on the lantern. Leather-bound books and cramped shelves surrounded them, the same as every day before, yet something felt different. He couldn't quite say what.

"Are you all right?"

"I'm fine." Cassi waved the question away. "The old man suspected nothing. I blubbered and apologized like a frightened little girl, so he gave me a lecture and moved on with his day. He didn't see you. And something about the dry way he spoke made me certain we weren't the first young lovers found in the tunnels late at night, just as I'd hoped."

"Good thinking."

"I try." She grinned, lighthearted and perfectly herself, though he couldn't help but notice the smile didn't reach her eyes. "So why were you trying to find me?"

"Why were *you* in the tunnels?"

"We're back to this?"

"Cassi."

"Fine." She sighed, her shoulders caving in. Dejection racked her body and she slumped against the wall. Xander eased onto the table behind him, careful to keep a distance between them. It made thinking so much easier. "I was trying to get into the archives. Is that what you want to hear?"

"No."

"Look, Xander. I know it was stupid and reckless and that I could've gotten into a lot of trouble. But if there was even a chance that I could uncover something that might help us find Lyana, I had to take it. Don't you understand that? I *had* to."

He closed his eyes, his anger wilting.

"When that owl came saying you had a messenger, I just knew it was bad news from home. I just knew tonight was my last chance to find something, anything, that might help us, and I had to take it. And I was right, wasn't I? We're going back to the House of Whispers, aren't we? Something's happened? You mentioned Luka?"

Interesting that she addressed the dove prince so informally. Xander stored that information away as he tried to steer the conversation back to his questions, her attempt at changing the subject not unnoticed. "Did you touch anything in the vaults, Cassi? Did anyone see you? Did you—"

"No," she cut him off gruffly. "I found a few doors, but they were all locked, and I was so deep into the tunnels I could hardly see a thing. Before I got lost, I made my way back out, which is when I ran into you."

Xander eyed the lumpy bag hanging near her hip. "What's in that?"

"A cloak. I thought I might be able to pass it off as an archivist robe in the darkness of the tunnels if I got caught."

"And that's all?"

With a dramatic sigh, she slipped the strap over her head and held out the bag to him. "You can check it if you don't believe me. I didn't take anything, Xander. I would tell you if I found something. We've been in this together from the start. Why would I start lying now?"

Why indeed...

She was doing everything right—the tone of her voice, the challenging gesture, as though she was daring him not to trust her. But that was the problem. He did trust her. He'd never had any reason to doubt her until now, and it was for no reason at all. It was just a feeling that her lips and her eyes were at war, and he didn't know which one to believe.

"No," he finally said. "No, I believe you. Of course I believe you. I'm just overwhelmed, I guess. The messenger tonight was Helen."

"Helen?" Her spine straightened and she stood alert, taking a step toward him as her eyes widened with surprise. Again, he couldn't help but feel as though she was simply going through the motions, as though there was an emptiness to her gaze. "What's Helen doing here? How is Luka involved?"

"The dove prince is camped outside Pylaeon with an army of a hundred men, demanding to see his sister. That's why I was summoned. We return to the House of Whispers at dawn."

"Oh, Luka." She dropped her forehead into her palms, shaking her head. "He's worried. I know him, Xander. He's not trying to start a war. All his life, he's protected Lyana, mostly from herself, and now she's gone. He's afraid, and he doesn't know how to handle it." With a soft groan, she dropped her arms back to her sides and looked up. "What are you going to do?"

"I—" Xander paused, frowning. "I don't actually know. We haven't discussed it yet. I wanted to find you first, so you'd have a chance to pack your things before we leave. Helen and I were going to figure out a plan after I got back. How long have we been gone?"

She grimaced. "Long."

"I should—I should probably go. Helen must be worried."

"You go. I'll wait here for a little while so no one sees us together, just in case."

"Good idea."

He didn't move. She didn't either. The air prickled with an awkwardness that had never existed between them before, the sort that came with crossing lines that weren't supposed to be crossed. They'd been faking. Those illicit moments in the tunnels were nothing but a ruse. Yet he still felt the outline of her lips on his throat, and he wondered if there was an invisible brand on her body too, one he didn't even realize he'd left behind.

Xander rubbed at the tingling spot on his neck, as though to wipe it clean. Cassi hugged her arms around her middle, and he suddenly remembered his fingers digging into the soft curve of her waist as he held her close. Chest tight, he looked away.

"Xander?"

"Yes?"

"I didn't— Before, I mean. I didn't—"

"I know."

"I was worried what might happen if you got caught."

"I know."

"It didn't mean anything."

"Of course not."

But it did. And they both knew it. Because that gentle kiss she'd pressed against his skin hadn't been part of a game. It was a stolen moment that had to stay buried in the dark.

He lifted his head, surprised to find a watery sheen to her eyes. Suddenly the hollowness in her voice became clear. She hadn't been lying. She'd been trying to face him while holding back tears. It was Cassi's turn to glance away.

"You should go," she said.

So he did.

34

CASSI

She was crying. Gods alive—magic alive—whatever damned curse in either world combined—why, oh why was she crying? Cassi wiped angrily at her cheeks, trying to stop the tears, but it was no use. They kept on coming. For weeks, she'd been stuffing her feelings away, pushing them down and down and down to the very tips of her toes, and now they were erupting with the unforgiving force of a volcano. It wasn't just Xander. It was Lyana, and Rafe, and Malek, and the sense that her world was crashing in all around her. Ever since that day at the edge of the House of Whispers, when she watched Malek sail away with her hopes and her dreams, she'd been struggling to maintain her control, balancing her problems like a stack of cards, using denial and excuses to keep the pieces afloat. One wrong move and the whole thing would cave in. Tonight, she'd made that move.

I never should've kissed him.

It wasn't even a kiss, really. Her lips hadn't touched his

347

lips, just the barest brush of skin. She didn't know why she'd done it, only that he'd been there, and so close, and she'd wanted to. She hadn't even thought he would feel it, but then his entire body had gone stiff, and she'd known she'd made a mistake. A horrible, horrible mistake. Because in that moment, she hadn't been Cassi, the grieving owl, or Kasiandra, the deceiving spy. She'd been the girl with no name, the one stuck in the middle with no best friend and no king and no loyalties aside from the wishes in her heart, and she'd wanted him to see her.

But that was ridiculous.

Because she was Cassi. She was Kasiandra. And what exactly would Xander see if he knew the real her? The woman who mutilated his brother? The woman who spent her entire life lying to his mate? The woman who helped a foreign king infiltrate his kingdom? The woman who was helping to destroy his whole world?

She'd told Malek she refused to kill Xander because he was good, because she didn't want to be a killer, because she wanted to be better. Lies. Xander was good, but so were the thousands of people hidden within the mist whom his very existence put at risk. And while she didn't want to be a murderer, it was a line she'd tiptoed before. The first time she'd met Rafe he'd been at the wrong end of her arrow, and she would have released it to protect Lyana if her friend hadn't ordered her off. So that left being a better person— better than whom? Malek? The dragons? The man with his head on an executioner's block? Good and evil were malleable concepts. In the world above, magic was a felony.

In the world below, it was a saving grace. There was no right and wrong.

The truth was far simpler, so simple, in fact, she'd been able to ignore it until the moment when her lips pressed softly against his skin and her heart pounded in her chest, with his arm wrapped around her waist and his breath against her neck, with their bodies so close there was no room left for denial. No noble reason stood behind her refusal to kill Xander. It was selfish—perhaps the most selfish thing she'd ever done. She didn't want to kill him because that day in Pylaeon, while the city burned around them, he'd held her close, much like tonight, and for a brief second in his arms, she'd felt worthy—of being saved, of being loved, of being seen—and she didn't want to let that feeling go. To Malek, she was a weapon. To Rafe, an enemy. To Lyana, a traitor. To Luka, a liar. To her mother, a sacrifice. To her father, nothing. But to Xander, she was worthwhile—and if she killed him, even if it was over quickly, with his dying breath he'd know he'd been wrong. And so would she.

It was a pretty poor reason to risk the fate of the world. She didn't need Malek to tell her so, just as she didn't need him to tell her what to do next. Xander had to die. Cassi needed to kill him, and Helen, and the queen. She needed to keep the truth from spreading before more avians decided it was time to explore the lands beneath the mist. And when all the murders were done, she'd take this diary to her king and go home.

Sucking in a breath, Cassi wiped her cheeks dry, then swallowed the knot in her throat. Once she was composed, she slipped from the library room and took to the streets, in no hurry to return to the castle. She walked and walked and walked, each step slow and steady, her thoughts a thousand miles away. The gentle *thud* against her ribs was the only reminder that she had a heart, though it felt like nothing more than a yawning void. The plan came together quickly —so quickly she couldn't help but wonder if maybe it had been in the back of her mind all along.

Tomorrow night, she'd be back in Pylaeon with Xander, Helen, and the queen.

Tomorrow night, while the rest of the city slept, she'd make her move.

35

RAFE

They arrived in Da'Kin in the dead of night, enshrouded by thick charcoal fog, a thin sliver of mage light guiding them through the dark. Brighty stood next to Captain at the wheel and whispered directions, her *photo'kine*-enhanced sight able to pick up the dull beacon far better than anyone else's. Their orders had been to take the dragon directly to a warehouse floating at the edge of the city where the king would be waiting.

Rafe wasn't surprised by the need for so much secrecy—it wasn't every day a dragon showed up in chains. The display would have caused a stir. The gods, he'd been staring at the beast for the better part of a week, and even he couldn't quite believe his eyes. Every morning, he woke expecting to learn it had escaped. Archer hardly slept for fear of the metal loosening. Pyro kept a near-constant watch for wayward flames. Brighty, too, seemed a bit more on edge than usual. He'd caught her glancing over her shoulder more than once, same as he, their eyes drawn to the eerie orange glow sifting through the fog.

Even now, a shiver ran down his spine at the sight of the fiery hues trailing behind the ship. The dragon's body burned with an inner heat no amount of ocean water could douse. Spout tried, again and again, but no matter how many waves crashed along the creature's back, the blaze returned, seeping through its scales, brighter with each breath, as though its skin contained liquid fire. Leech was itching to take samples. Rafe had seen the *agro'kine* stand at the stern with a vial in his palm and a longing look in his eyes more than once, but Captain forbade it. The dragon was for the king alone.

Rafe, for one, couldn't wait to be rid of it.

My wings. My wings. For the past few days, he'd been repeating the words like a prayer, to keep his mind focused and his heart steady, but now they brought a giddy lightness to his chest. *It's almost time to get back my wings.*

He left the dragon behind and turned toward the city, catching the hint of shadows through the mist. As they neared, the hazy outlines gradually sharpened. Four figures stood before a looming warehouse, their faces lit by mage light. One was clearly a *photo'kine*. His palm glowed a brilliant white, and beneath his flopping crimson hair, he had the same milky eyes as Brighty. Next to him was the sharp-faced *ferro'kine* Rafe recognized from his brief meeting with the king. He wouldn't soon forget the face of the woman who'd forcibly dragged him through the halls, metal binds digging into his wrists and ankles as he stumbled behind her. The other two he didn't know. One was a short woman with brown hair in a knot atop her head. The other was an older man with wrinkled olive skin.

Rafe leaned closer, frowning as he searched for another form in the shadows outside the halo of light, but there was no one else.

Where the gods was the king?

If he didn't come—

If he doesn't show—

No. Stop.

Rafe squeezed his eyes shut, forcing his doubts to the bottom of the sea. They had a deal. He'd get his wings back. The king was there, somewhere. And if he wasn't, Rafe would rip this city apart to find him.

"Rafe," Patch bellowed across the deck in his deep voice. "How about you quit staring and make yourself useful?"

With a sigh, Rafe pushed off the rail and hurried to help with the sails. It was strange to think that there had been a time when he could hardly stand on the ship, his feet unable to adjust to the constant rolling of the sea. Now he sidled up the nets without problem, loosening knots and retying them. Squirrel dropped a line down to him, and he passed it down to Jolt, no words required as they worked. When he jumped back onto the deck, he didn't need to wait for orders. Brighty stretched her arm back without even looking, expecting his presence, and Rafe took the rope and tied it to the cleat. Together, they hefted one of the thicker ropes over the edge and tossed it to the mages waiting on the dock. Within minutes, the ship was secured.

As soon as the gangplank was lowered, Captain and

Patch marched to the waiting mages. Rafe itched to run after them, but he knew when he wasn't wanted. Instead, he took his spot by the rails, leaning his forearms against the damp wood as he stared, not bothering to hide his interest. They spoke in hushed tones, their gazes ever so often darting to the ship or the dragon floating just behind it, but never once landing directly on him.

Where is the king?

Why isn't he here?

Brighty nudged him with her shoulder as she took the spot next to him. "You sure about this?"

"As sure as I've ever been about anything."

"Because I like you just fine without the wings."

A smile played over his lips as he turned to consider her, but she kept staring at the docks. "How do you know you won't like me better with them?"

"Eh." She shrugged. "I've gotten used to this whole grumpy, forlorn, completely lost aura you give off. I'm not sure I could handle a peppy version of you."

He snorted. "Don't worry. You have nothing to fear. My wings were the least of my problems."

"I meant what I said." She finally glanced at him, a quick there-and-gone before he could read the emotion in her eyes. "We'll always have room on this ship for you, if you need it."

"Brighty—"

He stopped short as Jolt sidled up next to Brighty, a bit of lightning crackling between her folded palms as she also leaned over the rail to stare at the meeting going on below. Leech took the spot next to her, and before long, the entire crew was lined up, eavesdropping unabashedly on what was clearly meant to be a private conversation.

"What do you think they'll do with it?" Pyro asked, a hint of sadness in her tone.

Rafe understood why. A solemn mood had followed them across the sea like a storm they couldn't outrun, leaving a heavy feeling in the air. Killing a dragon was no kindness, but for some reason, this felt worse. High in the sky with flames barreling up its throat, the beast had seemed unstoppable, but bound and broken, it seemed just as vulnerable as any other living thing. Rafe didn't like to think of what fate they'd doomed it to.

"Tests, I'm sure," Leech finally said, somewhat wistfully. He had the decency to look sorry as they all glared at him, but nothing could dull the intrigue in his eyes. "Probably using magic, first, to see how the dragon interacts with the different elements. I'd imagine they'll take samples of its scales and wings and blood. My guess is, it'll be dead before long, and that's when things will get truly interesting. I'd want to dissect it as soon as possible. They'll probably remove the organs one by one, starting with the heart and the lungs in search of the fire source, but personally, I'd be more interested in cutting along the stomach to release the bowels—"

"I think I'm going to be sick," Spout interrupted, clapping a hand over her mouth.

"Here we go again," Brighty muttered.

"What? Why? All I said was I'd want to release the bowels to search the intestines for evidence of a food source."

"Leech," Jolt cut in, bumping him with her hip. "You're a madman."

"I'm a scientist."

Brighty met Rafe's gaze and whispered, "Is there a difference?"

"I heard the king likes to bathe in dragon blood."

Silence descended as they all spun to gape at Squirrel, who was perched on the net above their heads, eyes wide with the wonder of youth.

"Oh, magic alive," Brighty grumbled. "Where'd you hear that?"

"At the brothels in Ga'bret."

"What were you doing at the brothels in Ga'bret?" Jolt snapped her face to the side. "Archer, he's only twelve."

"Don't look at me," the *ferro'kine* said, holding his hands up in defeat. "I didn't take him."

"Who did?" The lightning at Jolt's fingertips crackled.

She played the seductress so often Rafe forgot it was just a ruse to hide her more vulnerable, nurturing side. There was an unwritten rule on this ship not to ask for what people didn't want to offer, but he had a feeling that if he pried, her history would reveal far more torment than she ever let on. He could see it in the way she sometimes combed her fingers through Squirrel's hair, a hint of longing mixed with the anguish of loss.

"Cook took me."

"Cook!"

"Wow." Brighty nudged him with her elbow. "I didn't see that one coming. It's always the silent ones."

"He said I was old enough to see a naked woman if I wanted to, and I used my own money. I'm allowed."

"The boy's got a point."

"Shh!" Pyro interrupted. "Captain's—"

"Here?" The sardonic drawl made them all jump. Captain Rokaro was back on the ship, standing behind them with her hands on her hips and her brows raised. "What did I ever do to deserve such an astute, hard-working crew?" She shook her head with a snort and stared at the boy still dangling in the nets. "Squirrel, you're not old enough to see a naked woman until she'll show you her body for free. If you need to coerce her, you're doing it wrong. I'll have a word with Cook. Now, the rest of you, listen up. Rafe, Brighty, Archer, and Pyro, come with me. The rest of you, stay with Patch and take the ship to her normal spot. We have a few things to settle here, and then we'll meet you on foot."

No one moved.

Was she done? Was there more?

Sometimes it was difficult to tell.

After a moment, Captain leaned forward, the colorful fabric swaths in her hair falling over her shoulders as she jerked her chin to the side. "What are you all standing around for? Go!"

They scattered like roaches in sudden light.

Rafe and Brighty got to the gangplank first, with Pyro and Archer not far behind. Captain waited a moment, making sure everything was in order, before she stomped after them. At the bottom, the king's mages waited, faces carefully blank, though he caught a hint of disdain in them.

The difference between their two sides couldn't have been more obvious—one rigid and controlled, their formal stances a mirror of each other, and the other loose and relaxed, with the swagger of rebellion. Rafe wasn't quite sure where he fit. In the world above, he'd been a study of constraint, constantly fighting to blend in, always worried he might say the wrong thing, afraid of the one moment when he'd reveal too much. In the world below, he'd learned a different way, a freer way that came from not having to hide.

As they stopped, Brighty leaned her elbow against his shoulder as if he were a doorframe and cocked her hip. Pyro crossed her arms, seemingly bored. Archer offered a slanted grin, as though fighting to hold back a secret.

"Jacinta," he offered sweetly.

The *ferro'kine* curled her lip, her features exactly how Rafe remembered—all severity, sharp edges and stark contrast, her bangs harsh against pale skin, her pointed chin acting as a frame. "Archer."

"Kal," Brighty said next, a bit of a challenge to her tone, though Rafe didn't miss the way she smiled. There was nothing the woman thrived on more than confrontation.

"Brighty." The *photo'kine* grinned, a dimple digging into his freckled cheek, then glanced at Rafe. "Who's your friend?"

"We call him Scowl."

"No, you don't." Rafe eyed her strangely, but before he could say more, Captain intervened.

"Brighty, Archer, Pyro, Rafe," she said, pointing at each in turn. "This is Jacinta, Kal, Isaak, and Nyomi, though I think most of you know each other already. Let's get it over with. I'm ready for a shot of dragon's breath and a warm bed."

"I'll handle the dragon," Jacinta said icily.

"You sure you don't want help?" Archer asked, a taunting current laced through the words.

She slid her gaze toward him, as though expelling any more energy than that would be a waste. "I'm the king's head *ferro'kine* for a reason."

"Let me guess," Brighty cut in. "Your charming personality?"

"Just stay out of my way."

Captain glared at Brighty and shoved Archer toward the warehouse. Clearly, there was a backstory here Rafe wasn't privy to, though Pyro didn't seem to have the same reservations. She looped her arm through Isaak's and held up her other hand as red magic sparked along her fingertips. An orange ball hurtled over the side of the ship and raced across the darkness to land in her palm. The fire expanded until it encased most of her bare arm, stopping just short of her sleeve. The older man offered her a friendly look as he dipped his fingers into the flames and pulled a burning ember free, bringing a matching glow to his palm.

The final mage had already walked away, leaving Rafe no clue as to what her magic might be. With a shrug, he followed Archer, Brighty, and Captain toward the warehouse, then helped them pull open the massive wooden doors. Inside, Brighty sent a dozen ivory flares across the room, leaving the mage light suspended in the air to illuminate the space, though the effort was hardly worth it.

No one was there—no king, no other mages, nothing at all, except for a few unopened crates piled in the corners. Where was he?

By the time Rafe glanced back at the doors, the dragon was already halfway there, its body floating on a wave of evergreen magic, carried aloft by the metal binds. He forced himself to watch even as a hollowness grew inside his heart. Despite their fears, they had no trouble moving the beast inside. In just a few minutes, Jacinta was done. The dragon didn't fight, didn't struggle. Its enormous chest just rose with resigned breath, the dust along the floor kicking up before its nostrils. The molten heat churning within its veins did little more than cast a fiery glow upon the four walls and roof now encasing it. Pyro almost looked disappointed. The enthusiasm in her eyes dampened along with the flames at her fingers, and she dropped her arm down by her side.

"That's it?" Brighty asked. "I mean, it's a little anticlimactic."

"You say that like it's a bad thing," Archer commented.

"Pyro, back me up."

"Enough," Captain cut in. "The king has his dragon. Tell him my crew and I are taking a few days to regroup. I think we've earned it."

With those words, a warm thrill shot down Rafe's chest as anticipation swarmed like a hive of bees through his veins, making his skin buzz. He'd done it. He'd actually done it. He'd brought the king a dragon, and now it was the king's turn to make good on his end of the deal.

"What about my wings?" Rafe asked. *My wings. My wings!* "Where's the king?"

"He wanted to be here to fulfill his end of the bargain, but urgent matters intervened," Jacinta said. "He's expecting you at the castle. There's a boat waiting out back. If you'll follow Nyomi, she'll take you." The *ferro'kine* jutted her chin toward the other woman, who stood waiting by a door. "To the rest of you, it's been a pleasure."

That final word sounded as though it had been torn from her throat by force. Archer laughed softly as she walked away, while Brighty wrinkled her nose. Rafe turned toward the captain, a knot in his throat that hadn't been there a moment before. He had only just realized this was goodbye. What would he say to her? How could he thank her?

"Captain Rokaro, I—"

"Save it," she said, holding up her hand. "I'm too tired and too cranky for this right now. We'll be docked for a few days. Come to the ship before you leave so everyone can gawk at you. I think they'd enjoy seeing a person fly. I know I would."

Relief flooded through him. His entire life had been one massive goodbye. He wasn't ready for another quite yet. Instead, he grinned. "Aye, aye, Captain."

"Archer, Pyro, with me. Brighty, we won't wait long."

As they walked off, Brighty clutched his arm and yanked him down so she could whisper in his ear. "I don't like this."

"Do you like anything?"

"I mean it, Rafe. I have a bad feeling about this." She

relaxed her grip just enough to stare imploringly into his eyes. That alone should have made him pause, but it didn't. All Rafe could think about were his wings, and the sky, and putting this one broken piece of himself back together. "Why didn't the king come himself? And don't tell me you believe some crap about an urgent matter. Why isn't he here like he said he'd be? And why do you have to go to him? Why won't he come to you?"

"Do you really think he ever goes to anyone? I only met him once, but he didn't seem the type."

"That's beside the point," she grumbled, her pleading expression turning to a glare. "The point is, I know you like to act first and think later, but maybe, just this once, use your head. Why is the king doing this? Why? He always has ulterior motives, Rafe—always."

"I know, Brighty," he said as he gently disentangled her fingers from his jacket. A longing no one of this world could ever understand filled him as he caught sight of the captain's caramel feathers. He was a bird. It was who he was, who he'd always be, and the sky was calling. "I know, and I don't care. I need my wings. I *need* them. I'll deal with the rest later."

Brighty squeezed his hands, words hovering on her lips and clogging her throat, the need to say them dancing across her opal eyes. She was worried, and she hated it, which was why, in the end, she dropped her arms and let him go. "Fine. But don't say I didn't warn you."

"Cheer up," he teased. "You're almost free of me."

"Ain't that the truth." She rolled her eyes and pushed him away. "Go, you big oaf. But you better come say goodbye, or I'll hunt you down. I don't care if you can fly. I'll find you."

He pressed a hand to his chest. "I'm honored."

"Just go."

A laugh was on his lips as he ran across the room to where Nyomi waited, holding the door open as he approached. He was still smiling as she led him down a dark hall and then back outside, where the mist welcomed him like an old friend. The smile faded the second he realized there was no boat waiting on the waves.

"Hey—"

Salt water slammed into his face, cutting off the question as it drove him stumbling back. The pressure was relentless. Liquid clung to his arms and legs, wrapping around his body. No matter how hard he fought, he couldn't break free of the current. Lost in the maelstrom, he fell back, only to be caught by another surging wave. He rolled with the flood, weightless and directionless, tumbling in the river, until his back crashed into something hard.

All at once, the water released him and he dropped, feeling rough planks beneath his hands as he fought to stand. The creak of a door closing drew his attention, and he spun just in time to see the last bit of light disappear, leaving him in darkness. Rafe ran to the door, searching for a knob, but it was smooth, without even a scratch into which to dig his nails.

"What is this?" he screamed. "What are you doing? Where's the king?"

No response.

"We had a deal!" He banged his fist against the wood. "We had a deal!"

Silence.

He kicked and shoved and yelled with all his might, but it did nothing to stop the heavy bolt from sliding into place, locking him inside.

LYANA

Malek was later than usual that morning. By the time he walked in, Lyana was already seated at her desk with a perfect sphere of water floating in the air before her eyes. Perhaps if she'd been able to do as he'd asked and separate her magic from her mind, to build a wall between her emotions and her power, his sudden appearance wouldn't have bothered her. As it was, the moment he strode through the door she jumped in her seat and the globe of water burst, splashing her in the face.

"Where have you been?" she asked as she wiped the droplets from her cheeks.

"That was good," he said, ignoring her question. "Do it again."

"Malek—"

"After. I promise, I'll explain everything after."

When he approached, she couldn't help but notice his pale skin seemed alive with color, the flush bringing a certain sparkle to his midnight eyes, as if the mist had cleared to reveal a starry sky. His blond hair was in disarray, both falling over his forehead and standing atop his head as though caught in a breeze.

Questions stirred at the back of her throat, but Lyana swallowed them. *Later*, she thought. *I'll ask him later.*

With a sweep of his hands, the water splattered across the table lifted in a flash of gold and returned to the bowl. Malek sat, pressed his elbows against the table, rested his chin on his folded hands, and watched her. The look on his face, ripe with so much expectation, made her stomach flutter.

Separate it, she chided herself. *Cut off my emotions.*

Lyana concentrated on the bowls, closing her eyes and reopening them to welcome her spirit vision, so the world shifted into an array of elemental colors. Then she called on her magic. The power responded immediately, dancing along her fingertips as her awareness extended beyond her. Malek's soul whispered, lonely and aching, yet rigid and strong, pushing her away before she even had a chance to reach out. There wasn't time to linger on why, as the souls outside her window called, yearning for her healing touch.

No. No. No.

The surge broke like a wave crashing over her, but Lyana fought to keep the water back, building a dam inside her mind, cutting off her heart and her soul, focusing only on the magic thrumming beneath her skin and the power alive inside her. The sensation left her cold yet tingling, as though she were back in her homeland high above the clouds, where the air was crisp enough to burn as she drew it into her lungs. She felt just as barren as that tundra, nothing but ice and rock, a proper queen bred of snow, no longer the warm and carefree princess of her youth.

As she stared at the blue spirals of water sitting still inside the bowl, the spirit between gradually came into view, subtle flashes of gold and silver like oscillations of light from the sun and the moon. She grabbed hold and commanded that essence to move. The liquid responded, trapped within the spirit, hers to do with as she willed. Ever so slowly, the water conjoined in a perfect sphere and rose to hover in the space between her and Malek, their eyes meeting briefly over the churning globe.

"Good," he said, no smile, no enthusiasm. "Now the fire, too."

Furrowing her brows, Lyana divided her attention once more, keeping some on the wall around her heart, some on the water, and some on the fire as she reached for that heat and tugged a loose flame into the air, letting it blaze beside the water.

"Now earth."

Again, Lyana stretched her senses, fighting for control as she dipped her power into the green-flecked soil and commanded it to rise. An *agro'kine* could have touched the seed hidden within and commanded it to grow, but her magic couldn't penetrate the plant itself, just the spirit hidden all around it, so rather than green stalks and leaves, a crumbly circle of dirt joined the other two elements in the space above the table.

"Now air."

Taking a deep breath, Lyana focused on the subtle yellow sheen circulating within the fourth and final bowl.

All she had to do was grasp it. She'd done it in the arena so many times, while Viktor stood across from her, the breeze whipping his clothes as his magic-laced gusts raced across the sands. Out there, it took little more than a thought to hold up her hand and halt the wind, to touch the spirit within the gale and command it. In here, a bead of sweat dripped down the side of her face, tickling her skin as it slid past her ear and down her neck, then sank into the collar of her jacket. Her focus split five ways, she reached for the air with one thought, fought the barrage of souls with another, and used still more to keep the earth and fire and water in her grip.

Lyana brushed the spirit of the air and it brushed back, whispering of escape and endless skies and freedom. Her wings rippled as a shiver pulsed down her spine, and just like that, her careful control shattered. The water fell in a glittering cascade as the soil landed with a *thunk*. The fire burned out to smoke, and the air exploded in a sudden rush that sent both Malek and her careening backward. Their chairs toppled, and they crashed to the ground.

With a groan, Lyana rolled onto her back and stared up at the ceiling. Back in Pylaeon, it would have been painted with clouds. Down here, it was nothing but gray stone, as uninspired as the mist always lingering outside her window.

From the other side of the table, Malek murmured, "You lost control."

It took every ounce of effort not to lash him with spirit. "I know."

"Still, that was better."

Was that a compliment? Am I supposed to be grateful? Her

patience for Malek was wearing thinner. Nothing had changed since their conversation on the boat, at least nothing she could see. He taught her. He reprimanded her. He doled out criticism far more easily than praise, and he showed no signs of listening to her concerns. The first thing he'd done when he'd walked inside her room that morning was silence her.

No more.

She'd told him she would give him time, but it was running out. Yesterday evening, in the solace of her room, she'd tested her wings and for the first time in weeks she'd flown. Not a subtle lifting of her feet from the ground, but true flight—the sort that sent her racing around the room, feathers ruffling as a grin widened her lips, the sort that made her dove's soul sing. Whether Malek knew it or not, he'd healed her wings. She wasn't his prisoner any longer. But if he showed her even an ounce of trust, she might yet be his queen.

I'll give him one more day.

One.

If he refuses to treat me as his equal, I'll force his hand and leave. If he really wants to save the world—the whole world and all its people—he'll know where to find me.

"Lyana?"

"What?" she grumbled.

Malek was stretched on his side, leaning up on his elbow and watching her with a small grin across his lips. "Are you mad at me?"

"No."

"You are. And I know why. But I thought a lot about

what you said, and I've decided to make a change, which is why I was running late this morning. Something happened last night, something I normally would've kept to myself, but I think you'll want to see."

She was on her feet in an instant. "What happened?"

"A man from your world was spotted in the mist—"

"Who?" Lyana blurted as her fear spiked. In a flash, she was across the room, clutching Malek's hands. "Where is he? What happened?"

"I don't know his name. He was captured by our dragon hunters and brought here. I thought you'd want to see him." He brought their joined hands together so his fingers encased hers and squeezed gently, his eyes probing. "I thought perhaps this would be the first decision we make together, as king and queen of a unified world. Though I warn you, the sight of him might shock you."

"Why?" she whispered, voice hardly there. "What happened to him?"

"There was a fight when he was spotted, and it took some force to restrain him. He won't speak to anyone, and if you weren't here, I admit, I would've ended his life already and removed the risk he now presents. But I knew you'd never forgive me for it."

Her heart sank and rose at the same time. He trusted her. He finally trusted her. The relief was overshadowed by a sinking in her gut. There was only one man she could envision plunging into the mist to come to her rescue—the man who'd sent his brother to safety while he faced a dragon, the man who'd bested every other prince in the realm, the man who'd caught a building on his back to keep it from crushing her.

Rafe.

It had to be Rafe. No one else would risk the wrath of Vesevios just to save her, no one else but that beautiful man who would do anything, give anything, for someone he loved.

"Take me to him. Now."

"Follow me."

Lyana wanted to fly. She wanted to soar down the halls as swiftly as the wind. Instead, she folded her wings tight to her back and kept pace with Malek as he walked steadily through the castle. Down they went, past the entrance hall, past the kitchens, into the very lowest layer carved into the cliffs. There were no windows and no fresh air. Moisture clung to the walls, forming beads along the stone. Slick layers of green algae coated the floors, so she had to watch where she stepped, until finally they reached a bolted door.

"Why wasn't he given a room?"

"This is the only place without windows, and I couldn't risk his escape."

"He must be terrified."

"He is."

"He must—" Lyana broke off, words failing her, and reached for the knob.

Malek covered it with his hand. "I warn you, this might not be what you expect. I tried to heal him last night, but he struggled against the magic, and witnessing his horror, I thought it better to leave him with the pain than to force my power upon him."

"He won't fight me."

"Lyana—"

"He won't fight me."

Her voice lashed through the silence like a whip, and Malek dropped his hand from the door with a sigh. "Then, by all means…"

Before he finished speaking, she'd turned the knob and stepped inside, greedily taking in the room, her eyes hungry to see him. The torch cast an orange glow across the darkness, so different from the white mage light she'd grown accustomed to. It took a moment for her eyes to adjust as they scanned the shadows. When her gaze landed on the figure hunched in the corner, his knees pulled into his chest and his body curled atop the simple wooden bed, she gasped.

She'd been expecting to find a man with moonlight skin and onyx wings, but instead she saw one with copper cheeks, sandy feathers, and a face as familiar as one belonging to her own blood. After all, he was practically her second brother.

"Elias?"

At the sound of her voice, he opened his eyes and sat up, wincing in pain as he moved. "Lyana?"

His voice was broken and hoarse, but it immediately summoned memories of home. The two of them twirling across the mosaic floor of the crystal palace. The two of them grinning mischievously as they snuck Cassi into Luka's rooms. The two of them swapping blows in the arena while they practiced for the trials. The two of them racing across the glittering city of Sphaira as little more than fledglings with Luka by their sides, carefree the way only children could be, before he'd been a guard with rules to follow and she a princess with expectations to uphold, back when the world was full of nothing but endless possibilities.

"Elias!"

Lyana ran to him and collapsed on the bed, drawing him into her arms. Elias melted into her embrace, hugging her waist and holding her close, as though he didn't quite believe she could be real. That alone was enough to prove his terror. The moment he'd become a guard, a formality had risen between them, the sort of wall only time could build, but now it lay crumbled at their feet, his fear blasting it away. In this moment, he wasn't a soldier with his princess but a man with his dear friend.

"I found you," he whispered. "I can't believe I found you."

"I'm here," she murmured, feeling him tremble against her. "I promise, I'm right here."

"Are you hurt? Are you injured?" He pulled back to study her in the firelight, a frown forming as he took in her unmarred skin and richly woven clothes, the cleanly braided rows of her hair and the pristine ivory of her wings.

"That's what I should be asking you," she said softly, taking his hands in her lap and holding them tightly. A bloody cut had scabbed over on his cheek. Dark splotches stained his clothes. She breathed in a distinct metallic scent. "Elias, what happened? Why are you here?"

"We got word that you'd gone missing during your mating ceremony. Luka went out of his mind with worry. He sent a guard to the House of Whispers who bribed the story from a raven in the middle of the night. They told us a royal bastard loyal to Vesevios stole you for his god and took you beneath the mist. If you'd seen Luka's face—if you'd been there, Princess, when he heard the news, you'd know why I'm here. I told him I'd find you, but I didn't— I never— I thought I was flying to my grave."

Luka. Oh, Luka.

She knew he'd be worried, but if he'd sent Elias beneath the mist—

Lyana shut her eyes against the image of her brother's face twisted in anguish, pain blossoming like a flower in her own heart at the very thought.

What have I put him through?

What have I put them all through?

Malek had taken her beneath the mist. He'd clipped her wings. He'd grounded her. Still, could she have done more to return to her home? While she'd been learning her magic, and enjoying that freedom, and exploring this world so foreign to her, could she have done more to protect the people she'd left behind? To save them from this fear?

"What is this place?" Elias's voice called her back. "Where are we? What have they done to you?" His tone turned more frantic, words flowing faster. "They have magic —magic like you wouldn't believe. I didn't stand a chance. As soon as they saw me, I didn't stand a chance. How many of them are there? We need to get out of here. We need to escape. We— We—"

"Shh," she soothed. The calluses on his hands scratched her fingers as she held on with enough force to draw him back from the brink. "Breathe, Elias. Just breathe. You're in shock. And you're hurt. Let me help you."

Lyana didn't even think. The magic flowed freely from her skin into his, invisible to his eyes as it traveled up his arms and across his chest, nothing more than waves of cool relief. After a moment, his panic dimmed and he followed her guidance, breathing in deeply through his nose and out through his mouth. His racing heartbeat slowed. Unable to stand the sight of the gruesome cut along his cheek, Lyana lifted her palm and pressed it to his face, warm umber against deep copper, the colors of doves. A few brushes of her thumb and all evidence of the wound melted away. Elias lifted his hand to the spot, blinking as though returning from a dream. As his fingers grazed smooth skin, he froze.

"Elias?" she asked softly.

Unhearing, he moved his palm away from his face, staring at his hand in mounting horror. His eyes widened as his chin shook, then his arm, then his entire body.

"Elias?"

The question was little more than a whisper, but it was enough to draw his attention. Where moments before there had been nothing but warmth in his brown irises, now there was electric terror. "Who are you?"

She reached for him, but he was on his feet in an instant, stumbling back until his wings crunched audibly against the wall. He dug his heels into the ground to get farther away. "You're not my friend. You're not the princess. Who are you? What have you done with her?"

"Elias," she said calmly, standing with her hands outstretched as a sign of peace. *Stupid!* She cursed herself.

That was so stupid! She'd been in this world beneath the mist for too long, surrounded by its magic. She'd forgotten to be afraid. She'd forgotten that in her world she was something to fear. "It's me. The same me I've always been."

"Who are you?" he shouted, so loudly she flinched.

"I'm Lyana. I promise, I'm me. Do you remember when we were learning how to fly and Luka fell off the staircase in the crystal palace? You thought he broke his leg, but then he got up and he was fine. That was me. I healed him."

"No." He shook his head with such ferocity she worried it might snap off. "No. That's a lie. Stop."

"And that time you slammed a practice sword into Cassi so hard you thought she broke a rib? You were horrified, and we snuck you into her room so you could apologize, but then she jumped out of bed and terrified you, uninjured and fine? That was me. I healed her too."

"No! I don't believe you!"

"Please, Elias—"

"No! Stop! No!"

"Please!"

With a scream, he clamped his hands over his ears, dropped to his knees, and crouched over, spreading his tan wings around himself in a cocoon. He swayed back and forth, murmuring to himself, "No. Don't listen. It's Vesevios. He's trying to trick you. Don't listen. No. Stop. No."

Lyana pressed her palm to her mouth as it fell open, trapping her cry inside. She reached for him, then paused, not sure if her touch would only make it worse. He was terrified. Of her. Of this world. Of the magic he'd been taught his whole life to fear. And right now, he was too deep into his panic to hear logic, to hear the truth. Right now, the only thing she could do was make him more afraid. No matter what she said or did, it would only cause him more pain. So she ran, out the door and into the hall, where Malek was waiting to catch her.

They didn't need words.

One look into her eyes and he knew.

One look into his and she did too—he'd been right to forbid her from returning to the world above to warn her people. They weren't ready, and maybe they never would be. Elias was like a brother to her, yet the first sight of her magic had brought him to his knees. If he didn't understand, what hope did she have of convincing anyone else? What could she do, just one person against a lifetime of fear?

Lyana clutched the front of Malek's shirt as she cried against his chest. He held her until her tears ran dry and long after. Their hearts beat as one, no sound in these dark halls except their ragged breathing.

There was no telling how much time had passed when she finally pulled away, but it was enough to feel a change in the air. As she found his stormy eyes, the space between them thickened. He stared at her the way he always did, as though he could see right through her, into her very soul. Heat flooded up her neck as Malek slowly lifted his hands to her cheeks and brushed her tears away. He slid his fingers through her loose braids, then settled one palm at the back of her head as the other came to rest upon the side of her throat.

She didn't know what to do.

Chaotic and uncertain, her heart ached with despair yet pulsed with a new sort of yearning. He was her king. She was his queen. This was what destiny had foretold. As he leaned forward, she couldn't move, trapped between the desire to give in and the voice in the back of her head telling her to run.

Malek paused before touching her lips, his breath tickling her skin as he studied her expression. He wanted this. She could feel it in his spirit, a longing he'd never quite been able to hide, but there was a certain disappointment there too. Still, he closed the distance between them, pressing their lips together, and she let him.

The kiss lasted only for a moment. He pulled back with a sigh and dropped his hands from her, releasing his hold. Lyana breathed as though coming up from the depths of the ocean for air. Had she been suffocating? Her chest burned.

"I—" Malek paused.

"I want to stay," Lyana jumped in quickly, not sure what he was going to say, but also positive she didn't want to hear it. "Here, with Elias, I mean. I want to stay and try to talk to him again once he's calmed down."

"Of course." Malek swallowed and stepped back. "I'll have someone bring you both food and whatever else you need."

"Thank you."

An awkward silence stretched between them.

"Lyana?"

"Yes?" she answered too quickly, too cheerfully.

"That wasn't what I wanted, for him to react that way."

He meant it. She could see the truth in his eyes. Though she also saw a confession—it was exactly what he'd expected. "And I'm sorry for you."

"I know, Malek."

He stared at her for another breath, then abruptly turned and walked away. Lyana fell back against the wall behind her, letting the moisture of the stones seep into her feathers and her clothes, the coolness welcome. When the sound of his footsteps faded, she lifted her fingers to her lips and touched them gently, unsure what to think. So she didn't. She just stood there and stared at nothing, finally doing what he'd always wanted as she built a wall around her heart to keep her unruly emotions at bay.

XANDER

elen spent the better part of the journey from the House of Wisdom warning Xander about the severity of the earthquakes that had wracked his homeland during his absence, but no words could have prepared him for the sight of Pylaeon as he crested the mountain ridge and saw the city in the valley below. It was in ruins. Stones lay crumbled, wood splintered. A haze hung in the air, thick with soot and dust. The river overflowed where the dams had fissured, flooding entire streets. Part of the castle wall had collapsed. The only sparks of color were the mountains of flowers deposited at the ebony arches throughout the city, the spirit gates leading lost souls to Taetanos's realm. They were offerings and prayers, a symbol of the suffering his people had endured but also of their unyielding faith in their god to come save them.

At a loss for words, Xander landed on an outcropping of rock and stared at the destruction, his heart aching for his home. He should have been here. If his mother had sent word, he would have returned in an instant. But, of course, that's why she hadn't. She'd wanted him safely out of harm's way. And a part of him hoped she'd thought that if she just gave him enough time, he'd come home with all the answers.

Instead, the only things he'd found were more questions.

"I tried to warn you," Helen said as she landed by his side.

"Nothing could've prepared me for this."

Cassi's boots scuffed on the rocks behind him, but she said nothing, perhaps just as shocked as he.

"You said it started before I left?"

Helen nodded and crossed her arms, brow furrowed as she stared at the city in shambles before them. "You were here for the first two earthquakes, both short enough to seem like aftershocks, which is exactly what we thought they were, until the next one happened a few days after you were gone. It was short too, but then a few days later another one happened, also short. The queen and I sat down with the advisors and tracked the timing, realizing they were happening closer and closer together. For the past week, they've been occurring daily, sometimes more than once or twice a day, almost as though leading up to something—but we don't know what. By themselves, they don't cause much damage, but with so little time in between, the structures are failing bit by bit. Even if the dove prince hadn't come, I would've gone to retrieve you. I was already preparing for the journey to the owl kingdom when he landed at our door."

As she spoke, Xander let his gaze drift along the river cutting through the center of the valley. In the late-afternoon sun, its crystal waters sparkled like a beacon for his eyes to follow, leading him to Taetanos's Gate. The gushing fall spewed with all the fury of a scorned god, white and chaotic. A fine mist curled into the air to catch the light, but the shadows were what interested him. Wet with moisture, the cliff face glistened like polished onyx. Hidden deep at its heart was the sacred nest that now occupied his thoughts.

"Have you kept a watch on the god stone?"

"We've been getting daily reports from the priests and priestesses, but nothing is amiss. It remains in the heart of the sacred nest where it's always been. The only thing that has changed is the level of Taetanos's fury. The priests and priestesses say that before every earthquake the stone trembles with his anger. They think he's making our world shake as a reminder to right the wrong done against him, to face Vesevios and bring Princess Lyana home."

The only time he'd seen the stone shudder was in the presence of magic. Had that man come back? Was he hiding in the forests? Was he using magic to affect the stone? And if he was, why? What did it all mean?

Xander closed his eyes and squeezed the bridge of his nose as his face twisted with frustration. He was close—so, so close—to understanding. The riddle was staring him in the face, taunting him. All the words were there, but he couldn't see between them. He just wanted someone to tell him the answer, to supply the epiphany that would make it all clear.

"We've been spotted."

His eyes popped open and he shifted his focus toward the area of the valley he'd been pointedly ignoring—the one littered with ivory tents and pale wings that didn't belong in a land built for ravens. It didn't take long to spot the dove racing toward him like an arrow aimed at his heart. Two more followed behind their prince, Aethios's avenging army coming to strike. Xander stood his ground and waited for the blow.

"Where is she?" Luka Aethionus shouted as he landed on the rocks below, then half jumped and half flew the rest of the way to the top. His ashen wings cut through the air like swords, the body beneath them athletic and strong. He was a warrior through and through, but the look on his face wasn't of anger or hate. The only emotion shining in his honey-hued irises was worry, a fact that immediately endeared him to Xander. They both wanted Lyana safe, and everything else was just politics. "What have you done with my sister? I want to see her now."

"I'm afraid that's not possible."

"Listen," Luka spat. He grabbed the front of Xander's jacket and yanked him so close their noses almost touched. Xander motioned for Helen to stay put, already anticipating her reaction. "We might have tied in single-weapon combat at the trials, but this isn't the arena any longer. Where is my sister?"

"Threaten me all you like, but it won't bring your sister back," Xander said smoothly. "And I'm afraid a duel would leave you sorely disappointed. I'm not the fighter I once was."

The fire in the dove's eyes dimmed as a frown crossed his lips, but he didn't move.

"Luka," Cassi admonished.

At the sound of her voice, the dove prince relinquished his hold and stepped back. His attention shifted briefly to Xander's missing hand before rising to her. News of his injury had traveled fast, exactly as he hoped it would, but that wasn't what had intrigued Xander. It was the way the dove's face softened as soon as he looked upon the owl. All those hard edges fell away, replaced with an intimate vulnerability that left Xander feeling like an intruder.

"Where is she, Cassi?" The words were quiet, barely there and on the verge of breaking. "What has he done to her?"

She stepped forward and took the dove's hands in hers. Luka responded to her touch by threading their fingers together and holding her palms to his heart, the look in his eyes fierce and scared, but most of all, loving. The two other doves showed no surprised at their prince acting so familiar with Cassi. Xander turned to Helen and a silent conversation passed between them that left a stubborn ache in his heart.

One answer, at least, had become clear.

Luka was the man Cassi had loved—the one who'd left her bitter and angry about women sacrificing all while men lost nothing. He was a prince who'd kept his kingdom and his home, who'd gained a new mate and a promising future, while she'd been banished to the House of Whispers, losing everything in the end, including her best friend.

And last night she'd kissed another prince bound by sacred duty.

He could still feel the impression of her lips on his neck. His fingers had repeatedly run over the spot, yet each time he was surprised to find smooth flesh instead of the outline of her kiss burned there like a brand.

No wonder she'd cried.

No wonder she'd told him to leave and hadn't met his eyes since, not on the long flight, and not now either, with his stare burrowing into her cheek.

"Xander hasn't done anything to her," Cassi murmured, all her focus on Luka. The sun did little to hide the wet sheen to her eyes. "I promise, the only thing he's done is try to help her."

"Where is she?"

"I don't know."

A long breath escaped the dove prince's lips as he tried to absorb the information. Then he nodded once, coming back to life. The frantic fear in his gaze cleared, replaced with awareness and the smallest shred of pain. He glanced down at her hands held against his chest and swallowed tightly before stepping back. Cassi pulled her arms away and let them fall to her sides as she bowed her head. Luka shifted toward Xander.

"My informants told me she was taken by your bastard brother. Is it true? They said he was an agent of Vesevios, and that if he has her, it means he took her beneath the mist."

At that, Cassi looked up.

Xander didn't know what to say. The panic in her eyes was surely a mirror of his own. He knew the rumors would get out eventually, but he wasn't prepared to face the truth, not yet. They still didn't have answers or a plan. And if the doves learned the truth, it was only a matter of time before Aethios's chosen took over the search. If they found Lyana, they'd never let her leave the crystal city again. His people would be left even more lost than before.

"I—" Xander started. "I—"

"He didn't take her," Cassi cut in without hesitation, her tone final. Xander's stomach flipped and he sucked in a breath. Of course she'd betray his secrets. For Lyana. To see her safe. Of course she'd want the doves involved in the search. It didn't matter to her if Lyana returned to the House of Whispers or the House of Peace—all that mattered to Cassi was that she returned. Or so he thought. "She left of her own accord."

"What?" Luka and Xander said the word in unison, one a stern snap and the other a whisper. Xander swallowed, hoping no one had heard. And no one had. Cassi's revelation had shocked them all numb.

She lied.

She lied…for me.

"She left?" The dove prince shook his head as though attempting to dislodge the thought. "She wouldn't do that, to me, to you. She would never just leave."

"Wouldn't she?"

"I don't believe it."

"Luka," Cassi said apologetically, as though sorry for

revealing the truth. "You know as well as I do that she never wanted this life. She's always seen her destiny as waiting just over the horizon, somewhere far, far away. I always thought I'd be the one to go with her. But she fell in love, and they ran away before I could stop her. I think maybe she knew that if she told me, I'd talk her out of it, the way I always did, but this time she didn't want to see sense. She only wanted to be free."

"So she just...left?"

"I'm sorry," Cassi insisted, her tone soft with sympathy yet hard enough to deter questions. "I never wanted you to find out. We kept it a secret to try to save her honor, to save Xander's honor, and we said she was taken. We hoped we'd be able to find her and convince her to come home before the rest of the houses learned the truth."

"Then why did you go to the House of Wisdom?"

"Xander and I were studying their maps for places she and Rafe might've gone to hide. We were relaying the information to the ravens so they could send guards to search. But we couldn't find them."

"And what about the dragon?"

"A coincidence. Lyana and Rafe snuck away in the chaos, and we used the presence of the dragon to help push the story that it was Vesevios who had taken her instead of Lyana leaving by herself."

"But— But—"

Luka searched for an excuse, the muscles in his throat tensing with the effort of defending his sister. But Cassi's story was convincing, so convincing even Xander almost believed it—he would have, if he hadn't been in the sacred nest to see that man with his own eyes. For every question, she had an answer. The lie had enough depth to come off as truth, filled with so many layers he had no idea how she'd come up with it so quickly. Not only that, but her voice, her expression, and her words all begged to be believed. Though he'd never known Cassi to be a liar, she clearly excelled at it, a thought that left an unsettling feeling in his stomach.

A memory emerged like a monster from the shadows, creeping slowly across his thoughts—of Cassi, her clothes stained red and her cheeks and hands still pink with faded blood, her eyes swollen by tears as, on her hands and knees, she looked at him in the city streets, nothing but smoldering fire and destruction around them.

She's gone, he'd confessed.

Cassi hadn't asked who, or how she vanished, or what had happened. It had never struck him as strange until right now that she'd accepted the words without question, that instead of demanding answers, she'd turned her face away to stare at the chunks of her vomit still on the ground. And even later, she hadn't flown to his room in the middle of the night to force a confession. She hadn't hunted him down for information. She'd waited for him to come to her in the practice yards the next day, almost as though she'd been expecting him.

"Ana." The rough whisper pulled Xander back to the present. He blinked away the memory and returned his focus to the dove prince, who stood rubbing his palms along his cheeks while he sighed, the tips of his fingers shifting from brown to pink with the force. "Oh, Ana."

"It'll be all right," Cassi murmured. "We'll—"

Luka gasped so loudly she stopped talking. He jerked his head up, his eyes going wide, as a single name erupted from his lips. "Elias."

"What about Elias?" Cassi asked, looking toward the two other doves. Her brows drew together when they pointedly averted their eyes. "Why isn't he here? Where..." She trailed off as understanding dawned, an understanding Xander lacked, though he recognized the horror in her sharp inhale. "You sent him into the mist to look for her, didn't you? Oh, Luka, you didn't, did you?"

The dove swallowed. "He volunteered."

"No," Cassi muttered with an anguish Xander didn't quite understand. Maybe this was a good thing. Maybe this Elias would come back with the answers they needed. Unless, of course, they weren't the answers Cassi wanted him to have.

Xander frowned, thinking back to their nights in the library and all the circles they'd spun in their endless debates, leading him nowhere. Was it possible she'd been argumentative on purpose? Not just thorough in her research, but deliberately leading him astray?

Why?

To what end?

He'd wished for an epiphany, but the one spiraling across his thoughts like a maelstrom, shredding his newly constructed illusions, was the last thing he'd ever wanted.

"I have to find him," Luka said.

"Luka, no. It's too dangerous."

The two of them were so wrapped up in each other, they didn't notice the way Xander stumbled, his knees going weak as something within him snapped. Helen grabbed his elbow, giving him support. Her touch was the only thing keeping him grounded.

"Excuse me," Xander cut in, drawing their attention. Cassi tilted her head, studying his face, but he refused to meet her eyes. "I'm sorry for hiding the truth from you, Prince Luka, but perhaps now it's best to let Cassi fill you in on the rest. Tomorrow, come find me in the castle and we can discuss the next steps we should take to find the princess. Until then, I've been away from my home for quite some time, and there are matters to which I must attend. Good evening."

"Xander," Cassi said, stopping him.

It took every ounce of strength he possessed to keep the mounting distress from filling his eyes and flowing over. "Stay, Cassi. Stay and help him. We'll talk tomorrow."

Her jaw clenched briefly, but he watched as she forced her lips to relax and nodded. "Good night."

Without another word, he left, making haste for the castle. The second he landed in his room, not bothering with the formal entrance, his mother was there. Xander hugged her, half his thoughts on their conversation as she filled him in on all he'd missed, and half his thoughts on the spool unraveling inside his mind.

Had Xander told Luka the same story, the dove prince would never have believed him. But he trusted Cassi, deeply and intimately, so from her lips the words held undeniable truth.

Lyana had also trusted Cassi, and now she was gone.

Rafe, too.

Xander had seen them together enough times in the practice yards to know the owl had broken through his surly brother's defenses, no small feat. He'd never thought to question why she'd bothered tearing down his walls, but now he did.

Now he was questioning everything. Because he'd let himself be fooled once by the people he loved most, and he wouldn't let that same dagger cut him again.

Why had she been so covered in blood on his mating day? Why had she decided to stay in his city? Why had she agreed to help him when she could have gone running to the doves with the truth? Why had she saved his life from an assassin's blade? Why had she gone with him to Rynthos? Why had she been lurking in the archivist halls? Why, oh why, had she kissed him?

The spot still burned.

As his mother bid him good night, Xander lifted his hand to his neck and rubbed at his skin as though he could wipe the sensation away. It no longer felt like a brand, but like a lie—one which had almost succeeded.

He should have gone to bed, but he didn't. Instead, he jumped off his balcony and spread his black wings, blending into the night. He didn't realize where they were taking him until he landed in the old rooms belonging to Rafe's mother, still smelling of smoke and ash. He hadn't thought to question the fire that had once more burned the lowest level of the castle. Like everyone else, he'd assumed it was the dragon. But looking back, he realized the fire in these rooms weeks before had been nothing like the one responsible for killing his father years ago. It had been small, contained, and easy to tame, unlike the raging, wild flames that had nearly claimed the entire servant's quarter in his youth.

Xander stepped into the shadows, using the bright light of the full moon to guide him as he shifted charred wood and hole-ridden curtains. The room was a mess, nothing but soot and broiled bits and broken parts. Still, he searched and searched, not sure what he was looking for until he found it. Deep in the fireplace, buried beneath the ash, sat a white feather with black spots, whose edges were stained red with blood.

CASSI

I t was late before Cassi was finally able to soar away from the war tents in the valley toward the stone castle glowing silver beneath the full moon. Luka had kept her far later than she'd wanted, going over every detail of Lyana's time in the House of Whispers and how she'd fallen for the bastard raven. Luckily, mixing the truth with carefully chosen lies was an art she'd perfected. As soon as she'd told Luka of her suspicions about Rafe's magic, he'd understood. All Lyana had ever wanted was to be free. Free of her responsibilities, yes, but mostly free of her double life as part fugitive and part princess. It was a desire Cassi understood, which was, of course, the secret to convincing falsehoods—basing them in something real. The confession in her voice was her own, but Luka heard it the way she wanted him to, as the carefully kept secrets of his sister.

Any other night, she would have enjoyed sitting with him in the privacy of his spacious royal tent, eating dinner beside a cozy fire. She would have enjoyed sharing the stories of their youth, listening to the warmth in his voice and seeing the love in his eyes, though that was all it was. They didn't touch. A respectful distance remained between them. Luka was a man of honor, and though his mate was back in the crystal city, her presence was as real as if she were sitting there beside him. Still, it was a scene in which Cassi could lose herself for a few hours and forget.

But not tonight.

Tonight, she had matters to attend.

Cassi swept through the open balcony and into her room, the curtains swaying in the breeze created by her wings. Not bothering to unclip the weapons strapped to her waist, her legs, and her arms, she fell onto the bed. As soon as her eyes closed, she sank into her magic and emerged as the dreamwalker.

Though she knew she should deal with Xander first, and Helen, and the queen, she figured she'd waited weeks to carry out that order and one more hour couldn't hurt. Elias was traveling into the mist right now, and if Malek didn't find him, it could mean disaster. Worse, if Malek did find him, it would mean Elias's death. Cassi wasn't sure what outcome she feared more, but maybe if she pleaded for his life, Malek would spare him. If she explained what he meant to Lyana, that he was like a brother to her—well, she had to try.

Wasting no time, Cassi imagined the scent of Malek's spirit. He was the King Born in Fire, but his soul had never smelled of smoke and ash to her, nor did it contain the salty essence of the sea. Even now, despite all that had passed between them, he was all open fields and endless skies, fresh grass and crisp air, as alluring as a flower, as dangerous as a wolf, drawing up the memories of youthful intrigue and fun, their long-ago laughter echoing in her ears.

Her spirit flew out the open window and sank into the mist, the world passing in a blur of bright stars and deep shadows, then endless gray fog. In a flash, she was floating above Da'Kin. Instead of leading her to the castle, as she assumed it would, her magic pulled her sideways, past groaning wood and flowing canals, toward the outskirts of the city. She found Malek beside a towering warehouse, the sort normally used to store food. His *photo'kine*, Kal, chased the shadows away as the two of them marched along wet planks toward the backside of the building. As they turned the corner, she found Jacinta and Nyomi waiting by the far end, power dancing along their palms, the green and blue sparks vibrant against the fog. Cassi dropped into the space between them, her spirit hovering at eye level.

Malek spared her a glance. "Not now, Kasiandra."

With a frown on his lips, he proceeded to walk right through her. Cassi grimaced. She was nothing but air and fog, invisible to all except him, but she still *felt* him. For a moment, his soul, his scent, his body mixed with hers, stunning her senses. It was different from passing through rock or wood, sentient in a way that left her reeling. Her mind sank into his, almost like falling into a dream but with none of the control. His thoughts spun through her head, making her dizzy.

Rafe.

Cassi froze.

The name lingered. Though the thought wasn't her own, she couldn't shake it free. The word clawed at her, digging in like a bear burrowing for the winter and making home beneath her skin.

Rafe. Why is he thinking about Rafe?

Malek was halfway down the building. Cassi soared past him and once again dropped into the space before his eyes, begging to be seen. Malek arched a brow and said nothing, not slowing his deliberate march toward the two mages waiting at the other end. When he passed through her, Cassi reached for his mind with her power. His magic whipped out, dislodging her, but not before an image cut across her thoughts. Rafe, sitting in a plush, high-backed chair, his hands gripping the arms with uncontained fury, the muscles in his neck straining against invisible binds. On the table beside him, a set of bound and bloodied wings, black feathers crusted over and glistening in the firelight.

Rafe was in Malek's office.

When? Why?

Cassi didn't bother being polite. This time she darted after her king, forcing her spirit into him in a way that felt brutal and wrong, but no worse than his magic stealing her sky.

Dragon.

Rafe.

Dragon.

Rafe.

All she caught were two words swirling in his soul. He gripped her with his power, the touch suffocating as he jerked her from his mind. With a gasp, she let go and he flung her across the fog.

Cassi had come tonight to help Malek, to warn him about a bird within his midst, to try to protect just one of her childhood friends. But all thoughts of Elias fled as she raced through the mist, her spirit a dagger crafted to pierce her king's defenses.

It was too late. He anticipated her attack, his spirit rising around him like a shield. She bounced from his skin and rebounded into the sea. By the time she emerged from the water, the door to a small back room was already opening. Kal's mage light cut through the darkness, revealing a figure slouched in the corner with his knees pulled into his chest and his face hidden behind crossed arms. The muscles in his body were slack with sleep. His dark hair spilled over his forehead as his shoulders rose and fell in a gentle rhythm.

Malek turned to Jacinta with a nod. The mage stepped forward and—

Rafe attacked.

Uncoiling like a spring, he launched through the air with the grace of a raven in flight and reached for the king. His chest expanded as he sucked in a deep breath. The barest screech escaped his lips before a golden aura enveloped him and he halted midstep as though frozen in time. The silence of his stolen cry pierced Cassi, making her realize just how much she'd wanted him to escape.

"Close," Malek murmured, his eyes going black as they landed on the raven. "Closer than I'd like."

Rafe's glare promised retribution, but he wouldn't get it. If there was anything Cassi knew about her king, it was that he always won. He got what he wanted, no matter the cost, no matter the consequences. And whatever he planned to do to Rafe, he'd do it. Even if she wanted to, she couldn't stop him. Not like this, with her spirit form as useless as her foolish heart.

"Jacinta," Malek said, the name sounding like a command.

With the flick of her wrist, the mage peeled a metal band off her coat and wrapped it around Rafe's skull, sealing his mouth and removing any hope he had of freedom. Without his raven cry, the battle was lost before it even began. The *ferro'kine* then unhooked the chain from her waist and used it to secure his arms behind his back.

Malek loosened his magical hold on Rafe's spirit, maintaining just enough of a connection to prevent him from slipping free. Then he turned toward Cassi. "I know why you're here. And I also know you have more important places to be. Your time is up, Kasiandra. Kill the boy, or I'll have someone else kill him for you. One way or another, you'll be home by tomorrow—as my soldier or as my prisoner. The choice is yours."

Rafe's head snapped to the side. He stared into the mist, his brow furrowed. All at once, recognition sparked like metal to flint. He screamed, the garbled sounds caught by his gag, but she felt as though she heard him.

Cassi! The embers burning in his eyes seemed to shout. *Cassi!*

A slowly mounting horror twisted his features, the reality of the king's words hitting home. His struggles doubled, tripled. Malek's golden power increased to keep the raven contained. The muscles of Rafe's neck bulged with all the words he couldn't say.

But he didn't need words.

His expression said it all—a mix of unabashed loathing and fruitless hope, as though his every nightmare lived in her, and his every dream too. His eyes strained with pleading, red veins pulling at the whites until tears began to form.

Don't do it, he implored. *Don't hurt Xander.*

Even now, without his wings and at the mercy of a cruel king, his own life in shambles and his future teetering on oblivion, his only thought was for his brother. Rafe could have been begging for his own life, but he wasn't. And somehow that broke her heart more.

"Kasiandra," Malek said, his voice sharp.

What are you going to do to him? she wanted to ask. *What did I agree to? What was I a part of?* Willing or unwilling, she was the reason Rafe was here, and it was her fault that, when morning came, he'd truly be alone in the world.

"Go," Malek ordered.

Her hesitation held her hostage.

"Go."

Cassi did—not because he said to, but because high above the fog, in the quiet stillness of a city asleep beneath the stars, she felt a hand upon her cheek, warm and loving, and it shocked her from the daze.

Xander?

At his touch, her spirit cut through the mist, leaving Rafe forgotten by the sea as her soul sped toward the clouds.

What's he doing in my room?

What's he doing on my bed?

"Cassi."

The word was hardly more than a whisper on the breeze, far away yet close enough she felt the subtle brush of his breath upon her skin.

Cassi raced through the thinning fog, her focus on the sky and the floating isle so high above it was hardly more than a dark spot blocking out the stars. As she neared, the shadows played with the moonlight, revealing jagged cliffs and barren rock, the rough underbelly of paradise. From this vantage point, it was clear the land had been ripped away from the world below, leaving nothing clean about the sharp and broken edges. By magic? By the gods? She didn't know anymore. She didn't care. All she cared about was the castle teetering on its edge, the gray stones luminescent, and the windows flickering with amber firelight. All she cared about was the boy waiting inside.

When she reached her balcony, she stopped dead.

Xander sat leaning over her sleeping body, one arm resting on the pillow by her head while the other brushed a stray lock of hair behind her ear. Even in her spirit form, she could feel the heat of his skin, the gentle tickle of his touch, the way he stirred something deep inside of her.

Was he going to kiss her?

Was she going to let him?

The dark shadows of the balcony were a precipice she didn't want to cross. The moment she returned to her body, it would all be over, whatever dream she was living. Like Malek had said, her time had run out. There was nowhere left to hide, nowhere left to run. For the good of the world, she had to kill him.

On the bed, her body flinched at the thought.

Above her, Xander paused.

"Cassi," he repeated, and from so close, she recognized the hollow despair in his tone. A sigh shuddered through him, his back bending toward her as his head dropped. With his hand still on her cheek, he finally whispered, "Who are you?"

Motion in the corner of the room caught her eye. Helen and five guards emerged from the darkness, blades gleaming as they stepped into the light. Cassi snapped back into her body. Before Xander could move, she grabbed his hand.

As their eyes met, time seemed to stop.

She'd never thought this was how it would end, with Xander poised above her on the cushions, his body a welcome weight, his skin upon her skin, their mouths so impossibly near touching. The plan had been to do it while he slept so he could slip from one dream into another, no pain and no awareness, no understanding of her treachery. But now questions haunted the violet shadows of his eyes. Cassi didn't want to know what lingered in hers.

Scuffling feet approached and she acted, more out of instinct than any desire to be free. Wrenching his fingers away, she rolled off the bed without letting go and pulled him to the ground with her. A mess of feathers and limbs, they struggled on the rug. Despite his size, however, Xander was no fighter, a fact they both well knew. In moments, she stood behind him with her knee against his spine and her arm across his chest. Cassi snatched the dagger still strapped to her leg and held it to his throat.

"Stop where you are, Helen," she ordered, not recognizing her own threatening tone. "Stop where you are or I'll kill him."

The older woman paused and tightened her grip on her sword, not looking at Cassi but at Xander as she replied, "Do it."

The hairs at the back of Cassi's neck rose.

A tingle slipped down her spine.

The blade in her hand shifted as Xander swallowed. He turned his face upward, something defiant about the motion. Against her better judgment, Cassi looked away from the guards and down at the prince at her mercy. She expected to find hate in his eyes, to read anger and loathing in their lavender hue. She expected his stare to confirm the one thing she already knew to be absolutely true—that she was unworthy of trust or of love. Instead, as she met his gaze, she saw the last thing she ever expected.

She saw compassion.

Xander was sorry for her, for whatever had brought her to this point, for the life she must have led, for the lies he didn't understand. And he was sorry for something else too.

Cassi shifted her focus down the straight line of his nose, past the soft curves of his lips, over the strong edge of his jaw, pausing for a moment on the spot where her dagger dug menacingly into the thin skin of his neck, then farther still, until she saw what Helen had. Though she held his arms securely against his chest, she'd failed to notice the way his elbow bent toward his biceps and the silvery edge of the arm guard poised to strike—the very one she'd designed to save his life, now a twist of his wrist from ending hers.

Or maybe she'd noticed, and she hadn't cared.

They breathed against each other, neither moving a muscle, the rest of the world still and waiting. It felt like one of her lessons, one of her puzzles. *Tell me how you'd escape my hold*, she might have said. *Tell me how you'd get away.*

Except this wasn't a game.

They weren't playing pretend anymore, if they ever had been at all. Cassi looked into Xander's tender eyes again, willing him to make his move, to take away this choice she'd never wanted. If the world ended because of her inaction, so be it. What had the world ever given her anyway, except heartbreak and despair?

Do it, she thought. *Do it!*

He didn't.

Even with the truth of her wretched soul laid bare before him, her dagger at his throat and her lies at last undone, Xander remained still. His wrist didn't move. No blade sprang free to slice her throat. Against anything she ever could have imagined, he chose to spare her. He chose to believe there was something within her still worth saving.

Was there?

Cassi dropped her weapon. It clanged loudly against the floor as she shoved him away. Helen was there in a heartbeat, yanking her arms behind her back and binding her wrists. Xander sat clutching his neck, his stare as tangible as any touch, but she refused to meet it.

"Someone else will come," she said as they dragged her toward the door. "Someone else will come to do what I could not."

LYANA

In the dank dark of the windowless corridors at the base of the castle, time ceased to exist. The outside world was far away, no mist, no sea, no city, nothing but the subtle drip of water and the gentle hum of silence. It would have been peaceful, this welcome break from the constant barrage of a thousand lost souls, if she were alone. But the crying spirit on the other side of the door cut into her with the precision of a trained fighter who knew just where to slice so as to elicit the most pain. Lyana had no idea what day it was, what hour, or how long she'd been stationed outside Elias's room, fighting to make him understand, but it hardly mattered. She wouldn't leave until she finally got through to him.

"I'm coming inside," she said through the wood to avoid surprising him.

As the door creaked open, she found him on the far side braced for battle, his hands coiled into fists. The wet sheen to his copper cheeks shone golden in the reflection of flames, and the undersides of his spread wings were stark against the damp gray stone.

Lyana sighed.

At least it was better than the last time she'd entered, when he charged the second she pushed open the door. Before her mind had time to catch up with her body, she'd grasped his spirit with her magic and frozen him in place, which had only served to heighten his terror. She was still cursing her folly. They'd trained together most of their lives —she knew how to fight him with her bare hands, how to wrestle him into submission, or at the very least, defend against his attack. Yet somehow, in these past few weeks beneath the mist, magic had become her first instinct. She blamed Malek.

No magic, she silently ordered. *Absolutely no magic.*

Though she'd spent the first eighteen years of her life hiding her power, stifling it took more effort than she liked to admit, as if she were trying to repair a dam after the river had already been unleashed. The magic ran through her, wild and rampant, just like her spirit, rebelling against any attempts to be contained. They'd both grown used to the freedom.

"I brought food." She dipped her chin toward the tray nudged against her hip and used her free hand to close the door behind her. "I thought you might be hungry."

Elias didn't move.

Those brown eyes bored into her as she stepped slowly and deliberately into the room, not making any sudden moves. She sat on the bed without looking at him as she adjusted the bowls and poured two cups of hot tea. She made a show of tasting the fruits and breads so he knew they were safe to eat.

"It's not as good as the food back home," she said conversationally. "They lack our variety, especially in seeds and nuts. Down here, they're too precious to eat. And I think something about the absence of the sun dulls most of the flavors. Even the ripest fruit doesn't have that juicy sweetness I love. But the tea leaves are just like the ones we used to import from the House of Paradise, with a spiciness that settles in the stomach. I find it rather soothing. And with the moisture in the air, nothing ever seems to go stale. Here, try a bite."

She ripped off the corner of her sweet bread and offered it to him. The dough was infused with bits of dried fruit, which mixed well with the salty flavor of the air. Elias remained still and staring. With a shrug, she popped the piece into her mouth.

"Suit yourself," Lyana murmured and curled her legs beneath her as she took a sip of tea, encouraged that he hadn't screamed or yelled or threatened violence. If she just kept talking, maybe he'd think they were in the lush halls of the crystal palace, not the dank dungeons of Da'Kin. Maybe she would too. "Will you tell me about Luka's mating ceremony? I tried to imagine what the palace looked like a hundred times, but the image keeps changing. His mate's feathers are auburn, if I remember correctly. And her name is Iris, right? I always wondered if they incorporated a few amethyst garlands to match the colors of her home, something I know my mother would understand. But I can't imagine Luka saying the vows in anything except the brilliant white and gold of our house. Aethios must've—"

"Don't say his name," Elias interrupted darkly.

"Who? Aethios?"

"Don't," he growled, taking two steps forward, his body hunched and hulking. She wasn't afraid. This was what she'd expected. He was a warrior loyal to the House of Peace, and he would defend it until the bitter end. "You're an agent of Vesevios and I won't have you speak the name of Aethios, highest of them all."

"Whether I'm living here upon the sea or up above the clouds or in a place beyond the horizon that no one's ever seen, I'm a daughter of Aethios, Elias. I always will be. And I won't feel sorry for saying his name."

"You're not. You're—"

"I am," she cut him off, keeping her body relaxed on the cushions despite the sternness of her tone. The calmer she remained, the better. "Is there anything I can say to prove it to you?"

"No."

"Please, Elias." She tightened her grip on the teacup, releasing her frustration as her magic coiled beneath her skin. "Ask me any question, and I'll give you the answer."

"I don't believe your lies."

"I know that when you were fifteen you tried to kiss Cassi at the summer solstice ball and she nearly broke your nose." An uncertain groove dug into his forehead. She kept going. "Luka made fun of you for days, until you finally told him I kissed Theo the same night. Then I was the one who didn't hear the end of it for weeks. All for an innocent peck on the lips!"

Lyana rolled her eyes and sighed, smiling slightly at the memory. Cassi hadn't even been sorry. It'd been another three years after that before Lyana had caught her kissing Luka in a weapons room off the side of the training arena. Now, that had been a shock.

"Oh, how about the first time you worked a night shift at the palace doors? You were trying to be a serious, disciplined guard. And you were doing a wonderful job, until Luka, Cassi, and I snuck out through the secret passage and spent the next hour making faces at you through the crystals. I've never seen your face so red. But you never tattled."

Lyana took a sip of tea and leaned farther back on the pillows, hardly even looking at Elias anymore, lost in the lightness of her youth. The past few months had been so heavy, the weight pressing down from all sides. It was nice to remember a time when life had been simple and carefree, when the worst she had to worry about was a not-so-stern lecture from her father or the sharp whip of her mother's wrath.

"Do you remember how excited we used to get when the front hall was open for market? This was before we could fly, of course. Only a handful of children lived in the palace, but on market days, everyone from Sphaira came to us. We used to run through the stalls, our laughter trailing behind. We used to hold hands, and spin and spin and spin, until we collapsed on the tiles, all giggles and downy feathers as we watched the adults soar overhead. I couldn't wait to join them. I couldn't wait for the sky to be mine. I spent hours staring through the crystals, studying the clouds and the stars, the painted pastels of sunrise and the vivid streaks of sunset, endlessly waiting for the day when I could fly beyond the horizon, to just go and go and go, with no palace walls to stop me."

Now, all she had were barricades.

The bed sank as Elias took a seat at the far end, the smallest ounce of his body balanced on the edge, as though he might spring up at any moment. He turned toward her, something soft about his gaze, like the barest sliver of sunlight slipping through a break in the curtains to welcome the day.

"I should apologize to you," she said, holding onto that warmth. "I was a bit of a bully, I'm afraid, in my stubborn pursuit of adventure, especially during those last few days. I should've never forced you to dance with me when you'd wanted to go to bed. I should've never tricked you into drinking all that hummingbird nectar, until you didn't know which way was up or down or which foolish promises you were agreeing to. I probably never should've snuck out of the palace at all. If I hadn't, maybe none of this would've happened."

Even as she said it, she knew it wasn't true.

Malek would have found her, one way or another. He was even worse than she when it came to getting what he wanted, and his Queen Bred of Snow was the one thing he wanted most of all. But no matter their magic or the prophecy or the desires of his people, it wasn't his lips that she still felt on her skin, or his touch that haunted her sleeping mind, or his voice she sometimes heard on the wind. And when she closed her eyes, it wasn't his face she saw.

No matter what she told Elias, she would never take it back. Not her sneaking out. Not the dragon fight on the sky bridge. Most of all, not those hours spent surrounded by firelight and magic, healing a boy with the deepest, bluest eyes who'd completely changed her world.

"Lyana?"

She swallowed and blinked the images away. "Yes, Elias?"

"Are you really…"

He trailed off, leaning forward as he studied her, the caramel highlights in his eyes glittering as they caught the fire. She willed him to believe her, to trust her, to let go of his prejudices and know that even with magic she was the same person he'd grown up with.

For a moment, she thought it had worked.

Then the curtains snatched closed, leaving him in darkness. The light in his eyes went out and his face sealed off. Spine jolting straight as a blade, he jumped to his feet and backed away.

"Get out."

"Elias—"

"Get out," he shouted, voice cracking. "I don't know who you are. I don't know what magic this is. Please, please, just get out."

She'd lost him.

"Eat something, Elias," she said as she stood from the bed and walked slowly toward the door. "I'll leave you in peace, I promise. But your body is weak, and you need strength to heal. So please, eat something."

After Lyana stepped outside, she collapsed against the wall, her legs going weak. The rough edges of the stones scraped against her feathers as she slid down, her body falling with her spirit, until she sat slumped against the floor. Drawing her knees into her chest, she let her head fall back and closed her eyes. It did nothing to stop the silent tears from slipping out the corners and sliding down her cheeks.

She'd been close, so very close, to breaking through his defenses.

But she'd failed.

No, Lyana thought, drawing a shaky breath through her nose. *No. I can't see it like that, like a loss. I almost got through to him. And next time, I will.*

Hope.

That was what she needed to hold on to, for herself, for Elias, for her world above the clouds and these souls within the mist—hope that if she just tried hard enough, eventually she'd make a difference. If she could change just one mind, then maybe she could change them all. It was like learning her power all over again, or learning how to fly, or learning anything at all, really. She just had to take it one step at a time. Malek had written her people off, but she couldn't. She wouldn't.

Not yet.

Lyana repeated the thought, over and over again, until it became part of her. She repeated it like a prayer, slowly falling asleep to the lullaby in the words, a song made of hope and promise. She repeated it so thoroughly that when a nearby spike in spirit magic saturated the air, raising the hairs on her arms and tickling her skin, she hardly noticed. The outside world ceased to exist and she slipped peacefully into her dreams.

RAFE

assi was there. Cassi had seen him. Rafe kept his eyes peeled on the mist, studying the ashen vapors swirling in the wind. The king had been talking to someone—someone who wasn't there, someone who'd been little more than spirit.

Kasiandra. Cassi. Kasiandra. Cassi.

They're the same.

She was a dreamwalker. That's what Brighty had called it. She could separate her spirit from her body in sleep. She could dive inside people's minds.

It was her.

It had to be.

So what? the bitter, broken part of him snapped. *She did this to you. She cut off your wings. She dropped you over the edge. You really think she won't do the same to Xander? Won't do worse?*

No.

No, she wouldn't. Gods alive, he hoped she wouldn't. He had to believe differently or he'd lose his mind. He'd never forgive himself for not doing more, for not finding some other way home, for not being there to stop her.

Please, Cassi. Please. Whatever your motives, whatever the king told you, please don't do it. Please spare him.

Magic wrapped around Rafe's legs and chest, dragging him forward. He stared over his shoulder, the muscles in his neck straining with the effort as his body turned away. Metal dug into his wrists and arms. Green sparks flashed and the metal clamp across his lips jerked, forcing his face to the side. All sight of the mist fled, replaced with darkness as he was led inside the warehouse. At the front, the king walked with his *photo'kine*, the man's fist encased in white light to lead them through the shadows. The ominous *thud* of a door closing echoed down the corridor, making goose bumps rise along Rafe's skin. Suddenly, he remembered Xander's life wasn't the only one in question tonight.

What did they want with him?

What were they planning?

They walked on, nothing but the stomping of boots and the soft jangle of metal clasps to fill the silence. The metal mage to Rafe's left was tall and lithe, a study in harsh edges and contrast, the same as her magic, while the water mage to his right was short and curvy, features as fluid as the element she wielded. Neither would look at him. Not that he expected their help, of course. They were the ones who'd trapped him here in the first place.

He wasn't a fool. He was alone, as he'd always been, no

one to save him but himself. And the chances of that were looking rather dire.

The king's magic was impossible to fight. Oh, he wanted to, and he'd tried, but it was futile. The power sparkled like stardust in the air, as beautiful as it was impenetrable, holding not to his body but to his soul with a grip Rafe didn't know how to shirk. Where Lyana's magic had felt wild and free, brimming with passion, the king's was as sharp and emotionless as a blade.

When they reached the end of the hall, Kal released his magic and the world went black. As the mage pulled open the door, an eerie orange glow crept along the wooden walls, casting the king in reddish hue, the pale contours of his skin taking on a gruesome edge. Over his head, Rafe caught sight of the dragon, still bound and chained, its back rising and falling with slow, unhurried breaths.

He'd known their destination, of course, but drew in a sharp breath nevertheless, a jolt of fear hurtling down his chest and settling in his gut like bad food. A burning scent filled his nose, drawing him back to that room and to his parents and to the blinding heat so severe it had stolen his sight, the pain so intense that even surrounded by flames he'd fallen into darkness.

Still, Rafe stepped inescapably forward.

One foot rose, then the other, again and again, as silent screams clogged his throat. The king's magic pulled him along as if he were a dog on a leash, until they stopped beside a table fitted with leather straps. Jacinta removed the metal chains binding his hands.

No. No. No.

It was useless. In his head, he kicked and punched, struggling with every ounce of strength he possessed. In reality, his body sank onto the tabletop and lay perfectly still as Nyomi secured the binds. The king leaned forward, his face cast in shadow and silhouetted by the fiery aura of the beast looming behind him.

"I know you're confused, Aleksander," he said quietly, tone so emotionless and flat Rafe wondered if the man even had a soul. "But you'll understand soon. If you remember the terms of our agreement, you promised to bring me a dragon and I promised to give you the sky. Well, I'm a man of my word, like I said, and tonight I'm making good on my end of the deal. Don't try to fight it. I assure you, you won't win. And in the end, it will only make things harder. Now, I'm not saying it won't hurt, because it will. But, *invinci*, as with every other pain you've faced, in time you'll heal."

A sick feeling turned Rafe's stomach. The words sat on his chest like a weight, crushing him until he had no breath.

What did that mean?

What was going on?

The king's magic filled the room, golden and glittering. The three mages stepped away from the table, back and back and back, until they were nowhere in sight. Rafe couldn't scream. He couldn't fight. His heart pounded in his chest, his lungs swelling as power saturated the air, making his skin tingle. The dragon stirred beside him, its dark scales shifting to reveal the simmering fire beneath its skin. Heat flared, not from without, but from within, as though someone had pressed a torch to Rafe's soul, setting it aflame.

He didn't understand.

And then, with horrifying clarity, he did.

XANDER

"Leave us," Xander ordered as soon as the door of the cell clanked shut. If Helen thought to protest, the expression on his face was enough to send her quietly away. The gentle scuffle of boots faded, followed by the soft *thud* of a door closing at the other end of the hall, leaving him and Cassi alone—if that was even her name.

She was right on the other side of the metal bars, but he found he couldn't even look at her to ask. The haunting feeling of her stare was too much. Instead he walked, back and forth, back and forth, his footsteps echoing loudly in the silence. His fists, one real and one invisible, were clenched so tightly the muscles in his arms trembled. Fury stole his sight, blurring the world so he could focus on nothing but the memory of her silvery eyes, as luminescent and mysterious as the moon, churning with a single thought—*kill me*.

Why?

Why hadn't she cut his throat?

Why had she left him the opening?

Why?

Why?

Why?

"Gods alive," he shouted, though the words came out guttural and broken. The sound reverberated off the walls, a monster brought to life. Xander slammed his hand into the bars, the sting upon his skin a welcome pain that stifled the emotions threatening to undo him. Questions, and questions, and more questions. He wanted answers, and for the first time, he knew exactly where to get them.

Slowly, his gaze shifted over the rough stone floor, traveling back and back and back, until it reached her leather boots, then higher, up the lean length of her legs and the slim curve of her waist, past the empty sheaths, to the soft brown waves framing her neck and the elegant arc of her throat. He followed the edge of her jaw, avoiding her lips, until finally he met those steely eyes which had never seemed to match the rest of her. She was warm, the golden undertone of her skin, the bronze highlights in her hair, the brightness of her smile. He'd been drawn to her like a moth to a flame, fooled by the brilliant display. But now he saw the real her reflected in those frigid irises, as cold and unfeeling as her home.

The fight in him gave out.

Xander wrapped his fingers around the metal bar, holding up his body as his legs went weak. Even as his heart seemed to spill from his chest, he didn't look away. His anger was the only thing keeping him on his feet.

"Who are you?" he asked. *Who are you that you could profess to miss Lyana with one breath and then hide her with the next? Who are you that you could befriend my brother one day, and then hurt him like I know you did? Who are you that you could press your lips to my throat one night, and then hold a knife to the same spot hours later?*

Who are you?

Who?

Cassi said nothing.

"Who are you?" he shouted, with a fervor that surprised even him.

She recoiled as though struck, but remained silent.

"What did you do to Rafe?"

His stomach sank as she hid her face.

"What did you do?" he said, hardly recognizing the rough and feral quality to his voice. But what had kindness ever gotten him? Overlooked by his father. Pitied by his mother. Betrayed by his brother. Deceived by his mate. And now this. Broken by the only woman he thought might have seen the real him.

Xander let go of the bar and pulled the black-and-white feather from his pocket. Cassi refused to look at him, so he tossed it through the cell toward the spot where her gaze met the floor and watched in silence as it swayed gently down, fluttering like a butterfly over a dark field. It was so quiet he heard the subtle swish of bristles meeting stone as the feather came to a stop. Its bloodied edge gleamed crimson in the light.

"I found this in his mother's old rooms, buried among the soot in the fireplace. Ironic, isn't it? The spot made for fire was the only one that didn't burn. I know you hurt him, Cassi. Why? And how badly? And where is he?"

The muscles in her jaw clenched, but other than that, she didn't move.

"Dammit, Cassi!" He slammed his hand against the bars again, this time with so much force they rang softly, sending a shiver down the back of his neck. This wasn't him. Maybe that was a good thing. "Tell me what you did to him. Tell me. Did he discover who you were? Did you—did you kill him?" He tripped over the word, his emotions getting the best of him as a clog formed in his throat. Xander swallowed it away. "I'm the crown prince of the House of Whispers, and I'm done playing nice. If you won't tell me what you did, I'll bring someone in who is trained in all manner of ways to force you to talk."

Cassi remained still.

There was only one move left he hoped might incite her, before he had to make good on that threat. "Tell me, Cassi. Tell me what you did. Or when I leave this hall, I will take to the skies, dive into the mist, and find him myself."

She finally looked up. "Then you'll give him exactly what he wants."

"Who?"

She didn't say. Yet finally, he realized it wasn't because she didn't want to. Fractures had formed in her icy irises, expanding like fissures on a frozen lake. The cracks revealed a deep pool of despair underneath. Someone had a hold on her, as physical as two hands around her throat, cutting off the words. One guess who.

"The man from the sacred nest," he said slowly.

She turned her face to the side as though worried her expression might expose the truth. It had. Perhaps not the one he wanted, but it was the one he needed now. Somewhere beneath the lies, somewhere deep inside, she was still Cassi—not a heartless, brutal traitor, but the woman who had made him feel like a warrior. Maybe not the sort he'd spent his life reading about in books, but a warrior all the same. And if she was still Cassi, then he could still be Xander, a fact for which he was grateful. Ruthlessness wasn't a weapon he knew how to wield. If it were, she'd be dead right now, bleeding out on her bedroom floor.

He thought back to that moment in her room, the point of her knife digging into his skin. Everything in her had been braced for a killing blow as her eyes slowly met his, but she hadn't been worried about a blade. She'd been terrified of what she'd see on his face—of his disgust, of his loathing. But he'd felt none of those things, and even now, despite the rage unchained from his invisible fist running rampant through his veins, he didn't hate her.

He couldn't.

Maybe that was the key to breaking down her walls. Not using force, like that man with his magic holding her hostage. But by tossing her a rope and inviting her to join him on the other side.

"Cassi, please," he whispered, the words as vulnerable as the heart he'd left strewn across the floor, one stomp from smashing in entirely. "This isn't you."

"You don't know me," she growled, as though trying to be tough, but all he heard was her pain.

At first, it struck him like a slap. What right did she have to ache? She was the one who'd hurt him, and Rafe, and Lyana, and probably everyone whose paths she'd ever crossed.

Then he breathed, and thought about his brother and his mate, and how their betrayal had landed like a dagger to the heart until he'd looked beyond himself to see the truth their lies had been hiding. There were always two sides to a story, and before he cast judgment, he needed to learn hers.

"I do know you, Cassi," he said gently, filling the emptiness between them with a tether he hoped she'd take, an invitation to step out of the shadows and join him in the light. "I don't know why you hurt Rafe, or why you're working with the man who took Lyana, or why you lied. I don't know what you're planning. I'm not even sure I know your real name. But I do know you, and I know you're not the terrible person you're trying so hard to be. You could've killed me in your room. You had the knife at my throat, and you could've won. But you retreated. Why? You knew I'd never hurt you, and you could've used it against me. But you didn't. Why? You chose to design that weapon. You chose to give it to me. And maybe it wasn't conscious, but when you held my arms to my chest and pressed your blade against my skin, you chose to give me that opening. You're too smart and too sharp to have ever let that happen by chance. You wanted to get caught, Cassi. And I'm not entirely sure why, but I can't help but think you wanted to get caught by me."

Her wings curled over her shoulders and she shrank back. This time there was nowhere to run, nowhere to hide.

The wall behind her was three meters thick, the bars before her unbreakable iron, but somehow he knew it was his gaze that held her trapped, the same way the dawning vulnerability in her eyes made his breath catch in his throat and his heart stand still.

"This is what I was afraid of," she confessed, the words escaping like a sigh. "Back on the beach, when I promised you a secret and you asked what I was afraid you might see, this right here is exactly what I meant."

On the beach...?

The dream came rushing back, the one which had been so real he'd thought he was losing his mind. They'd been side by side on a sandy shore, the waves washing over their legs, the sun on their faces. It had seemed so real. She had seemed so real, lying beside him, the ocean soaking through her hair, the droplets glistening on her feathers. Yet even in his imagination, there had been a wall around her heart.

What are you so afraid of? he'd asked. *What are you so worried I'll see?*

Her expression had been inscrutable as a single word fell from her lips. *Me.*

"But that was a dream," he murmured, shaking his head.

Cassi shrugged. "That doesn't make it any less real."

Magic, he realized in a moment of perfect clarity. *She must have magic. Just like Lyana. Just like Rafe. Just like that man. All of them have magic.*

There was still something missing, a piece he couldn't quite see.

As he opened his mouth to speak, Cassi cut in.

"Let me ask you a question now, Xander," she said in a grave tone. Suddenly, he could see her teetering on the edge of her wall, one jump from crossing over or one slip from falling back inside. "Would you change things if you could? Not just for Lyana. And not just for Rafe. But even for people like me, a traitor and a spy, and for all the others who live in fear, the ones you'll never meet and the ones in your own city who turn away as you walk by, worried what their prince might see. Would you help us, if you could?"

He knew his answer immediately, but he didn't want a wall of iron between them as he spoke this truth, so he dipped his hand inside his pocket and pulled out the key. Cassi watched with a fierceness that made his fingers tremble. When he opened the door, she could have run. She could have overpowered him and escaped.

She didn't.

She stood frozen as he stepped inside, frozen as he walked closer, frozen as he took one of her hands in his, cursing his disability for the millionth time in his life as his right arm hung limp by his side. As though she could read his thoughts, Cassi finally moved, just enough to reach out and grip his forearm, connecting them in every way, their eyes locked, their limbs entwined, their bodies close, and the outer edges of their wings brushing. Nothing seemed to exist outside of them and this moment, and the answer waiting on his tongue.

"You might not believe me, but I know what it is to live in terror," he said, the words raspy and raw. "Maybe not the way you do, or the way Lyana did, or the way anyone with magic does, but in my own way. The moment I found Rafe buried beneath the charred bodies of his parents, my own father burned beyond recognition, his skin blackened and crisp, I understood true terror. When I pulled my brother from the wreckage, his skin boiling and raw, yet still fleshy and pink, I knew he was different. And I knew that even with all my power and all my privilege, if the truth came out, I would never be able to save him. Ever since then, I've lived in terror that one day I'll have to be the one to give the order, that I'll have to watch in silent horror as the executioner's blade falls, that I'll have to spend the rest of my days knowing I was the one who killed him. If there's a way to keep Rafe safe, and Lyana safe, and you, and however many others there are like you, then I'd take it if I could. If magic isn't the enemy, then please, Cassi, tell me what is so I can learn how to fight that instead."

She closed her eyes and took a deep breath. He waited and watched, not sure if his words, as honest as they were, would be enough to change her mind.

"I hope you mean that," she finally said, opening eyes as gray, opaque, and shrouded in mystery as the only sea he'd ever known. Then, meeting his, her gaze caught the reflection of the flames, and the clouds in it dissipated until her face shone like the sun after a storm. "It's a long story, and I'm not sure where to begin, but I guess I'll start here. My true name is Kasiandra'd'Rokaro, and I was born beneath the mist."

42

CASSI

I t turned out that betraying Malek, his people, and the entire world beneath the mist was far easier than Cassi had ever imagined. Once she got started, she didn't know how to stop. It was as though she were a dummy in the practice yard, filled with beans, and Xander had punctured her rough exterior, sending all the lies that once filled her cascading out.

She told him of her early years in the House of Peace, torn between two worlds and two best friends. She told him of Malek and his prophecy. She told him of the dragons and the rift and the spell holding the isles aloft. She told him of the cities shrouded in mist and the magic keeping those people alive. She told him of Lyana and her destiny. And finally, at long last, she told him of Rafe.

A strangled noise escaped Xander's lips as she described cutting off his brother's wings and dropping him over the edge. It was the only sound he made before clasping his fingers over his mouth, a worried groove digging into his forehead. Though he swayed on his feet, clearly shaken, he let her finish.

"So I stayed behind with my orders to kill you, but I didn't want to, Xander. I fought with Malek, and I struggled, the two sides of myself at war. I'm ashamed to say I don't know what I would've done if you hadn't come into my room and interrupted my plans. But you did. And now here we are. You have your answers. You have the truth. The only question left is what you're going to do with it."

Silence stretched between them.

Xander stared at the floor, still gripping his jaw, as the words washed over him. She didn't know if he even realized he'd been stepping back, slowly, inch by inch, with every new secret she told. Now he was all the way across the cell, his onyx feathers pressed against the iron bars, as though he were the one trapped with nowhere left to escape.

Cassi, on the other hand, felt free. There was no pain, no guilt, no remorse, like she'd always imagined there would be if her lies were revealed. Malek had warned her so many times of the risk, holding the fate of the world over her head like a cudgel about to drop, and now that it had, she felt unburdened rather than destroyed. Only time would tell if her actions had sacrificed the world or saved it, but for the first time in her life, she felt as light and weightless as a bird, as fierce and uninhibited as the sea, the two sides of her finally joined. Though she knew Malek would be furious, Cassi had no regrets as she stood staring at Xander and waiting for him to speak. No matter what he said, she'd found a strange sort of peace in knowing all her terrible deeds had finally come out in the light.

"Cassi..."

Her name had never sounded so terrible coming through his lips, scratchy and strained, as though it had been pulled out by some hideous force. She braced herself for what would come next. In a few short minutes, she'd destroyed his entire way of life. The gods he believed in so deeply? Nothing but magic. The kingdom he loved so dearly? Hanging on a dying spell and ready to fall at any moment. The mate he wanted to save? A woman who was never meant to be his. And the mysterious man he wanted to fight? A king of prophecy he could never hope to best.

"Rafe," he said after a prolonged silence, staring at the uneven stones along the ground as though the pressure of his eyes alone could smooth their rough edges. "Where's Rafe?"

Of course, she thought, releasing the breath she'd been holding. The tension in her muscles melted away. *I should've known his first thought would be for Rafe.* "He's in a city called Da'Kin, being held hostage by my king."

"Alive?"

"Alive." She nodded, even though he wasn't looking at her. She wasn't even sure he was looking at anything in this room. His focus was both sharp and distant, as though by fixing his eyes on the tiniest crack in a rock, he'd somehow gained access to an entirely new world.

"Could Lyana heal him, if they were brought together? Could she fix him?"

"I don't know," she said softly. "I don't think she understands how."

"But she could learn?"

"In theory."

"Then I have to save them."

She jerked upright, her wings expanding in protest. "You'll never get through Malek."

"I don't care. I have to try."

"Xander!"

The sharpness of her voice finally drew his attention. She saw every emotion swirling over his features, the confusion and the anger and the despair. The only thing she didn't see was hate, but she saw the yearning for it, as though he wanted to curse her name but couldn't quite form the words. Gone was the prince with lavender starlight in his eyes, his irises sparkling with mirth as she pressed him up against a wall, glittering with joy as they debated across a table laden with open books, glowing like the vast night sky as they held each other close in the darkness. Cassi might not have killed him, but she'd killed a part of him—the part that maybe, someday, might have loved her.

It was for the best.

She wasn't a creature made for love, anyway.

"Malek will kill you."

"Then at least I'll die fighting for the people I love, which right now, Cassi, seems like more than I can say for you."

"That's not fair."

"Isn't it?"

She looked away. His gaze bored into her cheek, so hot it felt as though a torch were pressed against the spot, burning her skin.

"You say you love Lyana, but you've done nothing

except lie to her for her entire life and then abandon her when she needed you most. You say you're sorry for what you did to Rafe, and yet you've done nothing to save him, to try to right the wrong. You say you care for this world among the clouds, but at every turn you've tried to bring it down. I might've spent my life buried in books, Cassi, but even I know that words mean nothing without action. You're a coward, and—and—" He released a heavy breath, some of the fight leaking away. "And, truth be told, I've always feared I might be too. But I won't let that be how my story ends. You say the isles will fall, and there's nothing I can do to stop it. You say the dragons are coming and an ancient prophecy is the only hope left to best them. In your eyes, I'm helpless, and maybe I am. But Rafe needs me. And I'm done running away."

"Xander..." Her voice faded into nothing. She wasn't sure what to say. He was right. She was a coward, but she'd never thought of him that way. He was kind, and noble, and full of honor, which was why it took no effort at all to imagine him flying to his death like a valiant knight from one of his books. But there was more than one way to be a hero, and this way would surely get him killed. "Xander, I—"

The ground shook and Cassi stopped abruptly. The rock walls grumbled as dust rained from the ceiling to cloud the air. Every other earthquake she'd experienced had been caused by a blast of magic, but this was different. There was no tingle in the hairs at the back of her neck, whispering of power. There'd been nothing to prompt it. The tremors were steady and slow, not the rough aftereffects of unleashed energy. This was something she didn't understand.

"Do you know why this is happening?" he asked over the noise.

"You were right back in Rynthos," she told him. "You were right, and I made you doubt yourself. When people use magic close to the god stones, it weakens the spell holding them afloat. But this feels different, Xander."

"Different how?"

"I can't explain, just different. That day in the sacred nest, Lyana released a lot of power. The spell might've been weakened. The stone might still be recovering. I don't know."

"I have to go."

"Wait!"

Somehow they were near enough, and she snatched his hand. Cassi wasn't sure when in the conversation they'd drifted closer, as though some unconscious force had brought them together. He swallowed as he glanced at the spot where her tan fingers wrapped around his fair ones, but he didn't move.

"Xander, please. Before you go, you have to promise me you won't say anything. Not to Helen. Not to your mother. Not even to Luka. I know you don't owe me anything, and I know I've lost your trust, but you must understand that this information will destroy everything. If the avians find out what lies beneath the mist, they'll gather armies. They'll charge headfirst into a war they can't win. The mages down there don't want to hurt the people of this world, but they will if there's no other option. Please don't make magic your enemy. It doesn't have to be. Lyana is the Queen Bred of Snow and I have faith in her. She loves her homeland. She won't let it be destroyed."

He closed his eyes so tightly little wrinkles sprouted at the corners, and then wrenched his hand free. "I have to go."

"Xander."

He ignored her plea as he turned and pulled the key from his pocket. After he crossed the threshold, he slammed the bars shut, the ring of metal audible through the subtle groan of the still-shaking earth. He bolted the lock, sealing her inside.

"More assassins will come," she shouted after him, pushing her cheeks against the iron as though she could squeeze through. He walked steadily away, his black wings spread for balance as the ground quivered. "They can be anyone. Don't drop your guard. Don't—"

A door thudded closed.

Cassi slumped against the bars, holding them with both hands to keep from sliding to the ground. Yet there was no time for pity, no time to question things. She pushed herself up with a sharp inhale and scanned the air, studying the dust still dropping from the ceiling and searching for a disruption. Of course there wouldn't be one. She knew that. Still, she couldn't help but feel as though maybe she wasn't alone.

"If there's a *dormi'kine* in here, I suggest you go to the sacred nest and check on the god stone. Something's not right, and I have somewhere else I need to be."

Without another word, she collapsed to the ground and

slipped into her spirit body, the one no walls, no bars, and no magic could contain.

Xander had been right.

Actions, and not words, defined a person. She could say she was sorry to Rafe, but what had she done to help him? She could say she loved Lyana, but what had she done to ease her pain? It had been easy in the House of Peace, to hold a bow in her hands and an arrow to her eye, and pretend that was all it took to help her friend, but those were lies she'd told herself. This time right here was what defined her. And what had she done? Hidden. From her orders. From her decisions. From her consequences. She would hide no more.

Maybe she couldn't stop Malek.

Maybe she couldn't save Rafe.

But she knew someone who could, and it was well past time to face her.

43

LYANA

Thick stone walls lit by staggered torches seemed to extend into infinity. As Lyana ran, the slapping of her feet echoed down the hall. The space was too cramped for flight. Her feathers scraped against the roughly cut blocks while she searched for the end, but there was nothing. No door. No window. No exit in sight. Just a straight passage that grew smaller with each step, the ceiling and the floor compressing in as she ran, and ran, and ran, going nowhere, until—

She fell.

The ground gave out beneath her, turning to liquid. She sank into shadowy depths as bright colors flashed. It felt like swimming, or maybe flying, the longer she hung in that void, spinning head over heels—or was the room spinning? Everything swirled. She was caught in the vortex, swept away. Then just as suddenly, the world sharpened into perfect clarity.

She was flying.

Crisp air stung her cheeks even as her muscles burned. She pumped her wings to cut across the sky, buoyed by the wind. The land below passed in a blur of dark jagged rock and a surface of frozen, crystalline snow refracting the sun into a glittering rainbow. Above, the world was painted a stark blue, broken only by fluffy clouds. Lyana laughed, snapping in her wings and plummeting to the ground, only to catch herself, then soar back into the sky. How long had it been since her world had been anything but gray? The silvery mist of midday that was almost too bright to look upon and thick enough to shroud the sun. The deep charcoal of midnight, so dark and foreboding, as though hiding a den of monsters. Her eyes almost hurt from seeing so much saturated sapphire, but it was a welcome ache, like coming to the surface for that first desperate breath.

Gray? She shook her head. *Why has my world been gray?*

"Lyana!"

"Come on, Cassi!" she shouted back to her friend. Up ahead, she spotted a crack in the landscape where the ground had simply fallen away. The sky bridge stretched across the opening, the clear stones glimmering in the sun. "We're almost there!"

"Lyana, wait!"

"I'll race you to the cave!"

Was that what they were already doing? She couldn't remember. Why had they left the crystal palace? What were they searching for?

Oh well. No matter.

She pumped her wings, a grin widening her cheeks as a wild thrill zipped up her throat. When she reached the canyon, she dove headfirst, cutting between two walls of sharp, uneven rock, her eyes on the gray fog blanketing the world below. The Sea of Mist. As usual, awe swelled inside her chest, along with the familiar ache of yearning. But there was something else too, something she couldn't quite place.

A memory tugged at the back of her thoughts.

Lyana landed just inside the shadows of their cave, her brows furrowed as she stared into the dark depths beyond. When she closed her eyes, the image flashed, of a man with brilliant blue eyes, and windswept black hair, and silky obsidian wings. Firelight flickered over fair skin as she pressed her dark hands to his back, his muscles writhing beneath her touch as though fighting a shiver. But there was something else there too, a subtle silver sheen rising up to meet the golden shimmer of her magic, two powers joining as one.

Rafe.

The name made her gasp. Recoiling from the darkness, she turned back to the light as Cassi swept into the cave. Behind her friend, the sky bridge loomed. It flashed red with blood, and a dragon sat propped on the stones, a beast made of onyx scales and fire, red eyes staring straight at her. But no, not at her. At the broken and bloodied raven clutched within its claws.

Rafe.
And the dragon.
And the trials.
And the House of Whispers.
And the mating ceremony.

And Malek.

The past few months came rushing back as she glanced at Cassi in mounting horror. Even her friend looked different now. Not sarcastic and spunky, her hip perpetually cocked to the side as she mocked Lyana's newest plan for adventure—but broken somehow, her eyes like a sword that had struck one shield too many, now shattered into pieces on the battlefield.

"I know you're confused," Cassi said, her voice warm and loving, yet teeming with fear. "It's always confusing the first time for someone with magic, someone strong enough to sense my presence in their mind. But you have to believe me when I tell you this isn't a dream. This is real."

"Oh, is it?" Lyana asked, her focus shifting from the rock beneath her feet, to the canyon outside, then back to her friend. "If this isn't a dream, then how are we here? How are we home?"

"Fine, we're in a dream." Cassi rolled her eyes, and the sight instantly relaxed Lyana. "But not the way you think of them. I'm here, inside your head. I'm with you. For real."

"How?"

"Magic."

"Good one." Lyana snorted and crossed her arms. "You want me to believe my best friend had magic our whole lives and didn't tell me?"

"Yes."

Lyana frowned as Cassi's gaze bored into her like a blade, cutting a fragile piece of her heart she'd never known she needed to protect. "I don't believe you."

"Has Malek told you of *dormi'kine* magic?"

How does she know that name? Lyana shook her head. *This is all in my head. I know his name, so she does too.* "No."

"We call it dreamwalking. It's the power to separate your spirit from your body, and to sink into other people's minds while they sleep to control their dreams. I have it. I've had it for my entire life, and I never told you, because I was using it to spy on you for my king."

"My father?"

"No," Cassi said, then swallowed, gritting her teeth as though trying to grind the truth to dust. "King Malek, the King Born in Fire."

"How do you...?" Lyana trailed off, shaking her head. "But you have wings. You're one of us."

"A trick," her friend offered slowly, as though worried she might run. "I was born beneath the mist, and at the age of three my mother walked into my room one night to find the skin above my heart glowing silver. My magic announced itself, and she did what any loyal soldier would do for the good of the world—she handed me over to the crown. Malek has probably never taken you to the aviary in Da'Kin, but they have birds from nearly every house, and they chose an owl for me. He joined our souls using his *aethi'kine* magic, then had his mages carry me to the world above, where his plan fell perfectly into place. You and I were best friends before I was old enough to even realize I was being used as a spy, and by then, it was too late. You know the prophecy. You know the stakes. So many times I wanted to tell you, but Malek swore me to secrecy. He said we had to wait until the arrival of your magic. He said we had to be sure. He said it was all in the name of saving the world, but lately...I don't know."

That sounded like him, dealing ultimatums.

But if this was true, it would mean her whole life had been a lie. Cassi was her best friend, her rock. She would never do this.

Would she?

"I don't believe you." Lyana choked on the words, her breath escaping her lips in rapid white puffs. She stepped back until her wings hit rock, and then back again until her feathers were crushed against the sharp edges. The pain kept her grounded. She felt like Elias, backed into a corner as his whole world flipped. She was caught in a rush of denial, staring at the broken pieces and certain she could make them fit. "This can't be real. It can't be."

"It is." Cassi was adamant, which left Lyana queasy. Her friend thrived on quick wordplay and playful banter. There was nothing she loved more than teasing and nothing she loathed more than brutal honesty. Perhaps there'd been a reason for that preference. "Please, Ana. What can I say to convince you I'm telling the truth? Ask me anything. Please."

"I— I—"

Lyana broke off, unsure. They'd grown up together. They'd spent their lives sneaking out of the palace, exploring the dove territory, sitting in her room braiding each other's hair, having entire conversations across a silent dinner table, needing nothing but the expressions on their faces to communicate. There was nothing she could ask this

Cassi that her subconscious didn't already know, nothing except...

"Where have you been?" The words tumbled out before she could stop them, ringing with an accusation she knew wasn't fair yet was there all the same. Where had Cassi been these past few weeks while Lyana was in the mist? Why hadn't she come to find her? What had she deemed more important than going after her best friend? "Why aren't you with me?"

Cassi sighed. The sound trembled in the air, rife with heartache.

"I wanted to be," she murmured, the words more vulnerable than any Cassi had spoken before, not in the hours they'd spent gossiping in their rooms, or chatting in their cave, or scheming in the shadows of the crystal palace. The raw honesty in them made Lyana shudder, highlighting just how dishonest her friend's voice had been so many times before. Cassi reached for her hand, then paused, as though unsure if she still had that privilege. "I wanted to be there with you more than anything, Ana. In all the nights and days and years I spent trying to figure out how I would tell you the truth, I never thought it would be like this. I thought I'd be by your side, maybe in the wooden depths of a royal ship or in the castle overlooking Da'Kin. I thought we'd be two birds discovering a new world together. A world without lies. A world where you were finally the queen I always knew you'd become, and I was whatever you needed me to be—best friend, loyal follower, faithful guard. That was all I wanted. It's all I've ever wanted. But the day of your mating ceremony, things didn't go as planned. I was supposed to be with you. I was supposed to be there when you woke up, to help explain, to help you understand. I was supposed—"

Cassi broke off as her voice cracked. She turned her face to the side, staring into the dark corners of the cave with so much intensity Lyana wondered what memory she saw within the shadows.

"When I got to the ship you were already inside," she said, voice hollow. "Malek told me Xander had seen too much, and ordered me to stay behind to kill him. I didn't want to, but he used his magic to hold me down until you were out of sight. I should've followed. I should've ignored him and raced after you. I should've done so many things, but I was afraid. Of facing you. Of facing the things I've done. I'm still terrified. But I realized something. If I stay frozen in my fear, it will never go away. The only thing I can do is face it head-on. You might never forgive me, and that's fine. I wouldn't blame you. But at least I'll know I tried. At least I'll know that for once in my life I did something I knew in my heart was right."

Cassi took a deep, shaky breath, finding Lyana's eyes. For her part, Lyana didn't look away as she let the words sink in, all the memories of her youth tumbling into versions she didn't recognize, with new questions she'd never in her life thought would be there. Cassi was a spy for Malek? Was that why she'd befriended her? Was that why she'd put up with her? Was their entire friendship a lie?

Then a less selfish thought took over.

What happened to Xander?

"Cassi, did you—" The panic in her voice cut the

sentence short, stealing her voice so she couldn't even complete it. But her friend understood.

"No. He's fine, Ana. Furious with me, but alive."

"You told him?"

"He caught me."

"Caught you what?"

Cassi's lips thinned, but she didn't answer. She didn't have to.

Lyana gasped, her hand coming to her lips to cover the sound. She'd seen Cassi protective before. She knew she was a fierce warrior. But she'd never seen a lethal intent in her eyes like the sharp glint that now shone there. "You didn't..."

"I tried. And that's not the worst thing I've done, which is why I'm here. There's something I haven't told you, Ana, something I don't think you'll be able to forgive."

Her heart lurched painfully. "What?"

"Rafe. I—" Cassi's mouth hung open, her chin wobbling as though fighting to say the words, to give them life. A pressure squeezed Lyana's lungs until she felt she couldn't breathe. Her throat burned for lack of air. Her head felt light. "The morning of your mating ceremony, I found him in his mother's rooms at the base of the castle. We fought. And I—I cut off his wings at Malek's bidding, then dropped him over the edge into the Sea of Mist where a ship was waiting to collect him."

Lyana swayed on her feet, her fingers clutching her chest as though to loosen the invisible binds holding her trapped. That day in Da'Kin, she'd been so sure she'd felt him in the crowd, so positive his soul had been one of the many calling out for her, but she'd been looking for a man with wings, for a raven. She hadn't seen. She hadn't known.

What if he'd needed her?

What if he'd been there pleading and she hadn't listened?

Oh, gods, Rafe. I'm sorry. I'm so sorry.

What had he been going through? Her wings had been clipped and that had been hard enough, but to lose them entirely? To lose the sky and his home and everything all at once?

And Cassi had done it.

Cassi!

Cassi and—

"Wait," Lyana spat, finally finding her voice, a fury erupting in her gut like a wave of dragon flames. "You said Malek. You said at Malek's bidding."

"Yes," Cassi answered, her voice no more than a whisper.

"He ordered you to do that to Rafe? He knows he's in the mist? He knows— He knows—"

"He knows everything."

Lyana shut down her emotions, locking them away before they had a chance to overwhelm her. Focus sharpened her mind. When she spoke, her voice was deadly serious. "Where's Rafe now?"

"That's why I came," Cassi said, bracing herself. There was a graveness to her voice, as though the worst had passed and now it was time to get to business. "I saw him earlier this evening, trapped in a warehouse on the outskirts of the city. Malek was there with some of his mages. I don't know what he's planning, but it has something to do with the dragon his hunters caught. And I'm worried—I'm worried for Rafe. I don't know what the king has told you while he's been teaching you. I don't know what you know about him or what you think. The two of you share something no one else will understand. But I know Malek in a way you never will, and I know that he's capable of anything, and I mean anything, that he sets his mind to. No matter how ruthless, no matter how cruel, if he deems it necessary, he'll see it done whatever the cost."

So be it. His voice slithered across Lyana's thoughts like a snake through the woods, creeping in and out of the shadows, winding through Cassi's words. When she'd said his plan would lead to war, that countless people would die, that her world would be destroyed, his answer had been, *So be it.*

"I have to go. How do I get out of here, Cassi? I have to go."

"Just tell yourself to wake up, and you will. Malek always could. I'll come back, if you want me to, if you want more answers, if you want anything at all. Just say the word and I'll come back as soon as I can."

Lyana didn't speak.

The words were stuck on her tongue.

Cassi had lied to her for their entire lives. Cassi had been spying for Malek the whole time. Cassi had tried to kill Xander. Cassi had maimed Rafe.

The friend Lyana thought she knew vanished before her eyes. The wavy brown curls and speckled owl wings were the same, but when she looked into Cassi's eyes, she saw nothing of the girl she loved. All she saw was a stranger.

Cassi's voice was weak, almost pleading, as she repeated one final time, "I'll come back."

Lyana couldn't find the will to answer.

Instead, she held her friend's stare and thought, *Wake up.*

The last thing she saw before the dream dissolved was a single tear leaking from the corner of Cassi's eye. Then she woke to the dimly lit halls at the base of Malek's castle. Lyana eased herself to her feet and brought her magic to the surface. Elias's spirit hovered peacefully on the other side of the door, but that wasn't all she felt.

Stunning, overwhelming power drew a gasp from her lips, the force of it strong enough to blow her over. And deep within that power, like a familiar song carrying on the breeze, was a soul she recognized, crying out for help.

44

RAFE

The world was on fire. Every inch of his body burned. Rafe couldn't see. He didn't know which way was up or down. He couldn't feel his limbs, but he could *feel* the flames. The blaze smothered him. The heat melted his every thought away. There was nothing he could focus on except the pain, which was more excruciating than any he'd felt before, as though his spirit had been tied to a spit and hung within an inferno. The fire wove through every fiber of his soul, like threads spun of flame being sewn to his skin.

Rafe waited for blissful oblivion, but it never came.

Every time his mind started to go dark, something prodded it back, and the process began anew—more burning, more fire, more pain.

On and on.

With no end in sight.

Until the agony transported him somewhere else, and suddenly he was a child again, buried beneath his mother's body as a sea of flames crashed into their rooms, setting his life ablaze. The acrid smell of burned flesh stung his nose. Screams of terror and pain tore through the air, a sound he'd never forget, replaced by a silence that was somehow worse, nothing but the crackle and pop of fire, the sizzling more familiar than any lullaby. He was broken, lying there and waiting for the end. He didn't try to move. He didn't try to run. He didn't want to leave his mother and father. He wanted to follow them to Taetanos's realm, and for a brief moment, as his world went dark, he thought he had—until he woke to find his brother above him, tears in his eyes and a smile on his lips.

Xander.

His name broke through the blaze.

Xander.

He was in danger.

He needed—he needed—

The thought disappeared as a wave of heat pulled Rafe under. There was another creature drowning with him, whose screeches he didn't understand, whose language was different, whose body was beastly, but whose mind cried out in a way that pierced him with recognition. They were together in this, whatever this was. Their spirits were entwined.

Save us, he pleaded, to the gods, to the mist, to whoever was listening. *Save us.*

But this time, there would be no Xander to pull him from the wreckage. This time, there would be no mysterious dove to heal his wounds. This time, there would be no ship full of strangers waiting to pluck him from the sky. Brighty had been right, back on the ship, spewing words he didn't want to hear. No one was worried about him. No one was coming. No one cared. Not anymore.

And then he felt her.

Like a winter storm, her magic blew in, wild and untamed, fierce and unforgiving, a brief respite from the heat as frigid air brushed against his skin.

Ana, he thought as the fire fought to claim him. *You came.*

45

LYANA

The warehouse shone with the brilliance of the sun, almost blinding as Lyana raced through the mist. Flames chased the darkness away, the scent of burned wood filling the air, but it was the golden current of Malek's power that glowed brightest. Her wings sliced at the fog. The muscles in her back burned with a familiar heat, making her feel strong as the city passed beneath her in a blur—houses and canals blending into a series of shapeless shadows flowing like a river. She wasn't moving fast enough. Against the maelstrom of a city full of aching spirits, Rafe's cries struck like lightning, so piercing that everything else was left in shadow.

Lyana's magic arched across the sky with a speed she envied, crashing into the warehouse, fueled by a single command—*Stop!*

Malek's response was a swift, *No.*

His magic hit her like a wall. Lyana ricocheted off the golden wave, flipping in midair as the blast shot her backward. But the sky was her domain and the wind her kindred spirit. Gusts whooshed by and righted her body, her feathers at a perfect angle to catch the breeze. Invisible currents carried her forward, faster and faster, unleashed and free. Lyana braced for another attack, but Malek must have been too distracted because it never came.

A moment later, she realized why.

Four of his mages waited on the dock in front of the warehouse. Isaak was the only one presenting her with his back, too busy containing the raging fire to worry about her. The other three, though, stood in a line, their shoulders squared as magic simmered at their fingertips—Kal, Jacinta, and Nyomi. They could have been back in the arena, preparing for a training session. But this was real, and it was Rafe on the other side of that door. If Malek had thought an army of three would be enough to stop her, he hadn't been paying attention.

Lyana collapsed her wings and landed on the wet planks in a roll. By the time she stopped in a crouch, their spirits had already been snatched by her talons.

Kal acted first.

The last thing she saw before the world went a blinding white was his crimson hair blowing in the breeze as a furrow appeared in his freckled brow. She closed her eyes against the mage light, fighting back tears from the sting. With her magic, she didn't need to see. No matter how much power Kal pushed into the air, burning up the mist, she could still feel his soul. There was no way to hide. She knew exactly where he was. One with the spirit of the air, Lyana pulled on the wind and sent a gust barreling toward him. It slammed into his chest, knocking him clean off the dock, and he dropped into the sea.

The ivory flare snuffed out.

Lyana lifted her head, daring Jacinta and Nyomi to face her. Green sparks flared and two daggers rose clean out of the scabbards around Jacinta's waist. Lyana hardly paid attention. She was the queen of prophecy, and she knew, no matter what Malek's orders, they wouldn't kill her. They wanted to scare her, but they wouldn't succeed. Fury had burned all her fear away.

A flute of water shot toward her.

Lyana lifted her palm and bid it to stop.

A dagger sailed for her throat.

She simply swatted it away.

Run, she thought, their bodies trapped beneath the weight of her command. *Run into the city, and don't come back.*

They did.

Swirls of green and blue magic filled the air as the two women sprinted past, but the attacks were too little too late. Lyana easily deflected the metal Jacinta sent soaring in her wake. The ocean surged, but she held it back. A beam of ivory light erupted from the sea, and she turned to find Kal had resurfaced.

Swim, she thought, her grip on his soul absolute. *Swim away, and don't look back.*

He did.

Lyana closed her eyes, feeling their souls drift farther and farther out of reach. Eventually, when they were at a safe distance, she'd release them. She didn't want them dead —she just wanted them out of her way.

As she stood, Isaak glanced over his shoulder, the wrinkles on his face harsh in the firelight. Red magic and flames enveloped his fingers as he fought to control the blaze attempting to swallow the warehouse whole.

"I suggest you let me pass," she said.

His light brown eyes darkened with defeat. "Very well, my queen."

Lyana soared across the distance and used a blast of wind to throw open the warehouse doors. As she tore inside, a sea of gold immediately swept her away. Malek's power churned like a cyclone, catching her in its vortex. She couldn't see beyond his magic. It was everywhere. He was everywhere. Embers scorched her feathers and her braids whipped across her face, making her skin sting.

"Malek!" she called, trying to fight through the chaos. "Malek!"

The fire was everywhere and nowhere, in the magic, in the building, in the air she breathed. She tried to reach for Rafe, but she couldn't feel him anymore. A man screamed and she fought with all her might to follow that sound.

"Rafe! Rafe!"

Her feet brushed the ground and she dropped into a run, but it was useless. The wind blew her over, sending her stumbling to the side as she struggled to remain upright.

Your magic.

Use your magic.

Lyana reached for Malek with her power, sensing his soul within the madness. He was too weak to shirk her hold. A scream ripped through the air, but this time she realized it wasn't Rafe—it was him.

What's going on?

What's happening?

Using his spirit as a guide, she took step after step closer, her magic swirling around her like a shield to deflect his power. Through the golden glow, the dark outline of a table came into view. She recognized Malek, his blond hair swirling around his face and his lips pursed. Boils spotted his cheeks. One had broken, the skin red and raw underneath. His hands were pressed against the table, his index finger burned down to the bone. And next to him— next to him—

Aethios help me!

Rafe was strapped to the table, only it wasn't Rafe. It was like staring at a reflection on the surface of a pond, the image shifting as ripples passed through the water. One moment he was the man she knew, and the next, black scales appeared over his skin. One moment his eyes were blue, and the next, they flared a monstrous red. Leathery wings flashed beneath his back, coming and going like phantoms. Every second he changed, there then gone. The only constant was the grimace frozen across his shifting features, his lips curled back and his eyes like slits. His mouth was open so far she could see his tonsils. In the hollow of his throat, a ball of flame churned. Lyana didn't want to know what would happen if he screamed.

"Stop!" she cried to Malek. "You must stop!"

"I can't," he said, the words coming out strained, as

though saying each one demanded a silent battle. "We've come too far to turn back."

"What are you doing to him?"

"Soul joining."

"I don't—"

She broke off as a flame shot toward Malek, bubbling red against the gold. Lyana caught it in her magic, the fire raging within her grasp. As the sizzle dissipated, she saw the beast chained behind him, snarling as it fought against metal restraints. Its body was like Rafe's, shifting every second, rippling as though covered by a sheer fabric caught in a breeze. Malek groaned and his spine bent forward as pain twisted his features.

He's joining that thing—

He's making Rafe—

"You can't, Malek," she snapped, her eyes finding his. "You can't do this to him. You don't understand what it means, what it will do—"

"It's already done."

"Then undo it."

"Lyana—"

Her name turned into a hiss and the golden power in the air dimmed. Malek gripped the table, his jaw clenching as he stared at nothing, too lost in his magic. Another boil sprouted on his cheek. Lyana realized in horror that whatever Malek was doing, he was losing—and if he lost, Rafe would be lost with him.

"Help me," Malek demanded through gritted teeth. "Help me or watch him die. Those are your only two options left."

Lyana opened her mouth, the answer caught in her throat.

Rafe will hate this.

To be bonded with a dragon. To be truly fire cursed. It was his worst nightmare come to life. The people of their world would never understand. He would be a son of Vesevios, an outcast. He would never be welcomed back.

But at least he'll be alive.

Maybe it was selfish, but she needed him. His bravery. His acceptance. His tender soul. And though she didn't know why, some part of her understood on a fundamental level that the world needed him too.

Lyana found Malek's midnight eyes. "What can I do?"

"Heal me."

With one more glance at Rafe, Lyana sank into her power and leaned across the table to grasp Malek's hand. Her magic disappeared into his skin, healing his wounds. The boils covering his face gradually sank back into his cheeks. The burns sealed. The raw and exposed flesh regenerated. Deeper than that, the fire burning his soul receded, her power providing the protection his couldn't. As he strengthened, the golden aura in the room did too, no longer pulsing as though at war, but sturdy as a wall. With his control regained, Lyana could finally sense Rafe's soul and the dragon's, half sewn together and half separate, neither sure if it should give in or fight to be free. The beast's spirit was pure fire, so hot Lyana burned just from being near it. She couldn't imagine how Malek had managed to control it on his own for so long. And Rafe's spirit—

Her heart lurched.

Rafe's spirit was just as she remembered, yearning and wounded, so tough on the outside yet so fragile underneath the hard exterior, his heart overflowing with all it had to give. If she closed her eyes, she could remember what it felt like to be the recipient of such steadfast devotion for that one brief night when she was his and he was hers, and nothing else in the world mattered.

Cassi's words came back to haunt. *Malek knows everything.*

"Did you do this because—" She paused to swallow. "Did you do this because you knew what he meant to me? What he still means to me?"

"No." Malek dropped his gaze to the table, not wanting her to see. "I did this because he's an *invinci*, and he's the only one who had a chance of surviving the transformation."

"I don't understand."

"Dragon souls are different from any other in this world, perhaps because they're not of this world," he said, his voice no longer strained as her magic coursed through him, healing him as fast as any new pain came. "They burn with a molten heat no human soul can bear, not even a *pyro'kine*. Trust me, former kings have tried. That's why I needed you to heal me. Using my power to hold the dragon's spirit also means allowing that same spirit to melt me from the inside out. It's how my father died—trying to hold onto a dragon for too long. But an *invinci*, well, the stories say nothing but time can destroy them."

"Why risk so much?" she asked, aching to brush her

fingers over Rafe's cheek but unsure if it would only cause more harm. "Why risk his life? Why risk yours?"

"My life was never in question."

An ominous silence lingered after his words.

You would've walked away, she realized. *If I didn't come, you would've saved yourself and left him here to burn.*

Lyana had known there was a ruthless streak inside Malek's soul—they'd been in too close of proximity for him to hide it. But she'd never imagined he could go this far, treating people as means to an end, as nothing more than pawns on a strategy board to be moved where he willed. She knew in her heart that he wanted to save the world. Malek was the King Born in Fire, the king of prophecy, the foretold hero. But he was also a monster. And she didn't know how to reconcile the two.

"Why?" Lyana finally asked, needing a reason.

"The dragons are our enemy, and now we'll have insight on them we've never had before. It's not pretty, but war seldom is, and I'll do whatever it takes to defeat them."

His voice was iron, so unbending, so unfeeling it might not have been human, but she understood. He'd done the exact thing he'd told her to do so many times before. He'd built a wall around his heart, separating his emotions from his magic, separating his soul from his mind to keep it from breaking under the strain. For the first time, she wondered if it weren't a cage.

They didn't speak after that.

Lyana funneled her power into Malek. Malek funneled his power into the soul joining. In the quiet, she studied his technique, trying to learn how this new aspect of her magic worked. She couldn't remember a time when the dove tied to her soul hadn't been there, when she'd been just a human and it a bird. They were as much a part of each other as the wind and the sky, interwoven so completely one couldn't exist without the other. The marvel of Aethios was alive before her, but it was twisted in fire and soaked in flames, a nightmarish version of the gift she'd always held in such high esteem.

I'm sorry, Rafe, she thought as the last bits of their souls were entwined, dragon and man united in a connection so complete, no force could tear it asunder. *I'm so sorry.*

"We should leave." Malek pulled his hands away from the table and wiped his hair from his brow. "I've done everything I can do."

Panic ensnared her. "What do you mean?"

"It's done."

"It can't be done."

Rafe's body flickered with every heartbeat, trapped somewhere between beast and man. Pressure pushed against her chest, not Malek's power, but Rafe's soul and the dragon's soul, battling for control. With each passing moment, the force grew, seeping from his skin to fill the air and tightening her lungs. It pulsed with increasing strength, again and again and again, like a wave that crested and crested but never crashed, the momentum only building.

Malek took her hand. "Let's go."

"No." She wrenched free.

"Lyana, haven't you ever wondered why some babies never make it out of the sacred nest alive? The end of a soul joining isn't always a pretty experience. Someone has to win dominance, and someone has to surrender it. The fight is in the raven's hands now."

"Rafe," she spat. "His name is Rafe."

A wicked glint flared to life in the corners of Malek's eyes. "Is that what he told you?"

"I won't leave him."

"I won't risk you."

Their magic crashed, the golden sparks flickering in his eyes as he demanded she come with him. But she was done being ordered around. Neither of them moved, their power pushing and pulling, leaving them frozen where they stood.

Behind her, the pressure mounted.

"Lyana, the entire building might collapse, and we both know the raven will survive."

"I won't leave him."

She reached back and found Rafe's hand, trying to ignore how his skin was smooth one moment, then rough and hot the next, then human, then beastly, again and again. His fingers tightened around hers, gripping so hard she bit her cheek against the pain, but she could take it. If it helped him, she could take anything. The pressure grew, pulling her away, but she held on, refusing to let go, refusing to let anything move her. Not Malek. Not a dragon. Not even Rafe.

"Lyana!"

She turned from her king and wrapped her other hand around Rafe's, so his fingers were completely enveloped by hers.

Please win, she prayed. *Please, please win.*

"Lyana!"

Malek's voice was softer, farther away. She wasn't sure if it was by her magic or by his own doing, or maybe by the force pushing against her chest, so strong she had to beat her wings to keep from stumbling back. Her feet rose off the floor. Her arms straightened. Her body stretched. Every muscle burned beneath the strain.

Leave. Leave. Leave, the very air seemed to whisper, wrapping around her limbs and pulling her toward the door. *Get out. Get out. Get out.*

But she wouldn't.

Not when Rafe still held her. Not when he still needed her.

"I'm here," she whispered, the words so soft she could barely hear them over the drumming in her ears. A tear leaked from her eye as her shoulder muscles tore, her arm bones about to pop from their sockets. Still she wouldn't let go. "I'm right here."

The pressure mounted.

The agony grew.

Their hands began to slip.

For a moment, time stopped.

Then the room exploded.

Gold and silver, flame and ash, all were released in a burst that stole her vision, turning the world dark. Rafe screamed. So did she. The dragon roared. In the chaos, wood splintered and groaned, coming apart with a deafening *crack*. Lyana scrambled onto the table and threw herself on top of Rafe's body, no time to wonder if it was man or beast below her, no time for anything at all.

46

RAFE

Rafe woke with a gasp, his lungs burning as he sucked in air. He waited for cool relief, but it never came. His throat was dry. His skin was hot. His chest boiled. Coughs spilled from his lips and the smell of smoke tickled his nose. Through it all, what he felt the most was the warm hand upon his face and the thumb tenderly brushing his cheek.

"Shh," a gentle voice whispered. "Shh."

Rafe didn't open his eyes. He couldn't. He was too afraid it would destroy the dream. Instead, he lifted his arm, trying to ignore how different his body felt, how unfamiliar, his muscles flaring and firing with a heat he didn't understand. When he neared her skin, he paused, curling his fingers into a fist.

"It's all right," she whispered. "I'm here."

He pressed his palm over her hand, their fingers entwining against his cheek. Her magic sank into his skin, and his magic rose to meet it. Their souls grazed in that forbidden place, and for a moment it felt as though no time had passed at all.

Rafe opened his eyes.

Lyana leaned over him, concern written in the grooves of her brow and the pursing of her lips, her face framed by deep ebony braids. Firelight caught her skin, enriching its dark color, and beyond her there was nothing but shadow. He studied the curves of her cheekbones and the elegant angle of her neck in a slow perusal of the face he'd seen so often in his dreams but hadn't looked upon in weeks. His imagination hadn't done her justice.

"Rafe."

At the sound of his name, he finally, at long last, found her eyes. He'd been afraid that maybe, after so long, she wouldn't look at him the way she had that night, his bed like a private world where the two of them could finally be free. Now he realized he had nothing to fear. A sparkle lit her emerald eyes. She still gazed at him the way no one else in the world ever had, as though it didn't matter that he was a bastard or that he had magic, as though his walls were as transparent as her crystal home and she could see right into his soul, as though all the things he hated most about himself were the very reasons she stayed beside him.

"Ana," he tried to say, but his throat was too dry.

The word tapered off into a cough, and his body convulsed, his lungs on fire. He rolled onto his side, wood crunching beneath him as he moved. Lyana kept a hold on his hand as the fit wracked through him. When it subsided, he realized they were sitting on a broken tabletop, surrounded by splintered pieces of burning wood. Flames licked the charcoal sky, ash and fog becoming one. The only spot not crackling with the blaze was the small circle where they sat unharmed.

"What...?" He trailed off as the memories rushed back. The king. And his mages. And the warehouse. And the dragon. Then magic, so much magic, and an agony that never seemed to end. "Where—" Gods alive, his throat was so dry. He needed water. It burned, but he forced the question out. "Where's the beast? Did it escape?"

"Oh, Rafe..."

The apology in her tone made him freeze. His back muscles spasmed as though fighting the awful truth, but he couldn't ignore the familiar weight beside his shoulders—familiar, and yet not. He didn't need to see them to know they were different. They were too heavy. There were too many bones. They were unlike anything he'd ever felt before.

They were still wings.

Give me a dragon, the king had said. *And I'll give you the sky.*

Rafe hadn't understood then, but he did now, the changes in his body too many to count. The unending heat. The extra weight of his limbs. The shifts in his senses. The trickster god had played with his fate once more, and like a fool Rafe had fallen for the bluff.

Taetanos, you bastard.

He jumped to his feet and dropped Lyana's hand as he backed away. Lured by fascinated horror, he glanced slowly over his shoulder. Fire rippled over onyx as his leathery wings, made not of feathers but of skin, expanded. Scales glistened along the top edge, the cracks between them glowing orange, and two sharp points jutted out like claws. He reached behind, slid his hand beneath his tattered shirt, and tentatively pressed his fingers to the joint where his wings met his back. The scales were smoother than he thought they'd be, like polished steel, and sharp enough to cut if he wasn't careful. Though he knew they must be hot, they didn't burn. At least, they didn't burn him.

Lyana tried to hide her hand within the folds of her ivory jacket, now speckled with spots of soot, but he saw. The pads of her fingers were slightly redder than usual, as though touching him had left a subtle mark.

"Rafe."

She reached for him, but he stumbled back. "Stay away."

"You don't scare me."

"I should," he snapped, the fire in his gut mixing with his fury and his pain, as though a dragon and not a raven was what he should have been all along. Smoke burst through his open lips as the heat in his throat flared. Rafe covered his mouth, his head shaking in denial, and spoke through his fingers. "I'm a monster."

"You're not, Rafe. You're not."

She stepped forward, and he stepped away, tripping on a piece of broken wood. His wings opened to stabilize him, but all he saw were the flames rippling with each motion. Needing the truth, he breathed into his palms and let the fire in his heart unleash. As he pulled his hands away, his fingers blazed.

Fire cursed.

He heard the taunts in the back of his mind, the ones he'd spent his entire life trying to ignore, trying to disprove. Yet the ravens had been right. He was exactly what they'd always feared him to be.

"I'm Vesevios come to life."

"You're not."

"How can you say that?" He stared at the flames encasing his hands up to his wrists, not burning him, though he could feel their heat. Then he found her eyes through the blaze. "Look at me, Lyana. Look at me."

"I *am* looking at you," she said, willing him to hear. "And I see the same man I've always seen, brave and loyal, with a kinder soul than he wants anyone to believe."

"You don't. You can't."

"I do."

Her magic shot across the distance between them, golden and godly, and enveloped him in its splendor. She wasn't trying to hold him or force him, just to reach him at a level no one aside from her had ever been able to touch. The fire simmering around his hands disappeared back into his skin. As she took one step after another closer to him, he could have moved, but he didn't. She stopped with no more than a few inches between them and brushed her fingers against his. Rafe flinched, pulling his arms away.

"Don't—"

Lyana reached out and took his palms, not letting him flee. No fear shone in her eyes, only that sparkle he never thought he deserved.

"I'm hurting you," he said.

"You're not."

"I'm burning you."

"You're not."

Holding his gaze, she moved their joined hands and pressed his palms against her waist. If his touch caused her pain, she didn't show it. They stayed like that for a moment, as though she was afraid he might try to run away. No matter the consequences, he'd never been able to run anywhere except toward her. Lyana lifted her fingers to skim his torso, then left one palm against his chest as the other continued to rise. She ran her fingers through his hair, sending a soothing shiver down his spine, and cupped his cheek. Her thumb brushed over his skin.

"Rafe," she said, her voice deep and dangerously alluring. "If there's one thing I know, despite everything that's happened between us, it's that you will never hurt me."

"I might."

"You won't."

"I—" He closed his eyes against the truth and dropped his forehead until it touched hers, breathing in her magic and her spirit, letting the sensation of her ground him as nothing ever had before. He'd spent so much of his life building his walls and hiding behind them, he still didn't know how to be open and honest. But there was nothing he wanted more than for someone to see him, to truly see him, and not turn away. "Ana," he murmured, his heart thumping in his chest. "I'm afraid."

"Look at me, Rafe. Please, look at me."

Her voice wrapped around him like a cocoon, so safe and warm that his eyes slid open before he could stop them.

He and Lyana were so close he could see nothing in the world but her, the dark planes of her skin, the vibrant greens of her irises, the ebony depths of her pupils made somehow bright by the emotions swirling within them.

"I'm afraid, too," she confessed, his breath halting at the words. "I'm afraid of so many things. I'm afraid I'll forever be trapped in a life I'm not sure I want. I'm afraid I'm not the person so many people need me to be. I'm afraid of my failure. I'm afraid of my success. I'm afraid I'll never be free. I'm so afraid, Rafe, and yes, I'm even afraid of you. But not of your wings or of this new spirit you share. The only thing about you that's ever scared me is the feelings you stir inside my heart, because I can't fight them, no matter what I do."

He inhaled sharply, finally remembering to breathe. A sting burned the corners of his eyes as his chest swelled.

"If you must be afraid of yourself," she whispered, "be afraid of the courageous and caring man I see when I look at you, because trust me, Rafe, he's a fearsome sight to behold."

He didn't know what to say, so he kept silent.

Rafe stayed where he was, holding her as she held him, willing time to stop so he could stay in this moment forever.

47

MALEK

A groan spilled from Malek's lips and he blinked the dark spots from his eyes. Ash filled his lungs as he sucked in a deep breath, then immediately coughed, his chest burning. Splintered pieces of wood clinked against the ground with the movement and sharp edges cut into his back, the debris of the warehouse. He'd finished the soul joining, and started to leave, then...

Lyana.

She hadn't wanted to come with him. She'd wanted to stay by the raven's side. He'd tried to force her to come, but she held him off, her power stronger than he'd ever felt before. As though she and raven were one force, he'd been pushed from the table, across the room and almost to the door, when the world exploded.

Lyana!

Ignoring his own pain, Malek jumped to his feet as his heart lurched. Why hadn't she come with him? Didn't she know by now she was more important than anyone else?

Especially a raven with no use beyond his magic? The world needed her. He needed her. If she was hurt— If she was gone— If—

Malek turned and froze, unable to process what he was seeing.

Lyana and the raven stood unharmed as the warehouse burned at their feet. Tendrils of flame reached up to lick the fog while ash flurries fell from the sky, a storm of smoke and fire billowing around a moment of perfect calm. One of Lyana's hands was pressed against the raven's chest and the other cupped his cheek as he held her close. Their foreheads touched, noses barely brushing, their gazes locked as though the rest of the world didn't exist. A white jacket hung to her knees, the silk stained with dark splotches of soot and the skirt in tatters. The raven's black shirt was shredded, his leather trousers scorched, though no burns showed upon his pale skin. Their wings fanned out in opposite directions, her pure ivory feathers stark against the night and his dragon scales simmering with heat. He was dark where she was light, and she was dark where he was light, like a mirror reflecting a perfect complement, as though they were two halves of one whole. They looked like…they looked like…a King Born in Fire and a Queen Bred of Snow.

No.

Malek stumbled as his knees grew weak.

No, he repeated. *No, it can't be.*

That was his fate. That was everything he'd spent his life working for. That was the air he breathed when he was drowning, the food he ate when he was starving, the only belief that kept him going when he wasn't sure he could make it through another day. It was the weight that buried him and the strength that buoyed him up all at the same time.

Lyana was his queen.

His partner.

The only one in the world who might understand him.

Every choice he'd ever made, no matter how tough, had been for her, for them, for their destiny. They were going to save the world. He believed that with every fiber of his soul. They were going to save the world, and when they did, everything he'd done would be worth it.

"Lyana!"

He had to break them apart. He had to reach her. What could an *invinci* do to save the world? Nothing. He was the *aethi'kine*. He was her teacher. He was her king.

"Ly—"

Malek broke off as a blast of magic shattered the air, so intense it stole the breath from his lungs. Before his eyes, Lyana and the raven tore apart, the moment between them broken. For a heartbeat, no one moved. Then, as one, all three of them lifted their faces toward the sky.

48

CASSI

Cassi was nearly back in Pylaeon when the magic hit, dispersing her spirit as it flooded through her with all the force of a dragon at full speed.

What the gods?

She cut across the night sky, crested the edge of the House of Whispers, and froze. The city was in absolute chaos. When she'd left her body behind, the earthquake was nothing but a subtle tremor, a nuisance, for sure, but not something to fear. Now the ground shook with such ferocity the population had taken to the sky. Ravens littered the air, their wings glinting silver in the moonlight. Their fear was palpable. Dust plumed from the streets. Booms reverberated, one after another, as walls and buildings toppled over, their foundations cracked and broken beyond repair. The river sloshed, sending wave after wave to flood the streets. Cassi followed the sparkling line back and back and back until she saw the pearlescent shimmer of Taetanos's Gate.

The god stone.

Propelled by her magic, Cassi raced over Pylaeon, ignoring the cries and shouts of a people in pure panic. Her spirit moved faster than a body ever could, and within moments she was across the valley and under the waterfall. Though she hated the feeling of passing through solid objects, speed was of the essence, so she forced her spirit into the thick cliff face, shivering as she fought the resistance of the rocks and went spilling into the sacred nest.

Something was wrong.

The power felt different. It vibrated across the harrowed walls with a rhythm she'd never experienced, not in all her hours spent spying for her king. Ravens screeched, their cries echoing in a deafening roar, the flutter of their wings like a living shadow as they swarmed the open air above the grove. Cassi floated through the trees, swerving around trunks, trying to hear over the groan of rock and the crunch of branches. The cavern shook violently. In its center, the priests and priestesses circled the god stone, their black robes a fluid curtain as they held hands and swayed in prayer, the gentle hum of their voices oddly calm. Only as she approached did she understand the problem.

The god stone had fallen.

The onyx orb no longer hovered in midair but sat against the dirt, leaning slightly to one side. It rolled with the movement of the ground, bouncing and tumbling, no longer held in place by the power of the spell. The surface didn't shimmer with an opal sheen. No magic played on its smooth curves, reflecting like light on polished obsidian. It was dull and dark, but Cassi could still feel the thrum of magic in the room, ancient and powerful, building with each passing moment. The priests must have too, their chants increasing with the same steady momentum. She moved closer, floating over their wall of bodies then sinking until her spirit pressed against the surface of the stone. There was something inside, something moving, something—

Cassi jerked back.

A fracture split the rock and expanded across the widest part of the oval stone, cutting a white line through the black, growing and growing, until it snapped and the two sides broke open. Onyx shadows spilled across the sacred nest, flowing from the stone as the rest of the world fell still.

The shakes wracking the cavern stopped.

The priests and priestesses fell silent.

Even the ravens halted their crying.

In the eerie quiet, a man emerged from the spreading darkness, his skin rippling like the surface of a lake on a moonless night, nothing but rolling shadow. Two wings extended from his back, so wide the priests and priestesses stumbled to keep out of the way. Scales covered his skin, onyx shards refracting the light. His eyes, when he opened them, were black.

"Taetanos," one of the priestesses whispered.

They dropped to their knees before the creature, and for a moment, Cassi wondered if the people of this world had always had it right. Maybe their gods had saved them. Maybe their gods had sacrificed themselves. Maybe their gods were magic, possessing a more profound power than she could ever understand. Could this possibly be

Taetanos, the god of fate, finally answering his people's prayers?

The deity stepped forward, shadows wafting off his frame to flow like a cloak in his wake. He knelt before a priest and lifted his arm to touch the man's chin. They rose together, one as inscrutable as darkness, the other luminous beneath his god's attention, hazel eyes wide and beaming. Black fingers covered in scales slid down the priest's chin to rest on his throat. Power stirred invisibly across the air and the priest's face went blank. A smile spread his lips as an expression of far-off awe overtook his features. The deity cocked his head to the side.

Snap!

It happened so fast Cassi didn't understand until the priest's body fell lifelessly to the ground, his head lolling against the dirt at an impossible angle.

His neck. It broke his neck.

Someone screamed. She didn't know who, but it didn't matter anyway. As quickly as it came, the sound was cut off with unnatural swiftness. Another body fell, then another, the darkness stirring as it rolled from the creature, cloaking the air so she saw nothing but flashes. The briefest glint of light on a scaled arm. The curve of a sharp wing. A spray of glistening blood. The beast was unlike anything she'd ever seen, as though formed by magic, as if the power of the god stone lived inside of it. The fight was over before it began. The creature made no noise. Its wings hardly stirred the air. The darkness clung to it, as though made for it, and it moved with all the swift stealth of night.

A priestess broke free of the carnage and ran across the

grove, jumping over roots as branches slapped her face, racing for the gate. Cassi didn't even see the creature move, but there it was, standing before her in the shadows. It used one sharp claw to slit her throat. Another priest ran and another died, on and on, until the sacred nest fell completely still. The beast opened its mouth, revealing white teeth and pink gums. Its forked tongue darted out to lick the blood from its fingers. The black eyes surveyed the room, shifting between the bodies littering the floor. Power leaked from its pores as though it searched for something. By its feet, the god stone was nothing more than a broken shell, hollow and emptied of all it contained.

An egg, Cassi realized with a mental gasp, studying the oval shape and the fissured edges, the delicate fragility now on display. *It was never a stone. It's an egg. They're all eggs.*

Her mind raced down this new path.

The prophecy played across her thoughts.

Beasts will emerge, filled with fury and scorn, fighting to recover what from their claws we have torn.

It was the piece of the puzzle they'd always been missing —what had they taken from the dragons? What did they want? Why did they keep coming back to this world?

Eggs. We took their eggs.

Cassi stared at the creature, its back to her as its head continued a slow perusal of the cavernous grove. Those wings. Those scales. Those claws. They belonged to a dragon, and yet not. Malek's face flitted across her thoughts, the hard, determined edge of his jaw as he marched Rafe inside the warehouse to where a dragon awaited. A sick feeling stirred in her spirit.

Soul joining.

The answer was as obvious as it was cruel. She didn't know why or how, but five hundred years ago, before the isles were lifted into the sky, dragon eggs had been fused to human souls, and this was the result—a creature stuck somewhere between the two.

I have to warn someone. I have to—

Cassi froze as the creature spun, its bottomless gaze landing on her.

It's not possible.

She was invisible. She was nothing but air. Grasping the tether to her body, Cassi pulled on that string to throw her spirit from the nest. Before she even moved, the beast was there, traveling with the speed of darkness. Claws stroked her soul, latching on as she fought to break away. Sharp edges cut, burning as they passed through her, but she didn't have a neck it could snap or a throat it could slice. It held her as though she were tangible, but she wasn't. In this form, she was nothing but a dream.

Cassi yanked on the tether, trying to slip free by using the connection to her body. She imagined the cell where Xander had left her, imagined her limbs sprawled across the floor where she'd fallen, imagined her speckled wings flared across the stones. If she concentrated, she could feel the damp cold against her cheek and the tickle of soot covering her feathers.

It was working.

Her spirit was like water, slipping through the creature's fingers. Her heartbeat pulsed down that line, *thump, thump, thump*, drawing her closer. That was the connection.

That was the tie. That was her freedom. *Thump, thump, thump.*

The creature released her.

Cassi flew across the sacred nest, her spirit passing through branches and leaves as she raced for the protection of the rocks. If she could just reach the wall, nothing would catch her. The trees gave way to empty air.

She was almost there.

Almost there.

The creature stepped from the shadows, blocking her path. It lifted a sharp claw, the point catching some unseen source of light as it gleamed across the darkness. With one swift jerk, it cut through the tether to her body and Cassi went tumbling into the wall at full speed. Her spirit rolled through the rock like a ship lost at sea, no anchor to hold it steady as the waves crashed and the wind howled.

Lost and adrift, she careened through the cliff and emerged at the splashing waters of Taetanos's Gate, her spirit coming to a stop in that wet, moist air as the falling river roared. No heartbeat stirred in the back of her thoughts. When she reached for the familiar warmth of her body, no matter how far she pushed her magic, nothing was there.

Cassi sped across the night sky, an arrow racing for a target. She didn't stop until she was back in that lonely cell at the base of the castle. Her body lay against the cold stone floor, as immobile and lifeless as an empty shell, nothing but mechanistic organs. She tried to touch her spirit to her skin, but they wouldn't connect. Like oil on water, the two refused to meet.

Was she alive?

Was she dead?

The horrible realization struck as swiftly as a hidden attacker, like two hands coming around her throat and cutting off air.

She was neither.

She was stuck, just like that creature, in some impossible in-between.

49

XANDER

That was the worst one yet, Xander thought as he stood on the castle wall and stared out at his broken city, surveying the damage as best he could beneath the moonlight. *Thank the gods it finally stopped.*

Pylaeon was in ruins. The river ran wild through the streets, glistening silver as it flooded over rock. Buildings were little more than rubble. A fire had started in the wooden sector where the peasants lived. Half his people had taken to the air. In the distance, ashen dove wings fluttered beneath the night sky. Xander wanted to help them, to save them, but what could he do to fix a magic spell he didn't even understand? What could he do when he could hardly think of anything except Cassi and all the things she'd told him? What could he do when he wanted to leap from this wall, dive over the edge of the isle, and see this world beneath the mist for himself?

Rafe.

His brother was alone right now in a foreign world, held hostage by some hideous king, abandoned and left to rot. And while Rafe had been down there, Xander had been up here letting the very person who'd condemned his brother to that gruesome fate wriggle her way into his heart.

How many lies had she told?

How many lives had she ruined?

All for what?

Xander tightened his hand around the ancient text he'd found in her rooms, buried at the very bottom of her trunk. It was bound by a thick leather string, the cover soft and worn, the text inside so old he couldn't read it. She'd stolen it, he knew, on the same night she'd pressed that gentle kiss to his neck. She'd looked into his eyes and lied through her teeth, the same way she'd done countless times before. His anger was a palpable thing, a bubbling, boiling fury he wasn't sure how to cool, but beneath that was a bottomless pit of hurt. He'd trusted her with his life, with Lyana's life, with his kingdom, and she'd betrayed everyone.

But she hadn't killed him.

In the end, she'd confessed.

Despite everything, he couldn't help but hope that might mean she wasn't beyond redemption after all. What sort of fool did that make him?

"My prince," Helen said as she landed by his side, pulling him from his thoughts. He hastily stuffed the stolen book into the folds of his jacket, pocketing it out of sight. "You should return to the safety of the castle. Too many dangers lurk under the cover of chaos."

"Is there anything more we can do to help them?" he asked, not taking his eyes from the city.

"Every guard is helping to clear the streets. Every healer is searching for more wounded. All the stores have been emptied and the servants are delivering food as we speak. There's nothing left to do until morning."

"So I should return to my silk sheets, rest my head on my soft pillow, and dream while my people suffer? I should run away and hide while they stare their greatest nightmare in the face?"

"What else can you do?"

"You don't—"

Xander stopped short, gritting his teeth to keep from revealing too much. It was a loyalty Cassi didn't deserve. But maybe the loyalty was to Lyana, this queen of prophecy who had for a brief moment in time been his mate. She'd saved his life. Given the chance, maybe she'd return and save his people too.

With a sigh, he studied the stones beneath his feet. *I'm the worst kind of fool,* he thought, answering his own question. *I'm the fool who chooses to believe even when all the evidence tells me otherwise.*

"I don't what?" Helen asked.

You don't understand. Our world is going to end. Our kingdom is going to fall. There's an entire civilization made of magic hiding beneath the mist, and somehow I have to make my people believe the thing that terrifies them most in the world is the very thing that will save them.

Of all the ravens, she was probably the one who would respond best to the news. On some level, she knew what Rafe was, and she'd still trained him when no one else would. But she'd also dragged men and women kicking and screaming down the streets of Pylaeon, her knife at their throats as she led them to the executioner's block.

"Nothing, Helen," he murmured. "Never mind."

"What did the owl tell you?"

The edge of his lip lifted—the woman missed nothing —but this was a secret he wasn't ready to share. As Xander turned to bid her good night, a distant squawking caught his ear.

"Do you hear that?"

Her golden eyes narrowed. Together, they turned toward the noise. Across the broken city and at the very end of the river, above the cascading waters of Taetanos's Gate which glistened silver beneath the moon, the darkness shifted. Xander leaned forward, his toes scooting over the edge of the wall as he strained to see.

"It sounds like—"

"Ravens," he cut her off as the dark cloud moved rapidly across the sky, revealing the subtle sheen of obsidian feathers catching starlight. For a moment, he thought he saw a man within the mix, but as the flock rose, the shadows fell away and he was gone. A trick of the eye. "There."

"What are they doing out of the sacred nest?"

"I don't—"

The ground lurched and dropped fifteen feet. His wings caught him before he fell, but nothing could prevent his stomach from sinking all the way to the base of his floating kingdom. By the time he looked down, the island had dropped again, thirty feet this time.

She was telling the truth.

Part of him had wanted to doubt the prophecy, to think it was just another lie Cassi had spun, but deep in his gut, he knew it was real. And somehow, it was happening. That earthquake had been worse for a reason. He didn't know if that king had come back to finish the job, or if some other work of evil had been at play, but he knew in his soul that the magic in the god stone had failed, which meant one thing.

The island was falling.

"Take to the sky!" he shouted as he pumped his wings to cut across the city. "Take to the sky, now! Gather your children! Hold them if they're too young to fly!"

A hand grabbed his arm. "What is going on?"

"There's no time to explain." Xander spun to face Helen, wild adrenaline coursing through him. "You must get to my mother, now. Tell her to take to the sky, and make sure she listens. I'll find you when it's over."

"When what's over?"

Xander held her gaze, his lips trembling, but he didn't know what to say. Instead, he turned and bellowed, "Take to the sky!"

The ground dropped again. He dove after it.

"Take to the sky! Take to the sky!"

His people were crying as they rushed into the night sky, wearing their nightgowns and underclothes, fear alive on their faces. Parents clutched their children to their chests, their fluffy wings unable to fly. The elderly struggled to remain airborne, the strength in their aged bodies already starting to give out. There were too many wounded to carry, so the unlucky lay stranded on the streets. All he'd ever wanted to do was keep his people safe, and he'd failed. The House of Whispers was dying before him, and there was nothing he could do but let it.

No, Xander thought, feeling as he had when he'd faced that dragon, as if he needed to go, as if he needed to do, as if he needed to scream at the world just to hear it bellow back. *No, this can't be the end.*

Maybe he couldn't fight with a shield and sword. Maybe all he had were words and heart, but they were weapons all their own. He was done waiting, done watching, done hoping for an answer to fall into his lap. There was no prophecy to his name. There was no magic in his skin. There was no noble fate written across the stars. But he was still a prince, these were still his people, and no matter how powerless the world deemed him, he wouldn't abandon them.

Somehow, someway, he would save them.

Before he had time to question, Xander hugged his wings to his back and plummeted headfirst from the sky, ignoring the shouts of his guards. Just as he reached the city street, the isle finally gave out. He gripped a black archway with both arms, hugging that godly gateway to his chest, a mix of prayer, determination, and fear alive inside his heart.

As his kingdom fell from the sky, he fell with it.

Together, they were swallowed by the mist.

"**W**hat was that?" Rafe asked, a tremor to his voice. They stared into the mist as though they could burn it away, hoping to catch one glimpse of the world above the fog.

"I don't know."

"But it was…"

"Yes."

They were birds. They knew without even trying which way was north or south, east or west, and they would never be so lost they couldn't find their way home. The magic had come from the House of Whispers. She'd bet her life on it, and the fear in Rafe's tone made it clear he thought the same.

"Lyana!" Malek called. She spun to find him behind her, golden power surrounding his fingertips as the flames parted to let him pass. "Do you feel it? It's begun."

"What?"

"The prophecy."

Rafe squeezed her hand, drawing her gaze. "What is he saying? What does he mean?"

"I'm not—"

"You know," Malek murmured darkly. His dark blue eyes were as wild as a raging sea, something unleashed deep within them. Rafe gripped her tighter, as though he too could sense the brewing storm. "You know exactly what I mean."

Lyana closed her eyes against the truth.

It couldn't be. Not so soon.

But as she dove into her power and reached with all her spirit for the rift, there was no denying Malek was right. The yawning abyss at the center of their world had grown wider. The spell fighting to keep it contained was weaker, no longer anchored by seven bright spots of magic but six. One was missing. One was gone. One had fallen. Now the other six dimmed, their lights already starting to sputter out as the strength holding them together unraveled.

"What will happen?" she whispered, still deep in her magic.

"The others will follow," Malek said, his voice grave. "One by one, until the House of Peace is all that's left between us and annihilation, unless you and I can find a way to stop it."

"What if I'm not ready?"

He didn't answer, but the sharp clench of his jaw said it all.

"What do you mean, until the House of Peace is all that's left?" Rafe asked, his question only for her.

Lyana turned to find his pleading eyes as Malek's stare burned a hole in her back. She was stuck in the middle of two extremes, a bastard and a king, her past and her future, her heart and her mind. As she glanced between them, the words stuck like a lump in her throat, because no matter what she said, it would come out sounding like a choice, one she wasn't ready to make. She needed Malek to save the world, but if she turned her back on Rafe, on her people, then what world would she really be saving?

"Ana…"

A whimper escaped her lips.

"Talk to me."

Unlike Malek's, the words from Rafe weren't an order. They were a prayer. He held her fingers tenderly, his thumb brushing over her skin, no demand in the motion, just vulnerability. The very fact that he gave her a choice made her ache to choose him.

"Rafe—"

"My liege!"

Their heads snapped toward the sound. Nyomi yelled from the other side of the burning rubble, blue simmering at her fingertips and sinking into the waves that sloshed against the dock. Her amber eyes were wide with a fear Lyana had never seen in them before—had never seen in any of Malek's mages. They were the sort who thrived on danger, as confident as Malek that their magic could save them from any foe.

Her chest constricted.

"The ocean," Nyomi called, her voice frantic and unsure. "Something's wrong. I can feel it racing toward us. I don't think we'll be able to stop it, not with all the magic in the city. It's moving too fast."

"The island," Lyana murmured, her mind spinning. When the island landed back in the sea, it must have displaced the water. It must have caused a surge.

"Let's go." Malek took her hand even as Rafe held the other. There was no question in his grip, only unflinching command as he pulled her toward him. "We must get to safety."

She dug in her heels. "What about the rest of the city?"

"The *hydro'kines* will do what they can."

"Nyomi just said it won't be enough. We can help, Malek. The two of us, together, we can stop it."

"We must get to safety first," he insisted. "Then we'll help."

"What if it's too late by then?"

His head dipped to the side, a bit of the hardness in his features leaking away to reveal a man of deep sorrow, the one she sometimes felt when she brushed against his soul, the one hiding behind his walls. He didn't want to make this choice. She wished she could somehow show him that he didn't need to. Before she had the chance, his defenses strengthened. His eyes hardened, shimmering like dark sapphires in the firelight, and in that reflection she saw his answer. *So be it.*

Lyana threw his hand away in disgust. She refused to be the queen of a drowned world. She refused to sit back and watch people die when she might save them. She refused to believe a prophecy made her more important than the poorest peasant on the street with no magic to his name. And she refused to quiet her heart when it had always been the one thing she could trust to guide her forward.

"Go," Lyana spat at her king. "Go, if you want, but I am *not* coming with you."

If Malek didn't want to help her, fine.

She would save the world on her own.

Lyana stepped through the fire, her power flowing out in waves as she reached for the spirit of the sea. Rafe let her go without a fight, watching her the same way he had on those long-ago nights in Pylaeon when they'd snuck through the city streets, as though she were the brightest star in the sky, as though she were invincible.

Tonight, she needed to be.

The spirit of the sea raged in quiet fury, the sort that built in secret, behind shut lips and closed doors, simmering in defiant eyes, alive in the souls of the silenced. Lyana tapped into that feeling as she pushed her magic deep into the rolling waves.

I hear you, she thought. *I hear you.*

The water kept on flowing, kept on coming. The onslaught traveled beneath the surface, rising and rising into a crescendo that would swallow Da'Kin whole.

No, she ordered. *Stop.*

It wouldn't.

The sea raced toward them like an animal unleashed, refusing to return to its cage. Her power wouldn't be enough to hold it. Not like this. Dividing her mind, Lyana reached for the air, ordering it to halt above the city's many canals and press together until it was so thick it could have been a wall. Still she knew it wouldn't be enough. Spirits clawed at her power, the way they always did, begging to be healed. She tried to push them away, to focus on the wind and the water, on the earth and the sea, but the humans were too loud to ignore. They drowned her in their cries. She couldn't fight the water and fight them. Her magic shifted, growing unwieldy. Her control fled as she struggled to keep it all contained, all compartmentalized, every element its own section inside her mind, until finally she thought, *Why?*

The world wasn't made of walls. It wasn't separated into neat piles. The elements were messy. They worked together.

So why was she always trying to divide them?

Instinct took over. Forgetting the lessons, forgetting the rules, Lyana ripped down the barrier keeping her magic from her soul, her heart from her mind. All that fear flooding her thoughts, all that terror, all that pain, she welcomed it into the deepest part of herself, making it her own. The spirits crying out to be saved were no longer strangers. They were a part of her, sewn into her skin, giving her the power not of one soul, but of a thousand. In that shift, she discovered newfound strength. There was no inner struggle, no overwhelming onslaught waiting to pull her under. Instead of flying into the face of a storm, she glided with it, her feathers catching the breeze until she moved faster and sharper than she ever had before.

Malek had been wrong. Her magic wasn't the only weapon she'd ever need. A sword was just a sword without a warrior to wield it. Power, by itself, was useless. But with her heart at the helm, no victory was out of reach.

The sea rushed forward.

With her magic and her soul united, Lyana rushed to meet it.

RAFE

She rose into the air as though lifted by strings, her wings spread but unmoving as the wind billowed through her feathers. Golden currents flowed from her outstretched hands, racing across the sea like a charging army, sinking beneath the ocean waves and rising to disperse the fog. If he was Vesevios come to life, she was Aethios, rising above the city like a goddess made of power and light, so bright he couldn't look away even as the sight stung his eyes.

"Lyana," the king said, the sound somewhere between a scream and a whisper, his voice gradually falling away in awe.

She doesn't need you, Rafe thought, a bit of pride swelling in his chest. *She doesn't need anyone.*

In the distance, a wall of water as high as a building surged toward them, like a ripple spreading across the sea, ready to devour Da'Kin whole. The *hydro'kine* stared at it, a frown twisting her features, fear bright in her eyes.

A scream pierced the air.

Then another.

The cries of the citizens without magic, the ones who couldn't see Lyana's power. If they could, they wouldn't be afraid. If they could, they would know, as Rafe did, that Lyana would protect them. Saving lives was what she did best. After all, she'd saved his too many times and in too many ways to count.

The dock dropped as the water beneath the city receded, pulled into the swell. Rafe flared his wings to catch his balance. Beside him, the king stumbled. Golden sparks sputtered at his fingertips, as though the motion had finally spurred him awake. His power flowed out, meeting Lyana's across the sea, but she didn't need it. Rafe couldn't say how he knew—he just did.

The ocean barreled forward, closer and closer.

Lyana jerked her arms, biceps flexed as though to push it back.

The water kept coming.

A hundred feet.

Then seventy.

Now fifty.

No, twenty-five.

Fifteen.

Ten.

Her golden magic flashed with the force of the sun, and suddenly the ocean simply stopped. Liquid bubbled and churned behind an invisible barricade. The water was so close Rafe's cheek became moistened by the spray, and steam erupted from his back as droplets fell on his wings. A wall of solid sea hovered, mere inches from crashing upon the city, but her power held it trapped. Inch by inch, Lyana lowered her arms, and inch by inch, the water receded, until finally it returned to normal, lapping up against the docks in gentle undulations. The power filling the air blinked out and she fell.

Rafe didn't hesitate.

Forgetting for a moment that he was a monster whose wings rippled with fire, he took to the air and scooped Lyana from the sky. It was strange not to feel the wind ruffling his feathers—strange, and yet not. This body, new as it was, belonged to him. He didn't need to learn it, the way he once had his raven wings, zipping across the palace courtyard with feathers little more than fluff. Something innate took over, something that perhaps had once belonged to the dragon now sharing his soul.

He landed on a knee with Lyana's body draped across his thigh and placed his arm behind her shoulders to cradle her head. With his free hand, he brushed her braids away from her cheek, tucking one behind her ear as he ran his fingers over her skin.

"Ana," he whispered. "Wake up."

Her eyes fluttered open. "Rafe?"

"Are you all right?"

"What..." She trailed off, her eyes going wide. "The water!"

"Shh," he murmured, trying to calm her. "You stopped it."

"I stopped it?"

A smile flitted over his lips. "You didn't even need to hide behind an overly large cloak this time."

Her brow wrinkled and he thought himself a fool for bringing up the nights they'd spent sneaking around Pylaeon, nights that might have meant far more to him than to her. But then the edges of her mouth curled upward and a sparkle lit her eyes. A grin pulled at her cheeks, widening and widening until her whole face seemed to glow. Watching her then, he almost thought it was worth it—all the pain, all the heartache, all the despair—since it brought him to this place and this perfect moment with her.

It ended far too soon.

As though a cloud had passed over the sun, her features darkened and a single word fell from her lips. "Xander."

Rafe snatched his palm from her cheek as though burned, the name more effective than a cold shower to douse his affection. If he closed his eyes, he knew what he would see—that look on his brother's face as Xander picked up Lyana's ring from his bedroom floor, the anger and hurt more scorching than a flame. So Rafe didn't close his eyes. He jerked his head to the side and stared into the fog, cursing himself for making the same mistakes all over again.

"No, Rafe," Lyana said with a wince. She reached for his hand, but he slid it away and eased her to a seated position, putting some distance between them. "I didn't mean— I wasn't—" She sighed heavily. "It's not just Xander, but the whole House of Whispers."

He glanced back to her, drawn by the grave tone.

"It's—it's gone."

"Gone?" The air left his lungs. "What do you mean gone?"

"I don't know what that blast of magic was, but I know something happened to the god stone. It stopped working, and the isle...well, it fell."

"Fell?" he asked, still not comprehending. *Fell?*

Then it clicked.

The water, the wave—it had been caused by something extremely large and heavy falling into the ocean, displacing it. And that large, heavy something was his home.

"Xander!"

Rafe was on his feet in an instant. His wings pumped and his body rose, his mind already a thousand miles away. Lyana grabbed him by the ankle, trying to pull him back down.

"Stop!" she shouted. "You can't!"

He ignored her.

"Rafe, they'll kill you!"

"No—"

He turned his face toward the sky and broke off at the heat simmering across his leathery wings. They stopped moving and he dropped back to the ground, landing hard on his feet as the truth pulled at him like a weight. He'd forgotten what he was, what he'd become. And she was right. They'd kill him.

Did it matter?

"He's my brother," Rafe said, just as Lyana took his hands, forcing him to meet her imploring eyes. "I have to go."

"He has wings," she argued. "He can fly. He's fine."

"What if he's not?" he asked, finishing the thought silently. *What if he's not, and I wasn't there to save him?*

Doubt flickered over her face, prompting him to recall the king's final words to Cassi as he'd been pulled into the dark depths of the warehouse. *Kill the boy*, he'd said. *Kill the boy, or I'll have someone else kill him for you.*

Rafe couldn't say how he knew, but he did.

They'd been speaking about Xander.

"Cassi's there. Cassi's with him."

"She won't hurt him."

"You don't understand—"

"I do," Lyana said, squeezing his fingers to pull him from his panic. "Cassi came to me in a dream tonight, and she confessed, Rafe, to everything. She tried to kill Xander, but he caught her. She won't hurt him, because she can't. She's imprisoned—"

A gasp stole her voice as a wave of conflicting emotions crashed over her face—hurt, betrayal, confusion, anger, but most of all, worry. *Imprisoned.* Her friend was imprisoned on an island that was at this very moment sinking into the sea.

It mattered little to Rafe.

Cassi could rot for all he cared.

"I have to go," he said, dropping Lyana's hands.

That broke her from the trance. "Wait—"

"Why?" he snapped. "Every moment I wait is another moment he might be in danger. If they want to kill me, let them try. Let them stick me with arrows until I stain the ocean red with blood, I don't care. It won't stop me. It never has before."

"And what will that do to your brother?"

It would break him. At least, it would have once. But Rafe preferred he be broken than dead.

"I'll go," Lyana stated. "I'll go in your stead."

He paused. "You would do that?"

"Of course."

"Why?"

She was a queen of prophecy. She'd just commanded the ocean to halt in its tracks. She dined with princes and kings. Why would she risk so much for him?

"Rafe." Empathy softened her tone. "Xander told me once that you pushed the world away because you didn't think you deserved any sort of love. I didn't believe him at the time, but I do now, and it breaks my heart to see it. Of course I'll go. Your life, no matter how invincible your body may be, matters. You matter. To me. To Xander. To more people than you'll ever know. So please, don't throw it away. You don't need to fight every battle on your own, not when I'm right here willing to help you."

"It might not be safe," he said lamely.

Lyana tossed him a pointed look. "I'm hardly defenseless."

"What will you tell them?"

"I'll make it up on the way."

"But—"

"Rafe," she implored, lifting her hand to his cheek.

He fought at first, resisting the urge to sink into her touch. He was good at being alone. He was used to it. But this—letting someone in, not for a single stolen night, but for real—this was something he didn't know how to do, especially when he knew she was right. When the ravens saw her soaring through the fog, they would cheer. They would hail her as their savior, returned in their time of need. If they saw him coming, it would only lead to more panic and fear, more things his brother didn't need.

"Go." The word spilled through his lips. "Please, go."

She put her other hand to his face, holding him so he couldn't look away. "I'll come back."

Before he could protest, before he could tell her to forget about him and to leave this world behind, she pulled him toward her and pressed their lips together for a fiery instant that was all too brief. The heat of her touch spread across his entire body, leaving his skin tingling and his throat burning even after she pulled away.

"I promise," she whispered, standing on the tips of her toes so her lips brushed against his ear and her breath played across his neck. "I promise, I'll come back for you."

Without another word, she turned, her ivory wings sending a cloud of ash into the air as they flapped. Just as her heels rose off the ground, a river of golden magic whooshed by. The power clamped around her limbs and trapped her in place. She froze with her face lifted and her arms outstretched, her entire body reaching for the sky.

LYANA

"**M**alek!" Lyana shouted, fury sharpening her tone. After expending so much of her power to stop the wave, she was too weak to fight his hold. Every bit of movement was its own battle, and it took all the magic she possessed just to turn around and face him. Though he stood as tall and proud as any king, the look in his eyes was full of jagged edges. "Let me go."

"I can't do that."

"You can't or you won't?"

"Lyana—"

"What's the plan, Malek?" she asked, so tired of having the same argument again and again. "You can't hold me like this forever."

"I don't need to."

A dark laugh escaped her lips. "So you'll clip my wings again, is that it?"

"If I must."

"Lock me in a tower?"

"If I must."

"Chain me to your wrist?"

Frustration rippled over his regal face. "Stop acting like a child."

"Stop treating me like one."

"The prophecy is upon us and you want to leave. What else am I supposed to do?"

"Trust me, Malek," she implored. His golden magic swirled around her, blocking out the rest of the world, entrenching her in his spirit. Beneath all that stubborn pride, there was hurt and most of all fear, a pining of the heart he tried hard to keep hidden. She wished he wouldn't. She wished, for once, he would let her in, but she knew it was useless even before she spoke. To Malek, vulnerability was a weakness. To Lyana, it was the essence of what made them human. "Trust that I want to save the world just as much as you, even if we have two different ways of showing it. Trust that I know what I'm doing. Trust your queen."

A war waged inside his eyes, but it was no surprise which side won. "You can't leave."

"I can't stay," she answered softly. "Not like this."

He clenched his jaw, brows drawing together as he stood his ground, refusing to release her. The power around her intensified until, one foot after another, she marched forward against her will. With each step her sympathy ebbed, replaced by determination. People weren't pawns on a board, and though it was a lesson she was embarrassed to have learned so late, actions had consequences—even

Malek's actions. If he wanted to be a king who knew no compromise, then she would be a queen who bowed to no one. The lines were drawn.

So be it.

Lyana unleashed her magic. Even depleted, she was still strong enough to fight him, and fight she would, until she had nothing left to give. Because she was done being what other people told her to be—a dutiful princess, a coerced mate, a silent queen. It was time to take her fate into her own hands. It was time to be who she was in her own right —Lyana Aethionus, free and unbound, guided by her heart and fortified by her magic, a woman who would save the world, the *whole* world, or die trying.

Malek braced himself as her power slammed into his chest, nearly knocking him over. He reeled, bending his knees and digging his heels into the wood planks beneath his feet to keep from flying backward. A frown flattened his lips as a hard look gathered in his eyes. The magic around her tightened. Lyana gritted her teeth, refusing to move another inch toward him. They were right back where they'd started, locked in battle. That wasn't what she wanted either, but if she had to choose, she would rather be his enemy than his prisoner.

"Lyana," he snapped. "We're supposed to be a team."

"You should have thought of that, Malek. When you turned my best friend into your spy. When you told her to cut off Rafe's wings behind my back. When you told her to kill one of the best men I've ever met. When you silenced me at every turn and refused to listen to my concerns. You should have thought of that, when you were lying and scheming and making plans without me, plans you never intended for me to find out. Don't put the blame on me for refusing to cower to your demands. Put the blame on yourself for doling them out in the first place."

"And what of the world? Will you let it fall in your pride?"

It took everything she had not to laugh. "Will you?"

They each attacked, neither giving, neither bending, back and forth and back and forth. *Aethi'kine* magic lit the sky. Her vision started to spot, her body weakening before her power, unable to hold on for much longer. Malek sensed it. He dug into her skin like a beast with claws, trying to drag her forward. A cry slid through her lips as she fought against him.

As quick as the pain came, it was gone.

She could breathe.

She could move.

Lyana blinked the dark splotches from her eyes, trying to understand. As her sight returned, all she saw was Rafe.

"Go," he grunted, his face twisting as golden waves of power crashed into his back and dissolved into his skin. His fiery wings were spread like a protective wall, catching Malek's magic before it could strike her.

"How…?"

"I don't know." His voice was labored, each word more taxing than the rest. Tendrils of flame flickered in his clear blue eyes as he stared at her, his biceps clenched and his feet braced, his every muscle straining. "Go," Rafe repeated. "I'm not sure how long I can hold him."

Lyana stepped back, but she couldn't quite turn away.

Something held her entranced—something she was only just beginning to see. Every man she'd ever met had wanted to cage her. Not all of them had meant ill, but they'd been controlling just the same. Malek had wanted to mold her into his perfect queen. Xander had held her duty-bound to be his mate. Even her brother, in all his protectiveness, had wanted to rein in her spirit.

But not Rafe.

He was here, fighting with every ounce of strength he possessed to set her free. And he always had been, right from the very start. When he'd been injured, he hadn't shied from her magic. He'd let her heal him. And when she'd gone to him with a foolhardy plan to save raven lives, he hadn't shut her down. He'd gone with her. And when she'd stood in his room that night, he hadn't asked for things he knew she couldn't give. He'd accepted any part of her she was willing to offer. He didn't take. He didn't demand. While the rest of the world tried to tell her who she had to be, he accepted her for who she was. Even better —he looked at her as though she were already perfect.

That was what held her.

That was why she'd never been able to let him go. Not upon finding out his true identity. Not in the face of a terrible betrayal. Not even after so many weeks apart.

That was why she loved him.

"Ana," Rafe rasped. "Please."

She saw the hopes and fears swirling in his eyes, the life he was entrusting to her safekeeping. *Xander. Save Xander.* He was putting all his faith in her, and for that gift, she wouldn't let him down.

With Rafe as her shield, Lyana ran from Malek and all the walls he'd tried to build around her. Untamed and untethered, she took to the sky.

53

XANDER

"Hello!" Xander shouted as he walked through the city streets, stumbling on debris and straining to see through the dense, shadowy gray. The ground swayed and sank, the sound of crashing waves becoming louder with each passing second. Wet air licked his cheeks, forming droplets along his skin. His clothes grew sticky and his feathers heavy with the dampness. "Can anyone hear me? Do you need help?"

"Here!" someone shouted. "I'm over here!"

Xander ran, biting his tongue to keep back a curse as he stubbed his toe on a fallen stone. His wings caught him as he raced forward. It was nearly impossible to see without the light of the moon. He'd never been surrounded by such thick fog. "Where?"

"Here!"

They shouted back and forth a few more times until Xander caught sight of movement. The man was stuck beneath a pile of crumbled stones, his legs lost beneath the rubble. He lay facedown with his wings outstretched, seemingly unharmed. When Xander got close, the man's eyes widened with shock.

"My prince," he said, trying to dip his chin even with his cheek squished against the street. "I'm honored you—"

"None of that," Xander cut him off as he knelt by his side. "Where are you hurt and what can I do? Most importantly, can you fly?"

"I think I can. It's my legs. The building fell and I couldn't get away in time."

"Stay still," he cautioned as he reached for the stones. Lifting the small ones first, he brushed as much debris away as possible. A boulder crushed the man's calves, a large piece of masonry held together with grout. The left leg was mostly untouched, but the right one was flattened beyond repair. He wasn't sure how the man was still awake, let alone aware enough to speak.

"Can you help?"

"I will." Xander frowned, staring at the bloody strips of the man's leg. He'd read books about medicinal practices, but he'd never thought he would have to use them in real life. "Do you have a belt on?"

"I do."

"Can I borrow it?"

The man nodded, a bit of fear seeping into his dark brown eyes. He gritted his teeth as Xander slid the leather strap free.

"I'm going to tie this around your thigh, all right? Don't touch it and don't try to remove it. As soon as you can slide your legs out, I want you to take to the sky. Fly as fast as you can for the House of Song. Don't wait for me. Don't wait for anyone. Just go. On the count of three."

The man swallowed.

Xander tried to hide his gulp as he used his teeth to secure the belt in place, tying it as tightly as possible to stop the bleeding. The leg was lost, but the man's life didn't need to be. Upon rising to his feet, he pressed his shoulder into the boulder and prepared to push.

"One. Two. Three!"

He shoved with every ounce of muscle he possessed, heaving as his heels dug into the ground. His feet slid on the damp rock. A grunt escaped his lips and he pushed harder. *Come on. Come on.* The stone gave, just a little, just enough. The man scrambled, dragging his arms and wings across the street as he screamed. *A little more. A little more.* Xander refused to give up. His legs and arms shook. His body burned. *Go. Go.*

The man was free.

"Go!" Xander shouted.

Onyx wings disappeared into the mist, and he dropped the boulder back to the ground with a *thud*. Xander rested his forehead upon it, breathing heavily for a few spared moments. With a sigh, he stood again.

"Hello! Can anyone hear me? Do you need help?"

On and on it went. Sometimes he stumbled upon nothing but bodies. Sometimes there were people he could help. Other times, the worst times, all he could do was provide a merciful end to the pain. He had no idea how much time passed, as the ground dropped and swayed beneath him. A few of the shifts were so great he took to the sky to keep from careening over, but the island always seemed to right itself before dipping the other way, as though two opposing sides were fighting for control. Eventually one would win, he knew, and then he'd have no choice but to abandon the people still left.

"Help!" a voice shouted, high-pitched with youth. "Please, help!"

"I'm coming!"

"Help!"

He followed her cries until he found her, a young girl of no more than twelve, still growing into her wings. But that wasn't what made him freeze. It was the tears streaming down her pale cheeks, the pain in her eyes, and mostly, the bloodied end of a metal shard sticking through her stomach.

"Prince Lysander," she cried. "Oh, please help me. Please!"

"Shh," he whispered, putting his palm to her brow to wipe off the sweat. She trembled beneath him. A knot formed in his throat, but he swallowed it and forced the soothing lie to his lips. "I'm here. I'll help you."

"I told my mother I was right behind her." The girl wept as she spoke. "She had my baby brother in her arms, and I told her I was right behind her. But I wanted the necklace my father gave me. I went back for it even though she told me not to. Am I going to die?"

"No, of course not," he murmured as he wiped her hair from her cheeks, trying to calm her. "Just close your eyes for a moment, and it'll all be over. You'll meet your mother with everyone else in the House of Song. Just close your eyes."

She nodded, believing him.

He wasn't sure if it was cruelty or kindness, but he didn't have time to decide. Xander slipped his hand to his waist and grabbed his dagger, already stained with the blood of the other lives he'd ended so they could soar in peace to Taetanos's realm rather than lie in pain for hours. The end, either way, would be the same. With a wound such as this, the girl would bleed out before she even reached the sky. Her wings weren't broken, but she'd never survive the flight. This was the true work of kings— bloody and gruesome, full of choices that would stay in his mind like a brand, images and people and deeds he would never be able to forget. But he would rather she die with her eyes closed, dreaming of her family, with him by her side, than alone in the fog as this foreign world pulled her under.

Xander lifted the blade.

"Stop!"

He turned toward her voice as his heart leapt to his throat and the dagger clanged against the stones. "Lyana?"

"I'm here," she said as she stepped through the mist, her ivory wings as luminous as ever, as though starlight lived within her feathers, breaking up the dark night.

She'd come.

Despite the prophecy, despite what Cassi had said about her destiny and her king, she'd come for him and for his people.

She'd come to save them.

"Princess!" the girl cried as she tore open her eyes. "You've returned."

"I have," Lyana crooned as she knelt beside the girl, nothing but sympathy and compassion in her eyes. "I'm sorry it took me so long, but I'm here now. And I come with Aethios's blessing to help the House of Whispers. I've been with him these longs weeks that I've been away, and he's gifted me with the power to save you."

"Oh, thank you. Thank you."

"You might feel a little pain, but it will all be over soon, I promise."

"Thank you."

Lyana lifted her green eyes to him, and for a moment Xander couldn't breathe. He'd forgotten what it was like to be in her presence, like looking at a goddess come to life, a woman so full of spirit and magic she shone as bright as the sun. But it was different now too. He thought of that beach where Cassi had taken him, of the tide flowing in and out, the sand slipping through his fingers with each passing wave. He no longer worried about trying to hold on to something that couldn't be bottled. She was meant for bigger things than him, and he was fine to simply sit and bask in her glow.

"Help me with her body," Lyana murmured.

Xander copied her movements and they each slid their arms beneath the girl's back. She hissed in pain, but the ache soon receded from her eyes. As they lifted her, she remained still, a serene expression on her face. He couldn't see Lyana's magic, but he could feel it like a static pulse in the air. The blood oozing from the girl's open wound slowed, and then her skin sealed, the scar shrinking and shrinking until it was nothing.

"In the name of Aethios, highest of them all, you're healed," Lyana said warmly as the girl blinked away her confusion, bright spots of wonder filling her gaze. "Go. Find your family and tell the ravens their prince and princess are coming to save them, with the power of Aethios and Taetanos combined. Go."

The girl raced off into the night.

"The power of Aethios?" Xander muttered, arching a brow.

Lyana turned toward him with a grin. "It sounds so much better than magic."

"Do you think they'll buy it?"

"I think they'll believe whatever keeps them alive."

He had so many questions, and not nearly enough time to ask them, but the answers swirled in her gaze. Her eyes were no longer clouded with secrets, but open and unafraid. He didn't know what she'd gone through down here in the mist, but one thing was clear—she was done hiding.

"Rafe is alive, Xander, and I love him. For that reason, and so many more, I can't be your mate. But if you'll allow me, I would still do everything I can to save our people."

The words were abrupt, but he'd known them already. He'd known them the second he looked into her eyes. The world was changed. She was changed. And so was he. Xander wanted more than a mate tied to him with shackles. He wanted more for his people, and more for himself. The feelings he'd once had for her had been a fantasy, crafted through daydreams, but he deserved something real. And someday, he would find it.

"Cassi." The name came unbidden to his lips, from some deep place he'd been trying to ignore, but now that it was out in the open, he remembered where he'd left her—behind bars. "She's trapped."

"I know."

"You know?"

"Xander," Lyana murmured, her voice soft enough to crush and yet strung with hope, a hope he didn't want to snuff out. "Did she truly try to kill you?"

He swallowed, thinking about the knife at his throat and the pleading look in her eyes. "I don't know."

"You don't know?"

"It's...complicated."

"She lied to me for my entire life."

"I know."

"She cut off Rafe's wings."

He winced. "I know that too."

"But still you want to save her?" Lyana stared at him, searching his face as though the answer might be written upon his skin. But there was no right or wrong, no simple choice. All he knew was that he couldn't let Cassi die like this.

"I do."

Lyana released a heavy breath. "Me too."

"Then follow me."

They raced across the city, stopping to help the injured along the way. Lyana moved toward them before he even heard them cry out for help, as though she could feel their spirits and knew where they were without needing to speak. One after another, they knelt together as Lyana worked her magic, healing his people and praising their gods, until even he started to believe she was working with some divine power. He was beginning to see what Cassi had told him. Magic and the gods were one and the same—all that mattered was how the information was framed. If they could come up with a convincing story, his people might think Lyana a messenger of the gods. After this, they would need something to believe in, and she could be that something, if they played their cards right. She could guide them through the storm.

"Xander!"

He was so entrenched in his thoughts, he didn't notice as the ground heaved, sending a cascade of debris off the side of a building. Lyana threw her arms up, and the rocks stopped in midair. With a flick of her wrists, she tossed them to the side. Invisible power raised the hairs on his neck. This magic was different from her healing. This magic made him question the very foundations of what was possible. But when he met her gaze, she was still the girl he knew, strong willed and brave, her expression daring him to say something.

"Thanks."

Her lips twitched. "No problem."

"We're almost—"

He broke off as the ground gave way again, but this time, there was no steadying push back, no gentle sway. The land tilted, slipping farther and farther to the side, until they had no choice but to take to the sky.

"What's happening?" he shouted.

"We're out of time," Lyana said, worry lines digging into her forehead. "I'm not strong enough to keep the isle from sinking. It's been bobbing in the ocean, trying to find its balance, and I think it just did."

"It's going over?"

She rolled her lip between her teeth and nodded.

"Do we have time?" he asked. The castle courtyard was visible through the fog, the stone wall normally hiding it from sight crushed beyond repair. Below those grounds, Cassi was locked behind bars with no avenue of escape, exactly where he'd put her. If the isle sank, she'd sink with it, and if she died, he might as well have put the blade through her skin himself. "Lyana, do we have time?"

Determination hardened her features. "We'll make some."

CASSI

It's a fitting way to die, Cassi thought as she watched her body roll across the moist stones of the dungeon, limp and lifeless, while the ground gave way beneath her. *Alone in the dark. Undone by my own lies. A creature of the sky swallowed by the sea.*

What a metaphor for her life.

She couldn't even be mad—she had no one to blame but herself. Her decisions had ruined lives. Her choices were the reason she was here. If she'd done what Malek had asked, she'd be in Da'Kin right now, safely by his side, still his favored spy.

She'd rather be dead.

At least this way she wouldn't go to her grave a liar.

Her one regret would be in not finding the courage to visit Rafe, to tell him to his face how sorry she was. She didn't expect forgiveness. She simply felt it was something he deserved to hear, and now he never would.

Of course, in these final minutes she could try to race

across the sea and dive into his dreams. It would probably be a better use of her time than this—hovering over her body, watching it slam into the wall as the isle tilted, unable to do anything. A cut split her forehead and the blood dripped down the side of her face, but she didn't even feel the pain. She wanted to. She'd rather feel the breaks in her bones and the cuts along her skin. She'd rather feel the burn of life in her lungs when the water rushed in and pulled her under. She'd rather anything than this horrible detachment.

Maybe that was why she couldn't leave. Even traitors and spies didn't want to die alone, and she couldn't bear to abandon her body to face the end on its own.

Or maybe it was because she was waiting.

Waiting for the impossible.

Waiting.

Waiting.

Waiting.

And then she heard it—the soft rumble of voices at the other end of the hall. If she'd had breath, she would have held it. This was too much to hope for, too much to dream of. Her story was one of abandonment. Her father left her first, before she ever had the chance to learn who he was. Then her mother, in a way, as she handed her toddler of three over to the crown. Then Malek, as he gave her wings and hoisted her above the clouds, only to drop her in the middle of vacant tundra where she cried and cried until a dove patrol found her. As a girl growing up an owl among doves, her caretakers had been plenty, shifting from one nursemaid to another, not a one sticking around for long. She'd learned that people didn't come back. They left.

Again and again, they did nothing but leave. Maybe that was why she'd loved her books—they couldn't get up and walk away. Maybe that was why she'd always been so afraid of telling Lyana the truth—in her mind, that would be the end. Of them. Of their friendship. Of their sisterhood.

She should have known better.

She should have known Lyana, her queen of prophecy, her best friend, wouldn't be like all the rest. And she should have known the man by her side wouldn't either.

Xander, Cassi thought. *You came.*

They flew down the hall side by side, flickering torches guiding their way through the dark depths of the dungeon. By the time they reached her cell, the room was nearly on its side. The door sat below them as though it were the floor, and through it, Cassi's body lay sprawled against the roughly hewn wall. Xander knelt across the bars, all his focus on the lock, but Lyana searched the darkness just beyond the halo of light.

"Cassi!" Lyana cried, spotting the body. "Xander, open the door. Cassi, can you hear me?"

"I've almost..." He worked the key, pursing his lips. "There!"

The heavy iron swung inwards, dropping down so fast Xander fell through the opening before his wings could catch him. Lyana followed more gracefully, arching her wings so she landed with control beside Cassi's immobile body. Golden magic erupted around her palm, quickly enveloping the entire room. The cut on Cassi's forehead sealed, along with any other physical injuries she hadn't felt. But no matter how much magic her friend funneled into her body, there was one break that wouldn't mend—the most important one.

"Are you healing her?" Xander asked from the other side of her body. It was strange to think that a power that was so blinding to Cassi was invisible to his eyes, nothing more than a strange current in the air he could feel but couldn't see.

"I'm trying."

"What's wrong?"

"I don't—" Lyana broke off, her brow furrowing.

"Is she...?"

"No."

More magic filled the tiny cell, so potent it saturated Cassi's spirit, sinking through her diaphanous form, as warm as the sun.

I'm here, she wanted to say. *I'm right here.*

"Cassi!" Lyana called, shaking her limp shoulders. If only it were that simple. Instead, her head lolled to the side. "Cassi, wake up!"

"What's her injury?" Xander asked. "Maybe I can help."

"That's what I don't understand. There's no injury."

"No injury?"

"It's like I can feel her but she's not there. She's somewhere else. She's..." Lyana trailed off as she lifted her face and scanned the room. The deep umber of her skin shone richly against the soft light of her magic. She was regal as a queen, and her eyes narrowed as her gaze landed on the spot where Cassi hovered.

I'm here.

This time Lyana heard her. Through her power she

sensed Cassi's spirit, and her fingers rose to cover her gasp. The shock on her face was quickly replaced by a realization —whatever kept Cassi from her body was a wound she didn't know how to heal.

"Lyana," Xander murmured by her side. His face was also lifted toward the iron door swinging overhead, though there was no way he could see what she saw. He saw something though, his brows drawing together in concern. Water glistened on his cheek. For a moment, Cassi thought it was a tear, but then another droplet splashed against his pearly skin. "Do you hear that?"

"What?"

He touched the water slipping down his jaw. In the silence, the subtle trickle drawing his attention was as loud as a rushing river.

Lyana's eyes widened, her voice panicked. "We have to get her out of here. You grab her legs and I'll grab her torso."

They moved with haste. Xander dug his elbows under her knees as Lyana did the same with her shoulders. By the time they lifted Cassi's body off the stones, grunting from the heaviness in her limbs, an unbroken stream of water dripped through the cell bars, landing with another splash by their side. It was awkward to maneuver her through the narrow door, one not meant for flying, but after a few tries they found a way. In her spirit form, Cassi hovered behind, wishing there were more she could do as they soared over the liquid cascading down the hall. With each passing second, the gush strengthened. When they reached the stairs, the splashes soaked their clothes, slapping against the walls and spraying the ceiling. With the isle on its side, the long winding steps from the dungeon went not up, but sideways. They rushed to carry her to safety, but the ocean water kept coming, thickening and strengthening, weighing down their wings as the narrow strip of air grew thinner and thinner. One by one, the torches lighting the way went dark. The castle descended into shadow, nothing but the subtle sheen of Lyana's magic to light the way.

"We're almost there," she called to Xander, whose world was utterly black. "Just keep following me. We're almost there."

Her power sputtered as she strained to hold the unceasing waves back. Lyana was weak, her magic pushed to the limit. But still she didn't stop. She didn't drop Cassi and leave her to drown. Even though Cassi had lied, and even though she'd done horrible things, her friend still fought with every fiber of her being to keep her safe.

They emerged into the mist just as the sea pulled the castle under, the stone parapets disappearing beneath the velvet darkness. Neither Xander nor Lyana stopped until they were clear of the drowning city and all its debris. Then they hovered, holding her between them as they watched the isle sink slowly into the sea. Tears did streak down Xander's face then, though Lyana was kind enough to leave him to his grief. She turned her head to the side and sent a golden current of magic into the fog.

Only a few moments passed, but they felt like hours before Xander finally broke the silence. "What now? Do you think we'll be able to carry her all the way to the House of Song?"

"No," Lyana murmured. "And it wouldn't do her any good anyway. I don't know how to save her, but there's someone who might."

Sharp as ever, Xander understood in a heartbeat. "The man from the sacred nest?"

She nodded. "I sensed a ship not that far from here. We'll leave her with them, and I'll order the captain to bring her to their king."

"He'll help her?"

"I hope so."

"And then what?"

Lyana tore her gaze from the murky sky. "What do you mean?"

"Will you go to this king with her? Will you come back home with me? Cassi told me about the prophecy, about who you are and what your life means. I know you have the whole world on your shoulders, but I also know our people could use someone to look up to, someone to believe in, and I think that person could be you."

"By the power of Aethios?" Lyana asked wryly, a joke Cassi didn't understand, but Xander got. He smiled.

"If that's what you want to call it."

"It won't be easy to change their minds," she cautioned. "We'll be up against five hundred years of fear and hate, and now that the House of Whispers has fallen, there won't be much time."

"We'll make time," he said, earnest conviction laced through his tone, the voice of a warrior. "Just like we did tonight, we'll make time. We were never meant to be mates, Lyana. I see that now, but that doesn't mean we don't make a good team. Between my book smarts and your cunning, we'll come up with something. We can do this. We can save them—not just the ravens, but all the houses. We can give them a future."

"One way or another, the islands will fall."

"Then we must give our people a reason to fly."

Something unspoken passed between them, something honest and true, the sort of exchange to which Cassi had never borne witness. Still, it shot through her, filling her spirit with a sense of purpose. They were good. They were noble. And somehow she'd found herself draped between them, carried aloft by their loving arms. She didn't know what she'd done to deserve such devotion, but she knew right then and there that she would spend the rest of her life fighting to earn it. If these two people had found her worthy of saving, then maybe, just maybe, she was.

As they raced into the mist, part of her wanted to scream, *No! Don't take me to Malek! He won't help me!* But that was the coward's way, and she was done being afraid. Instead, she thought, *Yes. Deliver me to the belly of the beast. Let me make home in the dark halls of his castle and the dank canals of his city, unheard and unseen. Let me fight the only way I know how.*

Spying was in her blood. That would never change. Lying and deceiving were her two greatest weapons, and it was time to turn them on a new target. If Cassi was a spy, let her be their spy. Let her help them bring Malek to his knees.

55

BRIGHTY

Brighty ran through the streets, keeping her gaze plastered on the fog as she studied the charcoal folds for the barest hint of fire, her *photo'kine* eyes more attuned to shifts in light than any others. *Come on, Rafe. Come on!*

She'd seen everything. The warehouse exploding. He and the queen rising from the ashes. The wave ready to crush the city. And then their fight with the king. She wasn't entirely sure what had called her from her slumber in the middle of the night, except to say she'd had a feeling, a very bad feeling. Before she knew it, she'd found herself dashing along the rooftops of Da'Kin, drawn toward the spot where she'd last seen Rafe.

And it was a good thing.

Because she was pretty sure the bloody idiot was lost.

Where are you? Magic alive, where'd you go?

He'd taken to the sky as soon as the queen was out of sight, his wings blazing with fire as he disappeared into the mist. The king's golden magic followed him into the air, but it hadn't been enough to stop him. She'd never seen anything like it. *Aethi'kine* magic didn't seem to penetrate his skin, or maybe it did, and the heat melted it away. Either way, he'd vanished, and she'd thought it had been for good, until she'd caught an orange flash in the sky. He'd dipped close to the city, seemingly searching for something, his body bobbing in the air as though it were a struggle to stay afloat. Golden power had chased after him as soon as he'd appeared, and he'd vanished again. They'd done that about six times since, and each time he looked weaker and weaker. He was searching for the ship with the circles he was taking, she knew he was, but they were in the completely wrong section of the city.

Come on, Rafe.

There. A blaze lit the sky, sinking rapidly toward the city, dropping faster and faster, as though he were...

Oh, for magic's sake!

He was literally falling out of the sky, his body burning like a comet as it shot toward a city built of wood. Brighty ran, forgoing stealth for speed as shingles slipped off rooftops, leaving a trail of shatters in her wake. Leaping from building to building, she made for the spot where he'd disappeared. The flames caught her eyes first, an angry glow stretching for the sky. The king would be there in no time, with his *pyro'kines* in tow. They'd grab him unless she got there first.

Brighty plowed into the fire, keeping her forearm raised to guard her face as the heat stung her skin. "Rafe! Rafe!"

There was no answer.

A few more steps and she nearly stumbled over his body. "Rafe!"

Magic alive, why did he have to be so large? He'd towered over her before, but now, with those wings, he might as well have been a giant as she tried to wedge her shoulder under his arm, careful to avoid the scales still sizzling with heat. Even his skin burned, a dull pain she'd be able to ignore—at least for now. She couldn't, however, ignore that he was heavy. Her legs shook under the strain as she tried to lug him out of the fire. They'd been lucky he'd landed in an open courtyard. If she'd had to carry him up a flight of stairs or fish him from the canal, they never would have made it. As it was, they'd never get to the ship before the king found them. She needed help. She needed a plan.

As they broke through the flames, Brighty studied her surroundings again. In her haste, she'd failed to notice which part of the city Rafe had landed in, but now that she had, she didn't feel much better. They were in the mage quarters, which meant there'd be no easy boat to steal here. Every house had a private dock to the canal, only accessible through the mansions lining the streets. Breaking in wouldn't be easy. Breaking in with a half-dead dragon man draped across her back would be impossible. There had to be another way, another option, another—

Her heart sank as an idea struck.

The king would never expect it.

She couldn't believe she was even considering it.

But there was no other way, and after tonight, with the image burned into her mind of Rafe and the queen standing in the flames as ash fell like snow all around them, Brighty knew this was bigger than the demons of her past. It had been years since they'd last seen each other, years since the heartache and the pain, though the thought of her still brought a throbbing that even time couldn't quite heal. Maybe it would be a good thing to finally face her.

Before she had time to question, Brighty stopped outside the home she knew better than any other in the city —its towering façade glimmering in the night, four stories of wood decorated with elaborate metal statues only magic could produce, starbursts and twisting rails, dragons and gargoyles, though her favorite had always been the climbing roses. The *ferro'kine* in charge of the city's elaborate plumbing system lived in this house, or at least he had. Brighty heard the man died two years ago, at which point his daughter moved back into her childhood home with her *ferro'kine* husband who took up the family business.

Brighty didn't expect her to sleep in the same room she once had, but she tried their old signal, just in case, and shot a beam of light into the third-story window on the left. After a moment, the curtain shifted just enough for her to catch a flash of pale fingers. With her heart in her throat, Brighty pulled her magic back beneath her skin and carried Rafe the rest of the way to the door. The latch unbolted. Her pulse raced. And just like that, she was looking at a face she swore she'd never see again, every detail just the same as she remembered. Her brown eyes were soft with sleepiness, the edges downturned and the lashes long. A delicate array of freckles covered the rosy skin of her rounded cheeks and button nose. Her auburn hair was pinned neatly atop her head and her elegant neck was covered mostly by her dressing gown, which had been pinned just below her chin.

"Thalyia?" she asked, shock making the word airy. It still managed to send a shiver all the way down Brighty's spine.

"Hi, Effie." She swallowed the knot in her throat, trying to fight the rush of emotions as her first love took her in, those eyes scanning every inch of her face before widening at the sight of the man draped across her back. "Can I come in?"

"Thalyia, what—"

"I wouldn't be here if it wasn't an emergency."

Effie bit her plush lower lip, then nodded and stepped back, opening the door to let Brighty inside. If the house weren't so full of fineries, she would have dropped Rafe the second she passed the threshold—he was heavy and her shoulder was starting to burn—but the last thing she wanted to do was light the pretty rug beneath her feet on fire.

"My ship is docked in the western edge of the city, near the gambling halls, and I need a boat—" Brighty stopped short as she took notice of the bundle wrapped securely in Effie's arms. Slack-jawed, she darted her gaze between the small angelic face visible within the folds of fabric and the feminine face watching her worriedly. "You have a baby."

Effie's lips twisted into a grin Brighty recognized. "I do."

Of course she did.

It was all she'd ever wanted.

I can't go with you, Thalyia. The words were imprinted like a brand across her chest. Brighty remembered every intonation, every lilt, every moment as they'd fallen like knives against her skin. *I'm going to marry him, I'm sorry. I can't go with you.*

Don't let your father win, she'd pleaded, taking the soft hands that had never known a day's work into her own callused ones, rough from a life of begging and stealing on the street. *We can go to another city. We can go somewhere he'll never find us.*

It's not about him, she'd said, her face tilting to the side as an auburn wave fell over her eyes. Effie had brought their clasped hands to her lips, then kissed Brighty's fingers once before dropping them. *It's about me. I want a family. I want children of my own, and I want them to live as comfortably as I do. I want stability. I don't want to run.*

It was the one thing Brighty never could have given her —a child. Oh, there were ways of course, men who could be hired, men who were willing to make arrangements, but that wasn't what Effie wanted. She'd wanted what she had right now, a mansion in the right part of town, a baby in her arms, a husband in her bed, a life with no surprises and no troubles. Brighty had been her brief stint of teenage rebellion, though it had taken her a long time to realize that when at the time Effie had been her whole world.

"I'm happy for you," Brighty said, surprised to find the words were true as she pushed the memories to the back of her mind.

Warmth entered Effie's dark eyes. "And I'm worried for you. What's going on, Thalyia? Who is this? Why are you here?"

"I don't want to get you involved. I just need a boat.

You can say someone stole it, or that it somehow got loose, but I need to get this man to safety. If you ever trusted me at all, please trust me now when I tell you it's important."

Indecision played across Effie's features, but it was over faster than Brighty expected. Perhaps their time together had meant something to her after all. "Follow me."

Effie led her down the hall and toward the back door of the house, stopping only once along the way to toss her a blanket made of metal mesh. "It'll stifle the fire," was all she said, and then they were outside. The gardens were just as she remembered, every bush carefully trimmed, every flower carefully ordered, the patterns intricately designed to be viewed from the home above. She should have known all along Effie would never run wild and free, not when this was her oasis. Brighty used to spend hours in the dark shadows of these groves. She'd use a borrowed boat to sneak in by the dock, where the gate was left unlocked. Effie would spin her *agro'kine* magic—nothing very fancy, she was just a low-level mage—and Brighty would shine her light along the petals to help them bloom. Sometimes they'd lose themselves, crushing the flower beds just to grow them again.

Those nights had been rare moments of peace in a life that had been anything but calm, all but the final night. Effie's father had caught them rolling around beneath the roses and demanded Brighty be exiled from the city. She ran, of course, positive she'd be able to avoid the authorities the way she'd done most of her life already. And it had worked, too, until the day of Effie's wedding. Like any imbecile in the throes of heartbreak, Brighty had gotten piss drunk and decided to use her magic to blast apart whatever metal structures she came upon, hitting four water main lines and two fountains before the final fatal blow. A young boy had been playing on the other side of the third fountain, out of sight while he leaned low over his marbles. She hadn't seen him until it was too late and he was little more than a body among the wreckage. A situation like that sobers one quickly. After scooping up his frail body, she'd sprinted for the castle and begged to meet with the king. *Photo'kines* were valuable, the only reason she was granted an audience. He offered her a choice right there—her life in exchange for the boy's. A few days later, she was handed over to Captain Rokaro and given a new home on *The Wanderer.*

Sometimes, such as now while she hefted Rafe through the metal gate and down the wet wooden steps to the dock, nearly falling on her ass in the process, she thought about that little boy whose name she didn't even know to remind herself the sacrifice had been worth it.

"Take this one," Effie said, indicating the smallest boat of the three with the fewest decorations. She bounced while whispering soothingly into her baby's ear. The sight brought both a pang and a peace to Brighty's chest. "Lay the blanket down first, and then wrap him in it. My father made them years ago to protect us in case of fire. It should keep the boat from burning."

Brighty did as instructed, first setting out the blanket and then unceremoniously dropping Rafe on top of it. The boat nearly capsized, water sloshing over the sides, and Brighty lunged to settle it. The last thing she needed was a swim in the canals to dive after him. There was no doubt in her mind Rafe would sink right to the bottom. When his limbs and wings were as drawn in as possible, she bundled the blanket around him, shielding his face and adjusting the folds until he looked like no more than covered cargo.

"Who is he?" Effie asked softly, her tone giving nothing away.

Turning around to face her one last time, Brighty settled by the oars. "A friend."

They stared at each other for a moment, time a fluid thing as their past and present merged, the years hanging between them while at the same time barely there. How many times had they been in this exact position? Murmuring goodbye with promises of "next time" and sweet kisses to last the days apart? There were no touches now, no lingering handholds, no longing glances, no declarations of tomorrow, but there was something between them—not the bright flame of young love, but affection, aged and more mature, just as they were.

"Thank you, Effie," Brighty finally whispered, her throat dry. "I won't forget this."

"Be safe, Thalyia."

It was done.

Keeping her baby to her chest, Effie disappeared behind the locked gate of the dock and Brighty started rowing down the canal, careful to keep her ears open for the sound of voices. The fire, it seemed, had caused enough of a distraction. The city had come alive, mages running to help contain the damage while the people whose houses were burning spat rage into the night. Boats drifted by, making her just another wandering soul in the dark. Her muscles screamed from all the paddling, yet with each passing moment her nerves settled. When she finally reached the ship, Brighty let out a high-pitched whistle. A second later, Archer's face appeared over the bow, his salt-and-pepper hair blowing in the breeze as humor twisted his features.

"Just the man I wanted to see," Brighty called, feeling herself again, this hulk of wood more a home to her than any she'd had before. "Rafe is hidden in this metal blanket, and I need you to bring him on board."

"Rafe?"

"Just do it. And toss me a rope."

The rope came first, followed by streaks of green *ferro'kine* magic. Brighty scrambled up with Rafe floating behind, until they were both deposited on deck. But the work didn't end there.

"Where is everyone?" she asked.

"Cook is below deck with Spout and Squirrel, all asleep last time I checked. Captain is in her rooms and Patch is with the rest in the city. Another ship of dragon hunters came in while you were gone, so the crew challenged them to a game of dice."

"*Dice* dice?"

Archer just grinned.

Brighty rolled her eyes. Of all the nights... "I'll take over watch. I need you to go round them up. We set sail immediately."

"You vying for my job?"

Brighty spun. "Captain!"

"I heard you through my window," the older woman

said, still a voice of authority despite being barefoot in loose breeches. Her shirt billowed around her waist, the ties mostly undone. "What's going on? And don't tell me that's a dead body."

"Worse." Brighty swallowed. "It's Rafe."

"Rafe?" A frown twisted her lips, making the wrinkles around the edges seem deeper. Captain Rokaro knelt and threw the blanket aside, a snarl coming up her throat the moment she noticed his leathery wings. "The king?"

"The king."

They shared a look. Captain stood and pointed at Archer. "Go round up the others and tell them we set sail as soon as everyone's on board. No delays. No dillydallying. Last one on deck cleans the privy for a month."

Archer ran off without another word, and Captain turned toward her.

"I'll take his feet," Brighty said, moving toward Rafe.

"Not so fast."

She froze.

"I said we set sail as soon as everyone's on board, but I never said we're taking Rafe with us."

"Cap—"

"Give me one good reason," Captain said, no malice in her voice, just directness. "One good reason why I should defy the king I've spent most of my life working for, the king we've all sacrificed for, the king with the fate of our entire world on his shoulders."

Brighty met her icy eyes. "Because Rafe's one of us."

"And in any other circumstance, that would be enough. But not this one."

They stared, neither backing down. After a few tense seconds, Captain arched her brow. Brighty broke, tearing herself away with a curse. Her thoughts fled back to the warehouse and the fight, but most of all, to that moment between Rafe and the queen that she still couldn't quite erase—their wings spread and their eyes locked as flames and flurries lit the skies around them. They'd looked like...like...

"What if there's another reason?" she offered slowly, lifting her head.

"What?" Captain narrowed her eyes, studying Brighty. "Spit it out."

The idea was ludicrous.

To even think it—to even imagine it—

"What if..." Brighty took a deep breath, picturing Malek's stone-cold face as he offered her a choice all those years ago, no passion in his gaze and no pain, nothing but steel. Then she thought of Rafe, the fear and worry and caring in his eyes right before he took that idiotic leap off the main mast to single-handedly slay a dragon. Maybe she wanted to believe a king was someone who would risk everything to save a life rather than callously send one away. Maybe she simply yearned for a leader she actually wanted to follow. Or maybe, just maybe, it was true. "What if he's the King Born in Fire?"

"Are you drunk?"

"I know it sounds like I've had one dragon's breath too many, but what if it's true, Captain? I saw him with the queen tonight. They're connected somehow. Their spirits are tied. I know it, and I think King Malek knows it too.

The way he looked at them—it was the look of a man whose world was falling out from under him. And if there's even a chance this might be true, don't we need to take it? If not for ourselves, then for the world?"

Captain lifted her fingers to her temples, features pinching as though in pain. Then in one swift motion, she knelt and hooked her elbows beneath Rafe's shoulders. "Well, are you going to help me or not?"

Brighty grabbed his feet and tossed the metal blanket over her shoulder. "Where are we taking him?"

Captain glanced to her right toward the gangplank, then to her left toward the door. With a sigh, she said, "To his room. And by the time we get there, I want to know every detail of what happened tonight. Understood?"

Brighty grinned. "Aye, aye, Captain."

While they carried him below deck, she described Rafe's moment with the queen, his fight with the king, and his not-so-graceful fall from the skies. As Brighty's story ran out, silence descended—unreadable, impenetrable silence. Not saying a word, they settled Rafe on the bed, making sure his fiery wings were carefully wrapped in the mesh before stepping back into the hall. Brighty almost flinched when the door clicked shut, unable to stand the quiet. But Captain just lifted her palm to the wood grains, staring as though she could see through them to the man sleeping on the other side.

"Do you—"

"Tomorrow, Brighty." Captain dropped her arm from the door and walked toward her cabin, her voice as heavy as her thudding steps, trailing behind her like a weight.

"When we're in the open seas, far away from the city, with some distance between us and the king's mages, we'll figure out the rest. Just give me until tomorrow."

Tomorrow, Brighty thought, her mood far lighter. She took the steps two at a time and burst through the door with a bang, weary and exhausted, yet somehow more alive than she'd felt in ages, as though seeing Effie had sealed a leaking wound and saving Rafe had closed another. Turning him into a king would be no easy job. Hell, he hardly passed for a sailor. But they'd find a way. If it was meant to be, the way she somehow knew it was, they'd find a way —tomorrow.

56

LYANA

As they flew to the House of Song, Lyana and Xander tightened their story. If anyone asked, they would say she disappeared during their mating ceremony as they pressed their palms to the god stone to murmur their vows. Xander had thought it was a trick played by Vesevios, some sort of magic he'd gotten Rafe to learn in order to spirit her away. But in truth, Taetanos had welcomed her into the spirit realm where all the gods were waiting to greet her. They said a terrible war was coming. They said she was chosen to help guide their people through these uncertain times. And they gifted her with the power of Aethios so she might see his will done. When the House of Whispers fell, the gods knew their time was running out, and Taetanos released her back to the world of the living.

"Do you really think they'll believe it?" she asked as they neared the northern edge of the House of Song, a dense canopy of trees visible just beyond the cliffs.

"You know what my mother told me once?"

He took her hand to stop her and Lyana turned. As they hovered side by side, the moonlight played on the skin of their joined fingers, a study in shadow and light. It had been so long since she'd seen the stars, since the sky had felt open and expansive rather than condensed and closed in.

"She said frightened gossip has the power to bring a kingdom to its knees, but I have something to add to that. Hope has the power to make a fallen kingdom rise." He swallowed and tightened his grip, his words like deftly wielded weapons cutting her doubts away. "You are that hope, Lyana. You'll be the bright spark to lead our people through the darkness. They'll believe you, because right now they need something to believe in. They've lost their homes, their way of life. Some of them have lost their families. They're terrified and adrift. Your arrival will be the dawn of a new day. Trust me. I believe that, and if you believe it, they'll believe it too."

He'd always had a way about him that made her feel special, but this was different. Now he made her feel strong. He spoke with conviction and authority. He spoke like a king—a true king, who led through faith and love instead of emotionless power. Lyana had almost forgotten what that felt like, but she was grateful for the reminder. "Thank you, Xander."

"Are you ready?" He lifted his chin toward the isle waiting just out of reach.

"No," she answered with a grin. "But let's do this anyway."

As they crested the edge and soared over the thick

forests of the songbird homeland, Lyana gathered her power, mulling over his words. If she believed, they'd believe. Though she was nervous and frightened and unsure, she couldn't show it. She had to be strong. She had to lead. There would be no more racing into the clouds, dreaming about the distant horizon and the adventure she might find there. It was time to grow up. For them. For the world. For herself.

It was time to become a queen.

They found the flock in an open clearing a few miles inland, the sea of raven wings looking like molten obsidian beneath the moonlight. Helen was the first to spot them, jumping to her feet as her hand rose to fight the glare. More soon followed, pointing and shouting as their prince and princess descended from the sky. Stealing Malek's favorite trick, Lyana sent her magic out in a wave of gold. It enveloped the lost ravens, filling their souls with warmth and love, that small trace of healing power just enough to enliven their weary bones. Without magic, no one would be able to see the subtle shimmer in the air. They'd just feel the slightest weight lifting off their shoulders. And anyone with magic, well, Lyana trusted they'd keep her secret. She was done being afraid, done hiding who she was, done pretending that power didn't run like blood through her veins.

"Helen," Xander called as soon as they landed on the soft grass. "Where's my mother?"

The captain of the guards dropped her gaze, and Lyana's heart dropped with it.

"Helen?"

"My prince," Helen said, apology thickening her tone. With her magic on full display, Lyana felt Xander's spirit freeze, as though his heart had stopped beating in his chest. "The queen didn't make it."

Xander took Lyana's hand, squeezing her fingers, and she squeezed right back, aching for him as the pain in his soul sank into her own, the sort of wound even her magic couldn't heal.

"What happened?"

"She was gone by the time I got to her room. The ceiling in the royal chambers collapsed during the earthquake, crushing her beneath it. There was nothing we could do before the isle fell."

Xander opened his mouth, then closed it, swallowing before he opened his mouth to silence once more. He was the boy who always knew just what to say, and now he was a man made speechless by grief.

"You did what you could," Lyana offered Helen, raising her voice so everyone could hear and strengthening the alluring pull of her magic. "All of you did what you could in the face of impossible horror. I know you're tired and confused. I know you're frightened and hurt. But Prince Lysander and I are here with the blessing of the gods to lead you through this terrible time. On the day of our mating ceremony, Taetanos welcomed me into the spirit realm and brought me before the gods. That's where I've been these long weeks. That's why I left. But now I'm back, and Aethios has gifted me the power to save you. If you would have us, we would be your king and queen. If you would have us, we would be the light to guide you through the dark."

At first, nothing happened. The ravens were wary and exhausted. They didn't know what to believe. But then the girl from the ruins of Pylaeon stepped forward with her mother and baby brother, faith a light in her eyes, making her glow beneath the stars. As one, all three knelt, bowing their heads to the ground. Beside them stood another man Lyana and Xander had saved. He knelt too. Then the next, and the next, starting with those they'd rescued and then spreading until the entire House of Whispers circled them, their foreheads touching the grass, not a sound in the clearing but the subtle rustling of feathers and leaves as a breeze swept through.

Lyana glanced at Xander. He stared back at her.

Are you sure? his caring eyes seemed to ask.

Are you?

Together, they lifted their clasped hands above their heads. A cheer erupted, full of so much hope and promise it stirred the rising sun.

57

RAFE

A blur of shadows and blood filled his vision. Red droplets glinted beneath the night sky. Tendrils of darkness swirled in the air. His clawed hand wrapped around a pale neck, and then his ebony scales slashed. Screams and screeches filled his ears, the chaos of movement, then silence.

Gilded metalwork arched overhead, the vast open air visible through the bars. With a leap, he pumped his wings and soared up, up, up, breaking through the cage as though it were little more than paper. Ravens surrounded him on all sides, their cries loud, the whoosh of the wind through their feathers even louder.

As they continued to arch into the sky, he banked left, pulled by a power calling out his name. He raced over the forest until the land gave way to sky, revealing the thick white blanket stretched out below, enshrouding what lay beneath. He dove, the distance disappearing in seconds as he sank within the *foggy folds, blending into the night. The ship broke through the mist with sudden clarity, a phantom cutting across the waves.*

He had to get inside.

Sticking to shadows and dim corners, he swam through the sea of darkness as swiftly as a spirit and snuck into the ship, then moved through unlit corridors and black-cloaked crevices until he was in the room. A boy slept on a bed, his dark hair spilling over his pale skin. They weren't the same, not quite, but he still smelled of fire and smoke, as familiar as a dream. He reached out his hand, his onyx scales silky as they closed the distance, and lightly ran his claw along that smooth cheek, waiting, waiting—

Rafe woke with a gasp and jerked his hand to his cheek. A line tingled across his skin, burning beneath his palm, almost as though it had been scratched. Heart thundering, he rolled off the bed and landed on his feet before scanning the room, but it was empty.

A nightmare, he thought, shaking his head. *It was just a nightmare.*

It had felt so real.

He half expected to see scales along his fingers, deep obsidian and oozing darkness, but his fingers were just that, fingers. No claws. No bloodstains. Just plain pale skin. Rafe shrugged off the heavy blanket across his shoulders, letting it drop to the ground with a *thunk* as he crossed the room to press his nose against the small circular window. Outside, waves slapped the sides of the ship in a soothing rhythm. The last thing he remembered was flying over Da'Kin in search of the ship. Then his vision had gone black and his memory blank until waking up here. Brighty must have found him. She must have brought him back.

I'm not a beast.

I'm not a monster.

The words quieted the pounding in his chest. For a moment, he'd thought maybe the dragon had won. That he truly had become all the things he feared. But the bloody massacre hadn't been real. He'd slashed no throats. He'd ended no lives. He'd saved Lyana from her king, then she'd saved Xander, and everything was fine. It was just a dream —a horrible, horrible dream.

Right?

The hairs on the back of his neck stood. Rafe rolled his shoulders, the window catching the reflection of flames as his wings shifted along with his muscles. A tickle slipped down his spine, the sense of being watched.

He spun.

There was nothing behind him but deep, impenetrable shadow.

ABOUT THE AUTHOR

Bestselling author Kaitlyn Davis writes young adult fantasy novels under the name Kaitlyn Davis and contemporary romance novels under the name Kay Marie.

Always blessed with an overactive imagination, Kaitlyn has been writing ever since she picked up her first crayon and is overjoyed to share her work with the world. When she's not daydreaming, typing stories, or getting lost in fictional worlds, Kaitlyn can be found indulging in some puppy videos, watching a little too much television, or spending time with her family.

Connect with the Author Online:

Website: KaitlynDavisBooks.com
Facebook: Facebook.com/KaitlynDavisBooks
Twitter: @DavisKaitlyn
Instagram: @KaitlynDavisBooks
Goodreads: Goodreads.com/Kaitlyn_Davis
Bookbub: @KaitlynDavis